C29 0000 0919 857

Elaine Everest

~

The Woolworths Girl's Promise

MACMILLAN

First published 2023 by Macmillan
an imprint of Pan Macmillan
The Smithson, 6 Briset Street, London EC1M 5NR
EU representative: Macmillan Publishers Ireland Ltd, 1st Floor,
The Liffey Trust Centre, 117–126 Sheriff Street Upper,
Dublin 1, D01 YC43
Associated companies throughout the world
www.panmacmillan.com

ISBN 978-1-5290-7806-0

1 3 5 7 9 8 6 4 2

A CIP catalogue record for this book is available from the British Library.

Typeset by Palimpsest Book Production Ltd, Falkirk, Stirlingshire
Printed and bound by CPI Group (UK) Ltd, Croydon, CR0 4YY

MIX
Paper | Supporting
responsible forestry
FSC® C116313

This book is dedicated to the memory of
my great-uncle Charles Sears, who perished
at Ypres on 17 August 1917, aged thirty-one.

I wanted to keep his name alive as he had no wife or children. I am the granddaughter of his younger brother, Edward Thomas Sears. The records show notification of Charles' death went to his parents, George and Jane.

If the name and date sound familiar it's because Betty Billington's fiancé, Charlie Sayers, also died on the same day at the same place. This is my way of remembering my brave family member.

There is a reason I changed Charlie Sayers' surname. Way back when he was born a few legal documents show the Sears name spelt as Sayers, a common error when census and registration documents were completed by hand, and so many people could not spell. In the area of Kent where I come from there are many Sears and Sayers families, with many distantly related.

Thank you to all those who have fought and died for our country. We owe you so much.

A Letter from Elaine

~

Dear Reader,

It doesn't seem that long since I last sat down to write a letter to you. In fact, it is longer than usual due to a rather scary problem with my eye. Burst blood vessels close to the retina meant I could hardly see with my right eye and trying to type, let alone read, was nigh on impossible. I honestly tried to write and have never known such frustration in my life. I tried all forms of dictation which made my storytelling worse – so much gobbledegook. My lovely agent, Caroline, stepped in and after discussions with my editor, Wayne, I was told not to worry about the next book deadline and to rest as much as possible. This is where decent sunglasses and Audible book downloads came into their own. Even so I was for ever squinting just to try and clear the constant fog. Of course, this mean *The Woolworths Girl's Promise* missed its October 2022 publication date, and for that I apologize. At this point I must thank you all for the constant stream of get-well messages, and to my friends for nagging me not to write.

Apart from my health problem, 2022 was a very special year as my husband Michael and I celebrated our golden wedding anniversary. I'm not sure how this happened, as I swear we've not been married that long – the years have shot by! I will claim to still be thirty-six though! We decided ages ago not to have a party but to fit in as many holidays as possible, something we have never done before. Henry went into his dog kennels where he was spoilt rotten, and we set off for Switzerland armed with maps and a good phone signal. In fact, we had such a good time we returned a few months later, this time booking with a rail-travel company – but came back with covid . . . We managed to fit in a trip with Henry to Cornwall and finished off the year with a short break in Bruges. It has been blissful! I count myself very lucky not only to have my husband still with me, but to have been able to celebrate such a wonderful anniversary. Some of my friends and family have not been fortunate enough to be able to celebrate such an occasion, and my heart goes out to you all.

With my eyesight eighty per cent better I'm raring to get back to my storytelling, and already there is another Woolworths novel completed for the autumn of 2023.

Thank you all for your support during what has been an unusual year.

Sending my love,
Elaine xx

Prologue

December 1938

Betty Billington looked up as trainee under-manager Alan Gilbert knocked on her office door before taking a step over the threshold.

'They're here, Miss Billington, and quite a motley crew, if I may say so. You may just find a few suitable Woolworths counter assistants to cover the Christmas period.'

Betty smiled at the affable young man. Even though her stomach was churning, she did her best to appear calm. Alan was a cheerful lad, always keen to lend a hand around the store. He'd been a godsend ever since she'd moved to the Erith branch, explaining to her what went on in the town, set on the south shore of the Thames, as well as sharing snippets of information about the staff and their families.

'Thank you, Alan. If you can give me five minutes, then show them in?'

'I'll do that,' he smiled in return, stopping for a moment before turning back. 'I hope you don't mind me saying it, but . . . don't be nervous. We all think you are the best staff

1

supervisor we've had here for a while. Oh, and Mum said she will send down a cup of tea shortly, along with a slice of her gypsy tart.'

Betty thanked him. She could have jumped up and hugged him, but it wouldn't be seemly now she was management, albeit junior management. She smoothed down her tweed skirt and straightened the lapels of the matching jacket. It felt strange not to be wearing a Woolworths overall, after all her years of working for the company. At least she was able to proudly wear the sweetheart brooch she had been given more than twenty years earlier by her beloved Charlie.

How the years had flown by since she was an innocent seventeen-year-old. Would she do things differently, if she could live those days over again? Perhaps not act so irrationally, or walk so blindly into situations over which she had no control? Her thoughts drifted back to a time when life had seemed much simpler. By now she could have been happily married with a family of her own, not a spinster who needed to work for a living. She shocked herself with the thought that if things had turned out differently, she could even be a grandmother, and then chuckled at the idea of herself, Miss Betty Billington, with a family.

Pulling herself up short, she reminded herself of the important position she held within the F. W. Woolworth company. It had been a struggle to reach this point and she had no intention of letting her employers down. She would treat her work seriously and not stand for any nonsense. Oh, yes, she knew what counter assistants and other members of staff could get up to; she'd learnt all the tricks while working her way up the ladder to where she was now.

She patted her severe bun into place, knowing the silver threads in her hair reinforced the impression that she was a stern taskmaster. At least none of the young ladies waiting outside were aware that this was the first time she had ever advertised and interviewed staff at the Erith store. She would make Charlie proud of her and all that she'd achieved, she thought, fighting back the sudden tears that pricked her eyes. 'Pull yourself together, Betty,' she scolded herself, straightening the paperwork on her desk and picking up a fountain pen in readiness for making notes.

'Are you ready, Miss Billington?' Alan popped his head round the door again.

'Yes, thank you, Alan, please show the candidates in. I will have a chat with the whole group before they take their tests.'

She watched as the women entered silently, giving her wary glances. Most seemed to be wearing their best coats and hats. One was dressed like a starlet from the silver screen; whatever was she doing applying for a position as counter assistant? Another applicant appeared to be no more than a child, a scrap of a thing whose clothes were worn, shabby and tired; very much like her expression, as she gazed at Betty through frightened eyes circled with dark shadows. It made Betty think back to the day when her own life had changed so drastically – when her dream of becoming a Woolworths girl had come true.

1

Christmas Eve 1916

'Oh, I've missed you so much,' Elizabeth Billington said as she threw herself into the arms of a sandy-haired man who was wearing the uniform of a corporal in the Royal West Kent regiment. He swung her around before leading her behind a high wall beside the entrance to Charlton Park, where he was supposed to be guarding the gates. Even though it was late afternoon with hardly anyone around, he was wary of being caught while on guard duty – not to mention sullying his beloved's reputation.

'Let me look at you,' he said, holding her at arms' length. 'You're a sight for sore eyes, even in the twilight. Is this for me, Betty?'

Elizabeth felt her cheeks start to burn. Only Charlie Sayers called her Betty; her mother would have a fit if she knew Charlie had shortened her name. Come to that, she would have a fit if she knew her seventeen-year-old daughter had slipped away from the house to meet a man the Billingtons had never been introduced to. Mrs Billington feared for

Elizabeth's virginity even more than she feared the danger of the Zeppelins.

She gave a small curtsy and held her coat away from her body so he could see the shell-pink gown, threaded with silver stitching. 'I chose it hoping you would remember me dressed in my finery; but it's really meant for a New Year soirée I have to attend with my parents. If only you could come,' she sighed.

Charlie snorted his disgust and reached for his cigarettes, lighting one for Elizabeth. She didn't like the taste and the smoke made her feel sick, but she wanted to share his love of smoking. In fact, she wanted to share everything he was interested in, including the way he worshipped the football team Charlton Athletic.

'You'd not get me near one of those highfalutin affairs,' he scoffed. 'No one in their right mind wants to waste time rubbing shoulders with toffs. That lot hardly get their hands dirty to earn a living – they all prefer to live off dividends from family shares, or inheritances. None of 'em do an honest day's work.'

Elizabeth pulled away. 'That's my family and their friends you're belittling,' she admonished him, even though she knew he was right. Her father did something in the City, but she wasn't sure exactly what it was – only that he left at eight o'clock each morning for the bank and always came home for dinner in a foul mood, before burying his head in his newspaper muttering about share prices and the state of the country. Perhaps Charlie had a point.

'Let's not fall out,' he begged. 'This'll be the last time we see each other for God knows how long. I don't want us to part at loggerheads so that you go running off with some other chap because you think I'm a miserable so-and-so.'

'Oh, Charlie – I'd never think of you like that, and I'd never even look at another man. I'm yours forever,' she sighed. She let her unwanted cigarette drop to the ground as he flicked his away, pulled her close and stopped her words with his lips.

After a few minutes, she wriggled free of his embrace. 'We ought to stop; you're crushing my gown. Besides, too much of this and I'll turn into one of those women waiting at the station for her man to return from the wars, holding a baby bundled in rags.'

'That's rather dramatic,' Charlie laughed as he turned away to light another cigarette. Then he took her arm again, pulling her further along the wall to where they could hide behind some bushes.

'Charlie, I don't think . . .'

'Sshhh. It's not what you think; here, I've got something for you.' He reached into the pocket of his khaki uniform and took out a small item wrapped in tissue paper. 'It's not a ring, but the chaps reckon it's just as important to a woman.'

Elizabeth unwrapped the tissue paper and squealed with excitement at the sight of a sweetheart brooch, the kind soldiers often gave to their loved ones. 'I know what this is!' she said delightedly, as she pinned the brooch to her coat. 'And it has your regiment engraved around the edge . . . Here, I have something for you, too – although it's nothing like your gift to me.'

'I should hope not,' he laughed as he took the wrapped packet she was offering. 'I'd look silly wearing a brooch on my uniform, or any other time, come to that. Why, these are just what I need,' he added, opening it to reveal a pair of knitted socks and a packet of tobacco. 'Thank you, my love.'

'And thank you again for my special brooch. I'll treasure it forever.'

'You know this officially makes you my girl,' he told her, wrapping an arm round her shoulders.

'I already was, Charlie. You didn't need to go buying me presents to prove it,' she said. She knew he liked to contribute as much to his family home as he possibly could.

'It'll do for now, until I get back and buy you that special ring. Then we can start to make our plans a reality. I just wish you'd let me ask your father for your hand in marriage before I leave for the front. I'd have something to remember you by,' he murmured gently, brushing her cheek with his finger.

Elizabeth knew that her father would not entertain Charlie's request and would simply show him the door. 'It's best we wait a little longer,' she said with a shiver as he ran his finger down her face and neck, stopping only at the neckline of her dress.

'I'm not sure how long I can wait,' he groaned before crushing her against the rough serge of his uniform.

'Just hold on to our dream of our own little greengrocer's shop,' she sighed as he kissed her just below her earlobe. She stepped back a little, fearing she would give in to his kisses as they became more demanding. 'Just hold on to that dream . . .'

'Where we'll live over the shop, until we make our fortune and can move to somewhere your parents would approve of.'

7

'Let's forget about them. Once we're married, it will just be you and me against the world.'

'Until the nippers come along, that is,' he said, giving her a squeeze.

Elizabeth was glad it was dark so he couldn't see her cheeks burning with embarrassment. 'There's time enough for that. I want to see you standing behind the counter of your own shop wearing a white apron and a straw boater, like they do in the food department at Harrods.'

Charlie snorted with laughter. 'I'd not know about that, love. You'll never see the Sayers family doing their weekly shop in places like 'Arrods. Dad's wages on the railway don't stretch to us shopping up town, and neither did my pay packet when I was a crane driver. It was barely enough to keep food on the table and a roof over our heads, especially when my stepmum was ill.' He hesitated, reaching again for the cigarettes. 'That reminds me; I want you to visit Dad and my sisters while I'm away, and . . . and, well, if anything should happen, you're not to be a stranger to their house, do you hear me?' he added in a gruff voice.

She clung to him. 'Please don't talk like that. You'll come back and we will have our little shop, and . . .' Her voice cracked, undermining her optimistic words. She'd seen the newspaper reports about what it was like over on the other side of the Channel, where Charlie had intimated he was about to be shipped off. Even though her parents forbade her from reading such things, she was aware of how terribly the war was affecting lives. There were houses in town with black wreaths hanging on their doors, denoting families that had recently lost loved ones. It was a common sight to see women in their widows' weeds, while poorer people wore black armbands to show their respect.

'We need to be sensible,' he said as he shook her arm roughly. 'Do you understand? I need to know everything is in place, in case I . . .'

'I promise,' she whispered. 'I promise, I promise, I promise. I'm yours forever and don't you forget it, Charlie Sayers. Don't you go running off after those French mademoiselles, either.'

'They don't hold a light to you,' he said, trying to keep his voice strong.

'How would you know?' she demanded, putting her hands on her hips.

'It's only what the chaps have told me,' he laughed.

Elizabeth didn't always know how to take Charlie; sometimes he made her want to answer back, to check his feelings for her. When they'd first met, she had been walking alone in the park; she'd dropped her bag and at first she'd thought he was going to steal it. But he'd handed it back with a charming smile and struck up a conversation, quickly convincing her that he was an upright citizen. He'd been so happy when she agreed to meet him the following week.

'Who goes there?' a voice boomed from nearby.

'It's only me, Sarge – Corporal Sayers. I was taking a piss. It's nippy out here and a long walk to the latrines.' Charlie pulled Elizabeth closer, signalling for her to be quiet.

'Get your arse out here this minute, you lazy good-for-nothing! You're supposed to be guarding the gates.'

Giving her a quick kiss, he pushed her towards the footpath that would take her in the opposite direction. 'I love you, Betty,' he said, keeping his voice low. 'Promise me you'll live a good life.'

'What a daft thing to say. I love you too, Charlie, and we will live that good life together,' she whispered urgently, feeling tears sting her eyes. 'Don't forget me,' she added, before hurrying away.

'Goodbye, Betty Billington,' he murmured as she disappeared into the night. 'Please keep your promise . . .'

2

25 August 1917

Elizabeth stormed out of the house. Blinded by angry tears, she slammed the heavy front door behind her and ran down the twelve steps to the pavement. Cuffing her eyes, she stopped for just a moment; which way should she go? She spotted a tram that would take her away from her parents' grand house in Charlton to the centre of Woolwich. Checking her purse was in her bag, she ran to join the queue.

As she waited to board she took a deep, shuddering breath, wiping her eyes again and hoping she didn't look as though she had been sobbing her heart out for the past hour. Try as she might, she couldn't pin a smile onto her face, even though she could hear the words of her late grandmother reminding her to do so when times were hard. Grandmother had always encouraged her to be brave what-ever the circumstances, and a smile would mean she was halfway there. She bit her lip to keep from answering back when an elderly man, stepping back to let her get onto the tram, told her, 'Give us a smile – you never know, it might not happen.'

Elizabeth mustered a smile and whispered her thanks before finding a seat towards the front of the car. Sitting down, she stared out of the window, oblivious to what was going on in the busy road ahead. The man was wrong: 'it' had already happened. To all intents and purposes, she was now alone in the world. Her future and her plans were shattered into a million pieces. Nothing would ever be the same again – whatever was she going to do?

Gradually she became aware of what she could see. The many men in uniform, an all too familiar sight these days; women in black; newspaper sellers waving the papers above their heads as they called out the latest headlines from this never-ending war.

Slipping her hand into the pocket of her smart navy blue serge jacket, she pulled out the hastily scribbled letter that had been delivered to her parents' house only an hour earlier. Already she knew its contents off by heart: the love of her life, her Charlie, had died of his injuries in a place called Ypres.

Reading the words again and again, she prayed it was all a dream, that she'd wake up from the nightmare knowing he was alive and soon coming home to her. Barely aware of what she was doing, she fumbled under the lapel of her jacket until she felt the rough shape of the sweetheart brooch he had given her at their last meeting. She'd often felt ashamed that the brooch had been hidden from view all this time. She had kept her love for Charlie a secret from her parents, knowing they would never approve of the man she loved and planned to marry. Now, defiantly, she removed it and pinned it to the outside of the lapel, where everybody could see the simple declaration of his love. She would wear it until her dying day – until she was at last reunited with the man with whom she'd planned to spend the rest of her days.

'Excuse me, love. I hope you don't think I'm being nosy, but I couldn't help noticing how upset you look,' said an older woman sitting nearby, wearing a faded blue coat that had seen better days. She moved from her seat to sit beside Elizabeth. 'I think you've had news of a loss; your husband, perhaps?'

Elizabeth nodded, unable to find the words to answer this kindly woman who had taken her hand and was patting it gently. It was clear she was a worker from her washed-out clothes and the scarf tied around her head. The basket at her feet contained what looked like sandwiches, wrapped in greaseproof paper. Charlie wouldn't have wanted her to ignore this woman. Charlie enjoyed anyone's company and would have chatted to her with ease; he would not have approved if Elizabeth had been rude.

'I received a letter myself just over a year ago,' the woman was saying. 'Still can't believe I'll never see my old man again. The kiddies don't understand what happened to him, as we have no grave to visit – that would've made things easier.'

'It was my fiancé, Charlie,' Elizabeth said. She passed the letter to the woman, who scanned it quickly and handed it back.

'You have my sincere sympathy, my love. At least you've not been left with little ones to provide for, like so many of us. It's a struggle to even put food on the table – and I have a decent job, unlike many poor souls. That's where I'm going right now. I'm a cleaner down at the Arsenal, that's the munitions works. My mother-in-law keeps an eye on the kiddies while I'm there.'

These words sank in slowly until the stark horror of her situation hit Elizabeth like a speeding steam engine. The family she'd planned to have with her beloved Charlie would never happen. Charlie had been quite amorous when he courted her, begging for them to be closer . . . more intimate. She'd laughed off his insistence, fearing for the consequences; if she were to fall pregnant and anything should happen to him, she would be ostracized by the society her family moved in.

She looked the woman square in the face. 'I wish I did have his child – then I'd have something to remember him by. I'm sorry if that sounds forward of me. I hope I've not shocked you.'

'There will be many women like you who dream of what life would have been like if this terrible war had not interfered. I know you probably think I'm daft, but you need to look to the future even though you're deep in your grief. Times are changing fast now. My mother-in-law gave me a right talking to when I wallowed in my self-pity. She didn't even allow me time to sit and sob because, as she pointed out, without money coming in we would all end up in the workhouse. Being an elderly woman, that was always her greatest fear and she was fond of saying, even when my Alf was alive, that we needed to keep our heads above water.' She shook her head. 'I used to laugh at her way with words – until I was left with five little ones and her to feed. It's been tough at times but I'm coping, as it's all I can do. No man is going to want to take me on, with five nippers and the old girl dependent on me. What will you do now?'

Elizabeth didn't feel the woman was being at all nosy; it was clear that she really cared. 'I'm not very sure. But I do know that I should shout my love for Charlie from the rooftops – I'll not hide his name a moment longer.'

'I'm not with you, ducks; what do you mean?'

'My parents don't approve of a girl my age having a romance. They had plans for me to meet the right kind of person. When I once tested the water by mentioning I had a male friend, my mother said she hoped he came from our class, whereas my father told me I was too young to think of marriage, especially with the war raging. But I'm seventeen and I know my own mind. I don't want to spend my life taking afternoon tea with Mother's friends and making social chit-chat with people I don't care for. What life is that? It's because of them that, until just now, I kept Charlie's love token hidden,' she said, touching the brooch with the rampant horse that was part of his regiment's emblem.

'Wear it with pride,' the woman said. She pointed to a badge of her own, no more than a button with a regimental name inscribed upon it. 'My Alf sent this to me in the last billet-doux I received from him. Of course, my mother-in-law wanted it, but I put my foot down. It was given with love from him to me.'

Elizabeth nodded. 'As was mine,' she replied softly.

'What about your Charlie's mother? She must be beside herself with grief. I know I would be, if my sons had been old enough to serve.'

'Charlie's mum died when he was ten. He's got two younger sisters by his dad's second wife. It was the older girl that brought this letter, from their dad,' Elizabeth said, folding the piece of paper and placing it back into the envelope. 'My goodness, I hope she's all right. I don't remember much after she was led into the drawing room and gave me the letter. The shock overcame me. Mother was firing off questions about why she was there; the poor child was overwrought. The proper notification had gone to Charlie's father, him being next of kin. Mother was pointing to the door . . . and then Charlie's sister left. It seemed as though the world had ended and I'm afraid I wasn't very good at hiding my feelings.'

The woman nodded understandingly. Elizabeth continued: 'Mother had to wave sal volatile under my nose, and then she started to press me about who Charlie's sister was, and what on earth a child like that would be doing bringing me a letter . . . She just wouldn't stop, and eventually I couldn't bear it any more. I had to get out, get away.' She felt tears welling up again, and fought them back. 'I need to decide what I'm going to do with my life from now on. I suppose that includes earning a living and finding somewhere to live, because I don't plan to sleep under my parents' roof for much longer.' Meeting the woman's gaze, she added, 'Does that make me ungrateful?'

'No, it doesn't, my love. I think, in a way, you've had a merciful release. I don't mean with your fiancé dying – I mean from your family. If you don't agree with the way they've been bringing you up, then now's the time to make the kind of life you want to live. Working-class girls of your age would already have been working for many a year. Now, I'm nearly at my stop, but if you're serious about wanting to find a job we always need people down at the Arsenal. It's hard graft but the money is good, and you're bound to be able to find some lodgings in the area. You only need to go to the gate and they will tell you what vacancies there are. I'm Maggie Jones, by the way. I didn't catch your name?'

'I'm Eliz . . .' She began to say Elizabeth, but stopped for a moment. From now on, she would use Charlie's name for her. 'I'm Betty – Betty Billington. And I can't thank you enough for your kindness,' she said, holding out her hand to Maggie.

Maggie ignored the hand, flung her arms around Betty's shoulders and gave her a sound kiss on the cheek. 'Come and find me if you start down at the Arsenal. Everyone knows me down there,' she chuckled, adding a cheery 'see you later' as she left Betty to her thoughts.

Betty had two more stops to go before her destination. Chewing her lip thoughtfully, she gazed out at the crowd of people heading towards the munitions factory. She spotted Maggie and followed her progress for a moment before the woman disappeared into the crowd. How could anyone work in such a place? She'd heard talk of the dangers of working in munitions, and the odd time she'd read her father's newspaper she'd quickly skirted past the news of the people at peril in such environments. Of course, it was nothing like fighting on the front, as Charlie had been doing . . . A shudder ran through her, and she reached into her pocket for the letter to read the words once more. Tears blurred her vision again at the thought that he had gone forever. 'I wish I could die and be with him,' she whispered as she wiped her eyes.

People had started to look at her, and although Maggie had been very kind, Betty didn't wish to discuss her private business with anybody else. Taking a few deep breaths, she composed herself, and even though she couldn't pin a smile on her face she did her best not to look traumatized. Getting to her feet, she pushed along the aisle in readiness to leave the tram when it pulled up. She managed a polite *excuse me* here and there and ignored a cheeky lad who whispered a lewd suggestion in her ear.

Setting off at a brisk pace, she soon spotted Charlie's home at the end of a long row of terraced houses. She knew these homes were mainly inhabited by railway workers. If she felt as though her life was over, how must Charlie's father be feeling? The man had brought up his children alone since his second wife had died giving birth to the youngest girl. All she knew of Harold Sayers was that he lived for his family, fitting in a full-time job as a train driver so as to keep a roof over his family's head and food on the table.

Walking the few steps up the path towards the front door, she inhaled the scent of hollyhocks and sweet peas in the small front garden that Harold religiously tended. It always delighted her to see him at work when she visited the house, but now his gardening implements lay scattered on the pavement and the front door had been left ajar.

Tapping on the door, she called out, 'It's only me, Mr Sayers; it's Betty.' Taking a deep breath, she stepped into the dark hallway and pulled the door shut behind her.

At once, the outside world was shut out and a sombre atmosphere all but smothered her. Up ahead there was a small living room, and it was there she found Harold with Charlie's younger sister, ten-year-old Peggy, sitting at his knee. The child was crying quietly and his hand rested on her head, gently stroking her blond curls. As Betty stepped into the room, Olive, the older sister, hurried over to hug her.

'I'm so relieved you made it home, Olive,' Betty said, holding the child tightly against her. 'And I am very sorry my mother was so rude to you – and that I wasn't able to respond to the shocking news.'

'It doesn't matter,' Olive answered, looking serious. 'I wanted to stay with you, but after being called a ragamuffin and told to leave, I thought it best to return home.' She gave an impression of maturity beyond her twelve years, despite being dressed in a child's frock that was slightly too small for her. Her sandy-coloured hair, a few shades lighter than Charlie's, needing washing. Betty couldn't help notice the way her eyes twinkled like Charlie's. 'I'm sorry Dad's note was such a shock. He wanted you here with us.'

Harold looked up. 'Fetch my coat, Olive, I need to see Betty's parents and explain . . .'

'There is no need, Mr Sayers, really,' Betty said. She didn't want Charlie's dad to have to face her parents. It was the last thing the poor man needed after the news he'd received today. As she thought about this, Betty crumpled and rushed into Harold's outstretched arms. 'What are we going to do without Charlie; whatever are we going to do?' she sobbed. He promised me faithfully he'd come home safe and sound, she thought to herself. He has let me down so badly.

Harold patted Betty's back as more tears overcame her. 'Go and put the kettle on,' he said to the girls after a moment, handing Betty his handkerchief to wipe her eyes before leading her to a chair. 'I should have gone to see you myself rather than send Olive with a note,' he went on, 'but Peggy was distressed, and I had no one who could sit with her. I do hope we haven't alarmed your mother – I understand she wasn't very happy about Olive asking to see you.'

Betty was ashamed of what she had to say. She looked at him with sad eyes but could not speak.

'They didn't know about Charlie, did they?'

'We did mean to tell them, but the time was never right. You see . . . they had such plans for me, and . . .'

'And the likes of our Charlie didn't fit in with their highfalutin ways?' he said, with a very small smile.

Betty nodded, embarrassed. How could she tell this man, who had just lost his son, that her parents were snobs who didn't consider any working-class person good enough for their only child?

'You've no need to explain, my dear. I'm old enough to know how strange some people can be. It's their loss that they never knew our Charlie, or how much he loved their daughter. I fear they will be no comfort to you in the days ahead. I'll say this now: there will always be a place for you under our roof. We only have a small box room, but you're welcome to it. You would have been my daughter-in-law one day, and before too long, the mother of my grandchildren. I can't turn my back on you now when we are all grieving.' A single tear ran down his rough face. He'd yet to shave that day, having been due to start a later shift at the railway, and he was in shirtsleeves and rough gardening trousers. 'We need to stick together,' he went on as he crossed to the table and picked up a letter from the green chenille tablecloth. 'This is the letter I received this morning. If you and Charlie had been married, it would have been sent to you as his next of kin.'

Betty was moved by his kindness, and surprised; Charlie had mentioned on more than one occasion that his father could be miserable and selfish. She shook that thought from her mind as she slid the single sheet of paper from its envelope, glancing past the official details of Charlie's rank and stopping for a moment to absorb the date of his death: 17 August 1917. Only eight days ago. It was a printed notification that would have been sent to thousands of bereaved families. She could get no comfort from the words, however well-meaning they were meant to be:

> *By His Majesty's command I am to forward the enclosed message of sympathy from Their Gracious Majesties the King and Queen. I am at the same time to express the regret of the Army Council at the soldier's death in his Country's Service.*
>
> *I am to add that any information that may be received as to the soldier's burial will be communicated to you in due course.*

Betty could not read another word. She replaced the letter in the envelope and handed it back to Harold, then sat, stony-faced. The words were cold and had no relevance to the Charlie she knew. 'They could be writing about anyone,' she said in barely a whisper. 'I wish there had been a letter from Charlie. I've received very little from him . . .'

'I don't know, my dear. I can't stop thinking that the official letter is a mistake, and our Charlie will come walking

21

through the door as bold as brass any minute with a cheeky grin on his face.'

'We can only hope your wishes come true,' Betty said. A deep shudder ran through her body as she tried to dismiss the image of her beloved lying dead on the battlefield.

Olive and Peggy came in, carefully carrying the tea tray between them. Betty was grateful for the hot, sweet tea; it did something to revive her.

'Are you going to live here with us, Betty?' Peggy asked.

Her father smiled gently; the child had no doubt been listening at the door. 'That's up to our Betty,' he said. 'She knows she's more than welcome to move in with us.'

Betty took a deep breath and gave them all a watery smile. 'I have things that need to be done – but I will return very soon. Please don't feel that because you've lost Charlie, you've also lost me: I'd like to think I will be part of your family for the rest of my life. I fear I won't be welcome at my parents' home much longer.'

Quickly finishing her tea and getting to her feet, she kissed all three of them, promising to be brave. Then she started the journey back to her parents' house.

3

Betty stepped through the grand front door of her parents' house into the cool interior. The black-and-white tiled floor, the walls painted in delicate shades of cream and green, and the ornate bowls holding aspidistra plants normally made her pause in appreciation of how lucky she was to live in such a place. Today, though, it did nothing to comfort her. She found herself thinking again about Charlie's dad's home, so welcoming to visitors.

'Is that you, my dear? I was beginning to worry. You hurried off in such haste,' her mother said, appearing from the drawing room. 'My goodness, what is this?' she cried, taking in Betty's tear-stained face and bedraggled appearance. 'Come here, Elizabeth, and explain yourself – and your association with that ragamuffin. I can't imagine a good reason for someone of that type to appear here asking for you.'

Betty opened her mouth to speak, but her mother hadn't finished.

'I'll have the maid bring in tea.'

Sinking into a plush red velvet armchair, Betty said, 'The maid's name is Vicky. I'm sure she'd like to be called by her name, don't you? As for the ragamuffin, she happens to be a very good friend from a respectable family . . .'

Agatha Billington drew in a sharp breath. 'Go to your room and make yourself presentable. I refuse to speak to you until you remind yourself of your manners, young lady.'

Betty wanted to shout at her mother – shock her with the double revelation that she had been secretly engaged, and her fiancé had perished on the battlefield defending their country – but she controlled the impulse. Instead she kept her eyes on the floor and hurried out of the room. Upstairs, in the cool of her room, she threw herself onto the bed and stared at the ceiling. Rather than the elaborate cornices and brass light fittings, she saw Charlie's face as he'd looked the very last time they met.

She pressed a hand to her lips, trying not to cry. If only she and Charlie had fulfilled their love for one another, she might have had something to remember him by; but it was too late now. The war had stolen him. She felt for the small sweetheart brooch pinned to her jacket. 'From now on, the world will know of my love for Charlie Sayers,' she whispered.

She sat up; her head was spinning. After a moment she went over to her decoratively carved dressing table and unlocked a small drawer, using a key she kept on a chain around her neck. Pulling out a bundle of letters and cards tied with pink ribbon, she took them back to her bed and gently undid the bow. The order of the correspondence followed her romance; from the very first note Charlie had slipped into her hand the second time they met, to the beautiful silk-embroidered postcard he'd sent on arrival in France. His correspondence had always been directed to his father's house so that Betty's family wouldn't see it. There had never been any question of them accepting him – Agatha Billington had high expectations for her only child's marriage, and her plans did not include a crane driver from a railway worker's family who had been called up to fight for his country.

Betty held the postcard to her cheek and wept. 'Oh Charlie, how can I live without you? We had such plans . . . I don't know what I'm going to do. But it's time the world knows we loved each other, and that you were going to care for me for the rest of our lives.'

She drifted over to the window and looked down at the busy road in front of the house. 'How can everybody still be going about their lives as usual, when mine has all but ended?' she wondered aloud. 'I do know one thing: I can't stay in this house a moment longer.' Taking a deep breath, she wiped her eyes with a delicate lace handkerchief and then replaced the cherished bundle of letters in their drawer, carefully locking it and putting the key on its chain back round her neck.

A glance at the ornate clock on the mantelpiece told her she would soon have to go downstairs; her father would be home from the bank before long and Mother would expect her to join them. Well, there were going to be some surprises, she sniffed to herself as she carefully removed her suit and took a green silk day dress from her large carved oak wardrobe. Laying it across the bed, she went to the washstand, tipped cold water into the bowl and splashed her face to calm her red eyes and burning cheeks. She patted herself dry on a soft towel before dressing.

Checking her hair, which was still neatly pinned back

from her face, she thought about how much Charlie had loved her soft curls. He'd always liked to see her hair loose when they were alone. Although fashion dictated she wore it pinned up during the day, she stopped for a moment now, turning her head from side to side before pulling out the pins and shaking her head. If Charlie liked her to wear it that way, then that was how she was going to wear it when she gave her parents her news. Rather than calling Vicky to help her fasten her dress, she fought with the buttons until she succeeded in doing it herself. Then, after taking a moment to compose herself, she raised her head high and went downstairs to the drawing room.

Her father was already home and settled in his usual chair. 'Ah, my dear, here you are. Your mother informs me you are out of sorts,' he said, lowering his newspaper onto a little table. He folded his hands and waited for an answer.

Agatha, sitting nearby, also waited, frowning slightly at the sight of Betty's unpinned hair.

Betty sat down, perching on the edge of her seat. Now that the time had come to speak her mind, she felt nervous. 'I'm still upset by the news I received today,' she began, not quite meeting her father's eyes. She gripped her dress with both hands, grasping the fabric tightly as she tried to compose herself.

'Perhaps you should explain that to your father,' Agatha prompted.

At last Betty looked directly at both of them. 'I was notified that my fiancé has been killed at Ypres,' she said, raising her chin defiantly.

Her father's mouth dropped open slightly.

'*Fiancé?*' her mother shrieked, startling Vicky, who was

coming into the room and dropped the tea tray. Betty hurried over to help her. The maid was the only person in the household who already knew about her secret love.

'I'm sorry, miss – I'm truly sorry for your loss,' she murmured in distress, hastily replacing the disordered contents of the tray and picking up broken shards of china.

'I'll have that taken out of your wages,' Mrs Billington snapped as the girl hurried out of the room. 'Elizabeth, please sit down and explain yourself,' she added, putting one hand to her chest and fanning her face. 'I feel quite unwell.'

Ignoring this, Mr Billington looked at his daughter with steely eyes. 'You do owe us an explanation, Elizabeth.'

Betty took a deep breath. 'My fiancé, Charles Sayers, has died. I found out earlier today. That is why I left the house,' she said.

There was a short silence while her father regarded her with disbelief. Then he said: 'I can only imagine this is some fanciful notion that has gone to your head, Elizabeth. You do read rather a lot of magazines; I've even seen you look at my newspaper on occasion. For you to have a fiancé, I would have had to meet the young man and give my approval. I do not recollect having done so. Do you know anything about this, Agatha?'

'Of course I don't,' she spat back. 'I would have told you. Any ideas you have in your head about marrying, you can forget,' she glared at Betty. 'There is a protocol to follow before we announce your engagement.'

Betty rose suddenly to her feet, the legs of her chair scraping on the wooden floor. 'I never told you because I knew you wouldn't approve of Charlie.' Agatha flinched at her words. 'My Charlie was a crane driver for the railway before he was called up and sent to France and his death.'

'My goodness,' her mother said faintly; then she stopped and frowned. 'How would you have met such a person?'

'That *person*, Mother, was the gentlest, most loving man you could ever know. I met him while out walking. We bumped into each other, and I dropped my bag and the books I was returning to the library.'

'You met him *on the street*?' Agatha Billington gasped.

Her father ignored the fact that Betty was on her feet ready to take flight. 'At least now, my dear, you can forget all about this silly notion. There are plenty of fine young men who would be glad to have you on their arm. You are our only child and you have prospects,' he said proudly.

'I'll never be seen with another man. I doubt I will ever marry, now that Charlie has died. He was the love of my life, and nothing you can say will take that from me.'

'While you live under our roof, you will do as we say,' her mother said. 'Now go and hurry that wretched girl along.'

Betty looked between her parents. Her father had resumed reading his newspaper and her mother was avoiding her eyes, clearly not wishing to continue the conversation. So that's it, she thought to herself. I've told them, and as expected, they neither sympathized nor enquired about my feelings. If fate had not been so unkind, I would have walked away from this house on Charlie's arm . . .

She frowned as she thought about her circumstances. She might not have Charlie by her side any longer, but she did have choices. She could still walk away. With her head held high, she turned and quietly left the room. Going to her bedroom, she pulled a small leather bag from the top of the wardrobe and quickly packed it, choosing only practical clothing and leaving behind the pretty lace gowns and frivolous hats. At the dressing table she opened a jewellery box and tipped its contents into the bag on top of her clothes before collecting her personal correspondence and tucking it in carefully among her possessions. Then she changed back into the suit she'd been wearing earlier, slipping her feet into boots instead of her silk evening slippers. Placing a coat over her arm, she picked up her bag and turned to go just as there was a quiet knock on her door, and Vicky appeared.

'Oh, Miss Elizabeth! I would've been up here sooner, but your mother is making a right song and dance about the mess I made,' she explained, before throwing her arms around Betty and pulling her close. 'I'm so sorry – your Charlie was a lovely man. I know I only saw him the once, but I could tell he loved you. What are you going to do now?'

Betty frowned. What was she going to do? 'My first thought was just to escape this house. I can't stay here any longer. I need to keep Charlie's memory alive, and I can never do that here.'

Vicky nodded sadly. 'Would his father not be the person to speak to?' she suggested.

'You're right. Mr Sayers told me I was welcome in his house,' Betty said, kissing her cheek, thankful that Vicky was on her side. The maid had been one of her only confidantes during her romance and had kept her secret faithfully, as well as helping by posting letters. 'I'll do my best to keep in touch with you,' she promised. 'I need to write a letter to my parents; I can do that at Mr Sayers' house and post it to them.'

Vicky took the bag from Betty's hand. 'I honestly think you should do it now, miss. I'll wait until you've left and then I can give it to them. The last thing you need is for them to be calling the police and searching for you and this way, even if they aren't happy about it, at least they'll know you are safe. Don't tell them exactly where you're going – that way you can take time to consider your future.'

Betty agreed, and went back to her dressing table. Using the notepaper she kept in one drawer, she wrote a brief letter explaining that she could no longer see a future living in her parents' house and wished to go away and be alone to think of her beloved Charlie.

'That will have to do,' she said as she folded the paper and slipped it into an envelope. 'Will you wait long enough so they can't see me if they look out of the window?'

'I'll wait until I've served dinner,' the maid promised, tucking the envelope into her apron pocket. The way the Billingtons treated her, she wouldn't have minded if they choked when they read the letter. It was only working for young Miss Billington that had kept her sane in this house. She intended to look for a new position very soon.

Betty pulled the door shut behind her as quietly as she could, saying a silent goodbye to her parents and to her younger self. Elizabeth Billington was no more; now she would be Betty until the end of her days. Her bag was heavy and she pulled on her warm coat – she didn't really need it but it freed up a hand. She headed down the steps, away from the view of the large bay windows that dominated the imposing house. Once at the corner of the street, she stopped to take a breath, knowing that from now on her life would change. Any money that she needed would have to be earned by her own hard work. In a way she was pleased; she'd always liked the idea of having a job and standing on her own two feet. The few times she'd mentioned it, her mother had had a fit of the vapours and refused to discuss the subject. She'd even suggested to her father that perhaps he could find her a small position in his bank? The look of horror on his face had answered her question and Betty had dropped the subject, feeling as though her life was destined to remain mundane and monotonous.

Meeting Charlie had been a godsend: he'd brought some much-needed normality to her world, and soon had her joining him for bus rides and walks down to the Thames to watch the busy shipping traffic. A couple of times he'd taken her to the picture house, and she enjoyed watching the silent movies, but it wasn't the socializing that she would miss; it was Charlie's very being, the closeness, his kisses and knowing that between them they shared something special.

Tears pricked her eyes, but she took a deep breath and stood tall. Whatever she did from now on, she hoped it would have Charlie's blessing. What more was there to hope for? His father had always said there would be a place for them in his house when they married, and hadn't he offered her a room only today? She prayed he'd really meant it – it would be rather unconventional, considering she wasn't even Charlie's widow.

Well, she'd soon find out how she stood, she thought as

she stepped down from the kerb and raised her hand, hailing a passing cab as it began to rain in earnest. She could start worrying about saving her money tomorrow.

The driver took her case and helped her into a seat. Sitting back while the vehicle headed towards Woolwich, she felt herself relaxing for the first time in hours. She'd asked to stop a couple of streets away from the Sayers home, in case they thought she was being frivolous with her money, and when they arrived she tipped the man generously.

First she visited a butcher's shop and then the grocer's next door, asking advice about the components to make a meal. If she didn't appear at Harold Sayers' door empty-handed, hopefully she'd be welcome for at least one night. She was surprised to be told that meat was in short supply, but when the butcher looked at the purse in her hand and winked, she got the message. There were still ways to purchase most things if you could afford to pay a little extra.

Her purchases were tied up in brown paper and she packed them into a straw basket she'd bought at a nearby general store – surely an item that she'd use often, now she no longer had a maid to fetch and carry her things.

Putting her case down on the pavement, she used her free hand to open the catch of the Sayers' gate and then made her way up the short path. She was ready to knock on the door when it opened and Charlie's father stood there, a broad smile on his face.

'Well, my love, I expected you to return, but not quite this quickly. Come along in before you get drenched.'

As Betty stood in front of him, her firm resolve to be

strong drained away and she fell into his arms, sobbing her heart out. He led her in and over to his own armchair, where he often sat looking out over the garden. Then he stood sadly beside her as she cried into her hands. He gently rubbed her shoulder, murmuring 'There, there,' until her tears subsided.

'I'm so sorry,' she said, looking up as the two girls joined them, peeping cautiously round the doorway. 'I'm not being very brave.'

'Don't go on so,' Harold said. 'You needed to get that out of your system. Big things have happened, Betty, and I promise that we three will be here to help you. I assume you've had words with your family?'

'Yes, but I left before they could say too much. I wondered . . . could you put me up for a night or two? Just until I work out what I'm going to do with myself?'

Harold shook his head and smiled. 'You are a one, Betty Billington. Like I said before, when you were here with Charlie – this will always be your home. It makes no difference that my lad's gone. To me you are still my daughter-in-law.'

'You can share our bedroom,' young Peggy said. 'It will be such fun.'

'I'd like that, thank you. Are you sure you won't mind?' she asked the child, with a questioning glance at Harold.

'Not at all. You can share my toys as well, if you like?' Peggy offered.

In spite of everything, Betty found herself laughing. 'That's very generous of you.'

Harold was thoughtful. 'If you don't mind sleeping top to tail with the girls tonight, I'll go down the road tomorrow and see what Fred Tomkins has got by way of a spare bed. Then we can set you up in the box room. Charlie shared a room with me until he was called up and I gave his bed to the rag and bone man, thinking I'd get a newer one once he was home; it was fit for nothing.'

Betty wasn't sure what sleeping top to tail meant, but she was glad of having anywhere to sleep at all. 'I can pay,' she said. 'I don't want to be beholden to anybody.'

'You're not – Fred owes me a favour, so put your purse away,' he scolded mildly as Betty reached for her bag.

Her heart filled with joy. 'Thank you all for being so kind.'

'Then let's set to and get you settled in, shall we?'

'I've brought a few things for your supper . . . but I'm not much of a cook. I've not had a chance to learn. That was something I planned to do before I married Charlie,' she added sadly, picking up her little basket of parcels.

'The girls can both cook,' Harold said gruffly. 'I leave all that to them.'

Betty thought it was strange that two children should oversee the meals, but she bit her tongue. Perhaps she would be able to help, once she'd found her way around the kitchen.

'It will be lovely to have you here when I come home from school,' Olive said, as she quickly put the meat Betty had brought into the oven and began peeling the vegetables.

'You do understand, though, that I'll need to go out and find work? I can't afford to be a lady of leisure,' Betty explained.

Olive giggled. 'How strange it must be, to be a lady of

leisure and not work for a living. Even with having lots of money – they must lead such boring lives,' she mused as she went about her work.

She could be describing my mother, thought Betty, and felt ashamed that that would have been her life, too, if she hadn't met Charlie. Marrying him, and helping to build a home and a business for them and their children, would have been all she needed. 'I'm going to have to search out work,' she confirmed, 'so if you can think of anything I might be able to do, please let me know.' Olive listened with her head cocked thoughtfully to one side. 'I met a lady earlier today who said there was always work at the Arsenal, but I'm not sure what I could turn my hand to there.'

'That is an idea – and from what I've heard they take on plenty of unskilled workers,' Olive said enthusiastically.

Betty smiled at her, thinking how much she resembled Charlie. Her hair was darker than little Peggy's, and she had Charlie's eyes . . . and her nose was the same shape, too. It made Betty wonder what their own children would have looked like.

'I'll start a list,' Olive said. 'I'm sure there's something you can turn your hand to. But it won't be working in a kitchen – not until I've shown you how to peel a potato properly,' she smiled.

Betty chuckled. 'That would be so helpful, as I have no idea whatsoever.'

The dinner was a resounding success. Betty was surprised how tasty the food turned out to be, considering Olive had given her only a short lesson.

'We'll have you cooking every day before too long,' Olive said, giving Betty a grin. 'You're a quick learner.'

35

Harold looked at her with laughing eyes. 'Perhaps I should marry you?' he chuckled.

Betty smiled at his joke, but Olive didn't look as if she appreciated it at all. 'I'll write down that list of work ideas after we've eaten,' she said rather pointedly.

'There's no need to talk to Betty like that,' Harold reprimanded his daughter.

'No, please, it's all right,' Betty said. 'I did tell Olive that I'm looking for a job. I need to pay my way from now on, and she's going to set down some ideas for me after supper. It will be a great help.'

'Yes, I'll go fetch my slate and make a start after the washing up is done.'

'We can do better than that,' Betty said. 'I'll give you a hand with the washing up if you help me unpack. I have a notepad and a special pen you are welcome to use.'

Olive's eyes lit up. 'May I really? I'm going to enjoy you living here.'

So am I, Betty thought to herself as she looked with fondness at Charlie's family. This is all I have left of him now, apart from my memories.

4
~

The next few days flew by as Betty settled into life at the little house on Railway Terrace. She'd imagined, what with the nearby Woolwich Arsenal factory working around the clock as well as the noise of railway workers and passing trains, that she wouldn't sleep well there. But as it turned out, snuggled down under the roof of the house that had once been Charlie's home, she slept soundly. It was only when she woke each morning that the horror of her beloved's death sought her out, eating into her soul as if she were hearing the news of his demise for the very first time.

Rather than dwell on her sadness this morning, she forced herself out of bed and quickly washed with cold water from the jug on the washstand in her room. Pulling on a cotton day dress, she clipped up her hair to keep it out of her face and headed downstairs, carrying the flower-covered china jug and bowl in order to clean it out.

She was about to take the jug and bowl back up to her room when she heard the rattle of the letterbox and saw a square white envelope lying on the doormat. Recognizing the smart stationery, she picked it up; it was addressed to her.

Betty truly hoped it would be a letter from her parents.

She'd written to them on her first morning at the Sayers' house, posting the letter straight after breakfast, knowing it would reach her family later the same day. She'd been able to tell them she had a place to live, and that she was as happy as possible considering the situation and would arrange to have her remaining clothes and possessions collected in the coming days. Being a dutiful daughter and knowing she was now free from their domineering clutches, she sent her love, saying she bore no grudge and hoped she would be able to visit them soon.

Betty had thought long and hard about telling them exactly where she was, fearing Charlie's family might suffer for it if her father's temper had not abated. However, Harold had told her in no uncertain terms that she should give the address. He'd added that the Billingtons were welcome in his home if they wanted to visit their daughter.

Her heart beat a little faster as she opened the envelope and unfolded the short letter, scanning the few lines. The writing was unfamiliar: neat and tidy, but badly spelt. It was a note from Vicky to say she would visit the following afternoon, as she had news to impart.

Although Vicky signed off with love and wished her well, Betty couldn't help feel that the cheerful maid must have suffered somewhat after Betty's parents discovered her absence. Her father was aware that they were close – he had lectured Betty plenty of times about fraternizing with the staff. Now, as she set about cutting bread and putting the kettle on the hob after collecting wood from the yard to feed the oven, her mind was full of ways to treat Vicky when she visited. Harold would be at work, as he was on a later shift tomorrow; and the two children would be in school, so Betty and Vicky would be able to chat freely. Betty felt she needed to prove to Vicky that she was able to cope alone and at the same time she wanted to show her appreciation.

Once the girls had been packed off to school she cleared away the breakfast crockery and wiped down the kitchen table. Outside the sun was shining, so, collecting her purse and basket, she took a short walk up to the parade of shops she'd visited a few days earlier. This time she wanted to find some sort of little present for Vicky, to thank her for her help. The idea kept her spirits up as she made her way along, stopping to purchase shin of beef and a kidney at the butcher's, along with suet to make a tasty pudding. With Olive's help she would be able to put together a decent meal later on.

With these thoughts running through her head Betty paused outside the window of what she at first took to be a jeweller's, although the windows were grimy and the contents old. She could see clothes inside on rails, and various ornaments and musical instruments. Looking up, she spotted three brass balls hanging from a bracket mounted above the door.

'Have you got something you'd like Uncle to price for you?' enquired an elderly man standing in the open doorway.

Betty hesitated, surprised. 'I'm sorry – I don't understand,' she said uncertainly.

'Mr Abraham will help you out,' a young woman said as she came out of the shop and gave Betty a nudge. 'Everyone needs money sometimes, and he'll see that you get a good price,' she advised Betty as she dropped a couple of coins into her purse and bade the man good day.

The penny dropped for Betty. 'Oh, you're a pawnbroker,' she said.

'I am indeed, my dear. And I haven't seen you here before. Are you new to the area?' he asked, noting Betty's smart clothing and general air of prosperity.

'I'm staying with friends,' she explained, as an idea started to form in her head. 'I wonder . . . I have a few trinkets and wonder if . . .'

'You wonder if I would be able to help you out? Please – step this way.' He guided her into the dark interior of the shop.

Inside, Betty was even more amazed by the variety of items stocked. She spotted a couple of stuffed birds and even an aspidistra in a china pot – which, going by its shape and the style of the handle, really belonged under a bed. 'What an interesting shop,' she said as she turned curiously this way and that. She stroked a fox-fur collar with one finger, causing tiny moths to fly into the air.

Flapping away the moths, Mr Abraham slid a bentwood chair out for Betty to sit down beside a cracked glass-topped display counter. He pointed a finger at the items below the glass. 'See here, my dear? These are the sort of things the gentry leave here when they pay me a call.'

'The gentry?' Betty echoed, looking at the strings of pearls and ornate brooches pinned to faded red velvet-lined trays. 'I had no idea.'

He tapped the side of his nose. 'Everyone trusts me, my dear. Now, what can I do for you?'

Betty delved into her bag. The jewellery she'd brought along when she fled her parents' home was wrapped in a silk scarf. 'I have these, and as I have found myself in a situation where I can't presently lay my hands on money, I wonder . . .'

Mr Abraham took the necklaces and brooches she held out and laid them carefully on the counter. Putting an eyeglass to one eye, he examined each item closely for several long moments, nodding occasionally. Eventually Betty, watching for his reaction, saw his expression become less friendly.

'Very nice, my dear. And where exactly did you get hold of them?' he asked coldly.

She was taken aback. 'Well, they're my property . . .' she began, reaching out to retrieve the items.

He pulled them sharply away. 'Not so fast: you haven't answered my question. I will not accept stolen goods. I have a reputation to uphold. Don't I, Sam?' he called over his shoulder.

'You do, you do,' replied a younger man, appearing from behind a rack of old coats. 'This is a reputable establishment. We don't want your sort in here.'

'My sort? Whatever do you mean?' Betty gasped. Their evident suspicion and disapproval so alarmed her that, unsure what else to do, she found herself almost pleadingly explaining who her parents were and where they lived.

She could see from the way they reacted that they believed her. Sam's expression became a trifle more friendly while the old man rubbed his chin thoughtfully.

'Sam, my boy – it seems we got this young lady wrong. Perhaps we should help her out after all.'

Betty felt her racing heart start to slow down. She'd half expected the pawnbroker to call for a constable and have her carted back to her parents' house. They would never,

never have forgiven her. 'Thank you so much – I do need your help . . .'

'And why would a pretty little thing like you be needing my help?' he said, giving her a piercing stare.

Betty drew a deep breath. The stakes were high: if this man trusted her, he would loan her money. If he didn't, he might well call the police. 'I currently find myself estranged from my parents and have very little money. I wondered if you would be able to help me out,' she said carefully, nodding towards the jewellery. Sam was now examining it. He nudged the older man and pursed his lips, making a sucking sound.

'What are you telling me, Sam?' Mr Abraham asked, looking concerned.

'It's mainly paste, Uncle, and really not worth much at all.'

Betty was surprised. 'But I don't think that can be right,' she exclaimed. 'Some of these pieces were given to me by my father, and the rings once belonged to my grandmother. They were left to me in her will. I feel awful having to . . .'

'Pawn them?' the young man asked, turning a brooch over to look at the back.

'If that's the correct word, yes; but doesn't it mean that I can buy them back once I'm not in such an embarrassing position?'

'You can indeed, my dear,' the man said, waving towards a grubby piece of paper that was pinned to the wall. 'The details are there for anyone to see. No one has ever claimed that I've tried to diddle them.'

Betty wasn't sure what he meant by 'diddle' and didn't want to ask. 'Oh, I'm sure you're very fair. Your business seems . . . to have been here a long time,' she added, glancing round at the moth-eaten garments and dusty surfaces.

'I am blessed that you are considering doing business with us,' the old man bowed. The younger man followed suit.

'If you could give me anything against them, it would tide me over until I find a job,' Betty pressed on, 'but I do wonder if perhaps I could retain the rings, as they have great sentimental value.'

'Of course you may,' he said courteously as Sam moved the rings away from the other jewellery, sliding them over the counter towards Betty. He watched carefully as she put them away in her bag.

'Thank you; that's very kind of you,' she said, feeling as though a weight had lifted from her shoulders. At least she would have some money in her purse to see her through the coming weeks.

It had crossed her mind to visit her father and request an allowance – that was, after all, the idea he'd fobbed her off with when she'd requested an actual position within his company. He'd said that instead he would consider letting her have a small allowance for 'fripperies'. The word had made her scoff, but now she just wished she'd pressed him more about it. Perhaps this was the right time to pay him a visit and remind him of his promise? At the same time, she could collect more of her clothes and personal items – and then she would be able to pay Mr Abraham back.

'You seem deep in thought, my dear,' Mr Abraham said as he pulled a box from under the counter and opened it, flicking through the money inside. He took out several coins and notes before scolding himself. 'Come, come, Abraham, you can do better than that for the young lady,' he muttered, then added several more coins to the ones in his hand.

Betty waited patiently, hoping the sum he offered would be enough to see her through until her future was secure.

'This is what I'm able to offer you, and it's more than any other person in my line of business would give. I'm doing this because I can see that you are a lady and will spend it wisely,' he said as he took one of her hands and placed the money into her palm.

Betty counted the money and then looked up at him, shocked. 'There's a little over two pounds here; I would have thought the value was much higher.'

The two men looked at each other before laughing out loud. 'You don't know much about the pawnbroking business, do you?' Sam cackled. 'You don't get the full value – otherwise we'd go out of business. We need to make a profit if we flog the stuff when you don't come back.'

Perhaps it would be best to accept the low offer, she thought, as it would be easier to buy the jewellery back at a later date. She could just about manage with the money he'd given her if she was prudent. 'But I will return,' she assured him.

Sam smirked. 'We don't know that, do we? You should be grateful to Uncle for being such a generous chap.'

Betty stood up and slipped the coins into her purse before placing it into the laden basket. She felt embarrassed. 'I'm so sorry; I didn't wish to offend you. I will be back to retrieve my items. You won't sell them to anyone else, will you?'

'I'm an honest man. Your trinkets will be here when you wish to collect them.'

Murmuring her thanks, Betty hurried out of the shop. It was a relief to be back in the sunshine. Glancing back, she saw Sam watching her from the doorway as another lad joined him, nodding in her direction. She set her course for the Sayers' home; so deep in thought was she, wondering if she had done the right thing, that she did not realize she was being followed. When she stepped off the kerb to cross the road someone pushed her sharply from behind and as she fell into the gutter with a cry, a dark figure grabbed her basket and ran away. Betty struggled to her feet as people hurried over to help her.

'Are you all right, ducks? He gave you a right shove,' a woman said. The young girl who was with her bent down to collect the few bits of shopping that had spilt from the basket.

'Thank you, I'm all right . . . but my things . . .'

'The dirty scoundrel's pinched her basket,' a man bellowed, and several people in the crowd of witnesses took off in hot pursuit of the thief.

The woman and her daughter helped to brush Betty down, and the man from the butcher's shop brought out a chair so that she could sit down and gather herself. She was shaking and rather confused. If only she hadn't put her purse into the basket!

'There's too much of it going on around here,' the woman tutted. 'Something needs to be done; it's a bad thing when a decent, law-abiding woman is accosted in broad daylight like this. Did you have much with you?'

Betty felt like an idiot. Had someone seen her leaving the pawnbroker's establishment and assumed she had money? 'Nothing of any value,' she replied, reluctant to be judged a fool for not taking more care. In truth, she felt as though all her worldly possessions had been taken from her. Thank goodness her letters from Charlie were safely in her room back at the Sayers' home – but now she was penniless. Whatever would she do?

The butcher's lad brought out a cup of water, which Betty gratefully sipped. Gradually the people who'd been interested in her plight drifted away. There was nothing to see here.

A red-faced man appeared and dropped the basket at her feet. He bent over, hands on knees, to catch his breath. 'Sorry, love, I chased him as far as I could; but he twisted and turned up the back alleys and I lost him. Not before dropping this, though. Do you want me to call a copper?'

Somehow, Betty didn't want anyone finding out that she had just visited a pawnbroker; and God forbid the police should turn up on Harold's doorstep because of her. She shook her head quickly. 'No, there was nothing of any great value in there. Thank you for what you've done,' she said, standing up. They shook hands as the butcher's lad appeared to collect the cup and the chair.

Betty took a slow walk back to Railway Terrace; at least no one had returned home yet, so she was able to sponge down her skirt and clean the grazes on her hand where she'd broken her fall. Making herself a cup of tea, she spooned in sugar for the shock, after which she put away her remaining shopping, thankful the meat had been well wrapped. With her purse gone she didn't have a penny to her name.

She would have to return to her parents' house along with Vicky tomorrow afternoon and throw herself on their mercy. She couldn't afford to argue with them any longer; perhaps, after all, she should just return to being a dutiful daughter.

Rather than try to appear jolly for the evening, she excused herself with a headache once the meal was over and went early to bed. Up in her little attic room she tossed and turned for hours, wondering what her future held.

5

It was a pale-faced Vicky who visited the following day – but before Betty could ask if the girl was poorly, Vicky took one look at her and said, with genuine concern, 'Has something happened, miss?'

This kindness was enough to make Betty burst into tears. Apologizing, she let Vicky lead her to a chair in the Sayers' comfortable living room. She'd held herself together the previous night while helping to prepare the evening meal and clearing up, before taking herself off to her bed. However, she'd woken full of aches and pains from being shoved to the ground, and meanwhile her head was filled with fears for the future. She didn't want to ask Harold Sayers for any more help; she was too proud to do so. The Sayers family had been kind enough taking her in, but now she needed and wanted to stand on her own two feet.

Drying her face with a handkerchief, she told Vicky everything that had happened the previous day. It was all she could do to put the experience into words, as it brought home to her what dire straits she was in.

'I don't know what to say, miss – I really don't,' Vicky

said. 'But I do know a cup of tea will help, while we decide what can be done.'

Betty insisted that she should be the one making the tea, but Vicky ordered her to sit where she was and not argue. 'I should think I know my way around a kitchen by now,' Vicky smiled, although Betty thought it wasn't quite her usual cheery smile; it didn't seem to reach her eyes.

Once on her own, Betty took deep breaths, forcing herself to calm down. She reminded herself that no problem was insurmountable. Besides, she wanted to find out if all was well in Vicky's life, rather than have her guest listen to her woes.

'Here we are,' said Vicky, returning with a tray. 'I used the best crockery; I hope that's all right?'

'Of course it is; I'd have done the same. I did buy a cake for us, but it was one of the things taken from my basket. I should have asked Olive to show me how to make another – but honestly, Vicky, it was all I could do after yesterday to behave normally in front of the Sayers family and not give them any sign that something was wrong. I don't want them to worry about me.'

'Have you spoken to the police? You never know, perhaps the thief has been caught. They sometimes know who these people are that do the robberies.'

Betty gave a harsh laugh. 'I doubt it very much. It happened so quickly! Several men did take chase but came back empty-handed, apart from my basket. I do wonder, though . . .' She paused as a thought came to her.

'Do you mean you have an idea who might have done it? You must report it if you do, because they need to be caught.'

'I doubt anything can be done, but ... I think what happened to me must have something to do with a lad I saw as I was leaving the pawnbroker's shop.'

'You've been to a pawnbroker?'

'Yes; you see, I have very little money left. I intend to find work, but I need to pay my way until then. I had some jewellery in my bag that I was unlikely to wear, and as I was passing the pawnbroker's a man invited me in. I thought it would be a good way of putting some money in my purse, and then I could buy the pieces back later on.' Betty took a sip of tea and frowned, thinking her way through the memory of yesterday's incident.

'It happened when I'd only just come out of the premises. I must have been watched, and the person watching me – I think it was the lad I mentioned – would have known there was money in my bag. I was going to say I'm penniless, but to be honest it feels more as though I'm destitute.' She took another sip of tea and forced herself not to cry again. Tears wouldn't achieve anything. 'Losing the little money I had has changed my future profoundly. I have made a decision.'

Vicky put down her teacup and looked at her expectantly.

'I'm going to accompany you back to my parents' house. I'll propose that I should be allowed some of the inheritance I'm going to receive when my father passes away. Under the circumstances, and now that he knows Charlie and I were engaged, he may not want me living under his roof. Paying me to go away, so to speak, may be the only answer. What do you think?'

Vicky hesitated, licking her lips nervously. 'There's something you need to know. I shan't be returning to work for your parents. I left my job the day after you left home.'

Betty shook her head in disbelief. 'Oh, Vicky – please don't say it's because of what I did? I couldn't bear it if you too were penniless and without a home. Please tell me more.'

'It's not quite as bad as that, although your parents did question me when I handed them your letter. I stayed true to my word and didn't tell them where you'd gone. I simply said you had asked me to hand them the envelope; which of course was true. However, your father didn't believe me. He was so sure that I knew something about your affairs, and he tried and tried to get something out of me.'

Betty raised a hand to her heart. 'I'm truly sorry you had to be put through that. Did he dismiss you?'

'No,' Vicky said. 'I've been thinking for a little while now how so many women are now working to help the war effort – I'd like to do that, too. And without you at the house, being the one cheerful face, it seemed as if the time was right. I told your parents that I would serve my notice, but your father raged and ordered me to leave the house there and then.'

'And did you?'

'Within a couple of hours. I went back to the kitchen and explained to Cook what had happened, and she suggested I get word to my young man, John – he knows my thoughts about doing war work. There was a boy out in the street and I paid him a couple of coppers to take a note to John. He was there within the hour.'

'He came to the house?' Betty gasped, imagining Vicky's young man facing her parents.

'He came to the scullery door and Cook let him in. By then I'd packed all my belongings and was ready to leave. It was Cook who suggested we fill a suitcase with more of your clothes and personal belongings, as once I left the house it might be hard for you to collect anything else – knowing the depth of your father's feelings.'

Betty's eyes lit up. 'You did that for me? I can never thank you enough! But what have you done with them?'

'John is coming to meet me and bringing the suitcase with him. It's mainly clothing. If only I'd known of your troubles! I would have collected all your jewellery and other valuables, and you could have pawned them.'

Betty chuckled wryly. 'After my recent experience, I'll never set foot in a pawnshop again. I'm just grateful for my clothing. I wonder, did you happen to pack my writing box as well as the beaded evening bag?'

'I did. Thankfully I took one of the largest suitcases from the attic and managed to drag it downstairs to the kitchen without your parents hearing. I know you're ever so fond of your writing box so I managed to squeeze it into the suitcase. The evening bag is so pretty, it seemed a shame to leave it behind.'

Betty smiled with satisfaction. 'I am thankful, but more importantly, I have a little money hidden away in that bag. At the back of my mind, I always knew that come the day when Charlie visited my father to ask for my hand in marriage, Father might well refuse him – so I had to start formulating a plan. Tucking a little cash away here and there meant I could walk out of the house with my head held high, on the arm of my husband – safe in the knowledge that I could help out at the beginning of our married life.' Her voice quivered a little as she remembered making these plans.

'Well, thank goodness I packed them,' Vicky said. 'I've been so worried about telling you what's happened, I haven't been able to sleep properly these last couple of nights. I'm surprised you didn't take that money with you when you left.'

'My mind was in such a muddle, I didn't even think of it until much later. At least I can put off going to see my parents for a little longer. But even the money in that bag won't pay my way for long – I really must think of something I can do to earn some more.'

'Why not give it a couple of weeks – that's if you can manage? I might be able to find a position for you alongside me.'

Betty hesitated. She'd never had any training and knew she would be useless as a housemaid; even though she thought the world of Vicky, it just didn't feel like the right job for her. How could she explain this without offending Vicky? The pause stretched as she tried to find the right words to reply.

Vicky chuckled. 'Oh miss, the look on your face! I didn't mean I was going to find you a servant's position. To be honest, I don't think you'd last five minutes.'

Betty chuckled too, relieved. She wasn't offended – Vicky was right. She'd never had to think about earning a living, undertaking household tasks. All she'd learnt about keeping a home was when she'd been able to slip down to the kitchen as a child and Cook had allowed her to stir up a cake mixture or lick the spoon. She had sometimes enjoyed putting on an oversized apron and pretending to dust the furniture in the servants' quarters, much to their amusement. That would not be enough to secure employment in one of the large London houses.

'I'm glad to hear it,' she said. 'I will miss Cook, you know, as she has always been so kind to me. She even took me to visit the neighbours now and then. Otherwise I wouldn't have known anyone who lived in our street.'

'Well, I've left service,' Vicky said defiantly. 'I'm going to get a job down the Arsenal; I'm staying with my John at the moment.' She had the good grace to blush. 'He says he'll marry me soon and until then, I have a small room at his lodging house. There's nothing underhand. Perhaps that's something you'd consider?'

Betty thought of Maggie, the kindly woman she'd met on the tram, and of the hundreds of people she'd seen pouring out of the munitions factory at the end of their shift. Could she work there? It was important work that would help bring this horrible war to an end – the war that had taken her Charlie from her.

Slowly, she nodded. 'I'll keep on living here for now, to help out the Sayers family; but yes, I'd like to get a job alongside you. You'll just need to tell me what to do to arrange it, as I have no idea how one even gains employment at such a place. Now, let me make some fresh tea while we make plans. You must tell me all about the munitions factory and the people who work there. And please, you must call me Betty rather than miss.'

Betty took a deep breath as she stood in line with a dozen other women, all waiting to sign on for work at the Arsenal. She was grateful that when Vicky's young man had dropped off her suitcase, some of her smarter outfits had been included. Even though it was a little warm she'd put on her best tweed suit with a crisp white blouse underneath. The frill on the collar framed her face and she'd pinned her hair up, leaving a few tendrils loose. Upon her head she wore a small green hat adorned with a feather.

She had hoped to see Vicky here but now, as she looked at the size of the works, she understood the employees numbered in the thousands rather than hundreds. It would be like searching for a needle in a haystack to find her friend. If only she had gone with Vicky to apply the day after their visit, rather than wait a week while she plucked up her courage.

She chewed her lip nervously, looking around her at the unfamiliar surroundings. There was a steady rumble of voices as workers came and went, as well as the smell of grease and something else Betty couldn't quite put her finger on. Perhaps it had something to do with the munitions she hoped to be working on. She'd never seen so many people heading into a place of work before and knew she could easily get lost and would have to keep her wits about her.

Glancing at the other women in the queue, she gave them a little smile. Several nodded curtly, while a couple of others turned away to laugh together. She frowned, wondering what they found so funny.

'It's your outfit, love. You're dressed a bit on the posh side for this place,' said a small, thin slip of a woman, giving Betty's suit an admiring glance.

'Oh dear, I've got it wrong already,' Betty said. 'I thought it was best to look smart when going for an interview. I've not done this before,' she added with a small grin at the woman's pleasant face. It was nice to be able to chat to someone; it helped calm her nerves.

'Love, you could've turned up in yer petticoats for all they care. If you've got two hands and a strong back, you'll do.'

Betty was surprised. 'I thought we'd have to sit an exam and fill out paperwork or something. As I said, I don't have much idea about these things.'

The woman chuckled. 'You'll soon learn. Just keep your ears open and your mouth closed, that's what my ma always told me.'

'How do you know so much about this place?'

'Half my family works here. I have three sisters and a mum and a couple of aunts bringing in good wages now.'

'Not as good as the men, though,' a woman standing behind her piped up.

'Don't start getting on yer soapbox,' another called out, 'or we'll all be sent packing.'

'She's right, though,' Betty's companion whispered. 'Many of the women do as good a job as the menfolk but have less in their pay packet come Friday. I'm not complaining, though, as it'll be more than I've ever brought home in me life. I'd have started here earlier if I could, but I had to serve me time with the people I worked for. They paid a pittance and worked me all hours. I'm glad to be shot of them.'

'Why didn't you leave earlier and not work your notice?' Betty asked. She didn't understand why the woman would have stayed in a low-paid job if there was a better job waiting for her.

She laughed. 'Because I'd not have been given a reference, and we all need those.'

Betty frowned; that was something else she lacked. Work experience and a reference.

'What brings you here?' the woman asked, looking Betty up and down. 'You're not the kind of woman who usually queues up to do munitions work.'

'I was due to be married, but my fiancé was killed at Ypres. I need to earn a living just like you.'

'I'm so sorry,' the woman said, reaching out and touching her arm. 'This bloody war has got a lot to answer for. One of my aunts told me the way we're losing so many of our young men, there'll be many of us never find a husband after the war.'

'I'm not looking for one,' Betty said, before biting her lip and falling silent for a few seconds. 'I'd rather there was no war, and I had my Charlie at home with me; we had such plans,' she went on. 'But I'm not the only woman in this situation. I just need to plan for my own future now.'

'That's the spirit, ducks. Besides, who knows what's gonna happen? You could walk out of this place and find some bloke who fancies you. Saying that, you might find someone in here,' she chuckled. 'Let's not take any notice of what my aunt says, she's a silly mare at the best of times. The way she goes on, she'll die an old spinster. It doesn't mean we have to. By the way, I'm Edna, Edna O'Leary. I reckon we'll be working together, don't you?'

Betty nodded and smiled at the eager young woman. 'I'm Betty Billington. How do you do?' she said, holding her hand out politely.

Edna shook it seriously, which prompted some of the

other women to start giggling again. 'Ignore them, Betty Billington, they're an ignorant lot and don't have any manners. Come on, let's move up in the queue,' she said, linking an arm through Betty's as they stepped closer to the gates.

6

Betty flinched as she and Edna entered the building. They were in a long passage, and the noise that assailed their ears almost knocked her backwards. She raised her hands to shield her ears, looking around; people were hurrying everywhere, intent on getting to their workstations.

'Hurry along there,' a man growled as he poked her in the back.

'I didn't expect all this noise,' Betty shouted to Edna, 'did you?'

'You'll get used to it. One of my sisters puts cotton wool in her ears as she reckons it helps a bit, but then she doesn't always hear her supervisor and gets into trouble. I suppose you can't have it all ways, can you?' Edna shrugged. 'Look out, we've got to go up that corridor. Old man Shaughnessy is a bit of a miserable git, so don't get on his wrong side. Just say yes, sir, when he tells you anything, and never question him. You'll be for the chop if you do.'

Betty did as she was told, hurrying along with the other women. Part of her wondered what on earth she was doing here, when she could have gone meekly back to her parents and not needed to work at all. But then she reminded herself of the reason she'd come to the munitions works: she owed it to Charlie to do her bit and help bring the war to an end. For all she knew, one of the explosives she worked on here might be the one that finished it all. There again, there could be a girl over in Germany just like her – how would she feel if another girl's fiancé was killed by a bomb that Betty had a hand in making? Deep in thought, she didn't hear a stern-looking woman snapping at her until one of her fellow workers alerted her with a jab in the ribs.

'You, girl! Are you an imbecile or something?' asked the stern woman. She was older than Betty and wore a severely cut suit. 'If you are, I don't want you working in here. You look as though you couldn't even roll your own sleeves up, let alone do a proper day's work. There aren't any maid-servants in here to help you posh girls,' she added with a sneer. 'The likes of you never last long here.'

Betty looked around for support, but all she could see were one or two other women in the queue giggling at her discomfort. She noticed that in front of her Edna had picked up the stub of a pencil and was scribbling on a card. Betty moved to her side and did the same, adding her name, address and next of kin. 'Is this it?' she asked Edna.

'Shut up,' the stern woman in the suit told her. 'Go get along the end there – Mr Shaughnessy will want to talk to you.'

Betty hurried along, doing her best to keep her wits about her. Now wasn't the time to get lost in thought.

Mr Shaughnessy was a large, thuggish man bursting out of his waistcoat and puffing on a cigarette. He had a bowler hat tipped to the back of his head, with bushy ginger hair sticking out in clumps below the brim. He loomed over

Betty, getting closer than she would have liked, and looked her up and down before licking his thick lips.

'You reckon you could put in a day's work?' he asked, without removing the cigarette from between his lips.

'Yes sir, I do believe I can. I'll do my best . . .'

'Did I ask you to keep talking?'

'Yes . . . I mean no . . .' Betty stumbled over her words.

'Are you fit and healthy? Is there anything wrong with you?'

'No, sir.'

'We'll have to see about that. Follow Mrs Granger and she'll sort out overalls and tell you your duties.'

'Does that mean I have the job?' Betty asked hopefully, crossing her fingers behind her back.

'You'd have been out the door by now if I thought otherwise,' he growled. 'But I can always change my mind. Hurry along there.'

Betty followed Edna, who had been waved through without being asked a question. 'What happens next?' she asked as they headed along another corridor into a larger room. Here, women were standing about watching as one woman stepped onto a small dais in the corner.

'We get told how to behave, what hours to work and how to try not to kill ourselves or anyone else,' Edna said, looking about in case she was overheard and told off.

'Good grief,' Betty said, putting a gloved hand to her mouth in shock. 'Kill ourselves?'

Edna sighed. 'Blimey, Betty, you've got a lot to learn. We're going to be working with explosives. If you cause as much as a spark, you'll blow us all to kingdom come.'

Betty chuckled, not quite believing Edna's words, but

then recalled what she'd heard about the many accidents in these factories. What had she let herself in for?

'I'm not joking,' Edna said before nudging her to be silent, nodding towards where the woman on the dais was clapping her hands together for attention.

'I didn't realize we'd be starting work today,' Betty said a short while later. After the introductory lecture on safety she and her fellow workers had been handed long overalls and told to change their clothes, removing every hairclip and piece of jewellery. She understood now why Edna had warned her about laughing; this was indeed a dangerous job. She was beginning to understand, too, what a sheltered life she had led. Most of the women around her seemed much more aware about the damage that could be caused if the workers didn't stay on their toes, constantly alert to danger.

There were different shift patterns, with the women working around the clock. Betty's shifts this week started at half past five in the morning and ended in the early evening. She straightened the rough calico cap that covered every strand of her hair, reaching into her bag for a grip to keep it in place.

Edna slapped the back of her hand. 'Haven't you listened to a word that's been said?' she snapped. 'If you haven't, I'm not working next to you. You're a danger to yourself, not to mention anybody else.'

Betty stammered her apologies. 'I'm sorry – it's all so new to me. I'll do my best, I promise.'

'Let's just hope you can,' Edna sighed, and she crossed herself and mumbled a prayer. 'Stick by my side and do everything I do. Understand?'

'I understand,' Betty said – although how she would iden-tify Edna she didn't know, when the dozens of women on their shift all looked so similar in their overalls and caps.

Betty and Edna, along with several of the others from the new intake, were led to a long wooden bench. Over the next couple of hours they were shown how to carefully fill shells with chemicals that could prove lethal if handled badly. To begin with Betty was frightened of doing some-thing wrong, but by staying vigilant and watching the women around her she was soon working at the same speed as the more experienced workers. She forced herself to concentrate fully on the task, knowing that just one slip would cause an explosion.

Betty had always thought herself dexterous, but as the hours passed her fingers grew numb and her eyelids began to droop. As hard as she tried to stay focused on the job in front of her, she began to worry about making an error.

'Oi, you – slow down,' Edna hissed, bringing her up sharp. 'You're making us look like slackers.'

'I'm sorry,' Betty said anxiously. 'I'm just not used to this; I'll try to improve by tomorrow.'

Edna's expression softened. 'You've not had a job before, have you?' she said, loudly enough for Betty to hear her above the din.

'I'm afraid I haven't. It's not through not wanting to, but my parents . . .'

'Your parents are snobs and they wanted to spoil you?' Edna said, not unkindly. 'I'll give you this, you've got guts turning up here to work. What made them give in to you?'

Betty grimaced as she almost dropped a small shell. 'They don't know.'

'They don't know?' Edna cackled. 'Don't you think that when you roll in late, tired to the bone and your skin turning yellow, they might be a bit suspicious?'

'The reason they don't know is because I ran away after I heard about my Charlie being killed at Ypres,' Betty explained.

'Even so, why come and work down here? You must be loaded?'

Betty gave a bitter laugh. 'I've not got a penny to my name. And what I did have was stolen from me.' She described her visit to the pawnbroker and how, if not for the kindness of Vicky collecting her belongings and Charlie's dad putting her up, she'd have been sleeping on the streets by now.

'Blimey. And I thought I had it rough having to share a bedroom with three of my sisters. What's it like living with an old man?'

'Mr Sayers is very kind and treats me like a daughter. Charlie has two younger sisters living at home; they've made me very welcome.'

'Well, you be careful. Some of these old men . . . What I'm saying is, they want more than a bit of cash for the rent,' Edna said, giving Betty a wink.

Betty had no idea what this meant and was about to enquire when the blast of a hooter interrupted them, echoing through the factory.

'Thank God for that. We've got a ten-minute break for our dinner. Have you brought anything with you?'

'No, I thought I was only coming for an interview,' Betty said. 'I wonder if there's time to go and buy something? Although I've only got a couple of coppers in my coat pocket.'

'You can share half of mine, but don't forget you owe me, okay? You bring something for both of us tomorrow.'

'I'll do that,' Betty said gratefully.

They wandered out of the building and found a low wall to sit on.

'Tell me, what do you mean about me going home being yellow?'

Edna sighed. 'Have you never read a newspaper?'

'No, not really. My mother didn't think it was appropriate for a young lady. I did have a look at my father's paper occasionally, but it was mainly about stocks and shares. Since I moved, I've borrowed Mr Sayers' paper to look at news about the war.'

'Then you keep reading, my love,' Edna said as she tore a doorstep-sized chunk of bread in half. 'There's only dripping on that, but it'll fill your belly. We can get a cup of water afterwards, there's a tap round the corner; my sisters told me about it in case I didn't see them when I started here.'

Betty bit into the bread and thought it the most delicious thing she'd ever tasted, but then she was starving hungry and anything would have tasted good. She sat listening as Edna explained that the chemicals they worked with, although they might not cause fatal harm, could do serious damage to the women's insides as well as turning their skin yellow.

'It's been said that those who don't get killed by this stuff could end up never having babies. That's pretty scary, eh? Me, I don't take much notice of it all, as I'll be earning more money than I've ever had in my life so far. I'll take my chances. Who knows – I might meet someone here and get a ring on my finger before I turn into a canary.'

'Even if you can't have babies?' Betty said thoughtfully. It wouldn't affect her, she thought; her chance of having a family had already passed her by.

'Come on, you lot – get your arses inside here. The bloody war will be over before you stop chatting to each other,' an older woman called to them.

Betty looked longingly towards the water tap, where there was still a queue of people. It was too late to get a cool drink now. Tomorrow she would bring a cup.

The afternoon dragged on. Occasionally women started singing songs and although Betty recognized some of the tunes, she didn't know the words. Gradually she picked up part of a verse and joined in. It lifted her spirits somewhat and made her feel more like she fitted in.

'That's the idea,' Edna grinned as Betty joined in with a rousing chorus of 'It's a Long Way to Tipperary'. 'What are you gonna do after work?'

'I'm going home to put my feet in a bowl of water.' Betty sighed at the thought. Although they'd been sitting down for most of the shift, her feet still ached; she was wearing her best shoes and they really weren't suited for a hard day's work.

'Why don't you come down the pub with me and my sisters?'

'Without a man to accompany us, do you mean?'

'Blimey, Betty, I know you've come from the dark ages, but around here a woman's money is as good as a bloke's any day of the week. No one is going to think badly of you for walking into a pub on your own.'

Betty couldn't think of anything worse. She wasn't a drinker, and hadn't been keen on the taste of sherry when her father had handed her one at Christmas – but she knew she would have to make an effort if she wanted to fit in here at the munitions works. The days would be long and arduous, and it would be a nightmare if she didn't get on with Edna and the other girls on their workbench. 'Perhaps another night?' she said. 'I'm supposed to have dinner ready for this evening; everyone will be in and wondering where I am, and why the oven's not on.'

'Blimey – he's got you by the apron strings, hasn't he?'

'Oh no, it's not like that at all,' Betty blushed. 'Mr Sayers is a good man. I just want to pay him back for giving me a bed and somewhere to live.'

'If you say so,' Edna chuckled, giving her another wink.

'Where have you been?' Harold Sayers demanded, as Betty almost fell through the front door of the house on Railway Terrace. 'We were about to go out looking for you.'

Betty summoned all her strength to stand up straight and give him a beaming smile. 'I found a job and started straight away. I've not long finished my first shift.'

Harold frowned. 'There was no need for that. I told you before, you can stay here; I don't want any money from you. You do enough helping around the house – that's good enough for me.'

Betty frowned as Edna's words – and that wink – came back to haunt her. Surely Harold wasn't trying to tell her how to lead her life?

'I need to do my bit for the war effort – we all do, otherwise it will never end. Besides,' she added, 'I want to be able to pay my way.'

He looked disgruntled. 'What is it, this job of yours,

that's so important there was no food on the table when I got home from work?'

Betty held up a newspaper bundle containing pease pudding and faggots. She'd had just enough coins in her pocket to pay for the food, not having wished to carry much money with her when visiting the munitions works. 'These won't take long to warm up – the girls told me you like them. As for my job, I've started work down the Arsenal. It's a bit dangerous, but the money is good,' she added as she turned to go into the kitchen.

Harold sprang to his feet and followed her; the two girls shrank away from him. 'That's no place for a refined woman like you.'

Betty put the kettle on the hob and dropped into a kitchen chair with relief. 'Mr Sayers – you have to remember, my family never knew about Charlie. I'm a working girl now and I must stand on my own two feet.'

Harold frowned. 'What exactly were you and Charlie going to do with yourselves after the war? I know I said the pair of you could move in here, but that was all talk. I expected your father to have set him up in something befitting your station in life.'

She shook her head, perplexed. Hadn't Charlie told his dad about their plans? Perhaps he too had thought her father was going to support them both . . . ? No – she wouldn't believe that of her Charlie.

'Charlie wasn't happy in his job. We talked about setting up in a shop somewhere. He fancied a tobacconist, or a grocery shop – and we would live over the top of it until we had a family, and then we'd find a proper home.' She looked up at Harold, hoping for his approval, even though none of this was going to happen now.

His face turned red. 'Well, well, well . . . that's completely different to what I believed was going to happen,' he huffed as the kettle started to boil. 'You'd better get that food heated up or we're going to be having it for breakfast,' he snapped before storming into his garden.

Betty was puzzled. Perhaps this was her fault – maybe she hadn't made things clear? She was too tired to think about it right now. Pulling herself to her feet, she set about preparing the meal. Hopefully Harold would soon calm down, and surely he'd be pleased when she was able to hand over some money each Friday for her keep. She needed to work out how to play her part in this household. If only she was a better cook! But everything about this new life was so unfamiliar to her.

'Oh, Charlie,' she whispered. 'Why did you have to go and die on me?'

7

'Shall I help you?' a quiet voice said from the doorway as Betty unpacked her shopping basket. 'I can cook, remember.'

'Oh, Olive, you startled me,' Betty smiled as the girl sidled into the kitchen. Once again she was struck by Olive's resemblance to Charlie. 'Yes, thank you – you can help by putting these groceries away in the cupboard. Your father gave me the impression he does a lot of the work around the house.'

'He just wanted to make a good impression.' Olive smiled as she picked up packets of tea and sugar and started arranging them on a shelf in the pantry.

Betty was thoughtful. 'There's really no need for him to do that. It's good of him to provide me with a roof over my head, and I'm more than willing to help around the house – it's just that I don't have much idea of what to do. I never had to lift a finger at home when I was growing up. Does that sound awful?'

'Of course not,' Olive said, sliding onto a wooden seat next to the table and gazing admiringly at Betty. 'It must be lovely to be rich and have servants.'

'I agree it's pleasant not to have to worry about money,

and my parents treated me very well in that respect. But in a way, you're the lucky one, because you have your freedom.'

'Whatever do you mean? Dad says that when you've got money, you're free to do whatever you want in life. He's always told us we should marry well. That's why he was so pleased when Charlie met you.'

Betty was surprised at Olive's words. 'It wasn't quite like that. Charlie had his own dreams and I wanted to share them. I wish my parents had been able to meet him and get to know him as I did,' she added, trying not to embarrass the girl. 'But now I'm just like your family. I must work for my living.'

She sank into the chair opposite Olive's. It worried her that the Sayers family thought marrying into money was the answer to everything. Surely Charlie had never thought that way? She recalled their long conversations about their future life together. No; she knew he'd wanted to work hard to achieve their dreams, and she would have worked by his side forever.

'Tell me more about your job,' Olive said. 'You look awfully tired, and your face is rather grimy. Would you like me to take some water up to your room so you can have a wash? I could carry on with the meal preparation while you do that, and have a cup of tea ready for when you come down.'

Betty sighed. 'Oh Olive, that would be wonderful, thank you. And I really would be grateful if you'd give me some more cookery lessons soon. I can't keep bringing in pease pudding and faggots from the shop – we've had it twice this week already.'

'Of course I will. You know I cooked most of our meals

before you moved in, and cleaned the house too, and I don't mind doing more of that. Besides, Dad says we have to learn, otherwise we'll make terrible wives when the time comes for us to marry someone and the babies come along. That's why Peggy helps me as well. We must think of our futures,' she said, sounding twice her age.

Oh goodness, Betty thought. Here I am, useless at every household chore, walking in and usurping the child. 'I'm so sorry, Olive. I didn't mean to take over all the jobs you were used to doing before I arrived. It's just that I don't want you girls waiting on me hand and foot, so I'd like to help you. However, you will be in charge and I will take orders. Just as if you're the housekeeper and I'm one of your servants,' she laughed.

Olive giggled. 'That's funny. I can see why Charlie loved you so much. We're going to miss him, aren't we?'

Betty's laughter caught in her throat. 'We certainly are. Now, let me go and tidy myself and then we'll chat over a cup of tea while dinner is cooking. We can plan how we're going to share the work. I'd hate you to fall behind with your schoolwork – even if you are going to marry and become the perfect wife,' she smiled.

Once the water was hot, Olive carried it up to Betty's room in a pretty china jug. 'I'll be down in five minutes,' Betty promised, before unbuttoning her jacket and shaking out the creases. She knew she really needed more suitable clothing for work – even leaving her things in a locker didn't stop them getting grubby, and they wouldn't last long. Besides, she didn't like to stand out from the crowd while she was walking to and from the Arsenal; she wanted to blend in with the other workers. After admiring Betty's leather bag Edna had advised her not to bring anything valuable like that in to work, just in case it was pinched from the locker room.

'I could have brought that down for you,' Olive said, as Betty returned to the kitchen carrying the dirty water from her ablutions.

'Thank you, Olive, but I'm perfectly capable of managing myself, and you're not my maid,' Betty said firmly before disposing of the dirty water and wiping out the jug. She joined Olive at the table, gratefully accepting a hot cup of tea. 'You have no idea how delicious this is,' she said before obliging the girl with a detailed description of her working day.

Olive's jaw slowly dropped as she listened to Betty explain how even a hairpin left in a worker's hair might cause a spark that could create an explosion. She didn't repeat all the stories she'd heard from other workers, as she didn't wish to frighten the child. She did say they'd told her that from where they worked on the south side of the Thames, they'd heard the massive explosion in January when the munitions works on the other side of the river at Silvertown had gone up and taken so many lives. Betty's colleagues had recounted some hair-raising stories about that, describing the deaths of women just like themselves, and yet they didn't seem unduly worried for their own safety.

'We heard it too. And I read about it in the newspaper,' Olive said, her face serious.

'Well ... let's hope nothing like that happens at the Arsenal,' Betty replied, pursing her lips.

'Working there certainly sounds different from anything

you've done before,' Olive commented as Betty sipped her tea. 'I'm not sure I could do it.'

'Needs must,' she smiled, not wishing to frighten the child. Reaching into her pocket, she took out a small notebook and pencil. 'Now, why don't we make some plans for sharing the housework and cooking? Between us we can work out a schedule to make life easier at home.'

The girl agreed, and for the next twenty minutes Betty noted down various ideas for meals as well as the timing of Harold's shifts over the coming week or two.

'I've decided I'm going to give you some pocket money,' she said to Olive, 'because it doesn't seem right that a child your age should be taking on so much responsibility around the home. I'll do the same for Peggy, so that she doesn't feel left out.'

'There's no need for that!' Olive was shocked. 'It's what we're supposed to do.'

'Well, I won't stand for it,' Betty said, looking serious.

'Dad won't approve,' Olive said.

'Then it will be our little secret,' Betty whispered, as they both heard Harold's footsteps approaching from the other room.

'Is the food ready yet?' he asked.

'Very soon,' Betty replied politely.

'I see you've had time to tidy yourself up,' he said approvingly, making her feel uncomfortable.

'I simply cleaned my face and brushed my hair after working all day.'

Harold harrumphed and turned back towards the front room, calling over his shoulder, 'Olive, you should've laid the table by now. Hurry yourself up, girl.'

Betty grimaced. Now that she'd been living here for a little while, it was becoming clear that Harold was often rather grumpy.

'He's always like that,' Olive said apologetically, seeing the look on Betty's face. 'When he was being pleasant it was . . . unnatural.'

Betty shook her head. 'I'll worry about that later. For now, let's get this food onto the table – and I must ask you a favour.'

'I'll help you if I can,' Olive replied, pleased that Betty needed her.

'I need some proper work clothes, and I haven't got much money.'

'But you look so smart in your outfit,' Olive replied, looking confused.

'It's very kind of you to say so, but it's not right for what I'm doing now. For one, the clothes will soon be spoilt and I can't afford to replace them; and for another, I really don't want to stand out. All I want to do is keep my head down, work and earn some money. So, Olive – I'm hoping you can tell me where I might find a shop selling suitable clothing for my job?'

Olive wrinkled her nose as she thought carefully. 'I've got it,' she said with a grin. 'We need to go to the market.'

'The market?'

'Yes, Woolwich market – there's a stall where they sell second-hand clothes.'

It was Betty's turn to wrinkle her nose. 'I'm not so sure about that – what if there are . . . fleas and things?'

'No, she's supposed to be very clean and only sells decent

clobber. We might be able to find you some sturdy boots as well. Yours are rather thin, aren't they?'

Betty nodded ruefully. 'I won't be able to get there during the break in my shift, it's only a few minutes – I'll have to go along after work.'

'She'll have closed down by then, I think,' Olive said. 'Look, if you'll trust me, I can go by myself and find you a few bits to tide you over. I've got a good idea of your size. Then I can bring them home and give them a wash, just in case there's anything hopping about.'

Betty grimaced at the thought, but she was grateful to the girl. 'But won't you be at school?'

'They won't miss me,' Olive chuckled.

'Well . . . if you're sure. Promise me you won't do this often, though. Learning is very important, you know,' Betty said, sounding more like the girl's mother than the sister-in-law she would have been if she'd married Charlie.

There was no time for further discussion, as Harold shouted from the other room: 'Are we going to get this meal before midnight or what?'

The next morning Betty had no choice but to put on her unsuitable outfit once more, but she made sure to leave off any jewellery. Olive lent her a bag that would not be missed if it was stolen.

'I can't help thinking that perhaps Edna exaggerated about things being stolen at work; but better to be safe than sorry,' she said as she handed over a few coins to Olive. 'If there's enough and you see anything for yourself, let it be my treat to you. Something to thank you for being so helpful.'

Olive gave her a broad wink, making Betty's heart lurch – it reminded her so much of Charlie. 'I'll see you this evening,' the girl said cheerfully, 'and don't worry about dinner, it's all sorted out. Thank goodness we sat together and made those lists!' Giving Betty a kiss on the cheek, she waved her off to work.

Betty was in plenty of time, so she decided to walk – she'd save her money and catch a tram when the weather was worse. It would take twenty minutes but needs must, she thought to herself as she strode out, thinking of what the day ahead would bring. As she approached the Arsenal, she thought about the war: how long would it be before it ended? And what would all these people do for work afterwards? she wondered.

Soon she joined the queue of men and women entering the massive building. When she reached the clocking-in machine, she placed her card in it just as the woman in front of her had done. There was no sign of Edna and Betty wondered if she was already there. She made her way to the room where her workmates were changing out of their day clothes into the rough cloth overalls and caps that covered their hair. Betty had counted how many pins she put into her hair that morning, and she counted each one again as she pulled them out and put them away safely. Checking she had a handkerchief in her pocket, she turned to go to her workbench and realized somebody was watching her.

'Oi, posh girl – you decided to turn up again today, then?'

Betty swallowed and pinned a smile onto her face. 'Good morning,' she said. 'I hope you are well?'

'I hope you are well?' The woman cackled at her own impersonation of Betty, showing a row of yellow tooth stumps. 'Who do you think you are, with all your prim and proper ways – Princess Alexandra?'

Fortunately, at that moment, Edna appeared, looping her arm through Betty's. 'Blimey, I was late getting up today. The last thing I want is me pay docked because I was fast asleep. Come on – let's get cracking before old Shaughnessy tells us off,' she said, marching forward and pulling Betty along. After a few yards, she slowed down. 'Watch that one. She's trouble, and if she decides to pick on you she will make your life hell. I noticed her watching you down the other end of the bench yesterday.'

'But I've done nothing to offend her,' Betty said. 'I don't even know who she is.'

'That's Eileen Swatkins. All the Swatkins are trouble, and there are plenty of them. They stick together like glue. Just keep your head down and stay clear of them. You could offend her just by breathing. She's a nasty bully, and the sooner somebody sorts her out the better.'

'You sound as though you've crossed swords with her before,' Betty said, glancing over her shoulder nervously.

'Too true, or rather my sister did. She answered back and they caught up with her going home from work, dragged her down an alleyway and almost beat her sense-less. If we hadn't been far behind and heard Fanny calling out for help, she could've been killed.'

Betty gulped. 'I only came here to work, I don't want to upset anybody. Perhaps I should tell her that?'

'No! Don't tell her anything, just get on with your work. I'll have a word with the others to keep an eye on you.'

'Thank you. I don't think I'd have lasted five minutes here if I hadn't bumped into you in the queue,' Betty said. She could feel her hands shaking and wanted nothing more to do than turn and run back to Railway Terrace – but what was there for her? Charlie's dad wasn't exactly friendly these days. Goodness, life can be so hard, she thought to herself as she sat down at her bench.

It was a relief when the signal came for their midday break. They made their way outside and perched on the low brick wall. Betty offered Edna a sandwich: 'It's only fish paste, but you're more than welcome to half.' She had also brought along a glass bottle filled with tea. When Olive had suggested the drink Betty had wrinkled her nose in distaste, but Olive had assured her it was what a lot of people took to work with them.

'Would you like a sip of this?' she said, holding out the bottle.

Edna swigged greedily and followed it with a loud burp.

Betty grimaced but said nothing. She'd noticed the manners of the women she worked with left much to be desired. However, she was no snob and would keep her thoughts to herself.

'Budge up,' a couple of women said as they approached Edna's end of the wall. Betty stood up to give them more space. As she did so she bumped into a different group of workers who were passing by.

'Look where you're going,' somebody said, giving her a hard shove. Betty just managed to stay upright, although the cold tea from the bottle she was holding slopped over the woman. Looking up to apologize, she realized with dismay that it was Eileen Swatkins.

'You silly cow, you've made me all wet,' the woman snarled. She grabbed hold of Betty's overall and pulled her until they were nose to nose, where she glared menacingly.

'I'm ever so sorry, it was an accident—' Betty began.

'I'm ever so sorry,' mimicked Eileen, laughing nastily just as she had done earlier. Then she lifted a hand and slapped Betty across the face. 'I'd watch your step from now on, girl. I'll see you sacked if it's the last thing I do,' she threatened as she released Betty and walked away, laughing with her companions.

Betty felt sick and giddy. She raised a hand to her cheek; it was hot and stinging.

Edna was at her side. 'My God, does it hurt?'

Betty shook her head miserably. 'Only my pride is hurt,' she said. She could see curiosity and laughter on the faces of other workers nearby. 'Why is it that just because I speak properly, people don't like me?'

'It's because you're different. Not in a bad way – it's just that they look at you and see the difference right away. Some are jealous. You need to start acting more like them. And dressing more like them. Even so,' Edna said disapprovingly, 'there was no reason for that lump of lard to clock you one like that. She's a nasty bit of work. There's talk of people leaving here because of her, and that's a shame because everybody needs to earn a living. Come on – let's go for a little walk so you can calm down.' She took Betty's arm and led her away in the opposite direction to the troublemaker.

Betty told her about the plan she had made with Olive to buy some clothes from the market so that she'd look more like her fellow workers.

'Don't go spending too much money.'

'I won't. She's going to a second-hand market stall,' Betty said, forcing a smile. It made her want to shudder when she imagined wearing clothes that had been worn by somebody else.

'I'd give them a good scrub first,' Edna winked.

'I'll do that,' Betty said, as if the thought wasn't already uppermost in her mind. 'Edna, what is it your sisters are doing? I noticed they're not working on the same job that we are.'

'They work in another department, filling the larger shells. It's heavier work; they have to hump them about.'

'There are so many departments here. I was hoping to find my friend Vicky, or Maggie, the lady I met on the tram the other day; but I've not seen either of them.'

'You'll be lucky – they could be on another shift, or working the other side of the building. It's like a blooming rabbit warren here. Come on, we'd better get back to work. It's bad enough getting told off for being late to our bench, but that Eileen will be reporting us if we're even a second late. Her not liking you is going to rub off on the rest of us.'

'I do apologize,' Betty said. 'If I'd done something really wrong I could put it right, but as you say, if it's a case of my face not fitting there's nothing much I can do, is there?'

'Don't you worry, ducks,' Edna said. 'We've got your back. Just make sure you've got eyes in the back of your head when she's about.'

Betty almost laughed; she didn't like to say that if everybody had her back, she'd best keep her eyes to the front of her head. Instead, she thanked Edna for caring enough to help her.

'Aw, yer not so bad,' Edna chuckled. 'And yer not to worry about tipping yer tea down her overall – it's the first decent wash it's had in a while. Oh bugger,' she added as someone coughed pointedly close by.

'What's the problem?' Betty whispered, seeing Edna's discomfort.

'That's Eileen's sister what heard me. All hell will be let loose if she tells her what I said,' Edna muttered.

'Let's just keep our heads down and get on with our work; then she can't cause any more trouble,' Betty said, glancing around to see who else might be watching them.

'That's a good idea. If we don't hang about, she can't nab us.' Edna peered over her shoulder at Eileen's sister, who was staring angrily at them with her hands on her hips. 'I should learn ter keep me gob shut.'

'You didn't mean any harm,' Betty consoled her, as they sat down at the bench to resume their work.

The afternoon flew by, with the girls kept busy. Gradually they began to relax a little, and Edna had just started to join in with a popular song when she was grabbed by the shoulder and pulled backwards off the bench.

Betty turned in alarm; it was Eileen, of course. She dropped her gaze quickly and climbed off the bench to assist Edna.

'I want a word with you,' Eileen was saying, and as Edna got to her feet Eileen grabbed the collar of her overalls and shook her. 'I'm sick to death of you making cheap jibes about me and my family.'

With Betty's help, Edna pulled away from the woman. 'If you did your work and stopped being such a bully, then you wouldn't have people saying things about you. You're the same with everybody – why, you even had a go at Betty here, and there's no one nicer than her. It's time you stopped it, Eileen. We're all here to do a job of work to get the war over and done with. We don't want to be frightened to come on shift because of the likes of you tormenting us.'

Betty gulped. Crikey – Edna was bold, but wouldn't this make things even worse? 'Perhaps we ought to get back to work,' she suggested, noticing the foreman marching over to them with a grim expression on his face.

Eileen shoved Edna away and turned on Betty. 'And as for you, you bloody snob – we don't want the likes of you taking jobs away from those of us that need them.'

Betty took a deep breath. 'I don't want any trouble. I'm as desperate to work as anyone else here.'

Eileen sneered. 'Well, you won't be here much longer if I've got anything to do with it,' she said, reaching for Betty's cap. Betty froze in alarm as Eileen tore the cap from her head; she felt her hair slipping free. Swiftly Eileen delved into the pocket of her own overall and pulled out a handful of hair grips. With the foreman getting closer by the second, she threw the grips across the floor and screamed: 'Look what Billington's got in her hair! She'll have us all dead before we know it!'

'But I didn't . . .' Betty started to protest. A look of horror crossed the foreman's face as he rushed towards the bench. Women nearby were shrieking and backing away.

'You silly cow,' he shouted, trying to avoid stepping on the grips without success.

Eileen moved back quickly, an evil grin on her face.

'Come away quick!' Edna snapped at Betty. 'Now's not the time to explain.' She grabbed Betty's arm, pulling her along. At that moment the foreman skidded on the hair grips and stumbled into a bench, sending casings half-full of explosive material crashing to the floor. There was a spark and a flash before one of them exploded. The foreman was flung across the benches to the other side of the aisle as workers ran screaming for their lives.

Betty had been shielded by Edna, and now it seemed as if her friend was frozen in shock. 'Edna, come along,' she shouted, tugging at her. Edna staggered and turned towards her, and Betty saw blood spreading across her overall. She cried out in alarm and somehow managed to drag Edna to the exit, holding her up. Outside, she knelt on the ground cradling Edna in her lap, calling for help.

All around them there was shouting and weeping. A member of Eileen's family was cursing Betty, calling her a murderer, as two women ran over to them: Edna's sisters. They quickly took over caring for her and Betty moved back, overwhelmed.

Even after Edna had been taken away in an ambulance accompanied by her sisters, Betty found herself struggling to comprehend what had happened. The shed where they worked had been evacuated and the injured were being tended to outside. The foreman hadn't been so lucky, taking his last breath before anyone could see to his injuries.

'It wasn't me – I didn't bring hairgrips into the workshop,' Betty tried to explain to an older woman who was giving her a cup of water to help her calm down. She was sitting on the low wall where she and Edna had taken their breaks. 'Now someone is dead because of Eileen Swatkins!'

The woman urged her to lower her voice. 'She got her

comeuppance – a piece of metal sliced open the side of her face. That'll improve her ugly looks,' she said grimly.

'But I don't want anyone injured, not even Eileen, even though she caused all of this . . . Does anyone know how Edna is? Will she survive?' Betty started to cry.

'With an arm missing, she may as well not,' one of the other women muttered. 'She won't be able to work now, and no man's going to want to marry her looking like that.'

Betty dropped her head into her hands, despairing. She couldn't understand what had happened. They'd all heard the stories of how a small spark could trigger an explosion. Surely Eileen realized that, and still she had thrown those hairpins, just to take revenge on someone she didn't like. 'She must have known people could be injured, killed . . . What was she thinking?'

'Who knows?' the older woman said, patting Betty's shoulder. 'Most people here are frightened of her family, so they won't speak out and say they saw her do it. I'm sorry to say, your days here are numbered. In fact . . .' She nodded towards where the works manager was marching towards them.

'Billington, a word, please.'

Betty got to her feet, wiping away the tears. She was barely aware of Edna's blood staining the front of her clothing and her hands as she brushed down her overall and thanked the woman who had helped her.

'Sir, it wasn't my fault,' she began. 'It was Eileen Swatkins. I don't know why she did it.'

He raised his hand. 'Stop your excuses: I don't wish to hear them. I knew you wouldn't fit in when you were taken on. Now I've lost my best foreman, and several staff will be off sick for a long time – some may never return. I want you to leave now. I'll pay you up to midday and you can collect your cards tomorrow. Be off with you,' he said, pointing towards the door.

'I just need to collect my clothes and my bag . . .'

'Come back for them tomorrow. I want you off the premises right now. You're a curse on the place,' he said as he turned to go. He stopped in his tracks and added, 'I suggest you find a job where you won't be a danger to other people. Being a shopgirl may suit you – perhaps a counter assistant at Woolworths. As long as it's as far away from here as possible,' he snarled before marching away.

Trembling, Betty risked a glance at the women around her, but they were turning away. Clearly, everyone was too afraid of upsetting the Swatkins clan. Edna, her only friend here, was lying in a hospital bed, and Betty was on her own.

She stumbled towards the gates, shocked to her very core, feeling as though the weight of the world had fallen on her shoulders. Life was going from bad to worse.

8

Betty stumbled along the road, oblivious to the odd looks she was attracting from passers-by. Her face was covered in brick dust and grime and her clothing was smeared with blood; her hair hung bedraggled around her shoulders. Her mind was far away as she tried to comprehend the enormity of someone doing this terrible thing purely out of dislike for her. Innocent people had been injured and killed – and not only that, but the production of vital bombs that could bring an early end to this awful war had been interrupted.

'Mind where you're going, love,' a man said as she stumbled against him. His companion muttered something about her having 'escaped from the looney bin'. Further along the busy street, a group of young lads jostled her and shouted rude remarks as they passed.

She stopped to draw breath, leaning against the window of a shop. She tried to pull herself together and looked at her hands; she must get home and wash off the blood. Was it Edna's blood or the foreman's? All Betty knew was that she was in some way to blame for what had happened. If she hadn't decided to look for a job at the Arsenal, no one would have had reason to hate her so much and cause this terrible incident.

Taking a deep breath and putting her hand to her chest to calm her fast-beating heart, she gazed up at the store sign. F. W. Woolworth: why did that sound familiar? She frowned. Oh yes . . . the works manager had told her to go and find a job at Woolworths. 'It would serve him right if I did,' she muttered out loud. A woman walking past gave her a startled look. Betty ignored her, as another thought crept into her mind. He would never know, as he'd dismissed her . . .

A small spark ignited within her sadness. It looked like a nice shop, she thought, peering through the gleaming plate-glass window. She could see busy shoppers standing at high counters that ran the length of the store. They seemed to be made of polished dark wood, with all kinds of wares displayed on top. Smiling assistants were placing goods into brown paper bags and handing them across to the customers. She could also see large brass cash registers.

I could do that, she thought to herself. After all, being helpful to customers and giving them a cheery smile would do a lot to raise spirits during the war. It might not be as important as making ammunition that would bring the war to an end, but there again, everybody needed to shop – and if there was a polite, well-spoken assistant to help them do it, all the better. Betty knew she could speak well as her parents had paid for elocution lessons, and even as a child she had been praised for her lovely manners. What more could be required? Yes, she would go in straight away and enquire about a position as a shopgirl. She headed for the two large doors that were continually swinging open and shut as shoppers passed through.

'I don't think you ought to go in there in your state, do you, young lady?' said an authoritative voice nearby.

Betty turned to see a policeman observing her closely.

'I don't understand,' she said. 'I want to enquire about employment.'

He looked at her for a moment, not unkindly. 'Perhaps now is not the best time. Why don't you go home and tidy yourself up? You look as though you've been in the wars.'

Betty was indignant and raised her chin, about to give him the sharp edge of her tongue, when she caught her reflection in the window. 'Oh, my,' she said, putting a hand to her mouth. 'You are correct, officer – perhaps I do need to go home and tidy up.'

His expression was concerned. 'Have you just come from the Arsenal? I heard there was a bit of an accident up there this afternoon.'

'Yes, there was an explosion in the section where I work . . .' she said, looking down at her overalls and remembering that she was covered in blood. Suddenly the full horror of what had happened came flooding back. She swayed on her feet.

'Whoops – mind how you go,' the policeman said, grabbing her arm to stop her falling. He beckoned to a lad nearby. 'Fetch a chair for this young lady, will you? She's feeling a little unwell.'

The lad dashed into the store and came out with two staff members, who fussed around Betty. One of them brought her a cup of water. Sipping the cold liquid reminded her of the day not so long ago when she had lost her possessions after visiting the pawn shop. Her life seemed to have become a sequence of alarming events, with people constantly having to step in and help her recover. Things couldn't carry on like this. Betty Billington, you need to pull yourself together, she thought to herself.

'Thank you, I feel a little better,' she whispered, noticing that the young women helping her both wore Woolworths uniforms.

'Are you from the munitions works?' one of them asked. 'You are brave to work there. I couldn't do that job.'

'I'm not sure I'm suited to it. I've only worked there a little while, and no one seems to like me very much . . . and then this happened,' Betty said, looking again at the blood on her clothes.

'Well, I can't imagine why they wouldn't like you,' said the other girl kindly, 'although your current state leaves something to be desired. Don't they let you change out of your overall and take a wash before you leave your shift?'

'I'm afraid . . . I'm afraid the manager sacked me straight after the explosion. He believed I was to blame for the accident. But I wasn't, truly. It was a woman who'd taken a dislike to me because of the way I speak. She kept saying I was "posh" . . . I was told to go immediately, and I've to pick up my cards tomorrow.'

'Why, that's awful,' the girl exclaimed. 'Anyone could see you're a cut above the average worker they take on down there; you seem very polite and you speak beautifully. Or rather, you'd be a cut above if you weren't quite so grubby,' she added, smiling to soften her words. Her colleague chuckled and Betty joined in with a weak smile.

'What are you going to do now, miss?' the policeman asked.

'I'm going home to my lodgings at Railway Terrace. I'll clean myself up, and then I'm going to sit down and think about my future. I really do need to find a job. I wonder . . .' she said, looking thoughtfully at the Woolworths store and then at the two girls. 'Would there be a vacancy here, do you know?'

'They always need workers,' the first girl said.

'Although it may not be counter staff they're looking for,' the second added.

'A job's a job,' Betty said, 'and it can't be anywhere near as horrendous as the munitions works. How does one enquire? Should I write a letter to the manager?'

'There's no need for that; you can just pop in and ask. You may need to wait a while to see someone, but it'll be worth it,' the second girl said.

'Thank you, then I'll do that tomorrow morning, after I've dropped these overalls back at the munitions works and enquired after my colleague who was injured.'

'Then we wish you good luck.'

The policeman gave a polite cough. 'I can escort you part of your way home,' he said, holding out his arm.

Betty took it gratefully. 'Perhaps if you could walk with me to the end of the high street? I should be able to manage on my own from there.'

The policeman wouldn't hear of it and insisted on walking her all the way to the gate and seeing her go inside. It was with mixed feelings that she bade him goodbye, hoping she might bump into him again while he was out walking his beat. He'd told her his name was Stan and he had only been a policeman for a short time, as a health problem had kept him from joining up to fight. Being reminded that there were people like Stan and the two girls from Woolworths in the world made Betty feel ever so slightly better after the shocking events of that morning. Just perhaps, life wasn't so terrible after all.

'What the hell!' Harold exclaimed as he walked into the kitchen of Railway Terrace. 'What are you doing in the tub when it's not a Sunday?'

Betty reached for the towel she'd left warming by the stove and held it to her breasts. 'Please, would you turn away!' she cried, horrified at the way he was standing and staring as she sat in the tin bath. The water didn't even cover her modesty.

'You should have said you'd be bathing and I'd not have come in through the back door. What's come over you, woman? You should still be at your work!'

'I no longer have any work,' she replied, stepping out of the tepid water and pulling the towel around herself.

'What do you mean?' he asked, turning again to look at her; at least now she was covered, althought not very well.

She pointed to where her overalls lay in a heap on the linoleum floor. 'There was an explosion, and I was dismissed.'

'You caused an explosion? I'd have thought you had more sense,' he replied, walking past her to the stove to check the kettle.

'It was most certainly not my fault. But being a new employee, and not liked by some of the women, I became the scapegoat.' Briefly, as she wanted to get away and put some clothes on, she explained what had happened.

Harold shook his head. 'I've heard some tales from down that place, but this takes the biscuit,' he said as he slid the kettle onto the stove to boil. 'Go get yourself dressed and then we can talk. There's something I'd like to speak to you about.'

Betty frowned. Whatever could he mean? Conscious of his eyes all over her nearly naked body, she hurried out of the kitchen and up the stairs to her bedroom, where she pulled on some clothing. This reminded her that she would need to collect her belongings from the factory in the morning. She wasn't looking forward to going back there, but she couldn't afford to waste any clothing now that she no longer had her parents to indulge her whims and fill her wardrobe. Vicky and her young man had delivered the suitcase full of clothes, but Betty couldn't help but think of what had been left behind; not the fashionable dresses and slippers, but sensible coats and shoes that she would soon be in need of.

Gazing into the cracked mirror on the wall, she hardly recognized herself: grey shadows outlined her eyes and her hair hung lank and damp around her face. You're starting to look old before your time, Betty Billington, she thought, and this will not do. What happened to that brave young thing who was going to forge her own way in life and not be beholden to her parents? You've made your bed and now you must lie in it, she told herself as she finished dressing. Then she returned downstairs to find that Harold had placed a hot cup of tea on the table.

'You didn't have to do that,' she said, noticing that the tin bathtub had been taken away and emptied. She could see through the window that he had hung it on its hook on the side of the shed.

'Carrying bathtubs and the like is a man's job,' he said,

before sitting down opposite her and taking a drink of his tea.

'You had something to say to me?' Betty asked, wondering if he was going to tell her to leave the house, especially now she didn't have any work to pay her way. After all, if she was no longer going to be his daughter-in-law she really had no right to stay there.

Harold cleared his throat. 'I've been toying with this idea for a little while now, but with the girls about, I've not been able to speak to you.'

Betty reached across the table and patted his hand in a comforting way. He's going to tell me more about Charlie, she thought.

He took her hand and turned it palm up, stroking it in a way that made her slightly uncomfortable, before gazing into her eyes. 'Betty, you probably know I've had two wives? Charlie's mother died in an accident.'

'Charlie did mention that,' Betty said.

'Olive and Peggy's mother died in childbirth when Peggy was born. I've been alone these past ten years – although I have had lady friends,' he continued, his eyes not leaving her face.

Betty wondered why he was telling her this. She murmured a few words about it being understandable.

'The thing is, Betty, I've started to feel it's time for me to marry again and perhaps even have more children. I'm still a young man,' he said, a smile crossing his face.

Betty's heart sank. Of course he'd made plans. What a fool she'd been to think she could settle into this family and carry on, as she would have done if she'd been Charlie's wife. There was no way a woman coming into this household as Charlie's wife would accept Betty staying on as a lodger. It would be hard enough taking on two young girls and the ghost of a dead son. 'I think I understand what you're trying to say.'

He gave a big sigh. 'That makes it so much easier. No doubt you've noticed that I have feelings for you. I hope you will do me the honour of marrying me – after a formal courtship, of course, as we are both still mourning the loss of Charlie?'

Betty froze. Whatever was he talking about? 'I'm sorry, Harold – I don't understand . . .'

'I'm talking about us. And our future,' he said, reaching out to take her hand again and holding it tightly as she struggled to free herself.

Betty felt a flutter of panic. Had she inadvertently given him some sort of encouragement, done something that he'd taken as a sign of her affection? 'But Harold, you are a father figure to me. You would have been my father-in-law if Charlie had come home. I apologize if I've given any indication that I was . . . that I was interested in . . . in marriage.' She felt bile rise in her throat at the thought of sharing a bed with Harold and took a deep breath, pulling her hand back quite forcibly.

Harold smiled. 'I know you are fond of me, and you treat the two girls as if they were your daughters. Mother-hood will come easily to you.'

Betty stood up, the chair crashing to the ground behind her. 'I'm sorry, I can't think about this right now. I've had a distressing day and this on top of everything else is too much for me to comprehend. If you'll excuse me, I will go to my room as I have things I must do.'

She turned to go and nearly bumped into Olive, who stood in the kitchen doorway with a bundle of clothing under her arm and a puzzled look on her face. 'I'm sorry,' Betty managed to say before hurrying past her and running upstairs.

Betty sank onto her bed, covering her face with her hands. Although she wanted more than anything to let go and sob her heart out, she knew she needed to keep her wits about her. Going back over the weeks she had lived at Railway Terrace, she couldn't see how she had encouraged Harold in any way. To her, he was an older man who had given her a roof over her head at a difficult time in her life. The only thing they had in common was their shared grief at the loss of Charlie. Had he misconstrued her compassion as something more?

'It's not your fault, you know,' Olive said, as she entered the bedroom and sat down next to Betty. 'He's always been a one for the ladies. He likes them young,' she added, showing no emotion. 'I heard your conversation. How he could even propose such a thing when you were in shock, I'll never know. Why, our Charlie hasn't been gone five minutes and you've scarcely lived here a fortnight.'

Betty was horrified. Olive was only twelve years old and shouldn't know anything about such matters, let alone be discussing them so casually. 'Your father is a good man. I think he must have become confused, what with having lost Charlie. I don't believe he truly wants to marry me. Perhaps he was simply thinking of my future?' she said, praying that this was true.

Olive shook her head. 'I may be younger than you, Betty, but in many ways I'm more worldly-wise. Dad has had a succession of lady friends ever since I can remember. I'm surprised Charlie never said anything to you?'

Betty thought hard. 'No, I can't recall him mentioning his dad's relationships. If truth be known, I had no idea that you and Peggy had a different mother for quite a while.'

'That was Charlie all over. He was too much in love with you to explain how things were around here.'

Betty smiled fondly as Olive spoke, her hand moving automatically to where the lapel of her coat would have been. 'Oh no, my sweetheart brooch – the one Charlie gave to me before he went to the front. It's pinned to the lapel of the coat I left at the Arsenal. What if someone has taken it? I'll never forgive myself if it's been lost, or even stolen.' This on top of everything else was enough to make Betty dissolve into tears. It took a little while for her to compose herself, with Olive patting her shoulder in consolation. Eventually she said, 'I must go there right away to look for it.'

'No, you're in no fit state to go anywhere,' Olive said firmly as she stood up, wagging a finger as if Betty was the child. 'Lie down and take a rest. I'll run down there – it's all right, I know lots of people who work there. I'll be able to slip in and out without anyone stopping me. Tell me what else you have there and where to find it, and I promise you I'll bring everything back.'

Betty wasn't so sure. She glanced towards the bedroom door. 'I don't know if I want to be here alone here,' she whispered.

Olive knew exactly what she meant. 'Don't worry. I heard Dad go out into the garden to work on the vegetable plot. Our Peggy is out front playing hopscotch and I'll have her come in and sit with you.'

'You won't tell her, will you?' Betty said, fearful at the thought of ten-year-old Peggy knowing how her father had behaved.

Olive chuckled. 'Don't worry, we've both grown up knowing about Dad and his lady friends. But I'll tell her to sit on the stairs quietly and make sure you're not interrupted while you have a sleep. I'll tell her about the munitions explosion, that will be enough for her to understand you need to rest.'

'That's very kind of you,' Betty said, although she also intended to put a chair in front of her bedroom door once Olive had gone. 'I wonder, would you do something else for me?'

'If I can, I will,' the girl said, getting up and checking her hair in the mirror.

'Do you think you could find out how my friend Edna is getting on? She was in a very bad way when the ambulance took her to hospital. Somebody told me she had lost her arm. The people down there may have heard by now?'

'I'll ask around. Bad news travels fast,' Olive said, again sounding much older than her tender years. 'Would you like me to pop into the office and collect your pay packet – then you've no need to go back there?'

'That's very kind of you, but no; I'll go there tomorrow morning to collect my money and my cards as instructed. I'd wait till then to collect my clothing, but I'm so worried about my brooch,' she said, again putting her hand to the place just above her heart where the brooch would normally be pinned.

'I do understand, and there's no problem. I'll go right now,' Olive said, bending down to kiss Betty's cheek.

'You are a good friend,' Betty said as she hugged the girl.

'I'd do anything for you,' Olive said, hugging her back. 'Our Charlie loved you dearly and you would have been part of my family. I don't want to lose you. You won't do anything daft, will you?' she asked, looking towards the closed door. 'We can deal with Dad, don't you worry.'

Betty wasn't sure exactly what this meant, but promised she wouldn't do anything rash. She thanked Olive profusely. 'You are my link to Charlie, too,' she said. 'I'll be here when you get back, never fear.'

The girl seemed satisfied with this promise. But as Betty watched her go, she knew she might not be able to keep it for much longer.

9

Betty checked her appearance in the Woolworths store window before pushing open the heavy glass door. Olive had encouraged her to wear her smartest suit, as it would make a good impression on the manager. The child had been so helpful as Betty forced herself to prepare for the interview.

'One look at you and he will hire you on the spot,' she had said as she brushed a loose strand of hair from Betty's sleeve.

'Charlie liked to see me in this,' Betty replied wistfully. 'I was thinking I would wear it on my wedding day.'

'Come along now, there's no time for tears today,' Olive chided her gently. 'You have Charlie's brooch, and you can imagine him by your side cheering you on. Now, are you sure you wouldn't like me to wait for you outside?'

'Thank you for offering, but I'd rather go alone. After the interview I'll walk down to the Arsenal and collect my cards and what pay is due to me. Why don't we meet when you've finished school? I'll treat you and Peggy to tea and cake – hopefully to celebrate my new job.'

Olive pulled a face; she wasn't one for attending school,

but the thought of a sticky bun made her smile. 'That sounds like fun. I supposed you won't need these after all?' She pointed to the second-hand clothes she'd purchased in the market.

'Well, let's not get rid of them just yet,' Betty said, wrinkling her nose at the two faded patterned frocks and the down-at-heel shoes. 'It was good of you to wash them.'

'If you sell them on you may get a few pennies more, now they're washed and ironed.'

Betty wasn't sure about that, but she admired the child's thinking.

Betty stepped into the store; it was still quiet, but even so the shop assistants were busy behind their counters dusting products and tidying up ready for the day ahead. A few had feather dusters and were flicking them over the more delicate stock.

She looked around to see if she could spot the two girls she'd met yesterday, but couldn't see them. She'd been hoping one of them would show her where to go to enquire about being taken on. As she stood wondering what to do next, an older woman in a similar uniform to the other assistants approached her.

'May I help you, madam?'

Betty cleared her throat; she felt so nervous. 'I was wondering who I had to speak to about being taken on as a shop assistant. I was informed yesterday that there might be a vacancy?'

The woman looked her up and down until Betty began to feel as though she was under a microscope. 'We don't employ management here. You would need to write to head office.'

Betty chuckled at the idea that anyone would think she was there to interview for the position of manager. Did Woolworths even hire women for management? 'Oh no, I was enquiring after a counter assistant's position,' she explained.

The woman stared hard at Betty, taking in her appearance and the way she raised her head high, looking back with confidence. 'I'm not sure you're right for the position, but you'd better follow me,' she sniffed, before turning on her heel and heading towards a door at the side of the store.

Betty hurried to keep up while dodging a few shoppers. Trying to ignore the looks from counter staff, she felt her cheeks start to burn and took a deep breath to calm herself. It wouldn't do to appear flustered when she met the person who was to interview her. The woman ahead of her moved faster up the steps, her heels clicking loudly as she hurried onwards.

Betty did her best to keep up, although she was becoming a little short of breath. The stairs were steep and there were many of them. She grasped the handrail to support herself, even taking a couple of steps at once to make faster progress. It was hard to hurry in her best shoes, which tended to rub her toes.

'This way,' the woman said in a sharp voice as she pushed through a set of double doors, allowing them to swing back into Betty's face.

'Ow,' she said as one door caught her chin before quickly recovering, straightening her hat and stepping through the doors. Already the woman was halfway along a corridor. She snapped over her shoulder, 'If you wish to work here you'd better learn to move a little more quickly. No dilly-dallying.'

Betty was beginning to think perhaps she wasn't right for working here if she would be expected to run about up and down stairs all day; but then she thought of the two girls she'd met yesterday. They had been so pleasant and helpful in her hour of need. If she was a counter assistant at Woolworths, she too would do everything she could to help people. Perhaps the woman ahead of her was just having a bad day. Who knew – she too might have had bad news from the front, and maybe her way of coping was to work hard. Betty's heart softened a little, until the woman looked back and glared at her. 'I told you to keep up,' she snapped as she rapped her knuckles on the door marked 'manager'.

Without waiting for an answer, she pushed it open. 'Excuse me, Mr West, there is a person here enquiring after the vacancy. Shall I show her in?'

Betty heard a mumbled reply, at which the woman turned and said to her, 'The manager will see you – you may enter. But look sharp.'

Betty squeezed past her and, after thanking her, looked around the room. It was covered from floor to ceiling in shelves, all lined with box files and ledgers, while in the middle of the room piles of paperwork covered a large desk. A red-faced, balding man looked up at her.

'I'm busy now, so please be quick.'

'Thank you for seeing me, Mr West,' she said as she sat in the vacant chair opposite him, straightened her skirt and placed her bag by her feet. 'I'm interested in a position as a counter assistant.'

Without speaking, he slid a sheet of paper across the desk and tapped on it. Betty looked at it; it was a form.

'Would you like me to complete this?' she asked.

Mr West frowned. 'You can write your name, can't you?'

'Of course I can,' she smiled and started to fill in her details. When it came to work experience, she wrote 'mother's help and munitions worker', not giving details or dates. She wasn't normally one to tell lies, but leaving out information didn't seem quite as bad as fibbing, and she had assisted her mother at times. She slid the form back across the desk and sat quietly, placing her hands in her lap as she waited for the manager's attention.

Moments passed in silence. She cleared her throat as he continued to scribble on his paperwork. She couldn't help thinking that if she had his job, she would have been a little more personable, even apologizing for keeping someone waiting; but of course it wasn't her job, and she was here hoping to be employed. She crossed her fingers as her hands lay in her lap. It would be so much better to work here in the store, keeping clean all day, and not having to worry about explosives going off at any moment. The biggest problem she could imagine would be an agitated customer, but then, as she'd always been told by her grandmother, pin a smile on your face and no one will be angry for long. She would have to remember that once she was working.

Looking around the room, she spotted a shelf with what look like folded uniforms, neatly stacked. She quite liked the maroon colour and thought the women she had seen downstairs in the store looked very smart. She was wondering who laundered them, and whether she would be given a spare, when the man gave a cough, shaking her out of her reverie.

'You have very neat handwriting,' he said as he scanned the page. 'Some of the women I interview can't even write their names.'

'I had a good education,' Betty replied. It seemed a little unfair of him to comment about other women who might not have had the opportunities she'd had. There again, perhaps he would look more favourably on her because she could write notes and add up sums of money while working behind the counter.

'I wonder if you're overqualified for this position. You look too smartly dressed for a shop worker,' he said, glancing up at the pretty hat she was wearing, his eyes sweeping over her smart suit.

Betty felt her temper start to rise. How dare he comment on the outfit she wore! A woman's outfit should have no bearing on the job she was applying for. 'I am capable of any work,' she said, wondering exactly what he was looking for in an employee. 'I'm more than happy to be trained, and I'm a willing learner. I like to think I would be an asset to the Woolworths company.' By then she'd uncrossed her fingers and was gripping the woollen fabric of her skirt. She sensed he didn't like her and was going to turn her down for the position she so desperately needed.

'There will be early starts, and you may be required to work late,' he said, looking her directly in the face.

'I'm willing to work hard,' she said, returning his gaze. 'I'm not fazed by hard work.'

'It can be dirty work,' he went on, holding the stare.

'Sir, where I worked before was more than dirty and I coped.'

'You would need to work fast. I don't like to see cleaning staff on the shop floor once the shop doors are open.'

Betty frowned. 'Cleaning staff? I was under the impression I was being interviewed for a counter position?'

A small smile crossed his thin lips. 'The vacancy is for a cleaner. I filled the one counter assistant position yesterday afternoon – take it or leave it.'

'But . . .'

He waved his hand as if to dismiss her. 'I sacked the previous cleaner for incompetence earlier this morning. Do you want the job or not?' he said as he started to pick up paperwork and move it around the desk.

Betty sighed. She knew she shouldn't have waited until today to apply – and now there was only a cleaning job. She chewed her lip. It would be so easy to stand up, thank him for his time and walk away; however, if she took this job and made it clear she wished to be a counter assistant, there was a chance she might be moved to the shop floor quite soon.

'I'll take it,' she said quickly, before she could change her mind. It couldn't be any worse than the Arsenal, surely?

Without acknowledging her answer the man bellowed, 'Bartram, get yourself in here now.'

Within a minute a tall, sallow-skinned woman hurried into the room. She wore a uniform like the counter staff but rather than the warm maroon colour, it was white. 'You wanted to see me?' she asked as she appraised Betty with steely eyes.

'I have a replacement for the cleaner I sacked. Get her kitted out and tell her the hours; she can start in the morning.'

'But sir, I did inform you I had someone lined up for the job – my cousin's daughter . . .'

'I don't have time to wait for you to find someone. We need another cleaner right now,' he said, dismissing them both.

A feeling of dread ran through Betty. She hadn't even started work yet and already this woman hated her – there was real malevolence in her glare. I fear you have a rocky road ahead, Betty Billington, she thought to herself.

Betty brushed stray wisps of hair away from her hot face with the back of her hand. Her knees ached from kneeling on the hard wooden floors of the store and her hands were red and sore from constantly dipping a scrubbing brush into a bucket of soapy water. In the two weeks she'd worked as a cleaner, she'd become aware that the other two women doing the same job tended to shirk their responsibilities; but she didn't feel as if she could complain.

When she'd returned to Railway Terrace after her interview she had been met with the expectant faces of Olive and Peggy, who'd wanted to know all about her new job at Woolworths. It had been hard to break it to them that she wouldn't be wearing one of the smart maroon overalls, nor serving customers. Olive had seen her sad face. Rather than comment, she had taken Betty by the hand and led her into the kitchen, putting a cup and saucer in front of her.

'The kettle's on and there's nothing better than a cup of tea,' the young girl had said with a smile. 'I'm proud of you, Betty, the way you've gone straight out to find another job.'

On that, Betty had to agree with her. And gradually, as

the tea warmed her and she told the girls about her duties and the early starts, she had begun to feel more positive.

'You never know – there may be an opportunity to become a counter assistant one day. You must just keep your eyes and ears open.'

Betty had promised she would, and for the past two weeks she had done just that. All she'd spotted so far, though, had been corners of the shop floor that were missed by the other women's scrubbing brushes and brooms, and she'd learnt to follow them to finish off their jobs. She knew the women were aware of what she was doing, but she decided to keep her head down rather than meet their sneering expressions. 'If a job is worth doing, it's worth doing well' became her motto. If she was to be a cleaner for the rest of her working life then she would be a conscientious one. She knew, when she collected the brown envelope with her pay in it on a Saturday morning, that she had earned every penny.

Looking up at the large clock on the wall of the store, she realized that the counter staff would be coming down to the shop floor soon to take the sheets off the counters and prepare for the day ahead. She stood up and dusted off the sacking apron she wore over her overall, straightening the large cap that mainly covered her hair, although there were always stray hairs trying to escape. She reminded herself to smile as she picked up her bucket of dirty water and moved it from the centre of the aisle. She'd decided she wanted to look like a member of the team, albeit a minor one, so she tried to always be as presentable as possible. Who knew when an opportunity might arise for promotion? When it did, she was determined to be ready. As she turned to go, she bumped into the two girls she'd met outside the store on the day of the explosion.

'Hello, Betty! I can't get over how you've completed a whole shift and we are just starting,' said Barbara, the taller of the two, giving her a warm smile.

'At least I have the rest of the day to myself,' Betty grinned back as she kept an eye out for Mrs Bartram, the supervisor, who had a way of appearing out of nowhere and picking holes in her work.

'I'm impressed by how you put up with that supervisor. I've heard she's a bit of a dragon,' Patricia said, as if she was reading Betty's mind.

'I'd better get on, then, in case she appears,' Betty laughed, wishing the girls a pleasant day. They both worked on the counter selling cutlery and kitchenware. If she was a little jealous, she didn't show it. A job is a job, regardless of what I do, she reminded herself as she continued on her way.

Heading through a side door that led to the storerooms, she emptied her bucket and wrung out her cleaning cloths ready for the next day. It was then she realized she'd left her broom behind in the store. If she was quick, she could retrieve it before the supervisors and floorwalkers appeared; they seemed to be the people to avoid, although mainly the cleaners and junior assistants were invisible to them unless there was a problem.

'Girl, what are you doing here?' a harsh voice snapped just as Betty had her hand on the broom.

'I'm sorry, sir, I . . . I . . .'

'I asked her to lend me the broom, sir,' Barbara said as

she stood up from behind her counter. 'It is a little dusty from where I was unpacking ornaments yesterday.' She took the broom from Betty and gave her a crafty wink.

'I can do that for you if you wish,' Betty replied with a grateful smile. Her new friends had warned her that certain floorwalkers liked to bully the female employees. 'If you like, I could help tidy up behind the counter. I have ten minutes before I need to clock off.'

'Then get on with it, girl,' the man snapped, 'but make it quick, I'm about to open the front doors.'

The two girls tried not to giggle as they hurried behind the counter. Betty looked around the little area with interest. There was just about enough room for two assistants to pass each other, while at each end was a shorter counter with just the one entry point for staff. She sighed. This was where she ought to be working – not on her hands and knees scrubbing floors. She looked at the shelves beneath the counters; what a mess, she thought to herself. If this was my section, I would keep it as neat as a pin. I'd put the different-sized brown paper bags into piles and have a box for the dusters. She noticed the counter covers: long stretches of calico fabric, bundled haphazardly and stuffed in at one end of a shelf. She imagined folding them and keeping them tidy, so they looked presentable when she shook them out at the end of the day to lay over the counter. One of the shelves held items of stock, including delicate china figurines and porcelain salt and pepper pots. Glancing up, she could see there was a space on the counter for them. 'Can I put these out for you?' she asked Barbara, who was examining her stockings and fiddling with a broken suspender clasp.

'If you wish,' she shrugged, 'but first, what can I do about this? It seems to have broken; I can't work all day with a loose stocking.'

Betty thought for a moment before reaching into her pocket and pulling out a small pin. 'Will this do?' she asked. 'It's quite clean. I found it on the floor, but I did polish it before I put it in my pocket.'

'You are a dear,' Barbara replied before making use of the pin and straightening her clothes. 'Are you sure you want to put these items out?'

'I'd love to. It's a dream of mine to work on the counters rather than be a cleaner,' Betty confided as she lifted each item, checked it had a price label attached and dusted it carefully before adding it to the neat row on the mahogany counter. She was admiring her handiwork and chatting to Barbara about the display when there was a sound of many footsteps on the wooden floor.

'Oh my, the customers are coming in,' Betty said putting a hand to her mouth. 'I'll be shot if I'm found here.'

'Quick – duck down here,' Barbara said as she reached for one of the counter covers and draped it over Betty, who tried not to giggle.

'I can't stay here all day,' she hissed, before pressing her hand to her mouth to choke a laugh.

'Shush, I'll tell you when it's safe to move. The floor-walker doesn't hang about this counter, it holds no interest for him. He'll be over by the vegetables very shortly as he's sniffing after one of the girls who works there.'

'I thought he was a married man?' Betty whispered. 'I've heard the girls mention his wife and children.'

'Believe me, that doesn't stop him,' Barbara murmured

before turning to serve a customer with one of the ornaments Betty had just displayed.

It was hot and stuffy under the dust cover. Betty loosened a button at the front of her overall and flapped the cloth about to create a draft. This made her nose tickle, and before she could stifle it she gave a loud sneeze.

'Please excuse me,' Barbara said to her customer, reaching for her handkerchief before bending over in a fit of giggles behind the counter. 'You need to be quiet or we will both get into trouble.'

It seemed an age before Betty felt a tap on her shoulder. 'It's all clear for you to go,' Barbara hissed, pulling back the cover. 'But keep down as much as you can in case you're spotted, and take the broom. That way if you're caught you can say you dashed back to collect it – you'll still get the sharp end of his tongue but at least it won't be so bad.'

Betty gave a sigh of relief as she reached the end of the counter on her hands and knees and stood up, looking to her left and right before dashing to the door of the storeroom. Closing it behind her, she went straight to the sink and turned on the cold tap, scooping water in her hands and drinking gratefully before dousing her hot face. She could easily have lost her job just for being on the shop floor at the wrong time.

'Haven't you gone yet, Billington? You should have clocked off half an hour ago,' her supervisor said as she entered the storeroom.

'I'm just on my way, Mrs Bartram,' Betty said, going to the locker where the cleaners kept their outdoor clothing. After pulling on her coat she made her way out to the street, smiling as she felt the sun on her face. It might have been dangerous for her to hide behind that counter, but for those few minutes when she'd been setting out the ornaments and lining them up, she had felt that she was truly a Woolworths girl. The thought gave her a real thrill and she resolved that one day, the job would be hers. At the moment the only fly in the ointment was Charlie's father. So far she had managed to avoid him, but she wasn't sure she'd be able to do so for much longer.

10

~

December 1917

'You look beautiful,' Betty said as she greeted Vicky, who was welcoming her guests in the church hall alongside her new husband. 'And the service was lovely.'

'Thank you, Betty,' Vicky said, brushing away a tear. 'We were fortunate the vicar was willing to overlook our forthcoming happy event. This was my sister's wedding dress – we had to let it out a fair bit.'

Betty smiled weakly; she'd spent the whole service trying hard not to look at Vicky's pronounced stomach. No one else seemed to have such a problem, with some of Vicky's family even patting the bump and giving her husband a wink as if to say 'well done'.

'I had hoped your parents' neighbour, Miss Hobson, would be able to join us, but it seems she has visitors,' Vicky said.

Betty felt guilty, as she hadn't given Miss Hobson a thought since leaving home. She had fond memories of going next door to visit the lady, along with Cook. 'I shall have to write her a letter and explain where I've gone. She was always kind to me.'

'That's a good idea. Now, you're not going to slide away, are you? Please stay and have a bite to eat with us – perhaps even a glass of port to celebrate my wedding day? I'll introduce you to my mum and my aunts and you can sit with them, so you won't feel alone.'

Betty thought Vicky must have read her mind, as she'd been planning to slip away once the service was over. She handed over a neatly tied parcel. 'Of course I will, and I would love to meet your family,' she said. 'This is for you – it's not much, but it's given with love. I hope you can make use of them,' she said, thinking of the hours she'd spent sitting up late, laboriously stitching the couple's Christian names onto two hand towels. 'It's something practical,' she said as Vicky tore open the paper wrapping and admired the gift.

'I'll use them all the time and think of you when I do,' she said, giving Betty a quick peck on the cheek. 'Now, come along over here and meet Mum and the aunts.'

Betty knew she would never remember the names of all the women, but between them they made up a bunch of flowers: Lily, Rose, Ivy, Daisy and Violet. She immediately lost track of who was who, and blamed the port for her fuzzy memory. They were honest, working-class people and even though she was becoming a little more worldly these days, Betty was aware that she didn't quite fit in. Her parents' horror of mixing with the 'lower classes' had made such an impression during her early years that she'd always been frightened of stepping away from the life she knew, and some of the old uneasiness still made itself known occasionally. If she hadn't bumped into Charlie that day, she would still be completely sheltered and would never have known love, let alone loss and friendship.

Her plate had been piled high with crusty bread and chunks of cheese and sausage. She tucked in just like those around her, using her fingers to eat. After Vicky's dad had made a speech and the nervous bridegroom had followed, a woman started to play the piano. Before Betty knew what was happening, she'd been dragged onto the floor to join in with a dance called the Hokey-Cokey.

As she was returning to her seat, hot-faced and laughing with the women around her, someone grabbed her roughly by the arm and she found a young woman hurling harsh words into her face. Blinking in confusion, Betty flinched back from the woman's hot, onion-tainted breath. 'I'm sorry, what is it you want?' she asked, trying to pull away.

'I said, it's all right for you, kicking your heels up and having a good time when our Edna is dead and buried. You're to blame for my sister's death.'

Betty gasped. She had tried to find out what had happened to Edna after the explosion at the Arsenal; Olive had helped her to ask around. From what she'd heard, Edna was healing, although she'd completely lost the lower part of one arm and three fingers on the other. What Olive had discovered was that Betty was not to blame, as several workers had reported what had happened leading up to the explosion. Betty had been relieved and had written to the factory manager with her own account of the incident, even though she'd yet to receive a reply.

'I'm sorry . . . I had no idea,' she said. 'I thought she was getting better – I tried to find out where she lived in order

to visit her. I didn't realize her injuries were life-threatening
... I'm so terribly sorry ...'

'You're sorry, are you?' the girl replied bitterly. 'Oh, it's
all right for you and you fancy ways, with your pots of
money. Our Edna didn't have a pot to piss in, and with her
injuries she'd not have been able to work again, let alone
have a chance of marrying a fella and bringing up a family.
She threw herself in front of a train down in Woolwich. It
was you that as good as caused that explosion and killed
her!' she shouted, before spitting in Betty's face.

An older woman joined them and put her arm around
the girl before leading her away while others consoled her.
Betty stood alone in the middle of the dance floor, frozen
in shock, until Vicky slowly came over to join her. Betty
could see by the look on Vicky's face that she didn't want
to be seen to take her side.

'I'm sorry that happened, Betty,' she apologized as she
took a handkerchief from her pocket and wiped the spittle
from Betty's cheek. 'I had no idea about Edna – you must
believe me. I'd have let you know if I had.'

'Of course, but it is difficult for you ... I'd better not
stay and embarrass you further.'

'Edna and her sisters are my John's distant cousins,' Vicky
tried to explain.

Betty nodded, unable to think of any reply that would
make things easier. It was time for her to leave the party.
She collected her bag and made her thanks to Vicky and
her parents; by the look in their eyes, they were glad to
see her go. As she walked out of the hall she felt every pair
of eyes in the room burning into her back. Fortunately, as
she made her way through the dark streets back to Railway

Terrace, no one could see the tears streaming down her cheeks.

The sound of carol singers on the corner of the road wishing everyone a merry Christmas only made Betty feel worse. Was she truly to blame for Edna's death? Could she have done more for the girl? Why was it that Edna's sister thought she had 'pots of money'? A few smart clothes left over from her days living with her parents did not make her a rich woman. Perhaps she'd better put these clothes away and not wear them again, she thought. As Railway Terrace came into sight she stopped for a moment and wiped her face. It wouldn't do to upset the girls. As it was, when she entered the house they were nowhere to be seen and Harold sat alone in the front room.

'Did you enjoy the wedding?' he asked.

Betty sat down on one of the wooden chairs by the table. 'It was a lovely service and Vicky's family were most welcoming.'

'Then why do you look so glum?' he asked, leaning over to light a cigarette from the fire.

'I heard some sad news, that's why I left early. Do you recall me mentioning Edna – the girl who was injured at the munitions works?'

Harold nodded slowly, watching her.

'It seems she took her own life on the railway line as she couldn't live with her injuries.'

'So that was her? I did wonder when I heard the news, but I didn't like to ask in case it upset you. Betty, you've got to realize that some people can't cope with what happens in their lives and I'm afraid the railway line is an easy way out. I've seen some sights in my time, I can tell you.'

Betty put her hand to her mouth; suddenly she felt sick. 'I had no idea these things happened on the railway lines.'

'Indeed they do. Us drivers learn to keep what we see to ourselves. We must find a way to cope with it, though, otherwise we'd go mad.'

'Oh God,' Betty gasped, thinking about the awful things he must have seen, and about Edna. She buried her head in her arms and sobbed. She fought to control herself in front of Harold, but the pain went deep inside her; she was remembering the happy, vibrant Edna she'd met that day in the queue, when they were both applying for jobs. To think Edna's life had been extinguished and her family blamed Betty for their loss! In some ways she blamed herself, too, even though she hadn't caused the explosion. How could she ever make it up to them?

She'd noticed some of the looks from other guests at the wedding as she'd been accosted by Edna's sister. They didn't know her, but they would know who she was now, and it was natural enough that they sided with Edna's family. Betty wasn't sure she could live with shouldering all the responsibility for what had happened. Would anyone else at the munitions works be carrying a burden of guilt? Probably not; they had all seemed more interested in inflicting damage and blame on others.

As her shuddering sobs subsided, she felt a hand on her shoulder – were the girls at home? Then the smell of tobacco came to her, and she realized it was Harold. She froze for a moment, knowing she was alone with him, and fear ran through her. There again, perhaps he was only being kind and consoling her, just as he would his own daughters.

Then his hand slid across to her neck, gently massaging with the tips of his fingers. A shiver of delight ran down her spine as she felt her shoulders start to relax. For a few seconds, in spite of herself, she relished his touch. It was only as his hand slipped down her back over the silken fabric, moving under one arm towards her breast, that she froze for a moment before trying to wriggle away from his grasp. It was hopeless, trapped as she was between her chair and the table. It was then that a scene flashed before her. Alone, bearing a child out of wedlock – or worse, married to Harold and having to put up with this every night. He was old enough to be her father, not her lover.

'No!' she shouted, pulling up her knees and then kicking out with all her might against the table leg to shove herself backwards. The back of her chair smashed into Harold's torso. He cried out in pain and doubled over, giving her a precious few moments to scramble away from him.

'I'm doing no more than my son would have done,' he said, reaching out a hand to her.

'My Charlie would never have done such a beastly thing,' she cried, outraged. Her head was thumping; suddenly she felt dizzy. Was it fear, or the port and gin she'd imbibed at the wedding? She dared not pass out as she feared the consequences.

'I don't feel I can live here any more,' she said, backing away from him. Even as she spoke, she realized she had nowhere to go. She would have to do something about finding a roof over her head. The fleeting thought that her parents might be willing to take her back kept her brave as she faced Harold down. 'I'm not going to be able to leave immediately and I trust you will cause me no embarrassment until I can. I'll pay my way and I will continue to help with the household duties, but you must accept that I have no love for you, whatever you think about me. I'm not going to be part of your future, do you understand?'

Harold returned to his armchair and sat down carefully, wincing as he did so. Reaching for another cigarette, he lit it from the burning grate. 'I hear what you say, but you must understand that if Charlie were alive you'd be part of this family and as such you'd be expected to join in with family activities. Saturday evening, I have my works do. I've informed my bosses that I will be bringing along our Charlie's fiancée. I hope you agree to that?'

Betty frowned. Under normal circumstances she would have agreed to accompany him, but now she was unsure. 'Do you promise not to touch me inappropriately again?'

He grunted his agreement while puffing on his cigarette, not meeting her eyes.

'Then I'll come along. But if you put one hand on me, I'll walk out, regardless of what your colleagues and employers think. Do you understand?'

He nodded again without speaking just as she heard the front door open, and the two girls came in.

'Hello there,' Betty said, smiling brightly.

Peggy ran to her side and took her hand. 'Was it a lovely wedding?'

'It was, and the bride was beautiful. I threw the confetti you made for me, and it floated to the ground like snowflakes.'

'Was there dancing?' Olive asked.

'Oh, there was, and I sat with Vicky's family, who were so welcoming.'

'Your cheeks are rather pink – did you have a drink?' Olive grinned.

'You've caught me out,' Betty said, knowing that in truth her pink cheeks were down to what had just happened in that very room. 'I was given a glass of port, which I rather liked the taste of, and Vicky's aunts gave me something called "mother's ruin". What do you think of that?'

The girls burst out laughing and Olive said, 'Oh Betty, you're such an innocent. They gave you gin – that's what they call it, mother's ruin. When we're alone,' she added, glancing towards her younger sister and then her father, 'I'll explain why.'

Betty laughed. 'It comes to something when a twelve-year-old must explain the ways of the world to me. I certainly am an innocent person,' she added, not looking at Harold. 'Now, if you'll excuse me, I'm rather tired, so I'm going to go to bed.'

'We will be very quiet when we come up,' Peggy promised.

As hard as she tried, Betty couldn't sleep for thoughts of what could have happened downstairs preying on her mind. Olive called her an innocent, and she certainly was. She wondered if she had encouraged Harold but really didn't think she had; just having her living under his roof seemed to have made him think she was available to him. Once again, fleeting thoughts of going back to her parents' house crossed her mind. If she did that, she wasn't sure they'd agree to her working at Woolworths – especially not as a cleaner. Having had a taste of the working life, though, she knew she could never go back to being just her mother's companion. She would need to put her foot down and remind them that she was an adult, even if she had yet to reach the age of twenty-one.

A little later the girls came up to bed and Olive crept into her room, tapping Betty on the shoulder to check she was awake.

'I know what happened earlier – or at least, I have a good idea,' she whispered. 'Dad has just asked me how I would feel if you were to be our mother. Betty, don't marry him,' she said, before kissing her cheek and leaving the room.

Betty lay still, pretending to be asleep. Now she knew that she really had no choice but to go back home. Harold had no intention of respecting her wishes; she would never feel safe as long as she was living in his house.

'Oh Charlie,' she murmured, 'why did you have to leave me?'

Her mind was elsewhere as she went about her work duties the next day. On two occasions she was reprimanded by a supervisor, who seemed to have made it her business to keep an eye on her that morning. The first time she'd left a bucket of dirty water where someone almost tripped over it, and the second time she was still on the shop floor when the front doors opened to the public.

Even the excited chatter about Christmas couldn't lighten her spirits. What did she have to look forward to? She'd lost the love of her life; the man who would have been her father-in-law had inappropriate ideas about her that she didn't want or need; and she hated her job. A dark thought flitted through her mind: maybe she'd be better off dead. Then she imagined what it must have been like for Edna, and the grief of her family. No, she couldn't do that to anyone, although there weren't many who would grieve for her passing; not even her parents, who would no doubt distance themselves from anything that brought shame to their door.

She looked around the staff room as employees arrived, taking off their coats and checking their uniforms and hair. The women she had most in common with here were the older ones, those who carried grief on their shoulders from being widowed or from losing sons in the war. But to them, Betty was just a young slip of a girl who didn't understand anything. If only she could talk and explain – but who talked to a cleaner?

Dejectedly she left the store, passing a beggar sitting on the pavement.

'Cheer up, lass, it might never happen,' he called to her with a grin.

Usually Betty dropped a coin into his lap, but now she hunched her shoulders and walked past him without a word. Around her people were going about their business. A newspaper vendor was calling out the headlines, but she deliberately blotted him out. To think that her Charlie was now just a statistic, a droplet in the endless stream of words generated in the press. She couldn't bear it.

Just then the sun broke through the clouds, and for a moment the winter light washed over her face. It warmed her soul and, for just a second, made it seem as if the world wasn't such a bad place. Perhaps there was a chance her parents would take her back and forgive her, seeing her engagement to Charlie as an indiscretion. She would never agree with that view, of course, but she had no choice but to compromise if she wanted to return to the family home. She would have to bite her tongue and not retaliate whenever her mother made barbed comments about the working classes. It would be hard, but she had no other options.

She stopped walking and turned around, going back to the beggar and dropping a coin into his cap before crossing the road to the tram stop. There's no time like the present, she decided.

11

Alighting from the tram, Betty took a deep breath before striding out towards her parents' house. If she'd allowed herself to stop and think about what she was intending to do, she would have turned around and fled. However, with life no longer bearable at Railway Terrace, she had no choice but to try and reconcile with her father. If he would listen, then her mother would have to agree to her returning to live with them. Betty had not considered life beyond that point, as now she feared for her safety.

All too soon, the steps that led to the Billingtons' grand front door were in front of her. Brushing away a stray hair that had escaped from the bun she now favoured while working, she ran up the steps and knocked sharply. Her heart beat fast as she waited to hear footsteps on the tiled floor in the hall behind the black-painted door. She stepped closer to listen . . . yes, someone was approaching.

Like a fool, Betty expected to see Vicky open the door, momentarily forgetting that the young woman no longer worked for her parents. She pinned a smile to her face as an elderly woman, wearing a floor-length black dress and a crisp white apron, opened the door.

'How may I help you?' the woman asked in clipped tones as she looked Betty up and down, sniffing through her long, pointed nose.

'I live here,' Betty replied. 'Are my parents at home?'

The woman barred her way. 'Oh no you don't, missy. I know your type – trying to barge into a gentleman's residence to steal his property. Do you think I was born yesterday? The master and mistress have no children – and if they did have a daughter, she wouldn't dress like that. Now, be on your way before I call the coppers.'

Betty felt a fury inside her she'd never felt before. How dare this woman speak to her so rudely, when she wanted no more than to enter the house where she'd grown up? 'Step aside. No one ever speaks to a guest like that in this house. When I tell my parents about it, they will not be amused.'

'I'll say this for you,' the maid sneered, 'you're a bloody good actress. You beggars and thieves will try anything to get into an honest person's house. Be off with you now.'

Betty knew that if she didn't make a stand now, she might never have the nerve to return. She poked the woman in the chest with one finger. 'Get out of my way now. If you want proof of who I am, you will find my portrait hanging on the wall at the foot of the main staircase. I am dressed in a pink taffeta gown with white ribbons in my hair.'

'Now I know you're telling lies,' the woman spat as she pushed Betty's hand away. 'There is no such portrait in the hall.' She swung the door back so that Betty could see the staircase. Her portrait had indeed been removed; in its place was a landscape she did not recognize.

'They must have moved it,' she said, momentarily

thrown. 'In that case, I will tell you that in the drawing room there is a portrait of my grandparents. My grandmother has her favourite dog sitting on her lap and my grandfather is holding a pipe.'

The maid sucked in her breath. 'If you've been snooping about, you would have seen that through the drawing-room window. I'll give you this, you're bloody good.'

'Look, my name is Elizabeth Billington. My mother is Agatha Billington. Surely you've heard my name spoken.'

'The master and mistress have never mentioned a daughter, nor anyone named Elizabeth. Do you honestly think they would have a daughter as scruffy as you?'

Betty glanced down at herself. So intent had she been on hurrying directly to her parents' house that she hadn't given a thought to what she was wearing, having come straight from work. She had on one of the washed-out cotton frocks Olive had purchased from the second-hand stall along with the shabby shoes that, despite their scruffy appearance, were comfortable and got her through her working day. Her confidence dropped. 'I've been working . . . I came straight here.'

The maid snorted and moved closer. Grabbing the front of Betty's dress, she shook her. 'I'll not tell you again – *go away*,' she hissed.

'Who is at the door, Andrews? There's a terrible draft blowing in. You could at least invite them in rather than hold a discussion on the doorstep.'

Betty recognized her mother's voice at once and pushed past Andrews. 'It's me, mother. Your daughter, Elizabeth,' she said, walking the length of the hall towards Agatha Billington.

Agatha froze. 'Good grief, look at the state of you. How dare you come to my house looking like this? Your father will have something to say about it, I can assure you. What has it come to, that you appear here dressed like a woman of the night and embarrass me in front of the staff?'

Betty couldn't help but smile; her mother had no idea how a 'woman of the night' dressed but she herself knew, from the few she'd seen wandering the streets of Woolwich, that if they were to wear clothes like hers they wouldn't pick up much trade. 'Mother, I've come straight from work. Yes, I have a job,' she said, as her mother made a horrified face. 'It's what women do to keep themselves. You might look down on people who work in Woolworths, but I'm proud of my job.'

Agatha Billington looked shocked and raised a hand to her mouth. 'Come into the drawing room. We do not discuss our private lives in front of the staff.'

As Betty followed her mother, she stopped and turned for a moment. With a sweet smile, she nodded to Andrews. 'Would you bring tea, please, Andrews? Thank you.'

The woman scowled, but didn't move until Betty raised her eyebrows without losing her smile. She always found it easier to make requests with a smile, rather than demand something.

Entering the drawing room, she was taken aback to see her father sitting in his armchair reading a newspaper. 'Why aren't you at your office?' she asked without thinking. It really wasn't her place to enquire, she realized as she said it.

He looked up at her and then turned to his wife, who had taken a seat opposite him. 'Did someone speak?' he asked her.

Betty shook her head as she sat on the edge of her seat. 'You know very well it is I who spoke, Father.' She was no longer willing to play his games. He'd often ignored her like this if she had been naughty as a child. Back then she would have thrown herself at his feet, begging to be forgiven and promising to be a good little girl, whereupon he would reward her with a toffee from a tin he kept on a side table. She doubted it would happen that way tonight.

'This woman dressed as a scullery maid is your daughter,' Agatha said. 'By rights she should have come in by the servants' entrance.'

'Remind me, do we have a daughter?'

'We did, my dear; but as you said recently, she is dead to us.'

He nodded his head thoughtfully and returned to his newspaper for several moments before placing it in his lap. 'Why is there a scullery maid sitting on our best furniture?'

Agatha was about to reply when Andrews returned with a tea tray. By the look on her face, she had overheard Mr Billington's last remark. 'Am I right to use the best china, ma'am?' she asked. 'I wasn't sure, considering . . .'

'Leave it there, Andrews,' Agatha replied with a nod to the nearest table. 'That will be all.' Regardless of what she thought of her daughter at that moment, she was not prepared to have a private conversation in front of a servant; they were known to eavesdrop and gossip with fellow staff. She did not air her dirty linen in public.

'Shall I pour?' Betty asked, leaning forward towards the table. She'd only just touched the teapot handle when the table sailed across the room, with the best china and hot water spraying everywhere. She gasped and recoiled as she saw that her father had jumped to his feet and kicked out at the table.

'Dammit, girl, you can't just walk in here dressed like a ragamuffin and offer to pour tea! What the hell have you been up to?'

'Please, control yourself,' Agatha begged, glancing towards the closed door. 'The servants will hear.'

'I don't give a tinker's cuss for the servants, when we have a working girl standing here purporting to be our daughter. I want answers, and I want them now.' He stamped his foot in anger and moved restlessly towards the fireplace.

'Don't do anything foolish, dear,' Agatha said, with an eye on the expensive ornaments lining the mantelpiece. 'Sit down. Let us have a sensible discussion.'

Betty righted the table and replaced the teapot before returning to her seat. 'I came here today to throw myself on your mercy,' she said, looking beseechingly at her parents. 'I need somewhere to live. It's no longer possible for me to stay at Charlie's home – I fear I may be in danger.'

'You're living with a man?' her father spat, his face turning dark.

'I didn't expect to hear that,' her mother said, gripping the arms of her seat.

Betty sighed. 'I do not *live with a man*. I'm living at the home of Charlie's father and his two sisters. Mr Sayers is a driver on the railway and we live in one of the railway cottages.'

'Oh, my goodness, this gets worse by the minute,' her mother flustered.

'They are decent, honest people who work for a living – just as I do.' Betty made an effort to smile and kept her tone persuasive. What she really wanted to do was shout at her parents to start thinking of others for a change, instead of sitting on their high horses and making unpleasant comments about the working classes; but she held back. 'My circumstances are such that I really do need a different place to live. Not having a penny to my name, apart from what I earn each week as a cleaner, I've come here to ask if you will allow me to live here again.' She looked between her parents for an answer. Her mother refused to meet her eyes, instead watching her husband.

'What do you say, my dear?'

Her father sat staring into space for several moments before shaking his head. 'It has been a constant worry to your mother that someone may have found out you were engaged to be married to . . . that man.'

'You mean the man I loved?' Betty said, gripping the arm of the chair so tightly she feared her fingers would go through the fabric.

'Allow me to continue,' he said, brushing aside her words. 'That man was not of our class, and neither are his family. What would people think?'

'Father . . . most people would think my Charlie was a brave man who died fighting for his country. If you know of people who would look down their noses at someone who was a crane driver on the railway before becoming a soldier, then I have no wish to associate with them and in my opinion, nor should you. I beg you; I just want my room to sleep in, and something to eat. I will even contribute to the household expenses each week from my pay packet if you like. I'll be no trouble to you; in fact, I will be out of the house most days working, and you won't even know I exist . . .' She stopped to draw breath before adding, 'I beg you to agree.'

She waited anxiously for him to reply, imagining what her future would hold if she lived at Railway Terrace for much longer. Would Harold Sayers attempt to interfere with her again, with expectations of making her his wife? Her stomach clenched and she felt sick at the thought.

'Remind me again, what is this position you hold? And are there any prospects?' her mother asked.

Betty wanted to scream. How many times had she explained? 'I'm a cleaner in a Woolworths store, and a very good one. In time I hope to be promoted to a position as a counter assistant.'

Her father groaned and dropped his head into his hands. 'I pray I shall wake up soon and find this has all been a nightmare.'

'Mother, what do you think?' Betty asked in resigned tones. She had a pretty good idea of what her mother would say.

'I'm very much in agreement with your father's thoughts. I was tempted to allow you to return if you forgot all this nonsense about working. However, you have managed to dig yourself a hole so deep I see no way for you to climb out of it and have a respectable future. What suitable man will take you on knowing that you've been a shopgirl – worse still, a cleaner? Or that you have lived under the roof of a man you're not related to? And on top of that, been engaged to a person who was a crane driver . . . ?'

'Mother, I have no wish for a man to take me on, as you say. I don't want that sort of life; and in any case, I would never be interested in a man who thought in that way.'

Mrs Billington shook her head in distress, making the neat curls adorning the sides of her face tremble alarmingly. 'Next you'll be telling us you're one of those . . . those suffragette women . . .'

'If I was, I don't see that it would be any concern of yours, Mother. Father, unless you say otherwise, I will be on my way,' Betty said, rising to her feet.

He turned the other way, not speaking to her as she walked towards the door. She was treading scattered pieces of seed cake from the tea tray into the precious Persian rug, but she didn't care. Desolation seeped into her bones, giving her just enough strength to open the door.

Andrews, by the look on her face, had heard much of the conversation. 'I'll show you to the back door,' she muttered, looking as superior as her employers.

A small flame of annoyance started to burn inside Betty. She pulled herself up and looked the woman in the eye. 'Please don't bother on my account. I know my way around this house. I suggest you go into the drawing room and clean up the mess – there's quite a lot of it,' she said politely before heading to the front door, knowing that she was unlikely to enter the house again.

Outside, she hurried down the steps before stopping to take a few deep breaths as she reached the pavement. Whatever would she do?

'Elizabeth, is that you? For heaven's sake, you look all in. Come along inside, you seem upset . . . Elizabeth?'

'Oh, Miss Hobson – I'm so sorry, I was deep in thought. How are you?' Betty smiled at the older lady who owned the small house next door to her parents'. She had always liked Miss Hobson, who would welcome her into her kitchen and give her a hot drink and talk to her with kindness and genuine interest when Betty was still a child.

Miss Hobson took her by the elbow and led her in through her front door, into the familiar homely kitchen. 'I can see you are troubled, my dear, and I will help you if I can. After all, we have been friends for a very long time, have we not? What is needed right now is a hot cup of tea. It is the cure for all problems; and I feel you have a problem.'

'I could do with a friendly ear just now,' Betty said as she went to the stove to warm herself. 'Your kitchen is always so friendly and comfortable. I remember with fondness sitting by the open fire in your front room and toasting bread for tea. What I wouldn't give . . .'

'What you wouldn't give for what, my dear?'

'Oh, nothing,' Betty said, shrugging her shoulders. 'Is there anything I can do to help you?'

Hortensia Hobson gave Betty a sharp look as she warmed the teapot. 'Nothing much gets past me, you know. I may be getting on a bit now, but I'm aware you haven't been living next door for some months. And now, seeing the way you are dressed and the way you fled down those steps makes me think all is not right in your world.' She appraised Betty with her birdlike eyes.

Betty sighed as she looked at the woman, who stood shorter than herself. For as long as she could remember, Miss Hobson had worn stiff taffeta dresses and a crocheted shawl around her shoulders. She was rather reminiscent of the late queen, with her grey hair pulled back in a tight bun.

'You're not wrong,' Betty said, sinking into a wooden chair at a scrubbed kitchen table. 'My life has changed in so many ways, and I'm very sorry I never came in to tell you the news, but . . . well, I'm afraid Charlie died fighting for our country.'

Miss Hobson was the only person apart from Vicky who had known about Betty's relationship with Charlie. She had bumped into the couple walking in Greenwich Park one afternoon, and Betty had felt it was her duty to tell the kindly neighbour about her fiancé. As she started to explain what had happened, Miss Hobson put down the teapot she was warming and opened a drawer in a wooden dresser. Pulling out a page from a newspaper, she placed it in front of Betty before returning to make the tea. 'I know about Charlie, my dear. I tend to follow news of the fallen, as so many of my friends have lost loved ones. I was most upset to see Charlie Sayers' name listed.'

Betty looked at the long list of names on the page before placing it back on the table. It was identical to the one Harold Sayers had kept and it was still too painful for her to read.

'Elizabeth . . .'

'Please, could you call me Betty? I left Elizabeth behind the day I heard the news about Charlie. He preferred to call me Betty, so it's Betty I will be from now on.'

'It suits you, my love. Here, drink up, we have a lot to catch up on.'

Betty gave her a grateful smile. Miss Hobson was so kind. As far as Betty could remember she had always lived alone and, although she seemed to be quite a private person, had often allowed Betty to help with her chickens and brush the coat of her little lapdog, who had long since passed away. Betty's mother had never socialized with Miss

Hobson, although she didn't know why not. Perhaps they just didn't have much in common.

Miss Hobson took note of Betty's appearance as she laid the table for tea. Taking a crusty loaf from the pantry, she held it under one arm, using a bread knife to deftly remove thin slices. 'Fetch the butter, dear,' she said, noticing Betty lick her lips. 'I take it they never offered to feed you?'

'The tea ended up on Mother's best Persian rug as I left.'

'I'd have paid good money to see that,' Miss Hobson grinned. 'Although I do not generally approve of rudeness, there are times when it is the only way to express oneself.'

'I was on my best behaviour,' Betty replied as she placed the glass butter dish onto the table and removed the ornate lid. 'My father was the culprit.'

Miss Hobson nodded for Betty to sit down at the table as she went to the pantry, returning with a plate of cold sliced mutton. 'It's nothing special, just something left over from last night's dinner, when I had visitors. As I always say, waste not, want not.' She placed the cold mutton between slices of buttered bread. Cutting the sandwiches into neat squares, she slid a tea plate and linen napkin across the table to Betty. 'Eat up, and we can talk afterwards.'

Betty needed no second bidding and tucked into the food as if she had not eaten for days. It seemed an age since she'd climbed out of bed at the crack of dawn, hurrying from the house before the girls, and more importantly, Harold, awoke. She dabbed at her mouth with the napkin. 'It's rather a long story.'

'I'm not going anywhere,' Miss Hobson said as she poured tea into two china cups. 'Start talking.'

Betty explained everything – from the moment Olive had arrived at her parents' door to inform her of Charlie's demise, to the events of the previous night. 'I'm so desperate that I thought I would beg to be allowed to live at home once more, even though it would pain me to do so. I like being independent and earning money to support myself, even though it is hard. Not that I'm afraid of hard work,' she added, looking down at her ragged clothing. 'I didn't even think to change out of my work clothes once I'd decided to come and beg for help.'

'That would have been your downfall,' Miss Hobson smiled sympathetically.

'It says a lot about my parents that the way I dress is more important than my safety.'

Miss Hobson shrugged her shoulders. 'Nothing surprises me any more. Some people cannot see further than the end of their noses. Now, tell me: do you really feel you will be in danger if you remain at Railway Terrace?'

Betty nodded, finishing her tea, and then told Miss Hobson a little more about Harold Sayers' advances. 'At first I thought he was just a lonely man, and sad because he had lost his son. However, Olive tells me he has had a few lady friends since his wife passed away. And all of them have been rather young.'

'And you have endeared yourself to him by making yourself indispensable, which no doubt added to his certainty that you would make a suitable wife?'

Betty looked down into her lap. 'I did nothing to encourage him. I've only ever loved Charlie, and we had decided to wait until we were married to . . .'

'There's no need to explain, my dear. I may not approve

of the way your parents have behaved recently, but I know they have instilled certain principles in you.'

Betty blushed. 'There have been times when I wish we had . . . especially now. I hope I haven't shocked you.'

Miss Hobson leaned over and patted her knee. 'As I said before, nothing shocks me any more. I would probably have done the same as you – there again, perhaps not quite the same as you.'

Betty wasn't sure quite what Miss Hobson meant by this, and felt it might be impolite to ask. 'I really must be getting back home,' she said, faltering over her words.

'But it is not your home, and you don't really want to go back there, do you, my dear?'

'I have nowhere else to go. If only my parents . . .'

'In many ways, I feel that would have proved to be the greater of two evils. Now,' Miss Hobson said, getting to her feet and brushing crumbs from her lap, 'I have an idea that might just help you. It's not perfect, but – well, follow me and see what you think.'

12

Betty was surprised how different Miss Hobson's house was from her parents' home. She'd known it was much smaller, but even so, the hall was narrower than she expected, as was the staircase. She followed Miss Hobson upstairs.

'Please do tell me if you're not interested, but I have a spare room that you're welcome to use. I would ask some sort of rental for it, but it will include food and everything you would expect – and I'm told I'm good company,' she laughed. 'The room will need sorting out, though.'

Betty's chin almost hit the floor as Miss Hobson pushed open the heavy oak door. 'Why, it's wonderful,' was all she could say as she looked around, ignoring all the things that were stored there. She could see that it was a pretty room, and she would be very cosy. The wallpaper was bright, adorned with cheerful sprigs of flowers; the chimney breast had a black grate that just needed lighting, and the two tall sash windows were hung with heavy damask curtains.

'Oh dear; I knew there were quite a few items in here, but I didn't realize just how cluttered it had become. I'm sure I can find homes for all of it,' Miss Hobson said as she went to the windows and opened them. 'The room just needs a little airing. If you wouldn't mind living alongside some of these things while I sort through them, we could clear the bed first and make it up so that you can move in as soon as possible. What do you think?'

Betty gasped, taking in her surroundings. 'Are you sure? I'd hate you to feel you'd been put on the spot.'

'My dear, I know my own mind, and I'd like nothing more than to offer you a room. Mind you, if you wish to think of me as someone rescuing a damsel in distress, I will not complain,' she chuckled.

Betty joined in with the laughter. 'In that case, I think I'm going to love living here,' she said as she ran her hands across the foot of the metal bed frame. She crossed over to the windows that looked out on the main road. 'There is just one problem – do you think my parents will be upset that I'm living next door? And will they be angry with you for taking me in?'

'I'm sorry to say that in all the years I've lived here, your mother has never stopped to pass the time of day with me. My house is smaller than hers, I have no place in society, and she frowns on me for being . . . well, for being single.'

'I thought she'd never spoken to you?'

'Oh, my dear – you can just tell what your mother thinks by the way she glances as she walks by.'

'Well, I for one think you're wonderful to take me in like this. I will never stop thanking you.'

'That could become tiresome and embarrassing. I'll accept your thanks, but if you keep on saying the same words, I'll show you the door.'

'I'll try not to, in that case,' Betty smiled. 'Would it be too soon for me to move in tomorrow? It's pointless today, as by the time I've gone back to Railway Terrace and collected my things and made my goodbyes to the girls, it will be too late to travel back here.'

'Whenever you wish. I'm not one for going to bed early.'

'Thank you,' Betty said, feeling a great weight drop from her shoulders. 'I do need to be careful not to bump into my parents. They seem to have whitewashed me out of the family, so I don't want to become an embarrassment to them, especially if I'm in my work clothes. I just hope they won't see me waiting for the tram – the stop is just over the road.'

Miss Hobson wandered over to join her by the window. She looked thoughtful. 'Tell me, my dear, have you ever ridden a bicycle?'

'A bicycle? Why do you ask?' Betty asked, feeling confused.

'Because it could be part of the answer to your problem.'

'I'm afraid I've never learnt to cycle – my parents didn't think it was necessary. What is it you're suggesting?'

'If you use the old bicycle I have out in the back garden, you could exit by the side gate and cycle to work each day. That's if you feel you're up to it? Your parents would never think to look twice at a girl on a bicycle – not that they'd see you, as you'd be cycling away from the house. It would also save you a few pennies in tram fares.'

Betty grinned. 'I will need some practice before I set off for work, otherwise I will be a danger to the public.'

'There's enough room in the garden for you to cycle up and down the path until you feel confident enough to ride on the roads.'

'Oh, that would never do. What if my parents, or the staff, were to spot me from one of the windows at the back of their house?'

'For one thing, they would never expect to see you out there, let alone riding a bicycle. If you're truly worried, you can wear one of my hats and borrow my coat. Your mother already thinks I'm a dotty old woman, so that would just confirm her view. Also, if you were to practise at dusk, they would be less likely to see you.'

Betty chuckled. 'Oh, Miss Hobson, it's going to be such fun staying here with you. I will do my share of cleaning and housework, just as I've done at Railway Terrace.' She clapped her hand to her mouth. 'Oh, goodness, I really must go back there – there's such a lot to do. If I hurry, I can be here by mid-afternoon tomorrow; that will give me plenty of time to practise on the bicycle . . .'

'That's a good plan. But I think you might have forgotten one thing, Betty,' Miss Hobson said, looking serious.

Betty frowned. 'I'm not sure what . . .'

'Didn't you say that you'd agreed to accompany Mr Sayers to his staff party this evening?'

Betty groaned. 'Oh, no – I can't see how I'm going to wriggle out of going. The last thing I want is for him to take out his anger on the two girls. What do you suggest I do?'

Miss Hobson went to a chest of drawers and rummaged. 'I know I've got a spare one somewhere,' she muttered before pulling out a large hatpin. 'I take it you will be wearing a hat?'

'Yes, I will,' Betty said.

'In that case, pin this in securely – and if Mr Sayers becomes a little frisky, you know what to do.'

Betty couldn't help laughing, although knowing she had something to defend herself with did make her feel safer. 'Oh, Miss Hobson, you are a card.'

By the time she got back to Railway Terrace, night was drawing in. Olive and Peggy were standing on the doorstep, looking up and down the road for her. Both hurried to hug her.

'Oh, Betty, we wondered what had happened to you! You're normally home by now. Dad's been fretting in case you didn't get here in time to go to his works do.'

Betty hurried them inside and closed the door behind her. 'There was no need for you to wait on the doorstep for me, girls – you'd have caught your death of cold out there without your coats on,' she said. 'Yes, I'm still going to his works dance just as I've promised, so there's no need to fuss so. Where is he?' she asked, looking around her.

'He said to tell you he's gone on ahead,' Peggy said. 'He had to give someone a hand with the crates of beer.'

'Typical,' Olive said with a grimace. 'If beer is mentioned Dad's off like a shot, even when he's said he'll take you to a dance.'

Betty frowned and thought for a moment. 'In that case, perhaps he doesn't expect me to join him after all – and I can stay home with you?' she said.

'No, he was most insistent that you should go down to the hall as soon as you were ready. He particularly told me to tell you . . . in fact . . .'

'In fact what?' Betty said, noticing the girl's troubled look.

'In fact, when his mate George knocked on the door to ask him for a hand, Dad said to him that he'd be able to meet his intended this evening.'

'Intended?' Betty asked, feeling worried.

'I did warn you, Betty. Once Dad gets a bee in his bonnet about something, there's no stopping him – and he does like the ladies.'

Betty shivered inwardly. It didn't seem right for her to talk to the girls about their father's advances and her fears, even though Olive was quite wise to the facts already. However, knowing she would soon be safely settled with Miss Hobson made her feel a little braver. 'I'll get myself ready,' she said with a smile. 'Will you girls be all right here on your own?'

'Of course we will. We're not young children,' Olive said, sounding too old for her tender years. 'You will tell us all about it when you get back, won't you?'

'Yes, of course,' Betty smiled. She would miss the two girls once she moved out, but would do her utmost to keep in touch with them if it didn't infuriate their father.

Hurrying up to her bedroom, she pulled her one decent frock from where she'd hung it behind the door, trying to erase the image from her mind of the last time she'd worn it – the day of Vicky's wedding, when Harold had molested her. 'This will have to do,' she muttered to herself, quickly washing and dressing. She ran a brush through her hair and pinned it back off her face before putting on her hat and adding the hatpin, as instructed by Miss Hobson. She pinched her cheeks, trying to add some colour, before dabbing a little eau de cologne on her wrists.

'I'm not there to show myself off. I'm doing this through duty, because Harold Sayers invited me,' she told her reflection in the mirror. Hopefully there would be a point during the evening when she could explain to him that she was moving out of Railway Terrace to go back to where she had come from. She wanted to make it as easy and pleasant as possible, and to make it clear that there was to be absolutely no romantic attachment between them.

It was as she pulled on her coat that she remembered it had only been a year since her darling Charlie had kissed her goodbye. 'Look at what has happened to me since then; my life has changed completely,' she murmured. She now worked for a living, and she had experienced suffering and seen things that she would never forget.

Why was Harold Sayers going to a party, when he should still be grieving the loss of his only son? Men could be so strange. Perhaps he preferred to grieve privately, she thought generously. Even though she was frightened of what he might do if they were alone together, she still pitied him for having lost his eldest child to war.

Calling goodbye to the girls, she set out into the dark night. The community hall where the railway staff were holding their Christmas get-together was only a few streets away and she hurried along, averting her eyes from passers-by until she approached the venue. Already there were people milling around outside, and she could hear music coming from the open door. Harold had told her they always had a band, although it was rather depleted this year what with so many younger men away fighting.

She had asked whether he really thought it right for people to be celebrating and enjoying themselves while the country was at war. Harold had been slightly affronted by her words, telling her that it was an annual event, a tradition, with the beer and food being paid for by the railway company. There was always a generous raffle, and the proceeds went towards parcels to be sent to loved ones at the front. Even so, Betty felt uncomfortable with it all, knowing that somewhere and only several months ago her Charlie, Harold's only son, had fallen while fighting for his country. As far as they knew, there wasn't even a body to bury. If only there had been a grave she could visit and tend, it might have felt as though Charlie was truly gone; but as things were, it still seemed as if he might reappear one day with a cheery smile.

Betty edged towards the open door, weaving her way through little groups of people standing chatting. 'I'm looking for Harold Sayers,' she said to a man standing at the door who was taking tickets.

'You must be his Betty. Come along in, love, you'll find him over near the beer table,' the man said, giving her an appreciative look. 'You can leave your coat over there.' He nodded towards a small side room.

She mumbled her thanks, quickly removing her coat and leaving it with a woman who handed her a raffle ticket that would serve to reclaim it later. Licking her lips nervously, she walked towards a row of trestle tables where men were being served with pint glasses of bitter.

'Ah, Betty, there you are, my love,' Harold said, putting his arm around her shoulders and kissing her cheek in an over-familiar way.

'I'm sorry I'm late, I got held up. I need to tell you all about it later,' she said politely.

'Not to worry, let's get you a drink. I'll introduce you to my friends,' he beamed, before leaning in close and whispering, 'You look rather splendid. I do like you in that dress.'

Betty flinched. The smell of beer on his breath wasn't pleasant, to the point that she held her breath before averting her head.

'A port and lemon for my Betty, and I'll have another pint,' Harold called to one of the men who was serving behind the table.

His Betty? That was rather forward, she thought; but she smiled politely, trying to wriggle away from the arm that he kept possessively around her. 'I'm pleased to meet you,' she nodded politely to the other men he indicated. Several of them turned to stare, until she felt uncomfortable.

'There you go, love,' one of them said, handing her a glass. 'If you want to sit with the ladies, my wife's over there,' he added, nodding to where a group of women sat chatting around a table. 'Here, let me take you,' he offered, as Harold was more interested in his beer.

As Betty threaded her way through the crowd with the man holding her elbow to guide her, she thought how strange it was that the men had all congregated together close to where the beer was, while the women had to entertain themselves. It was as if the man had read her thoughts.

'It'll liven up later, when the music starts properly and we all have a dance,' he explained. 'Molly, my dear,' he called to a dark-haired woman seated at the table, 'this is Harold's young lady. Would you take care of her until the dancing gets going?'

Six pairs of eyes turned her way as she took the empty seat the man had dragged across from another table.

'I'm pleased to meet you,' Betty said as she placed her drink on the wooden trestle table. 'Thank you for allowing me to join you. I don't really know anybody here apart from Harold.'

'From what I've heard, you didn't take long getting to know him,' remarked an older woman sitting next to Molly.

'Mother!' Molly hissed, before giving Betty an apologetic look.

'I've known Harold for over a year,' Betty tried to explain, although several of the other women were exchanging knowing glances. 'My fiancé, Harold's son Charlie, was killed at Ypres this August just gone. Harold kindly invited me to move into Railway Terrace.'

'Only days later, from what I was told,' the old woman continued, ignoring her daughter's sharp elbow. 'Then you worked down the Arsenal until they sacked you after that tragic accident . . .'

'She topped herself,' one of the other women joined in.

'Tragic,' a few of them murmured, as Betty watched them all discuss her life as if she wasn't there.

'Now you're scrubbing floors at Woolworths,' the old girl cackled, emphasizing the word 'scrubbing' in a way that caused some to laugh with her. 'When's the wedding to be?' she asked pointedly, looking at Betty's stomach.

If not for her strict upbringing and having been taught good manners from the cradle, Betty would have given them a tongue-lashing. As it was, she rose to her feet and gave a polite smile. 'If you will excuse me, I need to speak to Mr Sayers,' she said, leaving them before they could comment again and walking towards the door. Outside, ignoring the cold December air, she walked round the corner of the building to a quiet spot and leaned against the wall, trying to clear her thoughts. Was this what people thought of her? What had she done to deserve having her reputation sullied like this? She didn't even know these women, but they seemed to know a certain amount about her – and they had twisted the truth and decided she was not a nice person.

As they often did when she felt low, her thoughts turned to Charlie. 'Why did this wretched war have to tear us apart, my love?' she murmured to herself. 'I know I made a promise to you that last time we met, but it's been so hard – so very, very hard.'

She crossed her arms over her body, starting to feel the chilly night air. She was just wondering if she could creep back into the hall to collect her coat and slip away to Railway Terrace to start packing, when Harold staggered around the corner.

'There you are; what got into you, disappearing like that? George's wife was none too pleased the way you walked off. They are good people, and we will be in their company a lot once . . .' Even in his befuddled state, he knew better than to say any more.

'Harold, there's something I need to talk to you about. The people in there have made certain assumptions about me – and I've already tried to make it clear to you that I'm not . . .' Her words froze in her throat as he lunged towards her. Thankful she'd not touched the port and lemon and had her wits about her, she stepped sideways, causing him to crash into the wall.

'What the . . . ?' he gasped as he righted himself and looked around for her.

Betty backed away from him and stood with her hands on her hips. 'Harold, you've got to understand – I'm not interested in a romantic liaison with you. For one thing, I'm closer in age to Olive than I am to you. And for another, I don't love you, and there is no attraction which could lead to love. Charlie was the one for me, and now I don't see a future with anyone else.'

'Don't talk like that. I'm offering you a roof over your head forever and a respectable marriage. What woman wouldn't want that?' he slurred.

Betty sighed, but kept her distance as he stepped towards her. 'Harold, the advances you have made towards me have not been romantic. They've been . . .' She stopped to think, not knowing what word to use. 'They've been unacceptable, and you put me in an embarrassing situation having to fend you off. I haven't felt safe in your house, and that's why . . .'

An angry look crossed his face. 'Why, you . . .' He raised a fist above his head. 'You ungrateful little . . . What woman wouldn't want me?'

'A woman who still loves your son, and will never love another,' Betty said, feeling brave. Even if he struck her, she was determined to finish the conversation.

'In that case, I'm done with you, you ungrateful cow. I'm not wasting good drinking time out here. Be off with you. When I get home, I don't want to see hide nor hair of you.' With that, he turned and staggered back into the hall.

Betty followed, keeping at a distance. She collected her coat and returned to Railway Terrace, filled with a confidence she hadn't felt in a long while.

*

'Oh, my dear, come along in,' Miss Hobson said, after opening the door carefully and peering out to see who could be hammering on her door in the early hours of the morning. She ushered Betty in and closed the door, replacing the walking stick she had taken from the umbrella stand to protect herself, and apologizing for welcoming Betty in her nightclothes. Straightening the voluminous nightcap on her head and pulling a colourful silk robe around herself, she reached out to Betty. 'Here, let me take one of your bags,' she said, ushering Betty into the front room. 'I'm assuming something must have happened to make you arrive on my doorstep at this ungodly hour – not that you aren't welcome.'

Betty placed her suitcase on the floor and sank into an armchair before pulling off her woollen gloves and unbuttoning her coat. 'I'm so sorry for arriving on your doorstep at this time of night. He has thrown me out,' she said, unable to utter another word. She'd walked all the way from Railway Terrace to Miss Hobson's house, unable to think of any other way she might get to her new lodgings in the middle of the night.

'Not at all, my dear; you look all in. I'll put the kettle on and come straight back so you can explain everything to me,' Miss Hobson said. 'And you can take that worried look off your face, young lady. I'm a light sleeper. In fact, I was lying awake thinking about how delightful it will be to share my house with somebody once more. It's been a long time,' she said distractedly as she hurried from the room.

Betty finished taking off her outer clothes and went over to the fire, raking over the glowing embers to encourage a little more heat. Sitting back down in the armchair, she closed her eyes for a few minutes, feeling the warmth of the room envelop her. It felt so safe here, so secure . . . She was just nodding off when Miss Hobson reappeared with a laden tray.

'I should have come and helped you,' she blurted as she jerked awake.

'Nonsense. Now, you can be mother and pour the tea while I take up this stone hot water bottle to warm your bed. I've already put on fresh sheets and made some room for your things.'

Betty poured the tea and helped herself to a biscuit. She hadn't realized how hungry she was. The last time she'd eaten had been here with Miss Hobson, earlier in the afternoon.

'Now that's done, tell me everything that's happened,' Miss Hobson said as she joined Betty, sipping her tea gratefully. 'I take it Harold Sayers was a problem? Not that I've ever known a man who wasn't,' she huffed.

'He was,' Betty grimaced, 'but to be honest, I don't really blame him. I honestly think he's a lonely man, and the shock of losing Charlie must have made him look on me as a suitable wife. It didn't help that he was full of drink when he told me to pack my bags and go at once.'

'He what?' Miss Hobson was outraged. 'This man has made your life a misery by putting inappropriate pressure on you, and now he demands that you leave at this ungodly hour? How dare he!'

'I think the drink had something to do with it,' Betty repeated, and she explained what had happened at the railway workers' dance. 'But I'm glad it happened – because

153

it meant I didn't have to explain to him that I was leaving. And I'm free of him now. I'm just upset about the two girls – I had to wake them up to say goodbye, poor things. The older one, Olive, is aware of her father's reputation with the ladies, but Peggy could only see that I was abandoning them. I've promised to keep in touch.'

'Have you told them where you intend to live? I'm worried he may come looking for you.'

'No; I didn't want him bothering you, and it wouldn't be fair of me to bring my problems to your doorstep. It's good enough of you to put me up like this even though I'm so close to my parents' house. The girls know where I work, if they need me urgently. And I intend to write to them.'

'You're not to worry about your parents. I've told you before, they have nothing to do with me. If you come and go by the back door, I can't see that your mother will ever know you are living within spitting distance of her.'

Betty giggled at Miss Hobson's turn of phrase. 'I'm going to like living here, Miss Hobson. I intend to pull my weight and hand over some money each week for my keep. I am an independent woman, you know,' she smiled.

'I approve,' the older woman replied. 'However, you really can't keep calling me Miss Hobson. It sounds so formal.'

'But I don't know your Christian name. Ever since I was a little girl, I've always known you as Miss Hobson from next door.'

'My name is Hortensia, but that's more than a mouthful and just as formal. You may call me what my friends call me: from now on, you can call me Hobby.'

Betty looked at her friend, sitting in her cheerful robe with her steel-grey curls peeping from beneath the nightcap. Her home was so different to the Billingtons'; there was colour everywhere, and so many interesting knick-knacks. She knew that she had a lot to learn from this kind woman and would enjoy her friendship.

'Now, young lady, I think we ought to get you up to your bed. It will be cosy and warm by now, and you have an early start. I take it it's work as normal tomorrow?'

'Oh goodness, I completely forgot about work with everything that's been going on.' She got to her feet and kissed Hobby's cheek, picking up her suitcase. 'I do have an early start, but perhaps I shouldn't attempt to ride the bicycle just yet. I'll risk using the tram and hope my parents don't look out of the window and spot me.'

'Pull the brim of your hat down over your face, my dear, and no one will be any the wiser.'

13

Christmas Eve 1917

Early the next morning, Betty stood at the tram stop. She did as Hobby had suggested and pulled down the brim of her hat, standing at an angle so that if anyone from her parents' house should look out of the window they would only see an unidentifiable woman. Thankfully the tram came along quickly, and she climbed aboard along with the many other workers who were heading into the bustling centre of Woolwich. Everyone would put in a day's work before going home to enjoy the festivities of the season as best they could, with Christmas overshadowed by war yet again.

She couldn't help thinking about how different this Christmas would be from the last. Her parents, although they enjoyed the season, had always spent it quietly: a visit to church and perhaps to a friend's house. There would be a trip to the theatre at some point, not to something gay and musical but to an improving play with a sombre theme. She wouldn't miss that at all. Hobby had told her she would have guests on Christmas Day, just a few of her single female friends. Betty had offered to go for a long walk and stay out of their way.

'Don't be daft, girl, you're as welcome as everybody else. Why, I want to introduce you to my friends, and it would be strange if I told them that my lodger had disappeared rather than meet them. You are as welcome as they are, and I hope they will become your friends too.'

Betty felt a warm glow sweep through her at the thought of that conversation. She just needed to get through her work today and then she could forget about Woolworths until Boxing Day, when she would be expected in early.

At least she would be able to pick out a few small gifts today to give to Hobby and her friends. The last thing she wanted was to join them empty-handed. Thinking of gifts, she felt glad that she had at least managed to leave some presents for Charlie's family at Railway Terrace. A sewing kit and a length of fabric, enough to make a dress, for Olive; and a pretty doll with real hair for Peggy. She had thought long and hard about Harold's gift, not wanting to show him any form of affection. In the end she had purchased a china shaving mug with a hunting scene on the front.

Although they had taken her in at a time when she'd had nowhere to go, Betty knew in her heart of hearts that it was right for her to have moved on, what with Harold expecting more of her than she wished to give. She shuddered, imagining his intentions. Thinking of the Sayers family made her heart ache. Only a year ago Charlie had given her a token of his love, which she now wore with pride on the lapel of her coat. Her hand moved to feel for the small brooch engraved with his regimental insignia. It was not a pretty piece of jewellery, but she valued it as much as any diamond necklace. To her, it showed the world that he had loved her.

She squeezed her eyes tightly shut. Charlie had gone, and she had to face a future without him. A man sitting nearby shook open his newspaper with a brisk rattle and she opened her eyes at the sound, then glanced quickly away from the headlines. They showed yet more news of death and destruction, while outside in the street people were going about their business ready for Christmas Day.

Alighting from the tram, she hurried along the street, entering Woolworths by the staff entrance at the back of the building. She would need to get quickly through her cleaning chores on the shop floor, as people were already hanging about outside waiting for the doors to open.

'Don't they know they've got an hour before the doors are unlocked?' she heard an older woman mutter behind her.

Betty turned and smiled before realizing the woman was talking to another staff member. Both of them worked as shop assistants; she'd spotted them on the counter where fresh vegetables were sold. The staff on the food counters always arrived early to set out their wares for the day. Betty had found them grumpy as a rule and very messy, leaving vegetable leaves and mud from the potatoes on the floor where customers would soon be walking. Even though she scrubbed it diligently, they spoke to her as if the floor hadn't seen a broom or a mop in days. Already Betty was getting used to these people and their high-handed attitude towards the cleaning staff. When she was given their section of the shop floor to clean, she made sure to only venture there once the women had finished displaying the produce; that way, she didn't have to do her job twice.

'Who do you think you're looking at?' the one who had muttered snapped at her.

Betty simply put her head down and hurried on. There was no point in replying; whatever she said would be taken the wrong way. Better to keep her own council, she thought as she entered the downstairs storeroom, where she could leave her coat and slip on the harsh calico overall that covered her clothes. She would have loved to be wearing the smart maroon outfit, greeting and serving the customers. She'd even thought about how she would style her hair so that the cap sat jauntily on top. Perhaps one day, she thought to herself as she picked up a galvanized bucket to fill with water at the sink nearby. Checking the day's work rota, she collected the rest of her cleaning materials and headed for the shop floor.

Thankfully she was nowhere near the miserable women working on the fruit and veg counter. As she scrubbed and polished the hardwood floor, she thought perhaps they had good cause to be miserable. After all, she'd feel miserable too if she had to weigh and sell muddy potatoes and slug-ridden cabbages all day long. Thinking about it, she was probably better off cleaning floors. She smiled to herself as she set to with her scrubbing brush, humming a Christmas carol.

'She wouldn't be so cheerful if she knew what a mess she'll have to clear up round here, now the other cleaner hasn't turned up for work.'

Betty stood up, stretching her aching back as she did so. She recognized the voice as belonging to one of the miserable women who'd followed her in to work that morning.

Out of the corner of her eye, Betty spotted one of them tipping the remains of a hessian sack onto the wooden floor. She sighed as she noticed mouldy vegetable leaves as well as a couple of rotten potatoes hitting the floor, rolling into the aisle where very soon customers would be walking.

Spotting Betty looking their way, the two women hurried behind the counter and turned their back on her just as a supervisor, Miss Dempster, walked by. Betty liked this woman, who was one of the more pleasant workers in the store and always had a friendly word for her. If only she covered Betty's work area, it would make her life a little easier.

'How are things going? Only fifteen minutes until the main doors open,' she said, looking up at the large wall clock.

'I just need to sweep round this counter and then I'm finished downstairs,' Betty replied. 'I decided to work the other way round today, as it makes a bit of a change.'

'I don't blame you. What is it they say about a change being as good as a rest?'

Betty nodded politely, thinking to herself that whatever way she worked it was still messy, backbreaking and quite depressing. However, it earned her some money to live on, and for that she was grateful. 'I can think of better things to be doing,' she answered politely.

'You should think about applying for another job, rather than continuing to work as a cleaner. You are a diligent worker, and that's the kind of girl we want working here.'

Betty's heart skipped a beat. 'That's very kind of you, but I don't really know how to apply. What would be required of me?'

'Any vacancies are pinned on the noticeboard in the staff canteen. If you are interested, keep an eye out during tea and lunch breaks. The assistant manager pins a card up as soon as a vacancy falls open.'

'I'll do that, thank you,' Betty said, before glancing again at the clock. 'I'd better get on, otherwise it will be my job that's pinned to the noticeboard.'

'I doubt that,' Miss Dempster smiled. 'I don't know about you, but I'm looking forward to a day off tomorrow.'

'I certainly am too. Although it's only a day, it will be nice not to get up so early and travel home exhausted – not that I'm not grateful for my job,' Betty added hastily. She picked up her broom and began to sweep towards the vegetable counter. The two assistants behind the counter giggled together as Betty worked steadily towards the pile of mess they had left on the floor. Without looking their way, she started to hum, this time choosing a Christmas carol with care. 'We Wish You a Merry Christmas' didn't seem to go down too well with the women, as she carefully swept the debris into an empty bucket.

'Well, I never,' one of them said in disgust as Betty smiled and hummed a little louder. She was in a good mood and felt she had a lot to look forward to. Two miserable women would not upset her in the least. She recalled her late grandmother's words about pinning a smile to her face regardless of adversity. She did just that, although she knew it would annoy the women even more.

'Huh! Who the hell does she think she is, with that cocky attitude? And as for sucking up to Miss Dempster, I reckon she's got ideas above her station,' the second woman said.

'Then we'll have to keep an eye on her and put her in

her place, if need be,' her friend whispered, loudly enough for Betty to hear.

Betty tipped the last of the debris into her bucket before bending down and picking something up. 'I do believe this is yours? You must have dropped it just now,' she said as she held out her hand.

'I'll take that, if you don't mind,' the louder of the two assistants said as she pushed past her colleague, reaching towards Betty.

'Happy Christmas,' Betty called over her shoulder as she walked away, suppressing a laugh at the shrieks emanating from the woman, who now held a large, slimy black slug. She'd probably created a rod for her own back by doing that, but it was worth it to be able to get one back on her tormentors. She hurried through the double staff doors just as a bell rang signalling the store was open for trading.

After disposing of the water and debris in her buckets, Betty washed her hands at the sink in a corner of the storeroom. She preferred not to go upstairs to the staff canteen, as she always felt so dishevelled after her shift; but now, knowing there was somewhere she could check for staff vacancies, it was all she could think of as she went to her locker to pull out a clean overall and run a comb through her hair. 'I'm going upstairs for my tea break,' she called to the storeroom men, who were brewing up their tea on a single gas ring.

Although the store had only just opened, the staff canteen was buzzing with employees who didn't work on the shop floor and had started their shifts earlier. She gratefully took a cup of tea and was surprised when one of the women serving handed her a plate containing a sticky bun. She reached into her pocket for her purse, knowing that she only had enough coins for her tram fare home if she wanted to buy a few gifts. She wasn't sure if staff would be given a pay packet until after Christmas.

'No, put that away,' the woman said. 'This one's on the house.'

'Even for cleaners and stockroom staff?' Betty asked, as her stomach grumbled with hunger. She hadn't liked to help herself to breakfast at Hobby's house that morning, especially as she had not yet handed over any money for her keep.

'Everybody who works here. They don't discriminate between jobs – otherwise I'd be bottom of the queue,' the woman laughed.

'You have a very important job. No one would survive without a hot cup of tea,' Betty said, thinking that management must be very kind to do such a thing. A little kindness goes a long way, she told herself. She would remember that, if ever she was in a position where she oversaw staff.

'We don't see you up here very often,' the woman said as she slid Betty's cup of tea across the counter.

Betty looked around to see if anyone could hear her, before speaking in hushed tones. 'I'm embarrassed to be seen in my dirty cleaning clothes when the shop assistants look so smart. I usually have a drink in the storeroom.'

'Why, bless you, love. You shouldn't worry about a thing like that. We're all honest workers here. Besides, your overall doesn't look that bad.'

'I had a clean one in my locker. It's not always possible to have a spare.'

'I can solve that problem straight away,' the woman

163

smiled, wiping her hands down her apron before stepping from behind the counter and approaching a woman sitting at a nearby table. 'Kath, do you think you can help young Betty here? She needs to keep a few clean overalls in her locker. She does a mucky job looking after us all and it's not fair for her to have to keep wearing grubby things, now, is it?'

'Why, bless her, she only needed to ask. I'll make sure she always has two clean sets in her locker. Is it down in the stockroom, lovey?'

'Yes, thank you,' Betty replied, marvelling at how helpful these women were. If only her day hadn't been blighted by the women on the vegetable counter!

'Sit yourself down here with me,' Kath said, pulling out a wooden chair. 'Don't forget your bun. Mine went down a treat.'

'I'll join you both for a few minutes, before it gets busy when the shop floor tea breaks start. I'm Lou,' nodded the woman serving in the canteen. She plonked herself down in a spare seat and took a gulp of her tea. 'So, what made you that brave you ventured up to join us today?'

Betty felt her cheeks start to glow. She wasn't sure she wanted to tell them about her dream of becoming a counter assistant. They might laugh at her, as she was only a cleaner.

'You may think I'm daft, but . . . I wondered about trying for a counter assistant's position, rather than being a cleaner. Not that I don't think being a cleaner is an important job, but now that I've moved to new lodgings it might be diffi-cult to manage odd shifts in the early morning or late at night,' she explained quickly, in case they thought she had ideas above her station. She wanted them to think of her as working class if at all possible, and she wasn't about to mention her parents were well-to-do.

'Why, you should have said before now,' Lou said. 'There's a board on the wall just over there where the management put cards about any vacancies. It's where my daughter, Sal, spotted they wanted someone to work in this canteen. I was in here like a shot.'

'Oh, you have family working here?'

'Sal worked on the vegetable counter. She did a good job and kept it spotless.'

Betty felt her stomach lurch. What if one of the nasty women was Lou's daughter?

As if Lou could read her thoughts, she continued, 'Of course, that was five years ago. These days, she's at home looking after her little ones while her husband's fighting the Hun. Do you have a young man?' she asked, peering at Betty's ringless left hand.

'I had agreed to marry my Charlie, but he was killed . . .' Her voice started to crack as the two women looked on with sadness in their eyes.

'Well, you're amongst friends here. We've all lost someone we love,' Lou said, squeezing Betty's arm to comfort her. 'Now, you eat that bun and I'll have a look to see what jobs are available on the board.'

Betty quickly pulled herself together and bit into the bun, thinking she'd fallen on her feet meeting Kath and Lou. It would be nice to spend her breaks up here in the warn canteen rather than the draughty warehouse.

'Lou lost her husband and two of her sons at the beginning of the war,' Kath explained quietly. 'Working here, looking after the staff uniforms and suchlike, has kept her occupied. She told me once that if she didn't have her job, she would likely have thrown herself off the railway bridge.'

Betty shuddered, thinking of Edna. 'It must be awful to be so low that you want to die,' she replied.

'That's when you need friends most,' Kath smiled. 'Now, I must get back to work or my job will be up on that board. Why, I do believe Lou has found something that may suit you,' she said, as the older woman hurried back to their table with a piece of paper.

'It looks as though this hasn't long been put up. There's a vacancy for a counter assistant. Take the card before someone else spots it.'

Betty felt a thrill of excitement as she took the square card and tucked it into her pocket. 'I'll write a letter this evening and pop it through the letterbox.'

'Don't be daft. Not only is it Christmas Day tomorrow, but the job might have gone by then. Word of jobs spreads like wildfire in this place. You drink up your tea and go and knock on the staff manager's door right this minute.'

'Now? Like this?' Betty looked down at her shabby overall before putting her hand to her head to try and straighten the calico cap that covered her hair.

'You'll do. He'll recognize a hard-working girl, and he can tell by your posh voice that you're a cut above the average person here.'

'I've never thought myself any different to other workers . . .'

'Well, you should, because it'll take you far. It's nothing to be ashamed of,' Lou said as she stood up and ushered Betty on her way, wishing her good luck.

Betty decided to remove her overall even though it was

clean. If she was going to enquire about a vacancy that would enhance her working life, the least she could do was to look presentable. Underneath she wore a dark green woollen dress; although old, it was clean and of good quality. She popped into the ladies' room to check her hair was as tidy as it could be after dampening her fingers to run through a few stray curls, even checking her teeth for any remaining crumbs from the sticky bun. That'll have to do, she thought as she straightened her dress. Holding her head high, she crossed the hall to the room where the assistant manager worked.

'Enter,' a deep voice called out after she had given three sharp taps on the door.

'I'm sorry to bother you, Mr King. I was enquiring after this vacancy,' Betty said as she placed the card on his desk. She watched as he lifted the card and read the words on it before looking up, taking stock of the woman in front of him.

'And you are?' he frowned, although laughter lines at the edges of his eyes showed him to be of a friendly nature.

'My name is Bet . . . Elizabeth Billington; I've been working at this store for the past few weeks but would dearly love to be a counter assistant. I'm clean, I'm conscientious, I'm never late, I can add up, and I always have a friendly smile on my face for the customers. I can also . . .'

Mr King raised his hand to stop Betty's tongue running away with her. 'Take a seat, Miss Billington, while I check my files.'

Betty took the proffered seat, lacing her fingers together while she looked around the room as Mr King went to a shelf full of leather-bound ledgers. His office was a long, thin room with tall windows overlooking the busy street below. She assumed he did not work alone in here as there were several other desks, each piled high with paperwork and not quite as tidy as the one she was sitting in front of. She swallowed hard, suddenly feeling as if she had a frog in her throat. She slightly regretted that last bite of her sticky bun and wished she'd finished her cup of tea.

'Ah, here we are. Elizabeth Billington. And you are currently employed as a cleaner?'

'Yes, sir,' Betty squeaked before coughing to clear her throat. 'I did mention at my interview that I would like to work on the shop floor at some point.'

He glanced back down at the page. 'There doesn't seem to be a note here about your request.'

Betty knew why; Mr West hadn't seemed to take her seriously at her first interview. 'Is that a problem, sir?'

'No, not at all, although you will have to sit a proper interview as it obviously wasn't done when you were taken on in your current capacity. Tell me, Miss Billington, are you one of our young ladies who are planning to run off and marry your beau?'

Betty immediately felt tears sting her eyes. She had not expected to be asked such a question, although it was understandable that the company wouldn't wish to train her and then see her leave to start a family.

Mr King reached into the top drawer of his desk and pulled out a laundered white handkerchief. 'I'm extremely sorry to have upset you,' he said as he passed it over to Betty, who dabbed at her eyes before composing herself.

'I'm sorry, sir; my fiancé was killed at Ypres,' she managed, wary of saying anything more about Charlie in case she began to cry in earnest.

'I am sorry for your loss. I hope that working for F. W. Woolworth will be a solace to you in the years to come. This war has been painful for so many people.'

Betty wondered why he'd not joined up, but knew she could not ask. She waited a couple of seconds before venturing to enquire, 'Does this mean that you would consider me for the position of counter assistant?'

'It does indeed, although you need to sit a proper interview. I fear the one undertaken previously was not as formal as it should have been.'

Betty could have kissed the man, she was so excited. 'May I be interviewed now?' she asked.

Mr King looked at the clock and thought for a moment, before saying slowly, 'I would very much like you to start work as a counter assistant on the Monday after Christmas, as we are in dire need of extra workers. Would you be able to return here at two o'clock? I appreciate that you had an early start today, and no doubt like many women you have a lot to do to prepare for Christmas. But if you can do that, we will be able to sort out the formalities before you go home.'

Betty's heart soared at these words. 'I would be more than happy to do that, sir,' she replied, knowing it would give her time to make a few purchases and finish her cleaning duties for the day. Mr King was so much more friendly than the general manager. If only she'd met him when she first applied for a job!

Her stomach churning with anticipation and excitement, Betty returned to the assistant manager's office at the allotted time. She had kept herself busy since her earlier appointment by tidying away buckets, brooms and cleaning materials ready for the next time she clocked on, assuming that she would be a cleaner for a few days more before beginning her job as a counter assistant on the Monday after Christmas.

Of course, it all depended on whether she passed this interview. Not wanting to appear overly eager, she checked the clock at the end of the hall and waited for two minutes to pass. During that time, she thought of the small gifts she had purchased from the store. They were simple trinkets she would be able to hand over to Hobby's friends when they visited on Christmas Day: lace-edged embroidered handkerchiefs, a small box containing sweets, and pretty combs for the ladies' hair. She spent almost every penny in her purse, leaving just enough for her tram fare home.

She smiled as she thought of her new home. Even though she'd only moved in the previous night, she found the house welcoming and homely; her parents' large house seemed as cold as a mausoleum by comparison. She was still smiling when Mr King opened his office door dead on the hour.

'Come along in, Betty, and let's get started. I've cleared a desk here so that you can complete a few forms and undertake an arithmetic test.'

Betty nodded and sat where she was shown, pleasantly surprised that he had remembered she preferred to be known as Betty rather than Elizabeth. She noticed two sharpened pencils next to the neatly stacked papers. 'How long should I take, sir?'

'As long as you wish, but do remember the store closes in two hours,' he grinned. 'I usually have a cup of tea delivered to me around this time and I've requested one for you as well. I find paperwork can be a thirsty business.

It's on the house,' he added quickly, noticing Betty biting her lip.

'Thank you, sir, it would be most welcome. I've been shopping for the past hour,' she said before picking up a pencil and looking at the application form.

Silence fell in the room as she pondered the questions. The application form was easy enough; she was thankful that she could now give Hobby's address as her new abode. She had very little previous work experience apart from the short spell down at the Arsenal, but thankfully there was no box to complete about why she'd left that job. A question about her education was simple to answer: her parents had provided her with a private tutor up until the age of fifteen, whereupon her mother had decided that any more education would be vulgar. She was able to write; she had a good grounding in arithmetic; and she hoped that her tidy handwriting showed she could write down and correctly spell anything that would be required of her as a counter assistant.

Betty had always been fascinated by the small notebooks and pencils that were secured to the waistbands of the shopgirls' uniforms. She had seen them noting down prices while serving customers, then ringing up sales on the large metal tills that sat on each counter. Another use of the notebooks was for the girls to make lists to restock their counters, handing the lists to the storeroom lads, who would bring the items back on small trolleys.

Betty might not have enjoyed being a cleaner, but at least she had used her eyes and ears to find out more about the running of the whole store. There were supervisors on the shop floor who terrified her. Although they had nothing to do with her job, they would comment if they thought she wasn't doing her work properly. There was one who Betty did all she could to avoid, who would kick the water-filled metal bucket as Betty scrubbed floors, causing more work when Betty had to stop and mop up the mess. She'd also noticed one miserable supervisor who often worked around the area of the vegetable counter but did little to supervise staff, instead chatting with them like old friends. It was all Betty could do not to shake her head at the sorry state of that part of the store.

Turning over the application sheet once she'd checked her answers, she looked at the two pages consisting of arithmetic and adding-up tests. Betty prided herself on knowing her numbers, but all the same she double-checked everything she wrote down. It wouldn't do to make a mistake and lose her chance at working on the counters at this stage of the interview. With Mr King sitting across the room from her she didn't like to use her fingers to add up, so instead she used a scrap of paper she'd spotted at the side of the desk. There were questions about how much change to give for purchases, and how much certain items would cost if a customer purchased a dozen. Questions about weights and measures made her stop and think before smiling to herself as she wrote down the answers. She was just checking her work one final time when there was a tap at the door and a tray of tea was brought in. She placed her pencil down with a sigh of relief and put all the sheets of paper together in a neat pile.

'Perfect timing,' Mr King said as he indicated a vacant chair in front of his desk. 'Shall I be mother?' he asked, starting to pour.

As Betty sipped her tea, she watched Mr King checking her answers. He'd taken a crib sheet from a drawer and was placing neat ticks against all but one answer. 'You've done very well, Betty. Only one wrong answer.'

'Oh dear, I'm so sorry – I did double-check everything. Does this mean I've failed?'

He laughed out loud. 'It means you've done exceptionally well. I've never seen so many correct answers; in fact, even your wrong answer is perfect, because if you had charged the customer this amount of money F. W. Woolworths would have profited to the sum of one farthing. I'm pleased to say that you, Miss Betty Billington, will be working as a counter assistant from next Monday, the last day of 1917.'

Betty beamed with pride. 'Thank you so much! I'm delighted. May I ask on which counter I'll be working?'

'With your exceptional arithmetic skills I will be able to place you on the vegetable counter, knowing our customers will be in safe hands. Congratulations, Betty.'

How Betty kept a smile on her face, she never knew; one moment her heart was filled with joy and the next it had plummeted to her boots. Of all the positions in the shop, to think she would be working alongside those two unpleasant shop assistants and that miserable supervisor!

14

~

31 December 1917

It was with some trepidation that Betty arrived at Woolworths for her first day as a counter assistant. Mr King had told her to wait for a supervisor to collect her from the staff room ten minutes before the store opened, so she made sure to be there five minutes earlier. It felt strange to be dressed in the maroon overall, after having become so used to her cleaner's outfit. As she stood there, she received a few quizzical glances as staff came and went. She kept glancing at the large clock on the wall.

'The time won't pass any faster if you keep looking at that clock,' Lou said from behind her counter.

'I was told to be here for twenty past, so a supervisor could collect me and take me to the counter and instruct me on my duties. I fear she is late; perhaps she is poorly and hasn't come into work. I wonder what I should do?' Betty replied, biting her lip.

'Where are you going to be working? I may know who the supervisor is,' Lou said as she too looked at the clock. 'They're going to be opening the main doors any moment and the bells will ring to remind staff to be ready at the counters. It won't do for you to be late on your first day . . . I'm sorry, I didn't mean to worry you even more.'

'Mr King is starting me on the vegetable counter – he said it's because I'm good with my arithmetic. To be honest, I don't know if I'm going to enjoy working there . . .'

'Hmm; you don't need to say any more.'

'I take it you know the staff on that counter?' Betty asked, sensing from Lou's expression what the answer would be.

Before Lou could reply the doors swung open with some force and a woman strode in, looking red-faced and angry.

'Where the hell have you been, may I ask? There are vegetables to clean, and we'll have a queue waiting to be served within minutes.'

Betty's heart sank. As she'd expected, it was the nasty supervisor she'd encountered during her cleaning duties. She decided to start as she meant to go on. She wasn't going to have someone browbeat her when she'd done nothing wrong. If it meant they reported her to Mr King, then so be it; she would rather be a cleaner than put up with these women for a moment longer than necessary. 'Mr King instructed me to be here at twenty minutes past eight and to wait for a supervisor to collect me,' she replied, lifting her chin defiantly before staring up at the clock. 'Whoever it was supposed to be, is late.'

The woman's mouth opened and closed, reminding Betty of a goldfish in a bowl. She fought the urge to laugh and looked back calmly at the woman, waiting for a response.

'You'd best follow me, I'm two staff down today. Mr King forgot to inform me that he had dismissed two of my best workers for being rude to customers.'

'I'm sorry to hear that,' Betty said as she followed the woman out of the staff room. 'I'll do my best to work quickly so the customers don't have to queue for long.'

'You better had.' The woman turned, breathing gin fumes into Betty's face. 'If you don't, you'll be out on your ear as well. You'll have a hard job performing as well as the two girls who have been sacked.'

'As I said, I'll do my best,' Betty replied, hurrying to catch up with her as they headed down the stairs to the main part of the store. 'I'm sorry – I didn't catch your name.'

'Doreen Dunkin – not that you need to know my full name. Mrs Dunkin to you.'

They stepped into the main shop just as two men were opening the front doors. Women with baskets on their arms flooded in; the noise was quite deafening. As Betty hurried to the counter it felt as though they were nipping at her heels.

'Right, wrap this round your waist,' Mrs Dunkin instructed. 'You'll need it, as those spuds are muddy as hell and we don't have time to clean them off. Annie, show her what to do. I'll have to call one of the warehouse lads to help us lay out the rest of the veg. I don't know how I'm going to cope with a new girl and a dimwit, and the hordes of people expected here today.'

Betty did as she was told, wrapping the empty sack around her waist and tying it with a piece of string just as she could see the other assistant, Annie, had done.

'Don't take no notice of her,' the wiry dark-haired girl whispered as she led Betty to the end of the long counter, which was heaped high with potatoes. 'I keep my head down and don't let her bother me. Besides, with her being short-staffed she's not likely to sack us, is she?' she giggled, giving Betty a nudge with her elbow.

'I'm Betty,' said Betty, 'and I have no idea what I'm supposed to do first.'

'Ooh, don't you talk posh? With a voice like that you should be working up in the office,' Annie cackled good-naturedly.

'I'm happy to be working here,' Betty smiled back.

'Roll the cuffs up on your overall, you don't want to be having to scrub them every night. Now, see the scales over there? When the customer says how many pounds of spuds she wants, you scoop them into the brass bowl and put it on the scales. Get the weight right and tell her how much to pay you.'

Betty nodded as she followed the instructions. 'That seems simple enough, but where do I put the potatoes afterwards?'

'Oh, you are joking, aren't you? Have you never been shopping before? Why you shove a bit of this newspaper in their shopping basket and pour the spuds on top so nothing underneath gets dirty. Do you understand that?' Annie peered closely into Betty's face as if she thought she was daft.

Although Betty had a little shopping experience from when she'd lived with the Sayers family, it would never have crossed her mind to use a piece of newspaper. 'Sorry – I'm a bit flustered but I'll manage, honestly.'

'Then best you get stuck in, as there must be a dozen queueing already. I'll be just up here with the carrots, parsnips and onions. Shout for me if you have any trouble.'

Betty reached for the brass bowl and smiled at the first lady in the queue. 'How may I help you, madam?'

'Blimey, you're a posh one. I'll have four pounds, please, and not too much mud if you don't mind. I was always having to remind the other girls that worked here. I'm glad to see the back of them, I can tell you.'

Betty was tempted to ask what the woman meant, but knew it wouldn't be appropriate to do so. She quickly piled potatoes into the bowl, rubbing off the hardened mud with her thumb as she did so. Placing them onto the scales, she could see that they weighed nearly six pounds and removed some until they matched the required weight. Looking at the sign pinned to the counter, she quickly calculated the correct sum of money and charged the customer. After wiping her hands on the sack apron, she went to the large brass cash register and pushed the keys; the drawer shot out, making her jump, and she took out the correct change and passed it to the lady. 'Thank you very much for your custom,' she smiled, starting to turn to the next one in the queue.

The first lady cackled with laughter. 'That's all very well and good, love, but you've not given me any spuds.'

Everyone started to laugh as Betty blushed. She quickly put the potatoes into the woman's basket after laying a sheet of newspaper down to protect her other purchases.

'You'll not make that mistake again,' Annie said good-naturedly. 'It's the way we all learn. I forgot to take a customer's money, that was much worse – but fortunately the woman reminded me,' she laughed before returning to her own customers.

With trepidation Betty served her next customer,

chanting to herself under her breath: weigh the potatoes, take the money, hand over the change, put the produce in the basket. Soon she didn't have to remind herself what to do and was working automatically, building up speed. Stepping back as one of the warehouse men arrived with fresh supplies, she watched as he cut open the top of each sack and tipped the vegetables onto the high counter. She did wonder why the highly polished counter with its glass edging was used for such dirty produce; it was the same as all the other counters in the store. To her, it would have been common sense to have a more practical counter. But hers was not to reason why – she was here to do a good job and to earn enough money for her keep.

'How may I help you?' she asked the next lady and was quickly serving her.

'I also want some of those onions, please.'

Betty was about to point out that the lady needed to be served by Annie, when she stopped and thought for a couple of seconds. What was the hurt if she served the lady with more than just potatoes? She quickly turned to her left and weighed out the pound of onions the woman requested, added the two prices together and charged the lady.

'That saved a lot of time and no mistake,' the woman said. 'I've never known why we have to keep moving about on this counter to buy different things.'

'Oi, keep your hands off my onions,' Annie laughed. 'At least it keeps my queue down if you serve your customers with some of my produce.'

Betty was thoughtful as she continued serving customers. A few of them asked for carrots and onions and she happily served whatever they wanted, making a note of each price in the small notebook attached to her waistband by a piece of string.

'I'm going off for my tea break,' Annie said as she started to remove her sackcloth apron. 'When I get back and the bell rings it'll be your turn to go upstairs for a cuppa. I was going to ask if you'll be able to manage while I'm gone, but you're working faster than I am, so you'll be fine.'

Betty nodded and carried on serving, finding it slightly easier not to have to dodge around Annie when she wanted to weigh other vegetables. Again, her thoughts played in her head.

By the time Annie returned there was just the one queue, which wasn't very long.

'You've either scared all the customers off, or had wings fitted to your heels. Don't go working so fast that they sack me for being slow, will you?'

Betty giggled at Annie's cheerful comment, but did wonder if the girl was subtly reprimanding her. She'd best be careful in future, but it pained her to have to work slowly and she knew the day would drag if she had to do so. Just then, a shrill bell rang through the store.

'Off you go, I'll take care of everything here,' Annie said, tying her apron round her slim waist.

Betty followed a small stream of fellow shop assistants as they headed towards the staff doors. Hurrying upstairs, she went into the ladies' room first and scrubbed at her hands. Try as she might, she couldn't remove all the dirt from below her nails. She made a note to purchase a nail brush on payday and keep it in her pocket, so she was able to keep her hands as clean as possible in between shifts.

'Ah, Miss Billington,' Mr King said as he passed her in the hall. 'How is your first day at work progressing?'

'I'm finding it very interesting, sir, as well as extremely busy,' she replied politely.

'Hmm, yes; we need to do something about that. I'm just glad that you were able to start work today, otherwise I would have had to move staff from other counters.'

'I was surprised to find you only have two members of staff working on such a busy section,' Betty said, itching to know what had happened to make him dismiss the two nasty women she'd encountered while she was cleaning that area of the store.

Mr King nodded thoughtfully. 'I wonder, would you be able to spare me five minutes at the end of your lunch hour? I don't want to hold you up now – I know how much you ladies enjoy a cup of tea in your morning break.'

Oh no, Betty thought. He must think I've spoken out of turn. 'Of course. Shall I knock on your door at twenty past one?'

'I'll see you then,' he replied, giving her a charming smile before entering his office and closing the door.

Betty hurried into the staff canteen, saying hello to Lou, who was working behind the counter. 'May I have a cup of tea, please, and a biscuit?'

'You may, my dear – how are you enjoying your new job?'

'Very much, it's been so busy,' Betty replied, before looking to see if anyone was nearby. 'There are only two of us on the counter – Mrs Dunkin said that the two previous assistants who worked there have been dismissed?'

Lou raised her eyebrows and bent over the counter,

getting as close to Betty as possible. 'The pair of them was given their marching orders when they went to collect their pay packets on Christmas Eve. I was collecting empty teacups from the office and just happened to overhear what happened. And it wasn't before time, I can tell you.'

Betty waited, not wanting to interrupt. Although she was sorry that anyone should lose their job, especially at Christmas, she couldn't help feeling her own life would be much easier without those two women making it a misery every day. 'Oh dear,' was all she could say.

Lou continued to lean close to Betty, cleaning the counter as she spoke. 'The pair of them were stood side by side; I've never seen them look so angry. Mr King told them he'd had enough of complaints from customers about their rudeness, and although he should dock their pay for all the free vegetables they've been handing to their family, he was, in the spirit of the season, going to give them their wages and allow them to leave there and then.'

'They were stealing? How awful that someone should do that to a good employer.'

'They stormed out afterwards, and the language they used out in the corridor was not what you'd expect to hear from decent women, I can tell you.'

'Goodness – well, I'm glad it was done and dusted before I started work,' Betty said. 'It would have been unbearable if they'd had to work their notice. I've had problems with them in the past when I cleaned in that area of the store. I dreaded doing my work with them standing watching me.'

'Oh, my love, you should never suffer in silence. Our Mr King may not have been here long, but he's a good sort and would have given you a sympathetic ear.'

'He has shown me much kindness, but I would never dream of bothering the management with my small problems. I was grateful to have that job, and now that I'm a full-time counter assistant, I can't tell you how delighted I am.'

'I'm pleased for you,' Lou said, patting her hand. 'Now, can I tempt you with a bit of braised beef and cabbage when dinnertime comes? There's a nice tender shin of beef in the oven, cooking away with some of the carrots and onions from your counter.'

Betty licked her lips. 'Yes, please; how much will it cost?'

'Staff get their meals cheap, and it's docked from your pay packet when you collect it on Saturday.'

'Woolworths certainly look after their staff,' Betty smiled before finding a seat. She relaxed for five minutes, sipping her tea and enjoying the biscuit, before heading back down to the shop floor.

'I'm glad you're back,' Annie greeted her. 'It looks like the world and their neighbour need vegetables today.'

'I'll be two ticks,' Betty said as she tied her apron on. 'May I suggest something that might help make the work easier?'

Annie screwed up her face as she looked at Betty. 'It won't get us into trouble, will it? I've only been here a couple of weeks and in that time, I've seen two women sacked. Mind you, they were nicking stuff left, right and centre. It's nothing illegal you want us to do, is it?'

Betty chuckled. 'If it was, I'd not do it. Believe me, I'm no crook. I just thought if we split the counter between us and each just sold all the veg at our end of the counter, we wouldn't be climbing over each other. And customers wouldn't have to queue twice.'

'I don't know about that. It would mean more adding up, and I'm not so good at that.'

Betty opened her notebook and held it out to the girl. 'All you need to do is write down each price. If you can't add it up, show me and I'll tell you the total. I'm quite good at adding up.'

'I'm not sure . . .'

'Let's try it for an hour or so. If you don't like it, we can change back to what we were doing before. What do you think?' she asked, conscious that several women in the queue were started to mutter about being kept waiting.

Annie grinned. 'All right, let's do it. I'll take this end of the counter and when the warehouse lads bring the next lot of stock down, we can have them tip the veg at each end.'

The two girls picked up the brass trays from their scales and called out together, 'Who is next?'

Betty inhaled the delicious smell of braised beef as she entered the canteen for the half past twelve break. 'That looks delicious,' she said as she reached the head of the short queue, watching Lou dish up the beef before adding cabbage and a large portion of mashed potato.

'There's nothing like serving up Woolies' own products to its hungry staff,' Lou smiled back. 'You sit yourself down and enjoy your meal. I hear you have an appointment with our Mr King?'

Betty was surprised that Lou knew this, but was too polite to ask how she'd found out. 'I do. I think it's just to find out how I'm getting on in my first day.'

Lou raised her eyebrows in surprise. 'You just be careful,

young lady; you look too trusting. It doesn't do to get too friendly with management, if you get my drift?' She gave Betty a knowing look.

'Mr King has been nothing but polite to me,' Betty said carefully, not wishing to get on the wrong side of Lou. 'But I will heed your words and be ready to flee if I have to.'

'You do that, my love. I've known of a few girls who had to leave their jobs and move away to get themselves sorted out.'

Betty frowned, unsure how to respond to Lou's knowing look. Mr King did not strike her as somebody she should fear. Whatever was Lou talking about?

Finishing her meal and refusing a cup of tea when she returned her plate and cutlery to the counter, she hurried to the ladies' room, knowing there wouldn't be time after she'd seen Mr King. As she stood outside his office door several minutes later, she noticed a few counter staff giggling and looking in her direction as they hurried by.

'Ah, Betty, come along in; you are spot on time, I see,' he said, checking his watch.

'I pride myself on my punctuality,' she said, sitting down in the chair he indicated. 'I'm intrigued as to why you wished to see me – is there a problem with my work?'

'No, nothing like that at all. In the short time I've known you, Betty, I have found you to be an intelligent young woman, and I was astonished that you came to work here on the shop floor – even more so that you took a job as a cleaner. However, I can see a bright future for you in this company.'

Betty felt uncomfortable. Perhaps Lou had been correct in her assumption and Mr King had an eye for the young female staff. 'I don't understand, sir – surely you know very little about me?'

'I can see from the tests you undertook at your interview that you have an eye for figures, and I observed you on the shop floor this morning as you worked. You seem to have formed a different way of serving our customers.'

Betty felt her stomach lurch. Was she going to be told off for interfering in the way the staff on the vegetable counter served customers? 'I'm sorry,' she said anxiously, 'perhaps I should have asked permission from our supervisor before making changes? Annie and I were tripping over each other. We found it easier to each serve a customer with everything she required, rather than have her queue twice for different purchases. By having a selection of all vegetables at each end, we seem to be able to work much faster and more efficiently. However, if we've broken any rules, of course we will go straight back to the old way of working this afternoon.'

Mr King raised his hand to silence her. 'There is no need for that – you have my permission to continue. I will notify your supervisor.'

'Thank you, sir,' she replied, feeling her whole body relax with relief. His next words had her tense up all over again as he watched her thoughtfully before speaking.

'If only you were a little older . . .'

Betty felt a trickle of fear run down her spine. 'Sir?'

'I was thinking of you as possible supervisor material, but at your tender age that is out of the question. You could not be expected to oversee women older than yourself on the shop floor.'

Betty let out a discreet sigh of relief. 'I'm happy in the

position that I have, Mr King,' she assured him. 'Eventually I would like to experience working on different counters, but as I've only been a counter assistant for half a day, I can see that it would be a little early and rather presumptuous of me to expect to move on.' She looked up at the clock on the wall. 'If there's nothing else, I must excuse myself, as I'm expected back at my counter,' she said, standing up and heading towards the door.

He followed her and opened it before she reached it. 'You're doing very well here, Betty, very well indeed.'

Betty thanked him quickly before heading down the corridor. She was unaware of her supervisor, Doreen Dunkin, watching her before being summoned into the office herself.

Once Annie returned from her own lunch break, Betty told her excitedly what Mr King had said about serving the vegetables.

'You mean we can carry on this way? I was sure that when Mrs Dunkin noticed, she would make us change back. Well done, Betty! I don't know how you had the nerve to explain it to him. I could never have done that in a hundred years.'

Betty finished serving a customer and turned to Annie. 'He asked me how I was getting on and mentioned he'd been watching us across the shop floor. So I found it quite easy to explain what we were doing – but I was so worried that I was going to get told off.'

Annie chuckled as she tied on her apron. 'I've heard he has an eye for a pretty girl, so I doubt he would listen to me.'

'I can assure you there wasn't anything inappropriate

about it – Mr King was a perfect gentleman and just doing his job.'

'If you say so,' Annie grinned, leaving Betty a little perturbed. She hated the idea of anyone assuming she would try to get ahead at Woolworths by encouraging a man. She would never again be interested in romance; Charlie had been the only man for her, and he would remain in her heart until the day she died.

15

11 November 1918

'You look pale, my dear,' Hobby said as she peered at Betty over the breakfast table. 'You've hardly eaten a thing. Perhaps you shouldn't go in to work today?'

'I must,' Betty replied as she picked at a piece of toast, placing a morsel into her mouth and forcing herself to chew and swallow.

'Are you sure you're not coming down with something? I've never seen you like this.'

'I will be fine; I just need to get through this day and put it behind me. If it means I wallow in memories and thoughts of what might have been, then so be it,' she said, glancing towards a newspaper Hobby had collected the evening before. The front page was full of the news of peace being declared imminently.

Hobby nodded her head. 'You are a braver person than I could ever be. In your position, I would take myself off to bed and hide under the covers until the celebrations were out of the way.'

The thought of her dear friend and landlady hiding away

from anything made Betty smile. 'I've never known a braver person than you,' she said. 'Have I not been present when your friends spoke of your days campaigning for the suffrage movement? You always seemed to be at the front of any march, rallying the women while waving your banner. You are also the only woman I know to have been arrested by a policeman as you stood up for the cause. I wish I could have seen that and taken part. Do you think you will be taking up the cudgel once more?' Betty asked, pushing her breakfast plate away.

Hobby shrugged her shoulders. 'In a way, I feel as though we've never stopped fighting for our rights. Look at how many women have taken on men's roles during this war. Does it not show that we are equal, and capable of more than keeping a house and bearing a man's children?'

'But when men come back from the war, will they not want their wives at home? Will they not take their jobs back? I fear things will go back to the way they were,' Betty replied.

'Hundreds and thousands of men around the world will not be returning home,' Hobby pointed out. 'I've heard it said that there could be a whole generation of young women who never find husbands, with so many young men having perished on the fields of battle. The war has a great deal to answer for,' she added sadly, shaking her head.

This observation was like a shard of ice to Betty's heart. 'I hadn't thought about it in quite that way. I suppose I would be counted among those women – even though I have no wish to marry now.'

'Oh, my dear – I didn't mean to distress you. I was letting my thoughts run away with me. Can you forgive me?'

'There's nothing to forgive,' Betty said with a sad little smile. 'I value your views on the world. Did you never think of marrying yourself, Hobby? You would have made a marvellous mother.'

Hobby shook her head, smiling wryly. 'I have had many male friends and enjoyed their company. However, I've never had any inclination to marry one of them. I'm happy the way I am. Under different circumstances I would have been a grandmother many times over by now, no doubt; but not all women are the same, and I chose to walk a different path. I was lucky to be left this house by a good friend and an inheritance meant I was able to do as I pleased. My one true love passed away some years ago. You may recall Mildred Holdsworth living here for a time, when you were still a child?' Hobby watched as Betty frowned, absorbing her words.

'Oh, yes – I do remember Mildred! You know, I had forgotten all about her; I must have been very little at that time. But . . . Oh my goodness, you mean . . . ?'

Hobby nodded her head. 'Yes, I do mean,' she smiled. 'I hope I haven't shocked you too much.'

Betty was thoughtful. 'No,' she said truthfully, 'but it really would never have occurred to me. You must think that very foolish.'

'Not at all, my dear – you are no fool but an innocent, and that's as it should be. You were not brought up to know the ways of the world. Your life changed suddenly with the loss of Charlie and only then did you start to have more varied experiences.'

'Tell me, do my parents know . . . ?'

'Let's just say your parents did not support my views on

women's suffrage and we had little in common. I've kept myself to myself as much as possible as far as our neighbours are concerned. Your parents lead a different kind of life to my own. I'm just thankful to have known you as a child, and that was mainly down to your cook. Did you know she was a distant cousin of Mildred's?'

'I don't think I realized. But I used to have such fun playing in your garden. I was left in Cook's care when Mother was busy; she never knew.'

'We were both pleased to make your acquaintance. At one time Mildred and I even considered adopting a child, and that was largely down to meeting you. We adored having a child under our roof, if only for a few hours. Then Mildred's health took a turn for the worse and we decided it was not to be. Oh, please don't upset yourself,' she said, as Betty burst into tears. She hurried around the table to hug Betty. 'There, there; don't you go crying over my circumstances! I've enjoyed my life. I learnt early on that we are all different, apart from one resounding factor, and that is: we all need to have experienced love in our lives, in whatever form. I've experienced that, and I'm happy with my lot.'

Betty wiped her nose and did her utmost to smile. 'It's just that . . . on more than one occasion I've wished you were my mother. I wasn't very happy at home; my life was lonely.'

Hobby burst out laughing. 'What a pair we are. At least we found each other in the end, so we can turn into old maids together.'

'And I'll think of you as the mother I should have had.' Betty kissed her cheek. 'Thank you for caring.'

'Never forget that I do care and will be here for you, regardless of what path you take in life. Now, I am going to boil an egg and I want you to eat every morsel before you go to work. Who knows, by the time you return home we may finally have heard the war has officially ended. Then we can face the next foe.'

'The next foe?'

'This terrible influenza. So many people are suffering.'

'I've heard customers say it's the soldiers bringing it home with them from overseas,' Betty said, looking worried. 'People are wearing masks to protect themselves; do you think we should do the same? I'd hate you to become ill.'

'That seems rather drastic. Let's not worry about it for now; I'm sure it won't be around for long.'

Betty agreed, and as Hobby bustled about in the kitchen she thought about her friend's words. She hadn't given a thought to all the women who would never marry because of the shortage of marriageable men. She herself was prepared for a life of spinsterhood and had accepted that she would always need to work to support herself; there would never be another love for her. But there must be plenty of other young women her age who didn't feel able to accept things in the same way.

It was with a heavy heart that Betty collected her bicycle from the back garden and set off for Wooolwich. Even at this early hour, people were starting to congregate in the streets in anticipation of the news that the war had ended. Their excitement and happiness was reflected on their faces and a jolly atmosphere was building up. Perhaps these people had loved ones who would soon be home from foreign shores, safe with their families once more.

Occasionally, though, she spotted women dressed in black, hurrying along with their heads bowed low – as if, like her, they were blocking out the early celebrations around them. Betty couldn't help thinking that the day ahead would be one of mixed feelings.

She focused on the road ahead and cycled as fast as she could; work would be her salvation. Of course she was happy the war would soon be over, but at what cost with so many people dead? She didn't profess to understand the politics of it all and would leave that to the men in Parliament to worry about. Her thoughts turned again to the influenza that seemed to be sweeping the country. Hobby might have said not to worry, but the fear remained on her mind. One of the younger girls at the store had said it was the work of the Hun, trying to kill them off. This had led to some hysteria in the staff room and the manager had eventually stepped in to have stern words with everyone, warning them he would not tolerate idle gossip. However, he was now off sick himself, along with a large number of Betty's colleagues. As she reached the store and left her bicycle outside at the back, she wondered yet again what the day ahead would bring.

Betty was straightening her overall and checking her hair was tidy when her supervisor came into the room. Although she was not particularly enamoured of Doreen Dunkin she did her best to remain pleasant and carry out the woman's wishes, even though at times she did tend to pick on Betty and give her the lion's share of any work.

'Ah, Betty. We are somewhat short-staffed today so I will expect you to take on more duties.'

Betty sighed inwardly. No doubt what Mrs Dunkin was

about to say was that she would be working on her own on the vegetable counter, while Annie and the other part-time staff member were moved to a different section. 'Of course, Mrs Dunkin, whatever you say,' she murmured, getting ready to walk out of the room and onto the shop floor.

'Not so fast, young lady. I have yet to tell you where you will be working.'

Betty froze. 'I do apologize – I assumed you wished me to work alone on the vegetable counter,' she replied, turning to face the woman. 'Where would you like me to work?'

'I would have preferred you to remain on your usual counter. However, Mr King has other ideas.' She frowned as she looked Betty up and down. 'He seems to see a side of you I have missed. But then, he appreciates a pretty girl.'

Betty was indignant. She'd never felt intimidated or unsafe in the presence of Mr King; he was always professional, polite and not overly friendly. 'I have no idea what you mean,' she said, biting her tongue before she could tell Mrs Dunkin what she really felt.

The woman gave a harsh laugh and shrugged her shoulders. 'You don't need to look at me like that – I wasn't born yesterday. I've seen the way you blush when Mr King talks to you.'

'I can assure you I have not encouraged Mr King in any way whatsoever.'

The supervisor looked affronted. 'Do not speak to me like that, girl. Get yourself downstairs to the household goods counter before I report you to Mr King. He will have to do something about you then, even if he has taken a fancy to you . . .'

Betty was about to speak back at the hateful woman when there was a sound from the doorway. She jumped as Mr King spoke. 'Is there a problem, ladies?' he asked, taking in the sight of Mrs Dunkin wagging a finger in Betty's flushed face.

'Nothing I can't handle, Mr King. I was just giving Miss Billington her duties for the day.'

'Very good. If you have finished, I'd like a word with you before you go downstairs, Betty.'

Doreen all but snarled as she nodded to Mr King before leaving the room. 'Don't be late,' she threw back at Betty, before closing the door behind her with some force.

Betty glanced at the clock; she had only a few minutes before bells would ring and she should be at her new workstation. 'You wanted to speak with me, Mr King?'

'Yes; could we go through to my office?'

Betty nodded in agreement and followed him across the hall; his office was as untidy as usual. He cleared a seat for her to sit down. 'I wondered, if you don't think it impertinent of me, whether you would agree to take a walk with me on Sunday? Perhaps a stroll around Charlton Park; I understand it is close to where you live?'

She felt a jolt of shock shoot through her. 'No, I couldn't do that . . .'

'I'm sorry if you think me presumptuous,' he replied, looking embarrassed.

Betty flapped her hand at his words. 'I'm the one who ought to apologize. You see, the very last time I saw my fiancé was when I met him at Charlton Park. I've not been there since . . . the memories are still too raw.'

'I understand,' he said as a silence descended between them.

It was Betty who spoke next. 'Greenwich Park is very pleasant, even though it will be a little chilly at this time of year. I'm sure if we wrap up warm, a brisk walk would be enjoyable.'

Mr King's eyes lit up. 'Then Greenwich Park it shall be,' he said. They quickly agreed where they should meet before Betty excused herself and went down to the shop floor. She reached her counter just as the warning bell rang and the store opened for business.

There was only time for a harassed assistant to let Betty know that they were short on scrubbing brushes – if anyone should ask, they would have a fresh stock in next week, along with more Jeyes Fluid – before queues started to form. Betty raised her eyebrows as she wondered why she was being told such a thing.

The girl smiled at her. 'You'll soon learn. This is the counter where everyone who's worrying about the Spanish influenza heads. You may find that after a while your eyes start to stream.'

'I don't understand.'

'Firstly, we're near the front doors, so when the street cleaners start disinfecting the pavements outside, your eyes will start to water. Then as you sell bars of Sunlight soap, Rinso and every other soap known to man, your hands will begin to itch.'

'And I thought selling muddy spuds was the worst job in the store,' Betty laughed. Spotting a neat pile of Yardley lavender soap, she picked up a bar and breathed in the delicate perfume. 'I adore this soap. I must get some to take home with me.'

'Make sure you put some Jeyes Fluid by as well. From

what I've been told, it keeps the flu at bay. We've already lost a few young counter staff, and I reckon it's because they didn't do enough to protect themselves. Drink plenty of cocoa as well. My dad told me some government bloke says it will keep us safe.'

Betty could see that cleanliness would go some way towards keeping people safe, but as for all the other claims, she wasn't so sure. She rubbed her eye and was immediately scolded by her colleague.

'Don't rub your eyes or they will smart. I made that mistake last week and they were red and swollen for days afterwards. The lad I'm stepping out with said I looked as though I'd gone two rounds in a boxing ring. I do have a couple of things that will help us.' She reached under the counter and pulled out a pot of Vaseline, along with a couple of squares of flannel fabric with tape attached at each corner. 'My mum made these masks; she nags all the family to use them. Someone at her church group told her about how they save lives. We tie them around our faces to protect us. Here, take one of these. I have plenty. Use the Vaseline to rub into your hands; it stops them becoming sore. I'm Jane, by the way,' she grinned.

Betty thanked her as she took the mask. She'd seen a few people wearing them and wondered if she should mention them again to Hobby. Her landlady was often out and about attending meetings; it couldn't hurt to encourage her to protect herself. 'At least it will keep some of the disinfectant smells at bay, although we may frighten the children,' she chuckled before asking a serious question. 'Why, if we are so busy on this counter, are there only the two of us?' She wondered if it had something to do with Doreen Dunkin.

'Two of the assistants who died of the flu worked on this counter. Another is off sick. We do have a part-time assistant who'll be here in a couple of hours.'

Betty looked at her in horror. 'When you said we'd lost staff, I thought you just meant they were all off sick,' she said, appalled. The thought of women who had worked in this confined space having died really brought it home to her how dangerous the influenza epidemic was. 'Is it safe for us here?'

Jane shrugged her shoulders. 'As safe as anywhere, I suppose. I'd rather be here wearing a mask than on the battlefields, like my two brothers were. There again, they are safe now too, so I can't complain.'

Betty felt a stab of pain to her heart. She would have to get used to talking with people whose loved ones had come safely back from the war. 'You are very lucky to have them back home,' she said, before turning away. If she gave in to her sorrow, she'd be good for nothing. She would just have to immerse herself in serving the bustling crowd of customers, and perhaps that would make her forget her troubles for a little while.

16

For the girls working on the household goods counter, it was a busy morning. Betty was glad of her mask, as the air was never free of the smell of disinfectant. She was amazed at the number of bars of soap that were sold; if cleanliness was truly next to godliness, the people of Woolwich would soon be sitting at the right hand of the Almighty. The constant handling of soap quickly dried up her fingers even though she used a little smear of Vaseline to soften them. When Sara, the part-time staff member, joined them later that morning, she showed Betty that by opening a paper bag ready for the bars of soap and putting her right hand inside another paper bag to pick them up, it saved her fingers getting so dry.

'Why did I not think of that?' Betty chuckled before pointing out the simple trick to Jane.

'It is certainly helpful,' Jane replied, 'but don't let Mrs Dunkin notice, or she'll no doubt tell us off for wasting the paper bag stock. If there is something not to her liking she always lets us know, and in no uncertain terms.'

Betty agreed, and cast her eye around the shop floor

for the unpopular supervisor. 'I wonder why she's so bad-tempered all the time; do you know anything about the woman?'

'I neither know nor care. I just wish she would smile occasionally, rather than making life hell for the girls on the shop floor.'

'Perhaps I should tell her what my grandmother told me when I was just a little girl. She would advise me to pin a smile on my face and hide the hurt and anger inside me.'

'That is wonderful advice,' Jane said, 'but if Mrs Dunkin smiled, she'd crack her face. We just need to learn to keep out of her way and if she tells us off for any reason, not answer back. If we don't fuel her fire it will burn out – that was my father's advice.'

Betty got back to work, making sure she had a friendly smile and a pleasant word for every customer. Many of the women she served were busy chatting about the end of the war, whether making a general comment about better days ahead, or confiding that they looked forward to seeing their loved ones home safely. Betty was generous-hearted enough to agree with them, even though her loved one's remains were far away in a foreign land. There would never be a grave to visit, a place where she could lay flowers and shed silent tears. Instead, she would keep Charlie in her heart forever.

She touched the underside of the collar of her uniform overall, where she'd discreetly pinned her sweetheart brooch. It had now been nearly two years since the day he'd given it to her. *If only we had married before he left for the front,* she thought to herself. This was a thought that never strayed far from her mind. Granted, she would have been a widow, but at least she'd have had the chance to be a bride.

With no one else being put on their counter to help them, Betty told Jane she would forgo her morning tea break and keep working. It wasn't until early afternoon that she was given permission to go to lunch by Mrs Dunkin.

'Make sure you are back on time. I'll be on my break myself, so I'll be watching you,' she said, giving Betty a stern look. 'Don't think for one moment that you're going to dilly-dally with Mr King; I know what kind of girl you are, Betty Billington,' she added, before hurrying away to bark commands at the women on another counter.

'Don't take any notice of her,' Sara advised. 'I've seen you at work both here and on the vegetable counter, and everyone else can see that you're one of the most pleasant and hard-working staff members we have. Woolworths should be grateful to have you working here. Don't worry about there not being enough cover on the counter – I'll stay another half hour until you're back down here.'

Betty thanked her but decided that once she had eaten, she wouldn't hang about and would get back to the shop floor early, so the kindly woman could get home to her family.

When the bell sounded for the last lunch break of the day she hurried upstairs, quickly visiting the ladies' lavatory and scrubbing her hands thoroughly in the china washbasin. Out of all the advice being passed around by well-meaning people, one piece at least made sense: she might not be able to avoid crowds while working as a counter assistant, but she could make sure her hands were scrupulously clean.

With enough soap on sale, that would not be a problem. Going into the canteen, she felt her stomach grumbling as she breathed in the delightful smell of stew. She'd added her name to the list for a hot meal and hoped she wasn't too late.

'Here you are, my love – better late than never,' Lou greeted her. 'I've kept a plate warm for you and added another suet dumpling. It's not fair that you have to wait so long for your dinner. If I had my way, you girls would be eating earlier. I may just mention it to Mr King, or perhaps one of the supervisors.'

'Please, Lou, don't worry yourself about me,' Betty said. If Lou had a word with Doreen Dunkin, it might make her even angrier and more impossible to deal with. 'This looks delicious,' she added, picking up the hot plate with care.

'The gravy is a bit dry around the edges of the plate so let me know if you want another dollop, I've got plenty.'

Betty assured her the food was more than acceptable. Once she'd eaten, she doubted she'd need anything more for the rest of the day.

As she tucked in, she listened to the excited chatter all around her. When one of her fellow shop assistants burst into the room waving a newspaper above her head and declaring that the war had ended at eleven o'clock that morning, she suddenly no longer felt hungry. Around her women were cheering, but deep inside her heart was aching.

Looking up, she spotted her supervisor sitting alone at a corner table. Doreen Dunkin was wiping her eyes and averting her face from the other staff in the room. Betty watched her for a few moments, then picked up her plate and walked over to her.

'Do you mind if I join you, Mrs Dunkin? Although I'm happy the war has ended, I cannot be as joyful as the others.'

Doreen looked up; Betty could see her red-rimmed eyes. She had been right to think the woman was upset. Doreen might well send her packing with a harsh word but at least Betty could try to be friendly, perhaps offer an olive branch – even though she didn't know what for.

'What do you mean?' Doreen asked quickly, wiping her eyes and picking up the cup in front of her, trying to act normally.

'I lost my sweetheart not much over a year ago,' Betty explained, lifting the corner of her collar to show the sweetheart brooch. 'We were to be married. I will never love another man.' She held her breath, waiting to see how the supervisor would react.

Doreen frowned for a moment. 'Well, it seems I got you completely wrong, Betty Billington.'

Betty decided not to ask what she meant. Instead she cut into one of the dumplings and put it in her mouth, forcing herself to chew and swallow. Now the food tasted of nothing whatsoever.

'I lost my husband and my eldest son on the same day, right at the beginning of the war,' Doreen volunteered. 'Anyone will tell you we didn't have the best of marriages, but we ticked along well enough. He gave me a hard time, but I gave as good as I got in our marriage. We were two of a kind. When our boy joined up the fool went along too, forgetting that at that time he wasn't expected to sign up to fight this bloody war.'

Betty quietly put down her knife and fork. Sliding her hand across the table, she tentatively patted her supervisor's hand. 'Don't be harsh on yourself, Mrs Dunkin. I'm sure every bereaved woman is looking back now and thinking how different things would have been if they'd only known it was the last time they'd be seeing their loved ones. Now, don't you think it would be a good idea to get some food inside you? As I understand it, you still have youngsters at home, and they need you fit and strong right now.'

'I definitely got you wrong.'

Betty felt brave enough to ask, 'I don't quite understand what you mean – have I done something to offend you?'

Doreen bent her head in shame, although she did grip Betty's hand more tightly. 'There were two staff members that were sacked just before you were promoted to work on the vegetable counter. I'd got friendly with them and when one of them told me that you had reported them to Mr King, I decided you couldn't be a nice person. Then when you appeared on the counter, having taken one of the jobs – well, it made me angry. I saw you as somebody who wanted promotion and I thought perhaps, if I wasn't careful, you'd be after my job next.'

Betty knew it wasn't the right time to explain that the two women Doreen was referring to had almost driven her away from her cleaning job. 'I promise you, I knew nothing about your friends' dismissal until after it happened. In fact, I fully expected to find myself working alongside them at the veg counter on the day I started. I hope they soon found suitable employment elsewhere – I'd hate for anyone to be out of work and their families to suffer.'

Doreen nodded slowly, accepting Betty's explanation. 'They both found positions down at the Arsenal munitions works. I've not heard from them since, but I hope they are well. It's supposed to be very good pay although it's not something I'd fancy doing myself.'

'The pay is very good – much better than at Woolworths. I was there for a short while.'

'Why ever did you leave and become a cleaner here?'

'It wasn't for me.'

'Stay there and finish your meal,' Doreen said. 'I'm glad we had this talk. I can't promise I will be any more lenient on the shop floor; I'm too set in my ways. However, I will do my best to understand my staff a little more in future.'

Betty nodded her head, not saying a word as Doreen left the room. If anyone had predicted she would find herself talking so confidentially with Doreen today, let alone advising her, she would have laughed at the suggestion. However, perhaps life from now on would be a little gentler if Doreen was friendlier to her staff.

Betty sat on the first bench inside the gates of Greenwich Park. She was wrapped up warm in her best woollen coat and hat; Hobby had lent her a warm knitted scarf with matching mittens. She'd been horrified to see that although Betty was dressed smartly, there was little to keep the biting cold from reaching the girl's bones.

'I know that well-brought-up young ladies like to dress in their finery to meet their young men, but in this weather you must wear more substantial clothing,' she scolded as she rummaged amongst the coats hanging in the hallway. 'Here, you may as well keep these. Blue has never done anything for me and it's a shame to waste such warm garments. A friend gave them to me as a Christmas gift. The colour matches your coat and hat perfectly.'

Betty hesitated. Of course she was grateful for the gloves and scarf, but it was the reference to her 'young man' that worried her. There was a short silence as she tried to work out how to reply. 'Do you not like the colour?' Hobby asked, looking up at her.

'I adore the colour and can't thank you enough. It's just that . . . well . . .'

'Spit it out, girl.'

'You called Mr King my "young man", and . . .'

'And he isn't. Silly me for saying that. I could kick myself for not taking more care with my words,' Hobby apologized.

'But if you think that way, won't others think the same?'

Hobby shrugged her shoulders as she tied the scarf around Betty's neck. 'Who is to know? I'm just a daft old woman who gets her words mixed up. Anyone who knows you must realize you still hold Charlie in your heart – and will continue to do so,' she added quickly, seeing Betty's questioning look. 'Now, be off with you before he decides you aren't coming and goes off home. No one will stand about waiting for long in this freezing weather. Why he wants to meet you in the morning rather than wait until the afternoon, when the winter sun would have had sense to appear, I don't know. And another thing, why couldn't he come here to collect you?'

'It was my idea to meet him at the park. I was afraid my parents might notice a young man calling here, and then see me leaving on his arm.'

Hobby shook her head. 'I completely forgot they still don't know you live here. After all these months it had slipped my mind. Silly me. Get along with you, now, before you're late.'

ELAINE EVEREST

Betty heeded Hobby's words and set off for Greenwich.
She wasn't about to cycle there so she took several trams
and arrived ten minutes early, giving herself time to calm
down and compose herself. She was looking forward to
meeting Mr King and being able to chat freely, away from
the constraints of the Woolworths store and any prying
eyes that would assume something was amiss. Mr King
was ten years her senior – that alone would make some
tongues wag.

'Ah, Betty. I hope you haven't waited long?'

Betty stood up and held out her hand. He shook it
warmly after removing a leather glove. 'I've not long arrived,
Mr King. I'm glad it isn't raining,' she said with a smile.

'You must call me Richard, especially as we aren't in the
office. Mr King seems so formal.'

'And please do call me Betty,' she replied, before remembering that he already had when he spoke to her as a
member of staff.

They both burst out laughing before he held out his arm
for her to take. 'Let's take a stroll, shall we? If we keep
moving it won't seem so cold. You must say if you become
chilly. I thought perhaps we could take lunch, that's if you
have time?'

'I can think of nothing more delightful,' she said as they
started to walk around the park. For a little while they
strolled in silence. Betty wondered if he had a particular
reason for inviting her to meet him, but she didn't like to
ask. 'Do you live far from here?'

'I've taken rooms above a small tea room in Belvedere
– I thought we might go there for lunch.'

Betty froze and stopped walking. Was he intending to

208

take her back to where he lived? She'd thought better of him than that.

Richard noticed the look of consternation cross her face and was puzzled, until the penny dropped. 'Oh, my goodness, no. I had no intention of luring you to my bedchamber like something out of a penny dreadful magazine,' he chuckled. 'Everything is quite above board. My cousin owns the building and runs the tea room. As delightful as you are, Betty, I have no designs on your virtue.'

Betty turned to face him, noticing the smile lines around his mouth. 'I'm not sure if that was a compliment or not,' she laughed as they started to walk again. 'I don't know Belvedere very well, but it's not very close, is it?'

'I have my vehicle close to the park gates; it won't take us long to drive there.'

'All right; shall we take a short turn around this part of the park and then depart?' she suggested, noticing for the first time that he was limping slightly. 'I confess I'm quite interested in seeing how a motor car works.' She didn't add that the only time she had travelled in one had been when her parents' chauffeur had driven them somewhere; her mother would never have allowed her to discuss the techniques of driving with one of their employees.

Richard's eyes lit up. 'I've not long owned mine but it really has been useful, living where I do. My dear cousin is afraid of travelling at speed, so I've not yet been able to show it off to a lady.'

'I would love to travel at speed, as long as it's safe,' Betty chuckled. 'My landlady has a couple of female friends who drive. They did offer to teach me, but so far I haven't been brave enough.'

Richard raised his eyebrows. 'Ladies who drive, eh?'

Betty realized she probably shouldn't elaborate too much about Hobby and her friends. There seemed to be so much negativity around women who'd never married or had a family. She decided to change the subject. 'Tell me, Richard, do you have any family apart from your cousin?'

'I do – and that is what I wanted to talk to you about. Come, I've had enough of walking and making small talk. I could do with a hot drink.'

17

~

'You seem to be experiencing pain in your leg,' Betty observed as they settled at their table in the tea room. She had decided she could no longer ignore Richard's pained expression after he'd grimaced as he held out her seat.

'It is kind of you to notice. Actually, it isn't my leg that pains me – I have no leg below the knee, having lost it during the first weeks of the war.'

Betty held her hand to her mouth. 'I'm sorry; I shouldn't have said anything. Please excuse my bad manners.'

Richard gave a wry smile. 'I much prefer it when people ask. So many people simply stare. To answer your question, it's the colder weather that pains me most.'

'I'm so sorry that you were injured. It was only today that I noticed. I do wish you hadn't invited me to go for a walk on such a chilly day. I would have been happy just to have enjoyed lunch with you. Your cousin has a remarkable business here,' she commented, looking around the room. It was busy with people sitting at tables covered with white cloths, enjoying each other's company. As they entered the building, she'd noticed separate double doors with a sign saying 'guests only' and assumed this was where Richard lived.

Richard beamed at her thoughtfulness. 'In that case, I will just invite you to dine in future rather than take brisk walks around the park.'

Betty raised her eyebrows at his words. Was there to be a next time? She felt flustered at the thought. Would it not be disrespectful to Charlie's memory if she made a habit of dining out with other men? Of course, there was nothing romantic about spending time with Richard. All the same . . .

A waitress approached the table and after consulting Betty, Richard ordered for them both.

'You said you have rooms here with your cousin – does that mean your home isn't in this part of the country?' Betty asked, trying to make polite conversation.

'It was convenient for me to stay here with Letitia while completing my training period at the Woolwich store. In fact, the news I wish to share with you means that I will not be returning to my family home for the foreseeable future. Perhaps one day it will be different.'

Betty froze. 'You're married?' She was about to stand up and leave, but was unable to do so as the waitress returned with a laden tray and her way was blocked. She waited for the young woman to finish placing their order on the table before starting to stand.

'Please, I can explain,' Richard said, noticing her concerned expression.

'Rich . . . Mr King, you know that I lost my fiancé at Ypres. I thought you were inviting me out as a friend and, believing you to be single, I felt that was appropriate, although at no time did I want to tarnish Charlie's memory by starting another . . .' She blushed, not knowing how to continue.

'Oh gosh, Betty. I am making a complete mess of this. I can see how you would think I have compromised our friendship; I do feel we could be friends in time, don't you?'

Betty nodded warily. 'Possibly we could,' she murmured. 'Please continue.'

'I have three young children. My wife met with an accident when the youngest was a baby. She died from her injuries. At the time, I was in hospital in France and about to be shipped home.' A bleak expression passed over his face. 'It was a dark period in my life. Harriet meant everything to me, and all I could think as I lay in a hospital bed in a foreign country was that I should be at home with my children. The two older ones were of an age to understand their mother was no longer there.'

Betty felt tears sting the backs of her eyes. This poor, poor man. Here she was mourning the loss of a fiancé, while his three young children had lost their mother. 'I'm so sorry for your loss . . . I don't know what to say,' she replied as she reached out and gently touched his hand, before pulling back quickly in case anyone noticed. 'Here, let me pour the tea.'

Richard cleared his throat. 'Thank you for your concern. Harriet's family stepped in to take the children until I was on the road to recovery. My father-in-law, although grief-stricken, pulled strings so that I could join Woolworths with a good position.'

'You are fortunate to have a supportive family. It cannot

have been easy for any of you,' Betty said. She couldn't help wondering why he wished to speak with her today; it must be personal, surely? Otherwise they could have had the whole conversation in his office. She prayed he wasn't about to ask her to be a nanny for his children. She had no experience of such a job and had hardly ever met any youngsters, apart from Charlie's two sisters. As she bit into a potted meat sandwich, a thought crossed her mind: perhaps he was looking for a new wife? She swallowed and said, 'I don't quite understand . . .'

'. . . why I wished to speak with you?' he asked.

'I did wonder.'

He chuckled before speaking. 'Don't worry, Betty, I'm not going to ask an indelicate question. As much as I admire you, my reason for wishing to speak with you is purely business.'

Betty had the good grace to join in with his laughter. 'I'm all agog,' she said. 'Please tell me more.'

'I have been offered my own store to manage,' he said, watching her reaction to this piece of news.

'Many congratulations,' Betty exclaimed. 'Of course, I will miss working with you,' she quickly added. Mr King was the only person in management at the Woolwich store that she was able to talk to. Her colleagues, too, would miss his friendly banter on the shop floor. 'Which store will you be moving to?'

'It's a little way from here. Do you know Ramsgate?'

'I'm afraid I don't. I have led quite a sheltered life. I mainly travelled into London for entertainment with my parents, but of course that was before the war when it was safe to do so.'

'It is on the Kent coast – quite a pretty little seaside town. My father works at head office and put in a good word for me. He knows how keen I am to move on with my career. My family live near Faversham, which means I'll be able to see so much more of the children.'

'It sounds perfect for your circumstances,' Betty said, thrilled on his behalf. She wished that she'd had a parent who was so interested in her life.

'Then when we have finished our meal, I shall drive you there and point it out to you. Afterwards I will deliver you home safely.'

'I would be delighted. It's such an achievement to manage your own store. You must be excited?'

'I am – and yes, it is quite an achievement for a man not yet thirty. With the war now finished, my feeling is this new world we find ourselves in is one where young people should be able to pursue the careers they're best suited to. And that is why I want you, Betty, to come and work for me in Ramsgate.'

Betty almost dropped her teacup. 'Whatever do you mean?' she exclaimed. 'I can't travel that far every day on my bicycle. Surely there must be plenty of competent workers living closer to the store?'

Richard set down his knife and fork and cleared his throat. 'Do you recall me saying, soon after you started working as a counter assistant, that I thought you would make a very good supervisor – but your young age was against you?'

'I do, and I'm still only eighteen years of age now.'

'And everyone you currently work with knows you have worked for F. W. Woolworth for just under a year.'

'That's correct,' Betty frowned, wondering what he was getting at.

'I know you are good at your job; you've come up with some excellent ideas in the time you've worked under me. Your fellow workers like you and there has never been a complaint about you.'

Betty tried to ignore the vision of Doreen Dunkin that appeared in her mind. Although she'd made her peace with the woman for now, she wasn't sure it would last. 'I do get along with most people,' she acknowledged, 'but what has that got to do with me transferring to another store?'

'I would like you to start work there as a supervisor. No one would know your real age, and you would be doing me a great favour if you never disclosed it. You could easily pass for someone of twenty-five.'

Betty laughed. 'To be honest, I don't know quite how to take that,' she said as she raised a hand to her cheek. Granted, her great sorrow had left its mark in the shadows around her eyes; but the suggestion that she could pass for someone seven years older still came as quite a shock.

'Forgive me – I didn't mean to imply that you look old, or should I say older than your real age. It's the way you carry yourself and the way you speak, and your reliability and intelligence, that make you appear older than your contemporaries. You have a clever head on your shoulders and in time, Betty Billington, you could progress to management.'

'Oh, my goodness,' was all Betty could say. She pushed her plate away and sat back in her seat as she contemplated his words.

After a delightful meal and having met Richard's cousin,

being introduced as one of his colleagues who was recently bereaved, Betty pulled on her coat and gloves and followed Richard to his vehicle. 'It was kind of you to introduce me to Letitia in a way that wouldn't compromise my reputation. I'm grateful for your thoughtfulness,' she said as he helped her into her seat and closed the door.

He walked round to the other side of the car and climbed in, turning to face her. 'I would never do anything to distress you, Betty – I want to be your friend. Knowing you are working in the store beside me will help me do my job well. I am simply being selfish by wanting to take my best staff member with me.'

'You weren't thinking of taking anyone else, were you?' she asked cheekily. 'Higher management might not like it very much if you start moving staff around the country to suit your own ends. As it is, I'm still unsure how I am to travel to work each day . . .'

He laughed as he started the engine and pulled out into the country lane. 'Management has nothing to fear. As for your other concern – why not wait and see what you think of the town first?'

Betty looked sideways at him, watching his face as he concentrated on the road ahead. In another time and place, she could perhaps have imagined Richard as much more than a colleague. She raised her hand to the lapel of her jacket, feeling for the familiar shape of the sweetheart brooch. Stop that immediately, she chided herself as she settled back to enjoy the journey. After today's events, she already had more than enough to think about.

18

'Are you sure you wouldn't like to have some refreshments first?' Richard asked as he helped Betty down from the vehicle, watching with concern as she pulled on her woollen gloves and tightened the scarf around her neck. 'You do look rather pale.'

Betty gave a weak smile. The journey had made her feel queasy. 'I'd much prefer to see the store first,' she said. 'It was good of you to break our journey so that we could take the air and I could stretch my legs. I had no idea what to expect, or how far we would have to drive to reach our destination. I must say, this is a pleasant spot,' she exclaimed, looking down the street to where she caught a glimpse of the harbour.

'This was one of the reasons I agreed to the promotion,' he said, standing beside her as they both took in the view. 'I hope in time to be able to find a house here so that the children can join me. The sea air can be quite invigorating, and although they do like the countryside around Faversham, I can imagine them thoroughly enjoying a life by the sea. Do you think you'd find this an agreeable place to work?'

'It's beautiful. And the journey here through the countryside, seeing all the hop bines and farms, was delightful,'
Betty replied, not adding that she'd found the trip tiring
and was still feeling a little carsick. 'However, I don't intend
to let my heart rule my head – I would need to see where
I might be working. And as it's such a long way from
Charlton, I would need to find lodgings, which worries me
a little. I love living with Miss Hobson; she has made me
so welcome in her home, and I'd hate to lose touch with
her . . . Where is the store?'

Richard gently placed his hands on her shoulders and
turned her around. 'There it is. What do you think?'

Betty stared at the building in front of her. It was only
the second Woolworths store she'd seen, and for some
reason she had expected it to look exactly like the one in
Woolwich. The shop sign was the same, bearing not only
the F. W. Woolworth name but also the declaration of items
costing thruppence and sixpence. Similar products filled
the shiny windows and although the store was closed
because it was a Sunday, there were still passers-by gazing
at the displays.

'It's much smaller than our store,' she said, as they crossed
the road to get a closer view. 'It looks like a new building,
as well?' she added, looking at the brickwork around the
windows.

'It is smaller, but then, many Woolworths stores are
smaller than our branch. I doubt very much they would
have offered me a manager's position at a branch the size
of the Woolwich store.'

'You sell yourself short, Richard. You are an admirable
manager,' she said, leaping to his defence. 'I wouldn't be

surprised if before too long our employers move you to an even larger store. In the short time I've worked for the company, I've seen a number of under-managers and trainees come and go.'

'You are correct, Betty; trainees and managers can be moved from pillar to post. It's meant to ensure that they receive as much experience as possible before they're either given their own branch or a permanent under-manager's job. Some even move to work in head office, if the powers that be declare them more of an asset behind a desk.'

Betty cupped her hands around her eyes, peering through one of the glass doors. 'It looks as though they have capable cleaning staff,' she approved. 'The wooden floors are positively gleaming.'

'And so they should be,' he said as he joined her. 'To answer your earlier question, the building is just one year old.'

Betty stepped back and looked at the other shops nearby. 'How strange – these other buildings seem quite old.'

'You would have heard the term enemy action? I'm afraid the premises that were here before suffered at the hands of the Hun.' He looked angry as he told her. 'It doesn't seem right that civilians should suffer in this war. It was a bomb dropped from a Zeppelin,' he explained.

'You mean – people died here?'

'Yes; there were two people who perished here. Would it bother you to work on a site where people had died?'

Betty thought for a moment, 'I'm shocked that it should have happened, but no, I'm not superstitious, so it wouldn't bother me.' She turned and looked again at the building. 'What a shame that we've travelled so far and can't take a look inside.'

Rather than answer her, Richard gave a couple of sharp taps on the glass door before craning his neck to see if anyone had heard. 'Jolly good – he heard me,' he said, giving Betty a wink.

Betty watched as a man not much older than Richard, but certainly more rotund, appeared at the other side of the door. He fumbled with a bunch of keys, unlocking it, and stepped out onto the pavement. 'Ah, you both made it, and the weather held out for your journey. You must be Miss Billington. I've heard great things about you,' he said, extending his hand before Richard could make any formal introductions.

'I am,' Betty said, smiling politely at him before turning to Richard with a lifted eyebrow.

'Er . . . Betty, may I introduce Bertie Green, who is currently temporary manager of the store. It's very good of you to open up so I can show Betty around her future workplace.'

'Not at all, old man, the pleasure's all mine. Shall I give you both the grand tour, or leave you to it? There are a few things need seeing to in the stockroom. I want to leave the store in as good a condition as possible when I hand over the keys,' he said, rattling the bunch he still held in his hand.

Richard glanced at Betty and shifted uncomfortably. 'If it's all the same to you, Bertie, I'd like to show Betty around on my own.'

'Come and find me afterwards, then, and I'll give you both tea in the office,' Bertie said affably, ushering them inside and locking the doors behind them.

Betty walked the length of the store, stopping to examine

221

a few items displayed on the counters. Richard followed, not saying a word as he observed her reactions. They reached the far wall of the store before she spun on her heel, giving him an angry glare. 'What are you playing at, Richard King? How did it come about that Mr Green knew I would be visiting today, when I had no idea myself until we met this morning? Couldn't you have informed me of your intentions when you asked me to join you for a walk earlier this week?' Her voice faltered slightly on the last few words as she remembered that Richard was still her superior; but as far as she was concerned, he'd overstepped the mark. She was so angry that it crossed her mind she might be better off not travelling home with him; she'd noticed a sign for a railway station, and hopefully there would be a train heading to London at some point today. She had enough money in her purse to pay for a ticket.

Richard ran his hand through his hair, looking downcast. 'I can't apologize enough. I got so carried away with the thought of you working here as my supervisor I jumped in with both feet and told Bertie. I felt that if you saw this lovely town and its shiny new store, you'd fall in love with it and agree at once. I didn't expect . . .'

'You didn't expect Mr Green to drop you in it, did you?' she asked, trying to remain stern, although her mouth was starting to twitch as she fought back a laugh. He looked so forlorn, rather like a little boy who had been caught with his hand in the biscuit tin.

'I suppose you want to go home now. I'll go out to the stockroom and ask Bertie to unlock the door so we can leave.'

'I thought you were going to give me the tour?'

'You mean . . . ?'

'I mean, I'm not happy about the way that you brought me here. However, if you'd sat me down in your office in the Woolwich store and explained everything, my answer would have been that I would like to see Ramsgate and the place where you are going to be manager.'

'Does this mean you aren't angry with me?'

'I'm jolly angry, but I would be daft not to think about my future working life. I'm not yet nineteen and that means there are many years ahead of me where I am going to have to ensure I can live comfortably – and on my own,' she added quickly. 'I'll explain my circumstances more fully on our journey home but for now, I would like you to give me a proper guided tour. Then we can have a cup of tea with Mr Green. I don't know about you, but I'm parched,' she said, as she slipped her arm through his and nodded towards the counters she had yet to inspect.

Richard didn't speak until she started to ask questions. Betty would be good for the Ramsgate branch. He hoped, in time, she would also be good for him.

It was almost midnight when Betty let herself into the house. She crept in slowly and quietly, not wishing to wake Hobby. However, after she had taken a few steps the door to the kitchen opened and Hobby stood there, resplendent in the Chinese silk kimono she liked to use as a dressing gown.

'I'm so sorry to be this late,' Betty said softly. 'I hope you didn't worry too much?'

Hobby shook her head. 'Of course I was worried; who wouldn't be? However, I know you're a sensible girl and I told myself you would be home before too long. I'll warm some milk for cocoa, then we can make ourselves comfortable and you can tell me all about your day.'

Even though Hobby had not scolded her, Betty felt guilty for worrying her friend. Why else would she have stayed up so late? She quickly joined her in the kitchen and sat down with her, explaining that she had been to Ramsgate with Richard.

'That's a far cry from going to Greenwich Park for a walk this morning. I take it he had a reason for the trip?'

'He wanted to show me the Woolworths store where he is being transferred. He's been offered a promotion and will manage the store himself.'

'That is wonderful news for the young man. I did not realize the pair of you were so close he would want to share his news with you outside the store.'

Betty sipped her cocoa, avoiding Hobby's eyes. How did Hobby manage to be so perceptive, seeing things even before Betty had noticed? But this time she was wrong – Richard was just a friend. All the same, Betty was reluctant to break the news that she'd decided to accept Richard's offer and move to Ramsgate to be a supervisor.

'I take it there is more you've yet to tell me, but it is late and you have work in the morning. We can discuss it over our dinner tomorrow evening.'

'Oh no,' Betty said. 'I'd like to tell you now otherwise I'd feel as though I had a secret I was keeping from you, and that isn't the case at all.'

Hobby went to the cupboard and took out a packet of crackers before going to the pantry for cheese and butter. 'I have a feeling this may take a little time, so we might as well have something to eat while we talk. Tell me straight away, my dear, is there more between you and Richard than friendship?'

Betty shook her head. 'Believe me, he is just a friend – a recent friend, but a good one. There's no romance between us and he knows I will only ever love Charlie. I made that quite clear. In fact, he's in a similar position to me. He had a wife who passed away,' she clarified quickly, as Hobby raised her eyebrows. 'He has three young children. And you can stop looking at me like that, because I have no desire to marry him and become an instant mother to his offspring.'

'You can't blame me for wondering,' Hobby said as she cut a slice of cheese and speared it with the cheese knife before placing it on a plate in front of Betty. 'Eat up. You must be starving after making that journey. You will miss him when he moves to the Kent coast. That is a fair distance to travel, even by train.'

Betty nibbled on a corner of the cheese before replying. 'He has asked me to go with him,' she finally said, looking at Hobby anxiously. 'I am to be promoted to a supervisor's position. Richard mentioned when I had my interview last year that I might be capable of that sort of work – but with everyone knowing that I was so young and with me being new to the company, it didn't seem possible. Besides, I really needed some experience of working on the shop floor before attempting anything further.'

'So by moving to another store in Ramsgate, you suddenly age?' Hobby asked ironically.

'No . . . it's more that I know my job, and I feel I could be an asset to the company if only I was given the chance.

With no one knowing my age, I can pass for someone a little older. No one on the shop floor will question me. It's also my chance to make a fresh start away from . . . Away from my parents,' she finished, as tears threatened.

Hobby was silent for a little while as she chewed on a buttered cracker. 'Yes, I can see that it would be a fresh start for you. Saying that, I'm going to miss you around the house. It's been like having my own daughter here; you've certainly brightened my days.'

Betty hurried to hug her. 'You are better than a mother to me,' she said as they both shed a few tears. 'In the year I've lived with you, I have grown up so much. I'm wiser and have learnt from your ways.'

Hobby sniffed into her handkerchief. 'Your words mean so much to me, although I don't think you've thought this through properly. You will never be quite like me and my friends, will you?' She chuckled.

Betty was confused for a moment, until the penny dropped and she joined in with Hobby's laughter. 'Perhaps not in the way you mean, although I admire you all.'

'I do feel you ought to explain to Richard about your parents and the way they've ostracized you. Perhaps even mention the strange lady you lodge with. Start with a clean slate,' Hobby advised.

'I already have. Richard knows all about me, not that I said I live with a strange lady, because to me you're not strange. You are to all intents and purposes my mother. I've also told him about Charlie, and how I plan never to marry. This promotion proves to me that my way forward in life is going to be as a working woman,' she declared.

'Never say never,' Hobby admonished her. 'You are only

eighteen, and goodness knows my own life has changed drastically since I was that age. At the moment you are still mourning Charlie, but a time may come when you meet someone you want to spend the rest of your life with. We never know what will happen; it could be tomorrow, or it could be twenty years from now. Believe me, when it comes, you ought to embrace the change in your life. Now, can you make us another cup of cocoa? I have something I need to find.'

Betty had not only finished making their second drink, but had washed the pan and cleared away the remains of the food before a red-faced Hobby reappeared. 'I thought you'd gone to bed,' Betty smiled. 'I was about to bring this up to you.'

'You know what I'm like, with my paperwork all over the place, and I wanted to tell you about this while we were being open and honest with each other. Tell me, what plans do you have for finding a place to live in Ramsgate?' she asked, sitting back down at the table clutching an envelope.

'I plan to take a couple of days off and go down by train. I'll look at lodging houses, and I may even be able to rent a few rooms for myself rather than book into bed and breakfast accommodation.'

'Then I will come with you. We can decide between ourselves what is going to be most suitable for you. It may be winter, but a few days by the coast will make a delightful change.'

'Would you really? That would be wonderful, I'm sure you know more about finding suitable accommodation than I do. When I go into work tomorrow, I will book my days off and we can plan accordingly.'

'There is something else,' Hobby said as she slid the envelope across the table to Betty. 'I want you to read this carefully.'

Puzzled, Betty opened the envelope and pulled out several sheets of paper. Her eyes widened as she read the first few lines. 'My goodness, this is your will; I should not be reading this, it is your own private business,' she protested as she began to push it back across the table.

'No, you are to read it, as it concerns you,' Hobby replied sharply. 'I'd rather you knew about this now rather than . . . Well, rather than later, when I'm gone.'

With shaking hands, Betty read through the document before placing it back on the table and looking up at her good friend. 'This is more than generous, and I don't deserve what is written here. You have so many good friends and support so many associations and charities . . . surely they should benefit from your will?'

Hobby shook her head. 'Not in a month of Sundays. All my friends are settled in their lives, and I have made bequests to charities. Did you not look at the date of this will? It was drawn up ten years ago. That is when I decided who I would like to leave my home and my possessions to. I took such a shine to the little girl next door and somehow, in my bones, I knew the day would come when she would need to make her own way in life. Even then, Betty, I could see that you did not share your family's way of looking at the world. This past year, with you living here, has been a joy – and just as you think of me as a mother figure, I think of you as the daughter I never had. So this is yours and I wish you joy, as I know you will use it wisely.'

'Oh my goodness,' was all Betty could say, as she slipped

the paperwork back into its envelope. 'I hope never to see these papers again for at least fifty years.'

Hobby snorted with laughter. 'That is wishful thinking. Everything is lodged with my solicitor. These are his details,' she said, passing over a square card with the name of the business printed in black. 'However, there is something else. Naming you in my will does not solve the current problem of where you are going to live. Do you understand that you will need to pay a deposit to whomever you rent rooms from? I know it wasn't the same in our situation, but that was different.' She rose to her feet and went to a large dresser that stood against one wall of the kitchen. Opening a drawer, she rummaged through the items inside until she found a small book. When she sat down again, she opened a page and pointed her finger at the balance. 'This is my savings account. I've been putting a little by along with the money you've given me for your keep each week. Call me a silly old woman, but I felt that if the day came when you found a young man you wanted to marry, I would be the one to provide your wedding gown and contribute towards the wedding. It's not as if we can rely on my next-door neighbours, is it?' She chuckled.

Betty was overcome as she looked at the figures in the book. It was true that she would have had very little money to establish herself in Ramsgate; she had hoped that as it was winter, she might find a cheap lodging house where she could stay for a few months while looking for something more permanent. But with this amount of money, Hobby had solved all of her problems. Laying her arms on the table, she rested her head and sobbed her heart out. She had never known such kindness in all her life.

19

The next morning, Betty cycled to work in a daze. If it hadn't been for Hobby shaking her shoulder and telling her she would be late if she didn't get out of bed immediately, she would still be there now. She had wanted to have a word with Richard before the bell rang to open the store. As it was, she barely had time to put on her overall and check her hair before scurrying downstairs.

'Billington, did you not see the notice in the staff room? I've had to move some of the counter staff to other departments now that so many are going down with this infernal Spanish flu.'

Betty sighed as she turned to face Doreen Dunkin. She'd hoped that after their chat the other day, the lady might be more pleasant. Instead, she seemed as snappy and miserable as ever. 'I'm so sorry, Mrs Dunkin. I was a little late this morning and I didn't get a chance to check the noticeboard. Would you like me to look now, or can you advise where I should be working?' She smiled sweetly.

'There is no need to be facetious, Billington. I'm putting you back on the vegetable counter.' A smirk crossed the woman's face as she walked off, checking a list as she did so.

'Oh, that's a shame,' Jane said. 'I did enjoy working with you. Why don't you put an application in to Mr King to ask if you can be moved to this counter permanently? You seem to be on good terms with him, from what I've heard.' She nudged Betty and gave her a sly wink.

Betty didn't want to be sharp with Jane, so she kept her tone light as she asked, 'What on earth are you implying?'

Jane shrugged her shoulders. 'There's no need to be so defensive. You were spotted in Mr King's car yesterday.'

'Oh, for goodness' sake! Is nothing private around here?'

'So it's true!' Jane giggled. 'Well done – setting your sights high and fraternizing with the management. Good luck to you, is what I say,' she added before hurrying behind her counter to pull off the dust covers, ready for the first customers of the day.

That will run right through the store like a dose of salts, Betty huffed to herself as she made her way across the store to the vegetable counter. She stood, hands on hips, surveying the mess. It looked as though the cleaner had not carried out her duties in that area of the store; the storeroom lads had left sacks of vegetables on the counters, with no one there to open and lay out stock. She rummaged around under the counter until she found a piece of sacking she could use to cover the front of her overall. Tying the string around her waist, she next located a broom and a dustpan and brush, then set to clearing the area around the counter so that customers wouldn't trip over the mess or slip on the damp patches created by muddy vegetable leaves.

It was surprising how quickly a counter could look untidy when staff were not vigilant, or couldn't be bothered to do their jobs properly, she thought to herself; at the same time wondering whether there would be any other staff working with her that day. When nobody had appeared after fifteen minutes, she concluded that she was on her own. She spotted one of the storeroom lads chatting to a girl on the next counter.

'I would like you to come over here and open the sacks for me, please,' she called out, not giving him a chance to refuse. 'After that you can take these empty sacks away, along with the rubbish I've swept up. Do you have any idea what has happened to the cleaners this morning?'

The young lad slunk over. Betty spoke in such an authoritative manner that he did not answer her back or give her any cheek. 'They're off sick, miss,' he muttered, before pulling a knife from his overall pocket and getting stuck into the job.

'I will be two minutes,' Betty said to him as she hurried to the household goods counter. 'Jane, may I have a couple of those masks you keep under the counter, and a bottle of disinfectant? I'll make sure the disinfectant is paid for, if you could make a note of it.'

Jane nodded in agreement and passed the items to Betty without speaking. As Betty turned to go back to her counter, she heard the girl start to giggle. She'd no time to give her a piece of her mind; she was more concerned with her own work. 'Here,' she said to the lad, 'put this on your face. And when you've finished what you're doing, bring me a mop and a bucket of water.'

'Been promoted, have you?' the lad smirked.

'And less of your cheek, if you don't mind. I'm going to mop around the counter to keep it safe for our customers.

When you've brought me what I need, I want you to check this counter every hour in case I'm running out of stock. It looks as though I'm on my own today, and I don't have time to go running after young lads asking them to help me restock. You may think it's funny, but have you not noticed how many staff members are ill and missing today? It could be you or me next.'

The lad watched Betty as she tied the mask around her face. Slowly the penny dropped, and he did likewise before hurrying off with a pile of empty sacks tucked under his arm.

Betty had served several customers by the time he came back with the mop and bucket. 'You have a choice,' she said. 'You can either step behind the counter and help me serve these customers, or you can add some of this disinfectant to the bucket of water and wipe the floor. You will have to dry it as you go, in case there is an accident. Here, take these,' she said, thrusting several empty sacks over the counter that he hadn't yet disposed of.

Although he didn't answer her, she knew by the look on his face that he wasn't keen on serving; judging by the way he held the mop, though, she wasn't convinced he would make much difference to the dirty floor either. 'Excuse me for just one moment,' she said to the next lady in the queue as she went round the counter to the lad, showing him how to swirl the mop in the bucket and clean the floor. 'If you put this sacking down, you can use your feet to slide it along to dry the floor as much as possible. Once you get close to where I'm serving, I will move to the other end of the counter to give you a chance to clean the last of the floor space. Do you understand how important this is?' she asked, giving him a warm smile of encouragement.

'Yes miss, this is like the council are doing in the streets, spraying the roads with that stinky stuff.'

'Good lad. I'm not sure if it will save us from this awful Spanish flu, but as the saying goes, cleanliness is next to godliness; and we all certainly need some help from God right now.'

'You tell him, love,' one of the women in the queue called out, while several other ladies clapped their hands to applaud her. The lady who'd spoken picked up the bottle of disinfectant and read the label. 'I think it's about time I started scrubbing my home. It won't hurt to throw a bucket of water with some of this in it down my path out the front as well. I don't know any Spanish people, but who knows when they're going to come knocking and bring that sickness with them.'

Betty smiled at the woman's comments; but who was she to say if the woman was right or wrong? 'I believe we have plenty of disinfectant in stock over on that counter,' she said, holding up the bottle with one hand and pointing to the household goods counter with the other. Several women left the vegetable queue and hurried off. 'We also have a stock of mops and buckets,' she called after them.

'Blimey,' the storeroom lad said as he stretched his back and wiped his brow. 'I'm glad you're on our side, I wouldn't have wanted to cross you out on no man's land. The way you're going, you're going to be running this place by next week.'

Betty turned to serve the next customer. She knew the lad was joking, but at the back of her mind she started to wonder: would it be possible for a woman to become a store manager? She would have to ask Richard if F. W.

Woolworth employed women in such positions. Betty thought it would be lovely if, in a few years' time, she could inform her father that she too worked in management. Granted, it wouldn't be in a bank, but running a high street store must be just as important? That would show him she wasn't just a dutiful daughter, to be married off and provide him with grandchildren.

Thinking of her father as she weighed out carrots and onions, she decided it was time to pay her parents a visit. She could time it for the last day before she moved to Ramsgate; that way, if they spotted her returning to Hobby's house next door, there was nothing they could do about the situation. She was unsure about whether to give them her new address once she had found a place to live. She would decide about that once she was settled in the new job.

If it hadn't been for Richard visiting the shop floor, Betty would not have managed a tea break that morning, and by then she was flagging.

'Surely you are not working here alone, Betty?' he asked as he watched her hand over a woman's change.

She lowered the face mask and took a deep breath. 'I have no choice in the matter – I'm alone here today. Young Ronnie here has been a godsend. I do hope he won't get in trouble for neglecting his own duties.'

Ronnie looked up from where he was tipping a brass dish of potatoes into a customer's shopping bag. 'Miss Billington has shown me how to serve a customer, but she does all the adding up for me and checks I've charged the right money.'

Richard looked thoughtful. 'Are you enjoying working on this counter?'

'I am, sir, it makes a bit of a change for me. I just hope I'm doing things right. Miss Billington said I am, but I'm not so sure.'

'You are doing remarkably well, Ronnie. I would have been lost without you this morning. However, I'm not sure I can leave you working here alone while I take my tea break.'

A look of horror crossed the lad's face. 'Please don't do that, miss.'

'Stop worrying, Ronnie,' Richard said as he removed his jacket and took Betty's sacking apron from her. 'There's no need to gawp, a manager must learn the ropes and work his way up from the bottom. I've done your job, and many others as well. Now, the pair of you go off and take your break while I serve these lovely ladies. Ronnie, I'll have a word with your supervisor and tell him that I have seconded you to vegetable duties for the foreseeable future.'

'Blimey,' Ronnie said as he followed Betty upstairs to the staff room. 'Perhaps one day I could be a manager, if I play my cards right.'

Me too, Betty thought to herself.

When she arrived home in the early evening, tired but happy with the work she'd completed that day, she found Hobby with paperwork spread all over the large table in the front room. 'Whatever are you up to? Are you and your friends planning a new suffrage campaign?'

'Nothing as simple as that,' Hobby chuckled. 'I've had a few ideas about your move to Ramsgate in the new year.'

Betty felt guilty. Apart from booking a few days off so that the pair of them could go to the coastal town to find somewhere for her to lodge, she had not given any thought to her plans. 'Shall I prepare us some supper? Then we can sit down and chat about what you've been up to.' She peered over Hobby's shoulder, but couldn't make head nor tail of what her friend was up to.

'Goodness, I've not given food a thought, what a terrible landlady I am. We do have some cold meat in the larder, and you will find some vegetables still in my basket from where I popped to the shops on Saturday.'

Betty kissed her cheek. 'Don't ever call yourself a terrible landlady. As far as I'm concerned, you are the best in the land,' she said, before hanging up her coat in the hall and heading into the kitchen. In the time since she'd moved out of her parents' house, she wouldn't say she had learnt much about cooking; but she could produce a few passable meals, thanks to Olive giving her a few lessons.

She found potatoes and cabbage, along with the remains of a pork joint in the larder. I know just what to cook, she said to herself as she pulled on an apron and started peeling the vegetables. Humming away as she worked, she couldn't help thinking how much her circumstances had changed of late. If someone had told her a year ago that she would soon be moving to an unfamiliar town to work as a supervisor, she would not have believed them. But here she was, not yet nineteen years of age and about to embark on the biggest adventure of her life. She would be sorry to move out of Hobby's house, as she was fond of living with the older woman; but even last night, as they discussed Betty's plans, it had been clear Hobby would be a frequent visitor.

'Our meal is ready,' she called out to Hobby. 'I thought we could eat in the kitchen so as not to disturb all your work. I can't wait to hear what you've been up to,' she said

237

as Hobby came into the kitchen and washed her hands at the stone sink in the corner of the room.

'You will have to wait a little longer,' she said with a sparkle in her eye. 'I may just surprise you with my idea.'

'That does sound intriguing,' Betty said as she put the plates on the table along with cutlery.

'And this looks intriguing,' Hobby remarked, looking at the plate.

'I do hope you like it. It's called bubble and squeak – it's fried potato and cabbage. Charlie's sister showed me how to prepare it. I sliced the pork and left it cold.'

Hobby tucked into the fried golden vegetables and slices of meat. 'Of course, I'd heard of bubble and squeak, but had never bothered cooking it for myself. When my friends visit they generally bring enough cake to sink a ship, so savoury food isn't usually called for. This could be something for the menu when we . . .'

'When we what?' Betty asked, as she laid down her knife and fork and reached for a napkin to dab at her mouth.

'Don't worry, I'll explain more later.'

Betty frowned, but didn't push for information. She hoped all would soon become clear.

They enjoyed their meal as they chatted about Betty's working day. Hobby was impressed to hear that Richard was encouraging young people to think of their future working lives with the company, and that he had mentioned management.

'Do you think the day will come when there are more women in management positions?' Betty asked her.

Hobby nodded her head vigorously. 'I certainly do. There is nothing to stop women running businesses, and indeed our country. Let's face it, they would probably do a better job than many men have. I shall congratulate this Richard when I meet him, and remind him that we women are as capable of doing a good job as men are. In fact, I'll remind him that women don't have to be in their dotage to be promoted to supervisor positions.'

Betty bridled at Hobby's comments. 'Please don't say anything to Richard. I'm well able to speak for myself,' she said before realizing she had spoken sharply. 'I'm sorry, I didn't mean to snap at you; it has been a tiring day. I'm happy to go along with his suggestion that I age five years while working at the Ramsgate store. Even then I'll be older than any of the counter staff.'

'All I'm saying is, you shouldn't need to pretend to be older. If you can undertake a competent job, then age does not come into it.'

'I do understand, and you're quite right, but the other staff will not see things as you do. They will put two and two together and make five. I'd probably think the same in their position.'

'That is very astute of you. You seem to have an under-standing of your fellow workers. All the same, I'm not sure starting a new job with a lie is the right way to go about things . . .'

Betty sighed. 'Let's not argue over this. You aren't likely to meet Richard, so there won't be an opportunity for you to offer your words of wisdom . . .' Betty saw a crafty smile cross Hobby's face. 'What is going on?'

'Come with me and I'll show you,' Hobby replied getting up from the table and holding out her hand to Betty. 'I hope this will be a nice surprise, as I too have been busy today. I've been to see several people and have developed a plan for our future, come,' she said, leading Betty into the front room. 'We can wash up later.'

Betty did as she was told, pulling out a chair to sit at the large table where Hobby's paperwork was spread out. She averted her eyes, as she had a feeling much of this was to do with Hobby's private finances and personal assets. She was still reeling from Hobby's declaration last night that Betty would benefit from her will when, God forbid, she passed away. Betty couldn't bear to think of that. It was still hard enough to comprehend that she would never see her Charlie again.

'Now,' Hobby said as she sat at the head of the table, lifting a single page of paper covered in her handwriting. 'I hope I can understand my own notes . . . Ah yes, Ramsgate and our move.'

'Our move?' Betty spluttered. 'Hobby, you don't have to come with me. I'd hate to see you leaving your friends and committees.' Had she not explained properly that she alone was going to take lodgings, and Hobby was only accompanying her for a few days, just long enough to enjoy the sea air and advise on the best rooms to rent? She took a deep breath, ready to explain again.

Hobby raised her hand to silence Betty just as she was about to speak. 'Please do let me explain; you can ask questions afterwards. Now, long before you moved in with me, I'd been thinking about the years ahead of me. Let's face it, I'm no spring chicken, and I'd quite like to move and enjoy my final years somewhere pleasant. I'd considered the countryside and the seaside before now; however, two things stopped me acting on my thoughts.

'One was the war: who in their right mind was going to up sticks, when the chances were we could have been invaded at any time? I'd even imagined moving to a beautiful little cottage in the country, only for one of those Zeppelins to seek me out and despatch me to oblivion. Secondly, you came along. Please don't think for one moment that you in any way put a halt to my dreams of moving. No, I've enjoyed having you live under my roof and joining in with the subterfuge of your parents not knowing you are here.'

'All right,' Betty said, looking worried. 'I'm pleased to know you are considering a move, but I'd hate to think that you only stayed here because of me.'

Hobby raised a hand to silence her. 'What I'm trying to say, young lady, is that with you working at Woolworths and settled in your life, I had decided to see my days out here in Charlton. There would always be time later to make friends if you married and moved away. Please don't look at me like that, young madam. I know how much you miss Charlie, and I also understand that there will be many women of your generation who never marry owing to the great loss of life during the war. But you are an intelligent young woman and very personable; any man would be a fool not to be interested in you as a partner for life. No one can see the future, and if your Charlie was half the man I'm led to believe he was, he would not deny you a happy life with someone else.'

'It's very kind of you to say that. As for me holding up your dreams of moving away, I can only apologize. Perhaps now I'll be living in Ramsgate, you will be able to find your cottage in the country. Is this what all the paperwork is for? Can I help in any way?'

Hobby roared with laughter. 'Let's forget about men for now, but as for us parting ways . . . you don't get rid of me that easily, my dear. Today I visited the lending library and looked up all the information they had on Ramsgate. I had a word with my bank manager and managed to speak to my solicitor. As luck would have it, my solicitor has a brother-in-law who sells property down in Kent, and I had a chat with him on the telephone. We really ought to get one of those contraptions; they are so handy,' she added.

'My, you have been busy! All I've done towards a couple of days by the sea is to book my time off from work. Do you mean to say you will follow me to Ramsgate, or perhaps somewhere close by?'

'Yes, exactly. Although at the rate things are progressing, I might well be there before you start work in January.' Hobby hooted with laughter. 'There is just one thing,' she added, a serious look crossing her face. 'Do you want me to accompany you on your fresh start in life?'

Betty thought for a moment. 'I had not given it a thought. If I'm honest, I was rather frightened of setting out on my own to live in a strange town. Not only that, but I would also be overseeing staff for the first time in my life, and the only person I would know would be Richard – and him living closer to his children means that he would have a busy private life – not that I would expect him to be part of my life. So, thank you; I can think of nothing more enjoyable than moving in with you. You have been the perfect landlady and I would like that to continue.'

'Thank goodness for that. My friends have often told me that I can be hot-headed and jump into things without thinking through the consequences. They will tell you that in times gone by they've had to bail me out when I've thrown a stone through a window during one of our campaigns, or knocked a bobby's helmet off in my excitement. You must tell me if I'm taking over your life. You will do that, promise me?'

Betty chuckled at the thought of Hobby's escapades. She had heard some of the stories when the woman's friends came to visit. 'I promise to do that. Why don't we have a few days by the coast and see how we get along as friends, rather than you being my landlady and stand-in mother? Then we can decide whether to proceed with whatever it is you've planned.'

'That's a wonderful idea. Talking of mothers, what are we going to do about yours? It would be rather nice to move away from this area knowing we've not left any secrets behind.'

'I agree with you. In fact, I have plans to go and speak with my parents and tell them all that has happened since I last crossed their threshold. I don't expect them to like what I have to say, but at least I'll have done my best to make my peace with them. Tell me, have you seen or heard anything of them recently?'

'Not a thing – which is strange, as I usually notice quite a lot of visitors' carriages coming and going, along with chauffeur-driven vehicles. With us both using the back entrance of this house to avoid bumping into them, I haven't given them a great deal of thought lately.'

'I will go next door and see them before we set off for Ramsgate. It shouldn't take very long. Now, what is all this about?' Betty asked, nodding towards the paperwork on the table.

'If I tell you my plan, and I'll keep it short,' Hobby smiled, 'then you can contribute your own ideas. My bank manager and my solicitor both agree that I can afford to purchase a very nice little property without having to sell this place.'

Betty's chin almost hit the table. She did not have much idea about property and prices, but to think that Hobby had enough money to be able to own one property, let alone two, almost dumbfounded her. 'But how . . .' she started to ask, before realizing the question she most wished to ask was too personal.

'If you were going to ask how I can afford to be able to do what I've just mentioned, then I will explain. My dear and much-missed Mildred was a wealthy woman who, apart from a few bequests, left everything to me when she passed away. It had always been in my thoughts to do the same with the money she left me. Until now, the money has sat safely in my bank. As I told you last night, my own will was prepared some years ago when I wanted to leave something to the charming little girl who used to live next door to me. It has been a problem deciding what to do with the rest of the money, and now I know. This house can be rented out; we will take a few pieces of furniture and personal effects with us, but the rest can stay here. My solicitor is changing my will so that this house will now be yours. He will expect you to visit his office to sign some papers. I will use my late friend's money to buy the property in Ramsgate, where we can live quite happily; that's if we both decide we can get along in a new town once we've spent a few days there. When I pass away the new property will be sold, and that money will go to charity.'

Betty fell silent as she absorbed Hobby's words. Coals settled in the fire, and she heard the faint sound of a passing horse and cart on the road outside. This was a cosy house and she had come to love living here. With the heavy velvet drapes pulled close against the outside world, she felt safe and secure.

'But Hobby, my parents are quite wealthy and I'm their only child. Even though we're estranged, I may still inherit from them. I have never known such generosity and I'm truly grateful, but I feel you should be doing something else with the money from this house rather than handing it to me.' She sighed. 'One of the questions I want to ask my parents is about their will, and how I stand. I don't want to appear ungrateful, but it would be helpful to know whether I should expect anything from them in the future. Whatever they say, though, it won't affect my plans to move and take up my new position.'

'Then speak to them, my dear. However, my plans will remain the same. Hopefully you have a long life ahead of you, and regardless of what your parents may provide, I will stand by my decision to make you my heir. I don't intend to argue about it,' Hobby said gently, as Betty started to object.

'I'm truly grateful,' she replied before kissing Hobby's cheek, 'and I promise not to argue with you. Now, why don't I give you a hand organizing all of this paperwork?'

20

~

December 1918

Betty took a deep breath before knocking on the familiar front door. It felt strange visiting the house where she had lived for seventeen years. This time she knew for certain that she was a visitor, rather than someone with a claim to live in this grand home.

A young woman opened the door and frowned at her.

'Madam will certainly not accept visitors before eleven o'clock,' she said, primly eyeing Betty up and down, taking in her smart attire.

'Madam will see me, as I am the daughter of the house. Please tell your mistress I will wait in the drawing room,' Betty replied, stepping past the maid, who looked puzzled. She could hear Hobby's voice in her ear reminding her to start as she meant to go on. Inside she was quaking, but to anyone watching her, she would have appeared cool and collected. She'd planned exactly what she would say to her parents, almost to the point of being word-perfect, with Hobby suggesting what they might say in return and priming her with suitable replies.

Betty waited for ten minutes before debating whether to leave the house; she would not be toyed with by her parents. Nothing much had changed in the room, although there was a small double portrait hanging on one wall that Betty hadn't seen before: a severe-looking man with a woman by his side. She walked over to look at it more closely. Who were these people, she wondered?

A polite cough from the doorway alerted her that someone had come to see her. Turning, she saw that it was neither her mother nor her father. She glanced back at the painting on the wall, then at the man approaching her. Whatever was going on?

'Cousin Elizabeth,' he greeted her, 'I am Egbert, your second cousin on your father's side. You were but a child the last time we met.' He took her hand and shook it politely. 'My wife, Kitty, would have come down to greet you, but she is currently attending to your mother.'

Betty was confused. 'I'm sorry, you have me at a disadvantage. Is my mother poorly?' she asked, completely ignoring his greeting.

'I'm afraid so,' he said. 'As you were out of the country, there was no way we could contact you to let you know of your father's sudden death. Your mother has, understandably, taken it very badly; she hasn't been herself recently.'

Betty felt her head start to spin. 'I don't understand . . .' she said faintly as Egbert helped her to a nearby chair. 'At no time have I been out of the country. My parents knew where I worked – I felt it was my duty to advise them, even though we were not in contact,' she whispered. How could her father's death have passed unnoticed when she and Hobby were living next door? Hobby knew plenty of other people who lived in their road; surely someone would have mentioned it?

Egbert looked perturbed. 'Your father passed away quite suddenly seven weeks ago, at his office. Your mother wished the funeral to be a small, private affair, since the country was still at war; so apart from myself, my wife and his work colleagues, there were very few people present. He was interred in his family mausoleum in Oxford.'

Betty nodded slowly, digesting his words. That would be why no one was aware of a funeral cortège leaving the house, she thought. It was strange, though, that her father's death seemed to have gone unnoticed in a road where the Billingtons had lived for so long. And why had her mother not at least written or sent a message to Betty's place of work? 'Thank you, Egbert. I'm sorry that you and your wife have had to be here caring for my mother when it should have been my duty. If only I had known . . .'

'I am sorry you had to find out like this,' he said benignly. 'We seem to have been at cross purposes with information about your whereabouts.'

'I'd like to see my mother,' Betty said, getting to her feet, although she still felt quite unsteady. She grabbed the back of the chair and closed her eyes for a moment.

'My dear cousin, please sit and compose yourself – you've had a shock. I will inform your mother of your arrival, but you must prepare yourself; she may not be as you remember her. The doctor has been very concerned for her state of mind.'

Betty gave a weak smile. 'That is very kind of you. It's I who should be taking care of her – you must have your own home and work to attend to,' she said. She would have to cancel her plans to move to Ramsgate, she realized; her duty now lay with looking after her mother.

Egbert gave her a questioning look as he left the room.

Taking a few deep breaths, she got up and moved across to the window. Life outside was going on as usual. She spotted Hobby on the pavement talking to their milkman; no doubt cancelling deliveries while they were away. That would have to be changed now. She considered opening the window to call down, but thought better of it; whatever would her parents have said to her calling out like that? A smile crossed her lips before she reprimanded herself for the thought.

She waited for what seemed like a long time, circling the room restlessly and gazing at her mother's various ornaments and paintings, before she heard the sound of approaching footsteps.

A slight, blonde-haired woman hurried into the room and quickly embraced Betty. 'My dear girl, please allow me to give you my condolences on the sad loss of your father. The shock has made an invalid of your mother. I fear she will not be with us much longer.'

Betty set aside that worrying statement for a moment; she felt she ought to return the woman's embrace, even if she had never heard of her before today. 'I'm pleased to meet you,' she said, stepping back. 'Egbert no doubt explained that we haven't met before – or if we have, I must have been very young. I have few memories of my family.'

'Then we must make up for lost time. I insist that whenever you are in the area you visit and take tea with me.'

Betty was confused. 'But this is my family home. If Mother really is so unwell . . . if she does pass away . . . well, I would expect the house to come to me,' she said uncertainly. It crossed her mind that if this happened, she would have to insist that Hobby should change her will and leave her own property to someone else. The Billingtons' house would be more than enough for Betty to inherit. Although her heart ached a little at the thought of her mother presumably on her deathbed, it was difficult for her to feel as much sorrow as she would if Agatha had not rejected her so completely.

'Shall we sit down?' Kitty said as she led Betty to a chair before ringing a bell. 'A cup of tea may help,' she added, sitting down next to her and taking her hand. The maid who had answered the door appeared. 'Tea, please, Jenkins, and a little something to eat, as Miss Billington has had a shock.'

The maid bobbed a curtsy and left the room.

'I don't even recognize the maid,' Betty said with a catch to her voice, conscious of how unfamiliar her childhood home had become.

'Jenkins came with us when we moved here,' Kitty explained.

'I'm sorry – I don't understand,' Betty said, pulling back her hand. 'Would you please tell me exactly what is going on?'

'It should be Egbert who explains everything to you – he is your relative, after all. But as he's had to hurry back to his office, let me try to fill in everything that has happened since you left home to travel abroad.'

Betty was indignant. 'I have not been travelling abroad,

and nor did I ever suggest to my parents that I planned to do so. If you explain the situation here, I will explain what has been happening in my own life since I walked out of the front door last year.'

'Very well,' Kitty said, as the maid entered the room with a laden tea tray. She set it on a table beside her mistress. After she'd gone, Kitty continued, 'You must have some buttered toast before it goes cold. There is also strawberry jam; I made it myself this summer. Can I tempt you?'

'Just tea, please. You were about to tell me why you are here.'

Kitty took her time pouring the tea before settling back in her chair. 'First, I want to explain that I did insist my husband and your father should try to find you, as it was your right to know that your father had changed his will. I understand how important it is that a woman's future is secure, so that she has no need to rely on finding a suitable husband.'

'Is that what you did – marry to secure your future?' Betty asked, and then regretted the impertinent question. 'I'm sorry, I shouldn't have asked.'

Kitty gave a small smile, setting her teacup back in the saucer. 'I don't object to explaining my circumstances; after all, we are family. I had known Egbert for quite a long time before we married earlier this year. We attended the same church. I wouldn't say he pursued me as such, but after we had walked out together a few times, we developed an understanding. I hope you won't think too badly of me when I say I wasn't prepared to marry a man with no prospects. My early life was not easy, and I wanted more for myself than having to count every penny.' She glanced towards the closed door as if she expected her husband to appear.

'I'm a little ashamed to say that when Egbert informed me he had an appointment to see your father – and later said that he was going to help him find a suitable position in his office for when he inherited this house – it played a part in my decision to allow him to court me. I came alone to visit this street and looked at the house. I imagined living here, bringing up a family. However, I implored Egbert to find you, as it didn't seem right that the Billingtons' only daughter should become destitute while I gained so much. I was assured that you were out of the picture and well provided for, and that I shouldn't worry about you. Do you hate me for not insisting we find out more?'

Betty watched as Kitty's fingers tightened around the delicate china cup. It seemed as if the woman was sincere. 'I don't hate you,' she said with a sigh. 'How could I? It sounds as if you were as much a puppet in all of this as I am.'

'Please, do tell me all about your life and why your father removed you from his will. I'll help if I can . . . although . . .'

Betty was concerned. She like this fair-haired young woman, who could only be a few years older than herself. 'What are you worried about? I won't say a word to Egbert, if that is what concerns you.'

'No, Egbert is a good man; he would not be angry with me. It's just that I am carrying our first child. My fear of being left homeless keeps surfacing. When I was told you were downstairs, those thoughts came flooding back . . .'

'Goodness, no, I would not do such a thing,' Betty said.

252

Drawing a deep breath, she began to tell Kitty all about Charlie and how she had fallen out with her parents.

As Betty finished her story, Kitty shook her head with an amazed look on her face. 'If I hadn't heard it with my own ears, I wouldn't have believed a woman could go through so much. As for your parents – well, I'll just say that I'm not entirely surprised. I do have sympathy for your mother in her present condition, but she can be something of a . . .'

'Tyrant?'

Kitty nodded her head slowly, a small smile crossing her face. 'Yes, that is the word I was thinking of.' She sat up straight, setting down her cup and saucer. 'What shall we do next, Betty? Would you like to stay with us?'

'It is very kind of you to ask, but I'll decline your offer, as I don't feel my mother would be happy with my being here,' Betty replied, looking at the ornamental clock on the mantelpiece. 'I will have to leave shortly as a motor car is coming to take me and Miss Hobson to Ramsgate.'

'On the next leg of your adventure. Oh, how I envy you,' Kitty said.

'Just as I envy you and Egbert,' Betty said. 'If Charlie had not perished on the battlefield I might well have been welcoming our first child soon, just as you are.' She allowed herself to imagine for a moment the life they'd planned, living over their own little grocery shop after marrying, looking ahead to a happy future. She gave herself a shake. 'It doesn't help to dwell on things that will never happen. I am happy that I've coped with what life has thrown my way. I shouldn't grumble – there are many worse off than me.'

253

Kitty gave her a gentle hug as she got up to leave. 'Please will you write to me once you're settled in Ramsgate? I'd enjoy following your adventures. Until then, please do visit, as I'd like to think we will be good friends.'

'Of course I will, but it won't be until January that I start my new position and age by five years,' Betty laughed.

'I'm sure you will carry it off admirably,' Kitty said, joining in with her laughter.

'When I return from my travels I will visit and tell you all about Ramsgate and my lodgings . . .' Betty stopped as a thought crossed her mind. 'What about my mother? Do you think she will approve of my visiting, or will you keep it a secret from her?'

Kitty took Betty's hand. 'Come with me. Don't you think it would be a good idea to see her?'

Betty pulled back, but Kitty held her hand imploringly. 'I don't think . . .'

'Please trust me,' Kitty begged as she led Betty up the wide staircase to the master bedroom on the first floor. Without knocking, she ushered Betty into the room.

'Agatha? Are you awake?' she asked, drawing back the heavy curtains to let grey winter light into the room.

Betty gasped at the sight of her mother, pale and gaunt, lying against the snow-white pillows. 'Mother . . . ?'

Agatha Billington squinted at her before an angry look crossed her face. 'Has that girl brought my dinner yet? She's getting later and later. Tell my husband to take her into the yard and thrash her. I won't have slovenly behaviour in my household,' she said, raising her voice with each word spoken.

'Mother, it is me, your daughter. Elizabeth,' Betty said. She stepped cautiously towards the angry, confused woman.

Kitty tried to pull Betty back as she approached the bedside to take her mother's hand. The woman lashed out, scratching Betty's face. 'Get away from me, you harlot. I no longer have a daughter. Now where is my dinner?'

Betty backed away and lifted a hand to her cheek before turning and stumbling out onto the landing, tears welling up in her eyes. Who was this monster in her mother's clothes? Behind her, through the half-open door, she could hear Kitty placating the confused woman.

'Come along, Agatha, let's get you settled. It isn't time for dinner just yet. I'll give you a little of your sleeping draught and you can rest until lunchtime.'

'You're a good girl,' Betty heard her mother say. That was too much and she ran downstairs to the drawing room, where she dropped into a chair and tried to compose herself. Kitty joined her a little while later, carrying a bowl of water and a cloth.

'Here, let me see to that scratch. I'm afraid I should have warned you. Your mother tends to lash out when she becomes distressed.'

'Which is often?' Betty asked, noticing for the first time that there were one or two faded marks on Kitty's face, too. 'You shouldn't be dealing with her alone, especially not in your condition. What if she hurts your baby?'

'We have a nurse who sits with Agatha and tends to her needs; unfortunately she has been delayed today. I've given her something so that she can rest. We can manage, believe me,' Kitty assured her as she started to dab at the mark on Betty's face.

'What exactly is wrong with her?'

'She had not been well for a little while before your

father's death. It was all so sudden. His collapse seemed to exacerbate her condition. Dr Stapleton told us it was a condition of the brain, and nothing could be done for her. All we can do is care for her and keep her warm and fed. She has lucid moments, but they are getting fewer.'

'I'm sorry I've not been here to help you,' Betty whispered, her heart aching for the mother she had never really known.

'And I'm sorry we didn't try harder to find you,' Kitty replied as she gently patted Betty's cheek dry. 'Life can be so unfair.'

'To think I've been hiding away next door all this time. It sounds ridiculous to even say such a thing.' Betty managed a trembling smile.

'Believe me, Betty, there have been times when I've wished I lived next door too,' Kitty said wryly.

They looked at each other for a moment, then burst out laughing.

'Oh, dear, it's wrong to laugh, but you must admit it's quite farcical. We could have bumped into each other at any time.'

'Very true, but we wouldn't have known each other and would have kept on walking,' Betty said, trying to keep a straight face and failing. 'Oh, dear; I do apologize,' she added, wiping tears of laughter from her eyes.

'Let me call for fresh tea,' Kitty suggested as they recovered themselves.

'As much I'd love to stay and talk, I really must be going. I have much to do before the car arrives. I would hate to hold Richard up after he kindly offered to drive us to the coast.'

'Richard? You did not mention him when you told me about your life since leaving home.'

Betty knew she should have objected to Kitty assuming that the mention of a man's name meant there was a possible romance. However, she liked her new cousin far too much to be offended. 'That is a story for another day, dear cousin,' she replied, giving her a hug. 'Here, this is where we will be staying, and if there is . . . if there's anything you need me for, please do telephone immediately.' She handed over a card with the name of the Ramsgate guesthouse where she and Hobby had reserved rooms.

Kitty nodded her head, understanding exactly what Betty meant. 'Rest assured we will never lose touch again.'

21

'Are you sure you still want to take our trip to Ramsgate? We can easily change our plans and wait a day or two until you feel more up to it. It would mean taking the train, but so be it,' Hobby said as she stirred an extra spoonful of sugar into a mug of hot tea before sliding it across the kitchen table to Betty.

'I'll be fine once I've drunk this tea.'

'I want you to eat something as well,' Hobby scolded her. 'We can't travel all the way down there with you looking like death warmed up – and no arguments,' she added as Betty began to object. She quickly fried an egg and put it between two thick slices of heavily buttered bread before cutting it in two. 'Hmm . . . I think I'll join you,' she said, cracking another egg into the frying pan.

Betty smiled. Hobby did like her food. Despite thinking she couldn't eat a thing after the distressing visit to her parents' house, she'd soon left nothing except a few crumbs on her plate. 'I did enjoy that, thank you.'

'You've got a bit of colour in your cheeks now,' Hobby smiled. 'Are you still prepared to head for Ramsgate, or should we put it off for a day or so until you feel more the ticket?'

'If we put off the trip it is highly unlikely I'll be able to get any more time off work. The store is already getting busy, which does surprise me.'

Hobby raised her eyebrows. 'Why are you surprised?'

'Perhaps I'm being selfish, but I honestly thought that with so many bereaved families mourning their loved ones now war has ended, many women would not wish to celebrate Christmas. I thought that meant the store would be quieter. Then of course there's the Spanish flu . . .'

Hobby was thoughtful. 'Did you not tell me how busy the household goods counter has been, with shoppers clamouring for things to clean their homes to ward off the flu?'

A sad expression flitted across Betty's face. 'It doesn't seem to be working, going by the newspaper headlines. Did you know they're saying the soldiers have brought this back with them from the front?'

Hobby shrugged her shoulders. 'Wherever it came from, it seems to be here now, and we need to be vigilant regardless of all the old wives' tales. I hear people are purchasing onions by the sackload as they're supposed to be a strong deterrent against illness. Who'd have thought it?'

'How strange, but it does explain why we keep selling out of onions. I wonder what they do with them?'

'By all accounts they chop them up and hang them around their necks in muslin bags,' Hobby laughed. 'But, getting back to Christmas, I hear tell that some people like visiting Woolworths just because it cheers them up. Even if they can only purchase something small, the women I meet want to make the most of the season. It is, after all, our first peacetime Christmas for quite a few years. Now, let's get ourselves organized and go to Ramsgate today. The bracing sea air will blow the cobwebs away, and hopefully the Spanish flu with them.'

'We can only hope so,' Betty replied. 'Also, we cannot let Richard down when he has been so generous in offering to take us. At least we don't have to carry our heavy luggage to and from the railway stations,' she grinned. Mentioning the railway made her think of the Sayers family. 'I must write to Olive and let the Sayers all know what has happened, and where they can find me once we move.'

'Why not send them a funny postcard from the seaside? I've received a few myself and they do make me chuckle.'

Betty wasn't so sure the Sayers family would like to know she was enjoying herself at the seaside. She'd seen a few of the risqué cards Hobby's friends sent to her, and they had made her blush. Perhaps a view of the sands and a message to say she was there on business would be more suitable. 'Come on; let's clear up the kitchen before Richard comes knocking.'

'Who in their right mind takes a trip to the seaside at this time of the year? Look at the rain; I reckon it's going to turn to sleet, possibly snow,' Hobby huffed as she dragged her suitcase to the hall, leaving it just inside the front door. 'I'm only glad your young— I mean, Richard has offered to drive, rather than us having to catch a train.'

Betty raised her eyebrows. Hobby still kept calling Richard her young man. She wouldn't be surprised if the woman was doing it on purpose. She decided to ignore Hobby whenever she did this; then, just perhaps, she would desist. 'It looks as though you've brought along the kitchen sink,' she commented, eyeing her friend's large suitcase.

'We are only away for four days. Are you sure you need as much as that?'

'You never know. The weather is so changeable at this time of year.'

'Do you mean it might snow rather than rain?' Betty laughed as she opened the door. 'Here comes Richard now. I'll carry your case out; we don't want you hurting yourself, do we?'

'I'm not that old and decrepit yet,' Hobby laughed as she lifted the case and started down the path towards the road.

'I'll take that, thank you,' Richard said, hurrying to relieve her. 'It does a man's image no good to see a lady carry a suitcase while he stands idly by.'

'I'll have you know I believe a woman can do as well as a man any day,' Hobby was quick to reply, although she let him take the case and thanked him for doing so. 'I shall repay you in another way. Perhaps you would dine with us?'

'I would be honoured,' Richard replied as he took Betty's smaller case and settled the two women in their seats, handing them tartan blankets to wrap over their laps. 'I can highly recommend a fish and chip restaurant on the seafront not far from your guesthouse.'

'That sounds perfect. We shall arrange that for tomorrow evening. I'm sure none of us will feel like eating much after being bumped about for hours on end during the journey.'

Richard pretended to be offended. 'Madam, please do not judge my driving. You will find the journey akin to floating on a cloud.'

As Betty snorted with laughter, Hobby muttered something unrepeatable.

*

'I must eat my words,' Hobby declared as Richard's motor car entered the town of Ramsgate. 'That was a most pleasant journey. Most pleasant indeed.'

'Aided by the splendid picnic you packed for us, Richard, but you really shouldn't have done.'

'Nonsense, Betty. We made better time by not stopping to find a place along the way for lunch. That's one of the joys of motoring: pulling over on a country lane to enjoy the view while dipping into a picnic basket.'

'It was quite cosy, nibbling on your cousin's delicious pies while watching the rain fall – and not one leak from the roof. Unlike our outhouse in bad weather,' Hobby said, rubbing the misted window with the cuff of her coat to peer out at the view. 'My goodness, is that the sea?'

'It most certainly is; and just up this next road is the guesthouse where we have rooms,' Betty said, as she recognized the street she'd travelled down with Richard previously. 'This is it, Albion Road. I must say these houses look in better condition than many of the buildings we've passed.'

'The town suffered terribly during the war. So many buildings were destroyed, and lives lost.'

'Who would have thought it could happen in a little seaside town?' Hobby said, in awe as they passed a row of bomb-damaged houses.

'I thought the same until I saw how this town had suffered. I honestly thought the enemy had only attacked London or were fighting our armies overseas. I really should have read the newspapers more,' Betty said, looking glum. 'I can't help thinking I've let other women down by not acting more like a man – devouring newspapers and talking about the war.'

'For goodness' sake, Betty, surely you've learnt something living with me and meeting some of my friends this past year?' Hobby tutted. 'My friends in the suffrage movement simply wish to be equal to men, with equal rights. We have no wish to be *like* men. You were young when the war started, and you were guided by your father. I'll not speak ill of the dead and blame him for closeting you away, but if the truth be known, your parents did not educate you as they should have in world matters.'

'I'm sorry – I had no idea you had lost your father,' Richard put in as he parked the car in front of a smart-looking guesthouse overlooking the sea. 'From what you told me recently, I understood your parents to be living next door to Miss Hobson's house.'

'I only found out myself this morning,' Betty replied as she prepared to alight from the vehicle. 'I'll tell you all about it later on; but Miss Hobson is fully aware of the situation.'

Richard hurried round to open the door for her. 'Well, please accept my condolences,' he said. 'You seem to have had quite a day already.'

'You could say that,' Betty smiled as she helped him to unstrap the suitcases from the rear of the vehicle. 'I never thought to ask – are you staying at your family home, or will you be lodging here in town?'

'At the moment I'm staying with my in-laws, to be close to my children. It all depends on whether I stay on as manager of this store. But don't worry,' he said, seeing the look on her face. 'No matter what I do, your position as supervisor here is secure.'

'Thank goodness for that,' Hobby said as she checked they were ready to enter the guesthouse. 'I'd hate for us both to have upped sticks and moved here, only to find Betty without a job. I've taken a fancy to living by the sea, so you'd best make a good job of running the store so as not to inconvenience us all,' she sniffed. 'Now come along; let us get settled in, so that Richard can be on his way to his family. As it is, he'll be driving in the dark – and we don't want that after he's been so kind in bringing us here.'

Richard gave Betty a puzzled look as they followed Hobby into the guesthouse. 'Miss Hobson is moving here?'

'I'll have to explain that later too,' Betty smiled before thanking him for his help.

'I'll be in the store tomorrow, if you'd like to come in and meet some of the staff. I hope you will be very happy here, Betty,' he said, giving her hand a friendly squeeze.

'So much has changed for me in the past couple of days – I feel as though I should pinch myself to check I'm not dreaming,' she replied, before watching him return to his vehicle and drive off. Entering the small but comfortable guesthouse, she gave a sigh. For all the exciting things that were happening in her life, she would give it all up tomorrow just to have Charlie by her side.

The next morning Betty rose early and managed to make use of the shared bathroom before the other guests were awake. She tidied her room, not wishing a maid to have to clean up after her, and decided on a brisk walk before breakfast; she had half an hour before she met Hobby in the dining room.

Albion Place gave a commanding view of the area. She paused in front of the property, wondering which way to head. They would be visiting the town today, so she decided to walk in the opposite direction, past a grand building that looked out over the sea. It looked like a hotel, and Betty was inquisitive enough to stay on the pavement and pass it closely rather than crossing the road towards the beach. As she went past a door swung open in front of her and, rather than guests exiting the building, she spotted several nurses assisting soldiers who looked to be injured in one way or another. One had his head bandaged with only one eye showing; another was limping, relying on a walking stick and leaning heavily on the arm of a nurse. A third was being wheeled in a chair. They spotted Betty and waited while she passed, all wishing her a good morning.

'Thank you,' she replied. 'It is rather a chilly one, but at least we don't have the rain we had yesterday. It must be lovely here in the summer months.'

'It is,' one of the nurses replied, while the man in the wheelchair remarked that he hoped not to be there by the time summer came along. 'Hopefully I'll be back home by then,' he said politely, raising his cap.

Betty lingered for a moment. 'May I ask where home is?' she asked, noticing the man's accent wasn't local.

'Canada, ma'am,' he replied. 'Josh and Jim here are from Ontario, while I hail from Toronto. My name is Bill.'

'That is a long way from home.'

'We hoped to be shipped back by Christmas. It will be a joy to see our families again,' the man called Josh replied. 'It's been far too long.'

'I wish you well. Godspeed,' Betty said, her eyes filling with tears. Meeting these brave soldiers had touched her deeply. Who knew – under different circumstances, her

Charlie could have been the one recovering in a foreign land, looking forward to being home with his loved ones.

'Hey, why the tears? There's no need to feel sorry for us,' Bill said, looking concerned. He nodded to Josh, who limped over to Betty and took her arm. 'Can we offer you a shoulder to cry on?'

Betty dabbed at her eyes and gave them a grateful smile. 'Please don't worry about me. You must take care of yourselves and get home to your loved ones.' She couldn't shake the thought of Charlie from her mind and without thinking, slid her hand up to the lapel of her coat.

Bill looked at the brooch pinned there, then back to Betty, drawing his own conclusions. 'You have my sympathy,' he said politely. 'Your husband?'

The other men stopped their conversation and looked her way as concern crossed their faces.

'And you no more than a child,' Josh, the older of the three, said sympathetically. 'This war has left far too many pretty young women weeping for their loved ones.'

'It was my fiancé. He died at Ypres in the August of 1917.'

The soldiers exchanged glances before Josh spoke again. 'You have our sympathies. It was a bloody battle, with many fine men lost.'

Betty glanced at her bare left hand. 'I call Charlie my fiancé, but really I never got to wear his ring. He was going to put one on my finger when he returned . . . but it wasn't to be. I only have this brooch. It denotes his regiment, the Royal West Kent,' she explained as they took a closer look.

One of the nurses stepped forward to see it, too. 'West Kent? Then you aren't a local?'

Betty was touched by their genuine interest. 'I live in south-east London. But I will be moving here soon, to work at the Woolworths store in the high street. I'm visiting for a few days just now, hoping to find somewhere suitable to live.' She shivered as a biting breeze swept in from the sea.

'Hey, we can't have this young lady freezing to death when she's been friendly enough to stop and talk with three foreigners visiting her homeland. Turn us around, ladies; let's invite her in and give her some tea. You do drink tea, don't you?'

Betty chuckled as she put her handkerchief away in her pocket. 'I would be delighted to join you for a cup of tea.'

Inside the building, she gasped at the large sitting room they were led to. High ceilings, elaborate cornices and imposing works of art adorned the hotel – which, she was informed, was currently being used as a temporary hospital and convalescent home for Canadian soldiers. 'What must this place have been like before the war?' she wondered aloud.

'A darn sight quieter,' Josh said.

'And very much tidier,' one of the nurses joined in, as she fussed about the three soldiers making them comfortable. 'I knew the building before it was taken over for the war. It was certainly a grand place. Not everywhere in Ramsgate is the same, but I hope you'll find somewhere nice to live.'

Betty thanked her as an orderly arrived with pots of tea and coffee. The men asked her to join them for breakfast but she declined, explaining that she had to meet a friend for a meal.

'I had no idea there were Woolworths stores over here,' Bill commented as he poured Betty's tea. 'Gents, we must

267

pay a visit so that when we go home, we can tell our wives and mothers we have something in common with the fine people of England.'

'We could buy some gifts there to take back,' Josh said enthusiastically. 'Ladies,' he said turning to the nurses. 'Ladies, will you escort us down to the town to visit Betty working in her Woolworths store?'

As the nurses agreed with their wishes, Betty was quick to clarify. 'I won't be starting there until the new year – and by then you will all be safely back at home in Canada. However, I'm sure the staff will make you welcome,' she said, hoping that was indeed the truth, as she had yet to meet her new colleagues.

The conversation turned to the work the men hoped to return to once home. Only one of them, Josh, worked in retail. 'Tell me the position you will be taking up when you start with your new branch?'

'I'm to be a supervisor on the shop floor; at the moment I am a counter assistant at a larger branch in Woolwich, which is on the borders of London. It was one of the first branches to open in England.'

Josh looked interested. 'Goodness, you seem very young to have a supervisory job. How do you feel about super-vising staff members older than yourself? I hope that question doesn't worry you,' he added with a smile.

'No, not at all. You're only voicing my own fears,' she said, and looked down into her lap, unsure of how frank she should be. It wouldn't hurt, surely, to see what these kind men thought? 'I've been advised to add five years to my age . . .'

He considered this for a moment. 'Yes, I can see how

that might help,' he said, without asking her current age. 'How do you think the other members of staff will assess your age?'

'Goodness, I'd never given that a thought. I suppose the way I dress and wear my hair will play a part . . . I could put my hair up a little more severely?' she suggested, glancing towards the three nurses for advice.

The youngest of the three replied, 'That would help, but I've always felt my superiors have a certain businesslike manner that only grows with experience and age. I'm not saying they aren't friendly,' she added quickly, looking to her colleagues for support.

The two women agreed, with the older one adding, 'Yes, it would be more your attitude that makes you appear older and in command. Also – although I'm sorry to say this, with you having not long lost your fiancé – a ring on your finger would make a difference . . .'

Betty looked down at her bare fingers. 'It could cause too many problems if I suddenly began wearing a wedding band. I would also need to add "Mrs" to my name, which is a lie too far for my liking.'

'How about an engagement ring?' Josh suggested. When Betty looked at him he added gently, 'After all, if Charlie had returned safely, you would be wearing one by now.'

The young nurse clapped her hands in delight. 'That would be ideal – and in a way it would still bond you to your fiancé, as I'm sure he would have chosen a ring that you like.'

Betty thought for a moment. 'You are right, but surely they're awfully expensive? It's not something I know much about.'

The nurse pulled a notebook from her pocket and scribbled a few words before tearing out the page and passing it to Betty. 'This is the name of a small jeweller's in the High Street. He sells second-hand jewellery as well as new pieces. Next door there is a pawnbroker's shop. You should be able to find something suitable in one of those.'

Betty gave a little shudder at the memory of her last visit to a pawnshop, but was sensible enough to know it was unlikely she would be robbed a second time. Her hand strayed back to the sweetheart brooch. Yes, many women who had lost a loved one wore them, but while in uniform she wasn't allowed to wear a brooch. A ring on her finger would still show she'd had a fiancé. It was a perfect solution. 'Thank you, I will do as you advise,' she said gratefully.

'Don't forget you should also carry an air of authority,' Josh reminded her.

That won't be a problem, Betty thought to herself. I am not my mother's daughter for nothing. I will transform myself into Agatha Billington, although I'll still be pleasant rather than harsh.

Promising to visit the men before she left Ramsgate, she thanked them profusely and hurried back to the guesthouse, where Hobby would by now be expecting her.

22

'There you are,' Hobby said, as Betty hurried into the dining room. 'I was about to ask someone to check your room. Wherever have you been?'

Betty quickly gave the hovering waitress her order and thanked her before taking a sip of the tea Hobby had poured into her cup. 'I went for a quick walk,' she said, going on to explain about meeting the Canadian soldiers. 'What do you think? Should I buy myself a ring? Will it make me appear older?'

Hobby was silent as she absorbed Betty's excited words. 'My first thought is that you will be opening a can of worms. I wasn't keen on Richard's idea to suddenly age you by five years; so much could go wrong.'

'In what way?' Betty asked, as the waitress returned with two plates of egg and bacon. 'This looks delicious,' she smiled at the young woman. She could quite easily get used to living in a guesthouse, she thought; it was lovely being waited on hand and foot. The plush surroundings and comfortable rooms felt safe and welcoming.

'In that if you pretend to be a different age, it will only take one member of staff to check the employee records

271

and discover you have told a lie. That could have far-reaching consequences. Why would Woolworths employ a liar?'

'Goodness, I'd not thought of that and I doubt Richard had either. I'm sure he isn't one to make up stories willy-nilly.'

Hobby raised her eyebrows. 'Well, I can't speak for Richard, as I haven't known him for long. Neither have you, come to that. I only know that you're not one to fabricate such details.'

Betty stopped eating and looked shamefaced. 'When you put it like that . . .'

'I don't wish to spoil your excitement about this new job, but lies can start to grow and take on a life of their own. You would have to be so careful. Besides . . .'

'Besides what?'

'Any undertaking founded on a bed of lies can all too easily crumble and come crashing down onto your head. You are better than that; you are a personable young woman who enjoys her work and tries to help others. Staff working beneath you in the store have no need to know about your private life; they are there to work, and you are there to guide them.'

'I can see your point, but I still miss Charlie so terribly and I thought that if I wore a ring, it would also help to ward off any advances from men. Please don't raise your eyebrows at me like that – I would never wear a wedding band – but surely a small, simple ring that showed I was engaged would give me a form of status?'

'Would your colleagues not ask about your intended?'

'Then I would tell them that he was killed at Ypres. I

am so terribly proud Charlie gave his life for his country – all these months on, I can talk about him more easily without bursting into tears.'

'I can see you have decided on wearing a ring, so I'll not argue with you. Once we've eaten, I want you to look at this. The envelope was dropped off earlier.'

'That looks intriguing,' Betty said, noticing for the first time a large envelope on the table close to Hobby's plate. 'Are these the details of our potential new home?'

'They are indeed. I've taken a quick look, and the agent has done well. There are details of six properties within my price range. I suggest we finish our breakfast and order a fresh pot of tea. We can decide which ones suit our needs, then arrange to view them. Perhaps while we're out and about, we can visit that pawnbroker you mentioned,' she said, which caused Betty to grin. 'Mind you, the weather isn't very good, so we will need to wrap up warm and do our best to keep dry.'

Betty gazed out of a window. It was now raining hard. 'Another pot of tea sounds good,' she said, trying to remember if she had packed her umbrella.

'If I have to view any more properties, I swear I'll scream,' Hobby said as she collapsed into her chair inside the quaint teashop on the harbour front.

'Be grateful for small mercies. At least the rain eased off and we did see some wonderful houses. There were several I'd gladly move into tomorrow,' Betty said as she raised her hand to catch a waitress's eye. 'I do wish we'd been able to look around them on our own. Meeting the agents was tiring. They both seemed so keen.'

'I suppose we can't blame them. I doubt they've sold many properties during wartime. The gentleman who showed us around the first three properties told me that home-buyers and holidaymakers have kept away since the Zeppelin raids in 1915.'

'One of the early casualties was the hotel that stood where the Woolworths store is now. Richard told me it was a very popular business. I wonder why it wasn't rebuilt, rather than Woolworths purchasing the land it stood on.'

Hobby shrugged her shoulders. 'No doubt some man in management decided it would be beneficial to sell off the land. Perhaps he feared the building would be hit again. That's men for you,' she huffed as she looked at the menu. 'The full afternoon tea for me, dear,' she said to the waitress. 'What about you?'

'I'll have the same, thank you,' Betty said, handing back the menu. 'Could we have extra hot water with the tea, please?' she asked, knowing how Hobby enjoyed three cups of tea with her food.

'Promise me something,' Hobby said, giving Betty a stern look.

'Goodness, where did that come from?' Betty asked with a laugh.

'Promise me that when you are in management, you will not act like some of these men who make such daft decisions.'

Betty knew it was better to humour Hobby when she made such comments, and promised she would think before she acted. 'Which was your favourite property?'

Hobby rummaged in her large leather handbag and pulled out the paperwork she'd been sent earlier. 'There were two that caught my eye, but I narrowed it down to one, as the smaller house was too close to the girls' school. It would drive me up the wall having screaming young ladies walking past my home all the time.'

Betty knew at once which property Hobby was referring to and agreed, although she thought it was a cosy home.

'It smelt of cats as well,' Hobby sniffed, tearing the details into four pieces.

'I would be happy with any of them, but I'm hoping you liked the house in Guildford Lawn,' Betty said, crossing her fingers under the table. The Regency house was on four floors and just around the corner from a rather impressive library building.

'Indeed I do. Although I almost tore up the details when that agent asked why my husband was not accompanying us.'

Betty grimaced. That must have been when she'd walked outside to admire the garden and left Hobby alone with the pompous young man. 'My goodness, whatever did you say to him?'

'I fell back on an excuse I've used often in the past. I told him the major was at home with gout and as I was an heiress in my own right, I had no need to discuss my purchase with my husband,' she chuckled. 'I did imply that the house would be my pied à terre, where I would entertain privately . . .'

'You are shocking,' Betty admonished her as the waitress appeared with a tea tray. 'Now behave yourself,' she said, nodding towards the young waitress. 'Excuse my elderly aunt,' she said with a twinkle in her eye. 'She likes to shock.'

The girl simply bobbed a curtsy and hurried away.

'That'll give her something to talk about with her friends. A scarlet woman taking afternoon tea,' Hobby said, letting out a loud belly laugh.

'What happens next?' Betty asked, keen to move Hobby on to a safe topic. 'Does it take long to purchase a property?'

'It won't take long at all. I made it clear to both agents that I would only look at properties that were vacant and could be moved into by the time you start work at Woolworths in January. If need be, we can rent until the paperwork is completed.'

'But what about your home in Charlton? Surely we will need to arrange for everything to be boxed up and moved down here. It will take so much time,' Betty said, wondering how she would manage to help Hobby sort out a lifetime's worth of clutter. The woman never threw anything away. 'I can help you after work each evening.'

'There's no need. This is where friends come in handy. Besides, I'm going to rent it out to Gladys Singleton fully furnished.'

Betty was confused. She knew Hobby had been thinking of renting her property, but why fully furnished? 'Won't you need furniture in the new house?'

'Don't you worry about a thing. I'm leaving enough sticks of furniture behind for Gladys to be comfortable, and I'll be taking the rest with me. We will need more, but it will be fun to find new furniture and furnishings here.'

Betty felt a thrill of excitement run through her. Hobby was quite bohemian in her tastes, and it would be fun to accompany her on shopping expeditions.

'Now eat up, as we have to purchase your engagement ring before the shops close.'

A crash of crockery and cutlery hitting the floor indicated the waitress had been listening to them.

Betty entered the Woolworths store, thinking how different it was from when she had visited before. Even with the inclement weather, the store was busy. No different to the Woolwich branch, Betty thought, as she showed Hobby some of the counters before they went through the door marked 'staff only'.

Betty waited at the top of the staircase until Hobby had caught her breath. 'The office is just here,' she said, worried that her friend looked rather red in the face. She tapped on the door and was relieved when she heard Richard's command to enter. Hobby's jitters had affected her.

'Hello,' Richard said, springing to his feet to assist them into the room. 'Have you enjoyed your first day in Ramsgate?' he asked, offering them both a seat.

'We have, and Hobby has found us the perfect home,' Betty said as she looked round the room. She had never seen so much clutter, and she itched to be able to sort out the room and put everything shipshape. She should ask Richard if her duties included doing any office work.

'Betty has something to show you,' Hobby said as she opened her coat, flapping her hand in front of her face to cool down. 'Don't be shy, love,' she said to Betty.

'What is it, Betty?' he asked as she shyly looked down into her lap.

Pulling off her glove Betty held up her left hand and showed him the dainty diamond solitaire ring on her ring finger. The pawnbroker had assured her it was tasteful and worth the extra money he'd wanted from her. 'It will last for many years,' he'd told her which made Betty shudder knowing it was not being worn for the right reason.

'An engagement ring?' Richard asked looking puzzled.

'We thought, rather than increase my age as you suggested, it would be better for me to wear a ring to show I am betrothed. If anyone enquires about the ring, I can explain how I lost Charlie at Ypres before we could marry, and I will never marry another. It will give me more gravitas as a supervisor to have had a past.'

Richard looked disappointed. 'Would it not be thought strange if you should meet another man who wishes to marry you?'

'Who knows what the future may bring?' Hobby said, watching Richard closely. 'The same could be said about you, lad.'

Richard stood up from behind his desk. 'I'll arrange for some tea to be brought in. You look as though you could do with a cup. I know I could,' he said, without waiting for an answer.

'So, I was right in what I thought . . .'

'What are you talking about?' Betty asked as she put her glove back on. She felt uncomfortable with the ring on view. Perhaps in time she would get used to wearing it.

'He has designs on you. The lad needs a mother for his children and no doubt a woman who can give him more kiddies. You mark my words, he brought you to Ramsgate for a reason.'

'Don't be daft,' Betty snapped back. 'We are friends and nothing more. Richard noticed I had potential to be a supervisor and saw an opening for me to advance my career.'

'The only career he sees for you is to wear his ring. Why

else do you think he blanched like that when he saw what was on your finger? Just be careful, my dear girl. You could lose everything by becoming chained to a man for the wrong reasons.'

Betty fell silent and was still contemplating Hobby's words when Richard returned to the office. She knew that her friend was different and would never marry, but why was she acting like this? Betty had made it clear to her over and over again that Charlie was the only man she would ever love. Richard was a good friend and nothing more.

Wanting to lighten the heavy atmosphere in the room, she gave a small cough. 'I wonder if you could tell me a little more about my duties. Will they be entirely on the shop floor, or could I help in the office?'

Richard gave her one of his charming smiles. 'A supervisor's duties would normally be on the shop floor, but as I am newly in charge here – and, as the saying goes, "a new broom sweeps clean" – I can't see why you shouldn't spend an hour or two each day assisting me. As you can see, there is a lot to sort out. My predecessor was a little tardy with his filing.'

Betty's heart fluttered with happiness as she gave him a big smile. She would learn all she could while working at this small store. Then if the day came for her to return to the Woolwich branch, or any other, for that matter, she would be armed with even more skills. 'I'd like that very much,' she said before glancing at Hobby, who stayed silent but whose look spoke a thousand words.

Later on, Betty could only look back on the days spent in Ramsgate as a blur of activity. She accompanied Hobby when papers were signed to get their house purchase rolling, and to a different house where the departing owner had items of furniture for sale. A country house sale just outside town had them snapping up curtains and bedroom furniture. Hobby also secured a stuffed boar's head, which she declared would look splendid in the dining room. Betty wasn't so sure it wouldn't put them off their food.

She spent an afternoon at the Woolworths store, getting to know her staff and fellow supervisors. Although Hobby and Richard were not keen on the idea of Betty's engagement ring, she found it helped to command a certain respect from the older staff and a sense of awe from the younger counter girls. Pinning her hair into a more severe bun at the nape of her neck, she felt both capable in her duties and a little more confident for her age.

'You seem to have been a success, just as I thought you would,' Richard said as she collected her coat at the end of the day and stopped in at his office to say goodnight.

'I've enjoyed myself. And I've already thought of a few ways we might make changes on the counters, to ease queues and take some of the pressure off our staff.'

'Our staff?' Richard grinned.

'Woolworths' staff, I mean,' Betty blushed. 'I apologize if I've spoken out of turn.'

He rose and walked round his desk to where she stood, taking both her hands. 'Betty, I knew from the moment I interviewed you that you would be an asset to this company. You are bright, friendly and full of excellent ideas. I can't think of a better person to work with me here.'

'I'm not sure about that,' Betty blushed.

'In fact, I don't know what I'd do without you,' he said, stepping closer to gently kiss her lips.

Betty froze, and was about to pull away when thoughts of Charlie and his wonderful kisses came flooding back to her. She closed her eyes, imagining she was in Charlie's arms. Her lips opened slightly as a feeling of contentment washed over her.

Richard let go of her hands and enveloped her in his arms. 'You have no idea how long I've waited to do this,' he murmured in her ear.

His words broke the spell. It wasn't Charlie kissing her – it was Richard. She wriggled out of his grasp. 'I'm sorry, Richard. I'll see you in the morning,' she said hastily, grabbing her coat and bag and rushing from the office.

Outside in the street, she stopped to pull on her coat and gloves. It was dark and an icy rain was starting to fall. 'Oh Charlie, I miss you so much,' she said quietly, as her tears blended with the rain running down her face.

Would it always be like this? Would she always be seeking memories of the man she loved? She stopped to look out over the harbour, which was lit by only a few lights from the fishing boats seeking shelter. Spotting a nearby bench, she sat down, oblivious to the rain and deep in thought. Would it hurt if she encouraged Richard?

The rain fell relentlessly, and eventually she put her head down and hurried back to the guesthouse. She'd left her umbrella in Richard's office, and she couldn't face him again after what had just happened. It was bad enough that he was driving them back to London tomorrow. At least Hobby would be with her in his vehicle, and she could pretend to sleep for most of the journey. However, before long she would be seeing him every day and working alongside him. How would she cope?

'Look at the state of you,' Hobby declared as Betty ran into the foyer of the guesthouse holding a copy of the *Evening News* over her head. A man had taken pity on her and offered his evening paper as she'd waited to cross the busy road in front of the harbour. 'Why did you not use your umbrella?'

'It's in Richard's office,' she replied, taking an already sodden handkerchief from her pocket and wiping her face.

Hobby frowned. 'Why, it's been raining all afternoon. You should have gone back to collect it before you left the store.'

'I never gave it a thought,' Betty said, unable to meet Hobby's eyes.

Hobby huffed suspiciously. 'I'm not sure you are telling me everything . . .'

Betty was relieved when the owner of the guesthouse appeared. 'Oh, Miss Billington, you must get out of those wet clothes. The bathroom is free, and there is plenty of hot water for a bath. You get yourself upstairs and have a long hot soak before you catch your death. If you leave your coat and clothes outside the door, I'll have them hung in our laundry room. They will be dry and ready to wear again by the morning. You have an hour before the dinner gong sounds.'

Betty thanked her profusely and hurried away. Already she was starting to shiver, and her head was throbbing. What she would feel like by morning, she did not know – and her life suddenly seemed to have become complicated once again.

23

If Betty had wanted to ignore Hobby's questions and Richard's advances on the journey home, she couldn't have done better than catching a chill. Bundled up in a blanket and feeling distinctly under the weather, she was oblivious to everything around her. When they stopped for lunch in a village close to Maidstone, she could only force a few sips of soup down her sore throat before a hacking cough had her pushing the bowl away.

Hobby hurried over to where a waitress was watching them and requested a glass of water for Betty. The manager joined them and whispered a few discreet words, prompting Hobby to storm back to their table. 'It seems our custom is not wanted here,' she said as she helped Betty to her feet.

'Whatever is the problem?' Richard asked, glancing over. Now there were two waitresses looking in their direction, as well as the manager. 'Perhaps I should have a word?'

'No, don't bother. That silly man seems to think Betty is carrying the Spanish flu. I tried to explain that she has simply caught a chill and we are transporting her home, but he seems to think he will lose custom if we remain.'

'I've never heard anything so preposterous in my life,' Richard fumed as he lifted Betty into his arms and carried her out of the restaurant.

'The soup was too salty,' Hobby declared loudly as she swept out of the door behind them.

'I'm so sorry,' Betty croaked as she was settled onto the rear seat, while Hobby joined Richard in the front of the vehicle.

'You don't think it is the flu, do you?' Richard asked Hobby quietly as they set off. He knew Betty would be unable to hear them over the sound of the engine, even if she was awake. 'It's come on so suddenly; she seemed fit and well in the store yesterday.'

Hobby looked sharply at him as he concentrated on the country lane ahead. 'She got soaked to the skin walking home from Woolworths. For some reason, the silly girl would not turn back for the umbrella she left in your office.' She saw him visibly pale.

'That may have been my fault. I . . . declared myself to her. She left very quickly after that. I gave no thought to the weather . . .'

'You declared yourself to her?' Hobby hissed, doing her best to keep her voice down. 'I just knew you had more than a professional interest in the girl. Why – you must be ten years older than her?'

'I am,' he said, looking back over his shoulder. Betty was dead to the world. 'And I adore her and wouldn't want a hair on her beautiful head harmed.'

'You've made a good job of that.' Hobby inadvertently raised her voice, causing Betty to stir and mumble inco-herently before dropping off again. Hobby held her breath

284

until she was sure Betty hadn't heard anything. 'We will continue this conversation once I've tucked Betty up in her own bed and called the doctor,' she said grimly. She spent the rest of the journey staring ahead in silence.

It was mid-afternoon and the sun was already sinking when the vehicle pulled up in front of Hobby's house. As she climbed down to the pavement, she looked up at the sky and cursed. 'The damned weather has followed us all the way home. Now, love, can you walk to the front door? You can take my arm,' she said as Betty tried to sit up.

'Kindly step out of the way,' Richard said as he leaned past Hobby and took Betty in his arms. Despite his war injury, he lifted her as if she weighed no more than a feather. 'If you can open the front door and point me to Betty's room, please,' he said between gritted teeth.

Hobby scuttled ahead of him and, after fumbling with a bunch of keys, pushed the door open. 'Top of the stairs, second door on the left,' she instructed. 'I'll start bringing in our cases.'

'Leave them, you'll hurt yourself. Besides, Betty needs a chaperone while I'm in her bedroom. I'd hate you to think I'd taken advantage of the situation.'

'Don't be daft, man. It's obvious we both care for the girl. Now, hurry up so I can settle her down.'

At the top of the stairs Hobby pushed past Richard and opened the door to Betty's room before pulling back the blankets. 'Lie her down there and I'll take off her shoes.'

He did as he was told, glancing round at the pleasant room with its chintz-curtained windows.

Hobby, who was fiddling with the buttons on Betty's shoes, went on: 'Now, I want you to go round to number twenty-six in the next road and tell Dr Barrowman to come as quickly as he can. You can explain what ails her. After that, bring our cases in and you can go,' she said hurriedly as she unbuttoned Betty's coat. 'Well, hurry up, don't stand there gawping. I need to undress her.'

Once she heard the front door close behind him she quickly undressed Betty, going to the airing cupboard in the hall and pulling out a freshly laundered nightgown. 'Let's get you into this and I'll go down to the kitchen and boil a kettle for a hot drink, and to fill a stone hot water bottle to warm your feet. Close your eyes and rest for a while,' she said, kissing Betty's cheek and pulling the bedcovers up beneath her chin. She shivered. 'It's a tad chilly in here. I'll light the fire,' she said, crossing to the ornate little fireplace. The fire had already been laid and was just waiting for a match to be lit and held to the kindling.

'There, that'll soon warm the room,' Hobby said, rubbing her hands together. 'I'll go down and put that kettle on,' she added brightly, although Betty failed to respond, looking deathly white. As she hurried downstairs, Hobby prayed the girl hadn't caught the deadly Spanish flu.

A short while later Betty tried to open her eyes, flinching at the low-set winter sunshine coming through her window.

'It's too bright in here, isn't it?' Hobby said as she closed the curtains. 'Is that better, lovey?'

Betty nodded her head slowly; how it ached. She tried a second time to open her eyes and succeeded, only to see three faces peering down at her.

'I'm sorry . . . have I been asleep long?' she murmured.

Hobby chuckled, pleased to see her young friend back

with them. 'Six days! And you've had us so worried. I can't begin to tell you how many hours we've prayed for you to wake up.'

Betty groaned, trying to sit up. 'Six days!'

'Please, Betty, don't try to move too much just yet.'

'He's quite right,' a third voice agreed.

Betty frowned. 'Is that you, Kitty?'

'It is indeed. Egbert sends his love and wishes you well; he is at his office this afternoon but he'll call by later. We've all been so worried about you.'

'That is kind of him,' Betty said groggily as she tried to remember what had happened. 'This is silly, but . . . the last thing I can recall is Richard carrying me upstairs. I hope I wasn't too heavy for you.'

'Never,' he exclaimed. 'I'd do it again in a shot rather than see you so poorly.'

'Richard has been such a help this past week. I take back everything I said about him.'

'Steady on, Miss Hobson,' Richard laughed.

'Credit where credit is due. You have been a godsend, what with running about for medicine and shopping for me and doing the heavy lifting, then sitting here with us for hours on end.'

Betty felt confused. Whatever had been going on while she slept? 'Heavy lifting?'

'Miss Hobson wanted to disinfect all the floors downstairs, and that meant moving some of the heavy cabinets.'

'It had to be done, as the removal men will be coming soon,' Hobby explained.

Betty raised one hand to her forehead – Richard was still holding the other – as she tried to understand what

287

was going on. Slowly the penny dropped. 'My goodness . . . we're supposed to be moving soon, aren't we?'

'There's nothing for you to worry about,' Hobby fussed. 'We can move to Ramsgate whenever you are fit and well. Richard has been popping into the house to check on things for me while he's been at the Ramsgate store. The lady renting this house is flexible with her moving-in date; besides, she wants to be sure that you are well and everything is dis . . .' She broke off at a discreet cough from Kitty.

From the back of her memory, Betty tried to understand why the word disinfectant sounded so familiar. Of course; hadn't she sold lots of it to people cleaning their homes so as to fight off the Spanish flu?

A fear like no other flooded over her. Gripping Richard's hand, she begged him, 'Please tell me, do I have the Spanish flu? And if I do, why are you three here in this room? Kitty, you must protect your unborn child.'

Hobby moved closer to the bed and sat down close to Betty's feet, where she could be seen. 'Betty, the doctor has visited several times. He is most experienced and has seen countless cases of Spanish flu. You are lucky – if I can use that word – in that you caught a chill sitting out in the rain, which turned nasty. The medication he prescribed has helped you to remain in a deep sleep while your body recovered. He decided this morning that we could reduce the dose, as you appeared much better.'

Betty thought over what Hobby had said. 'You mean to say, that chill I caught made me so ill I've not known what's been happening for nearly a week?'

'I blame myself,' Richard said, looking distraught. He lifted her hand and kissed it gently.

'No, it was no one's fault but my own. I should have returned to your office and collected my umbrella, rather than sit by the harbour getting soaked. Or I should have hurried back to the guesthouse. I've put you all to a great deal of trouble. I'm sorry,' Betty managed, before succumbing to another bout of coughing.

Hobby held a glass of water to her lips and told her to sip slowly while Kitty stepped forward and rubbed Betty's back.

'I do not deserve all this care,' she said once she could relax again.

'I think we should let Betty sleep for a while, she looks exhausted,' Kitty said. 'I am going to return home, and I will see you in the morning, dear cousin. I feel perhaps Egbert should wait until tomorrow before paying you a visit; what you need now more than anything is plenty of rest.'

Betty murmured her thanks as her cousin's wife kissed her cheek and bid her goodbye.

'You ought to leave as well,' Hobby told Richard. 'Betty needs to sleep, and surely it's about time you returned to work otherwise people will talk.'

Richard nodded his agreement, and then he too kissed Betty's cheek before bidding her a good afternoon.

'Thank goodness for that,' Hobby said as she took the vacant seat next to the bed. 'Having visitors is all well and good, but it can be so tiring. Look at you; you've had non-stop visitors since the day you fell ill, and you've done nothing but sleep,' she laughed. 'You look so much better already, my dear. There was a time when I feared the worst.' She reached for her handkerchief, tutting. 'Look at me, acting like a daft old woman. What have you done to me, Betty Billington?'

'Please don't cry,' Betty said softly, 'or you will set me off. I'm so grateful. Now I'm back in the land of living, I'm going to do as much as I can to be healthy once more and get back to work. We have a lot to look forward to with our move to Ramsgate.'

'You are right; we both have a lot to look forward to. Now, can I tempt you to something to eat? How about a boiled egg with some bread and butter?'

Betty licked her dry lips. 'I'm not sure how much I can eat, but my grumbling stomach is telling me I need food.'

Hobby laughed. 'You are certainly on the mend.'

The days passed slowly as Betty regained her strength. It was another three days before she was allowed out of bed, although the doctor told her it was too early for her to be going downstairs. Without her knowledge, Richard had spoken to the manager of the Woolwich branch of Woolworths, and it had been decided that Betty would not return to work until the new year when she and Hobby had settled in Ramsgate. In some ways, this news made Betty sad; however, she knew it made sense. While she was still so weak, it could have been dangerous for her to be on her feet all day.

Richard visited most days and always came bearing gifts. One day it was perfume and cream for her hands; another day, a box of chocolates; and once he brought her a book of poetry, which made her exclaim with delight. Although she thought often of the kiss they'd shared in his office, he did not attempt to kiss her again apart from a perfunctory peck on the cheek on arrival and before he left. Betty started to look forward to his visits, and on the odd day when he didn't appear her heart sank. She ignored Hobby's comments about him being more than just a friend.

A few days before Christmas, Egbert appeared at their front door. By then, Betty was sitting in the front room near a roaring fire. She had seen him walk up the path towards the front door and falter for a moment before he knocked. He was alone, and Betty immediately began to worry that something had happened to Kitty. It was still too early for the baby to arrive and in the couple of minutes before he was let into the front room, she prayed fervently that the young woman was well. She had grown to love her like a sister.

'Egbert, how nice to see you. Won't you please come and sit by the fire? I hope everything is all right next door?'

Egbert removed his coat and took the proffered seat, holding his hands out to the fire to warm them before rubbing them together. He cleared his throat before speaking. 'I'm afraid I come bearing bad news . . .'

Betty's first, dreadful thought was that she had been right: something had happened to Kitty.

'. . . I'm very sorry, cousin, but it's your mother. She slipped away quietly during the night.'

A surge of relief for Kitty went through Betty, followed immediately by guilt. Not once since she'd been taken ill had she thought about her mother next door.

Hobby bustled in carrying a tea tray with her best china upon it, as if Egbert were somebody of great importance. She always seemed a little intimidated by his blustery ways, to Betty's amusement. Seeing Betty's distressed expression, she quickly set the tray down on a side table. 'Whatever has happened?' she asked, as Betty burst into tears.

'My mother . . .' was all she could say.

24
~

Betty held on to Egbert's arm as he assisted her up the grand staircase of her parents' house. She was still feeling quite wobbly, as she hadn't walked far since being allowed out of bed. Kitty stood at the door to Agatha Billington's bedroom.

'You poor dear, an orphan at your age,' she said, coming forward to give Betty a quick hug. 'She went quite peacefully in her sleep. There is no need to upset yourself by imagining that she had a bad death.'

Betty couldn't help but think that any death was bad. How could anybody know her mother had had a good death? She wasn't likely to come back and tell them how it had gone, was she? 'Thank you for sitting with her. It can't have been easy, especially in your condition.'

'It was an honour to care for her. Betty . . . I know your mother was a very difficult woman, and I will not judge you for walking away from the family home. In a fair world, your Charlie would have come home from the war and would have been welcomed into the Billington family; but we do not live in a fair world. Before you go into that room to pay your respects to the woman who gave birth to you, I want you to consider this. Until my child is born, there are only three Billingtons remaining. Wherever we may roam, I want us all to promise that we will always keep in touch with each other.'

'I promise I will do that,' Betty said.

'We will be in the drawing room when you're ready to join us,' Egbert said. 'Please call out to me if you require help down the stairs.'

Betty paused at her mother's door and nodded her thanks, then stepped into the darkened bedroom.

Agatha lay peacefully in her bed, her head resting on white pillows. There was a sheet pulled up to her chest and Kitty had placed a chain with a gold cross in her hands, which rested across her body.

Betty gazed at her. Her mother looked as though she didn't have a care in the world: her frown lines were gone, and there was no sign of the tightly compressed lips that had preceded many a sharp word aimed at her daughter. Betty sat down on a chair beside the bed and took Agatha's cold hand.

'Mother, despite us not getting along, I wish to thank you for giving me a good life and for keeping a respectable house for my father. If there is a heaven, and I hope there is, I pray my Charlie will seek you out and introduce himself to you. You would have liked him, Mother. He was a decent, honest, hard-working person. He may not have come from the middle classes, but he'd have made something of himself . . . and he would have loved your daughter until the end of time.'

She kissed Agatha's hand before gently placing it down. 'Goodbye, Mother,' she murmured, and left the room without looking back.

Standing at the top of the staircase, she prepared herself to rejoin her cousin and his wife. She wished them well living in this mausoleum of a house. Perhaps they would sell the property and move to somewhere they could bring up their child without having a daily reminder of her parents. It was never a happy home, she thought as she took each step carefully until she reached the hall. Drawing a deep breath and pinning a smile on her face, she went in to Egbert and Kitty.

'I hope that wasn't too painful for you,' Kitty said sympathetically as she poured tea.

'It had to be done,' Betty said. 'I need to thank you both again for caring for Mother in her final months. I fear she would not have accepted me back into this house. But of course, it is your home now, and I hope you have many happy years ahead either living here, or selling up and moving elsewhere. I have very few happy memories of this as a home. I've been much happier living next door with Miss Hobson.'

Egbert sat back in his armchair and looked at his cousin. 'When will you be moving to Ramsgate?'

'Because of my illness putting our arrangements into disarray, we will now be moving at the beginning of January. Richard has told me I may start work at the beginning of the second week of the month.'

'That is good, as we have arranged your mother's funeral for the day after Boxing Day, depending on whether you were well enough to attend,' Egbert said. 'I informed the funeral director of a possible change of date. I hope you don't mind that we went ahead with the arrangements.'

'Of course not,' Betty said, although she noted that he

hadn't let the grass grow under his feet, what with her mother only having passed away the previous night. 'I applaud you for being so organized.'

Her tone was a little sharper than she'd intended, and Egbert looked slightly taken aback. Before he could reply, Kitty explained, 'Mr Farrow, the owner of the company, was a friend of your father's; they were members of the same club, and he handled the arrangements when your father passed. Egbert kept in touch with him when it was apparent Agatha was not long for this world. Your parents' solicitor had informed us that your mother would be interred with your father when the time came. With Christmas fast approaching, plus the inclement weather, we thought it prudent for Egbert to place a telephone call through to Mr Farrow this morning.'

Betty felt awful. How could she have questioned her cousin's intentions? 'I'm sorry; I do apologize if I spoke out of turn. I'm still not quite myself.'

'It's understandable,' Kitty said kindly, and Egbert agreed. 'You have been very ill, and now you've had this news about your mother just when you are back on your feet – not to mention your imminent move to the coast. If it was me, I'd not know if I was coming or going.'

'You're too kind. Will you tell me if there's anything I can do to help?' Betty said.

'There is something . . .' Kitty glanced at her husband as if for support.

'In fact, there are two things,' Egbert said.

'Please say what it is, and I'll help if I can,' Betty said, wondering what they were about to ask. If it was money-related, she had some savings . . .

'The most important is that we would like you to be a godmother to our little one when he or she is born. We want all our family to stay close, and I can think of no one better than you to be our first choice for a godparent,' Kitty said as she gently laid a hand on her stomach.

'I would be delighted,' Betty grinned. 'Although I'm afraid I may spoil the child and turn into one of those dotty relatives who take their charges to the seaside to play in the sand and ride on donkeys.'

Egbert chuckled. 'As long as the child's father can join in as well.'

'You're all very welcome to visit me in Ramsgate once I've settled in, and when the weather is better we can explore the town. It is brimming with history,' Betty said excitedly, before remembering that her mother lay dead upstairs. She cleared her throat. 'What else was it you wished to ask me?'

'Well, Miss Hobson explained that you will benefit from her will when she passes. We had many a long chat while you slept in your bed,' Kitty explained. 'We both thought that as you're moving to a new home, you might like to take some of your parents' furniture and belongings with you? By rights, anything here that you'd like should be yours,' she said, waving her hand at the contents of the room.

Betty, who had been looking forward to purchasing more items to furnish the house in Ramsgate with Hobby, was surprised by this suggestion. Did she really want anything that would remind her of unhappy times in this house? As for family heirlooms, who would she pass them on to when she reached her dotage? 'That is very generous of you, considering everything was left to you both. Hobby's new house isn't as large as this and she is bringing along some of her own furniture, so we won't really need anything sizeable. Hobby has already negotiated with the owner of the house to buy some of the things he's leaving behind when he moves abroad. My first thought is that everything should remain here for you to do with as you please; or perhaps even leave them for your future children, when the time comes. What do you think?'

Egbert scratched his chin thoughtfully. 'What you say does make sense, but surely there are some family mementos you wish to take?'

'Perhaps the small oil painting of my parents? And there used to be one of me hanging at the foot of the stairs,' Betty said. 'I did wonder what had happened to it.'

'I found it recently when I was looking in the cellar,' Egbert said, looking uncomfortable. 'I did wonder why it was down there. I assumed your parents had stored it there when you fell out.'

'That is probably what happened,' Betty said, with a small smile at the absurdity of the situation. 'There is also my mother's small writing desk. It would sit very well in my new bedroom; that's if you don't want it, Kitty?'

'Oh no, I'm not one for writing; although I promise to write to you often when you move away. Are you sure you wouldn't like to take your mother's sewing box?'

Betty chuckled. 'Hard as my mother tried to train me, I never could thread a needle, let alone partake in embroidery. But I've noticed that you enjoy it,' Betty said, nodding to where a partially completed piece of embroidery lay on an occasional table near Kitty's chair. 'You would get more use from it than I would. That's if you do not have your own sewing box?'

'I must say, I have admired it ever since we moved here,' Kitty replied. 'It is very generous of you and will remind me of your family.'

'There is plenty of time, if you change your mind and wish to take any other items with you,' Egbert said. 'I will have the paintings and the writing desk securely packaged for transportation to Ramsgate.' He glanced round as there was a sharp knock at the front door. 'That will be the undertakers,' he said, looking at the small ornamental clock on the mantelpiece.

'If you don't mind, I think I'd like to go back to Miss Hobson's house now,' Betty said, not wanting to watch as her mother was taken away.

'Of course, I'll walk back with you. We can leave Egbert to oversee matters here,' Kitty said, rising to her feet with care and linking her arm through Betty's. 'Come, cousin, we'll help each other walk the short distance next door.'

'And you must stay with us for a little while until everything is completed here,' Betty said, thinking that in her condition Kitty should not be distressed by seeing Agatha Billington's body removed from the house.

Egbert gave her a grateful smile as he helped them on with their coats.

Back at the house, Hobby fussed around the two women, making sure they were seated comfortably next to the fire in the front room. She discreetly closed the curtains at the front of the house as a mark of respect, even though she'd never had any time for Mrs Billington. 'Good riddance,' she muttered to herself as she went upstairs to close the heavy brocade curtains in her own bedroom. 'I doubt anyone will miss her.'

'My goodness, Richard, do you never put in a full day of work?' Hobby said when Richard appeared early the next morning while they were still finishing breakfast. 'I suppose you haven't even eaten, have you?'

'I wouldn't say no to a cup of tea,' he said, joining them at the table and pinching a slice of toast from Betty's plate. 'It won't be long before I've moved out of my cousin's premises and down to Ramsgate permanently. As far as I'm concerned it can't come soon enough. My car knows its own way back and forth from the coast, I've been there so many times lately.'

'To what do we owe the pleasure of your company at such an early hour? Although I'm grateful that you have taken so many of our bits and pieces down to the new house each time you've travelled to Ramsgate. Have you seen much of your children?' Hobby asked, keeping an eye on Betty's face as she did so.

'Yes, and that will be the most enjoyable part of working so close to them. My mother and father-in-law have been very good caring for them, but the time has come for me to be more of a father than a stranger who turns up with toys and sweets.'

'It must be hard for you, as well as them,' Betty said as she thought that if she had a family, she would never leave them.

'I am driving into London this morning to purchase some Christmas presents for the children and I wondered if you would like to accompany me? I would think you must have some shopping to do for yourself, having been laid up?'

'I would adore that, thank you for asking. I was beginning to wonder what I could do about presents for Charlie's two sisters. I could do that while you shopped for your children's gifts. I can be ready in ten minutes,' she said.

'Then I shall finish your breakfast for you while I wait,' he laughed, pulling the half-eaten meal towards him and starting to tuck in.

25

~

'I've never seen anything so wonderful in my whole life,' Betty said as she gazed around the Lyons tea room situated on the Strand in London. 'It's like no other tea room I've ever seen before.'

Richard chuckled as they were shown to a table. 'There was I, thinking you had been to some extremely smart places with your parents . . . I'm sorry. That was thoughtless of me when your mother has just passed away.'

'Please, Richard, you don't have to tread on eggshells around me. Of course I mourn my mother, but we never saw eye to eye and so I shall not wear mourning clothes or avoid speaking of her; or my father. Besides, I have no recollection of being taken anywhere as beautiful as this.'

'Lyons' teashops and restaurants are springing up everywhere,' Richard said. 'Perhaps we should visit some of them? My children would enjoy that.'

Betty wasn't sure whether he meant she was to be included in this imagined outing, so decided to say nothing. 'I did enjoy shopping with you, Richard. We made so many purchases.'

'It's I who should thank you. I would never have thought

302

of a dolls' house for the girls, and the hobby horses with real horsehair manes will delight them.'

'Thank goodness the store delivers, otherwise we would have struggled to fit everything into your car.'

'And they're going down to Kent to my in-laws, with strict instructions not to allow the children to see them.'

'That would be a catastrophe,' Betty said before giving a small yawn. 'Excuse me; this is my first outing since my illness, and although thrilling, it has left me rather tired.'

'I can take you home right away, if you like?' he said, concerned.

'Oh no, I wouldn't hear of it. Besides, I wouldn't miss a delicious lunch for all the world.'

Richard bowed his head in agreement, although he still looked thoughtful as they placed their order with a waitress. 'I wonder, would you like me to drive you to Woolwich after this, so that you can deliver your gifts? That's if it wouldn't tire you too much?'

Betty's eyes lit up. 'Would you really? That would be so helpful. I was unsure about going by public transport in case it exhausted me. I feel so spoilt with you driving me; I could get used to it,' she chuckled. 'If you're worried about me being tired, don't be. I'll feel completely rested by the time we've eaten. However, you must remind me to buy some boxes of those chocolates we spotted as we entered. Hobby and Kitty would love them.'

'Then I would be delighted to drive you there,' he smiled as their meal arrived.

Betty looked back at Richard sitting in his motor car outside the house on Railway Terrace. She raised a hand to assure him that she was all right before knocking on the door. She wasn't sure the family would be at home; it could be that Harold Sayers was working a shift on the railway. However, surely at least one of the girls would be in? She needn't have worried; Olive opened the door and exclaimed in delight at seeing Betty standing there. She flung herself into Betty's arms before leading her inside.

'Look who's here,' she called, as they came into the cosy front room. Peggy also hugged Betty, although Harold sat in his armchair without saying a word. 'We were only talking about you yesterday, weren't we, Dad?' Olive added, trying to encourage her father to speak. 'We have something we feel you should have; I said ages ago that one of us ought to take it to you.' She nodded to where a small box sat on a side table.

'We weren't sure if you still lived at your parents' house,' Peggy said. 'I walked down to Woolworths to see if I could spot you, but you didn't seem to be at work, and I was too frightened to ask anyone.'

Betty was delighted to see the girls, less so Harold, but she was prepared to let bygones be bygones now that she no longer lived under his roof. 'I live next door to my parents' house now, although both of them have recently passed away. I do have news, though; I'm moving to another branch of Woolworths down on the Kent coast. It's at a place called Ramsgate – I'm not sure if you've heard of it? I move there in a few weeks, along with my landlady.'

'Isn't that on the line you work on, Dad?' Olive asked.

'It's one of them,' he replied, watching as Betty placed her parcels on the table before removing her gloves.

'I've brought along a few small gifts for you for Christmas,' Betty said, 'and to wish you all the best for the season.'

'All the best? It's not that long since we lost our Charlie. Or have you forgotten that, as you stand there spreading your Christmas cheer and dressed up in your finery?' he spluttered.

'I've just come back from London. I couldn't exactly go in my work clothes, could I?' Betty said evenly. She was not afraid of Harold any more.

Olive slipped her hand into Betty's. 'Don't take any notice of him,' she whispered. 'His latest lady friend left him for someone else.'

Betty sighed. It was no life for these two young girls, having a father who was always chasing the ladies. Thank goodness Charlie had never been like that. If only . . . if only he had written and told her that he still loved her. She'd heard nothing from him for ages before the letter notifying his family of his death. She wondered for the first time if he had lost interest in her a little.

'I'm sorry,' she murmured, not knowing what else to say.

Peggy had moved to the table and was looking at the parcels wrapped up in pretty tissue paper. 'They do look interesting,' she said. 'Thank you very much.'

'That's all right, my dear. I just wanted to remember you and wish you a happy Christmas,' Betty replied, lifting her hand to stroke the girl's hair fondly.

Harold Sayers sprang up from his chair. Reaching out, he grabbed Betty's hand where she still wore the ring she'd purchased from the pawnbroker. 'What do you call this?' he asked. 'You come here handing out gifts, when all the time you are betrothed to another?'

305

'I can explain,' she said, snatching back her hand. 'It's not what you think.'

The two girls shrank back as their father bellowed, 'And who's the toff in the motor car out the front? Is that not what I think either?'

'He's a friend,' Betty answered, knowing her reply sounded feeble.

'Get out of my house right now,' Harold snarled. 'God knows what our Charlie would have thought of you. He's not cold in the ground, and you're running around with some other bloke. You're nothing more than a tart.'

Betty was shocked by his violent words. She wanted to stand up to him and ask what sort of example he thought he was setting for his young daughters, running after every woman in a skirt, many of them no better than they should be. However, she knew he could strike out with his fists when drunk, and she could smell the beer on his breath even at a distance. She didn't want the girls to witness anything worse than they already had.

'I'll go. But your assumptions about me are wrong.' She turned away from him and hugged both the girls before heading towards the door. As she reached into her pocket for her gloves, her fingers touched a card. Slipping it into Olive's hand, she whispered, 'If you ever need me, I'll be there to help you; please do keep in touch.' A sob caught in her throat as she ran from the house back to Richard, who was now standing by the side of the car. 'Get me away from here, please.'

Richard drove slowly, knowing better than to ask for details until Betty had stopped crying. He pulled over eventually, and reached into his pocket for a clean hand-kerchief. 'Do you want to tell me what that was all about?'

Betty wiped her eyes and nodded. 'Yes, I would like to tell you about the time I spent living with Charlie's family.'

As the words poured out of her – about Harold's approaches to her before Hobby took her in, and his accusations this afternoon – she was taken aback by the sheer horror on Richard's face.

'Tell me, Betty, did he ever . . . did he ever put you in a compromising position? If he did, I'll turn this car around right now and go back there to sort him out.'

She could see the whites of his knuckles as he clenched his fists; she had never seen him look so angry. 'Please, could you just take me home? What I want is to put all of this behind me. I have a lot to look forward to, and it's time I stopped looking back.'

Richard put his arms around her and kissed her gently. 'You mean a lot to me, Betty, and I'm a patient man; however, I want you to know that one day I'll be asking you to be my wife. Please; there's no need to say anything now as you are upset and tired. Perhaps I shouldn't have said anything, but I want you to know that I'll always be here for you,' he said as he kissed her once more.

Betty closed her eyes, and this time she wasn't thinking of Charlie. Instead she was thinking of Richard and how much she admired him. It might not be possible now, but just perhaps in time they could be happy together. She'd ignored her feelings for so long. Maybe her future was with Richard . . .

Hobby was at the window as they arrived back at the house. 'Thank goodness you're here! I thought something had happened to you, you've been gone so long. You look rather pale, girl. Are you feeling poorly again?'

'She's had an upset,' Richard said as he helped Betty inside the house and led her to a seat in the front room. 'I'll just go out to the motor and bring in your packages.'

He took his time outside, and when he returned Hobby gave him a thankful glance.

'I'm only glad that you were with her when she went to the Sayers' house. I dread to think what it would have been like if she'd gone back there on her own. I'm not saying he would have hurt you, Betty; I was thinking more of you coming home on your own and in a state. Good riddance to all the Sayers,' she muttered darkly. 'The sooner we get to Ramsgate, the better.'

'Please don't hate them,' Betty begged her. 'They are, after all, Charlie's family; I don't want anything to tarnish his memory.' She saw a shadow cross Richard's face and took his hand. 'I can't thank you enough for today. And I mean all of it,' she said, looking into his eyes and giving him a gentle smile.

'I'll go and put the kettle on. I take it you're staying for tea, Richard?' Hobby said, not waiting for an answer as she left the room. She closed the door behind her.

'I'll go if you are tired?'

'No, please don't. I've enjoyed our day, well most of it, and I don't want it to end.'

He moved closer and swept her into his arms. This time she didn't protest as his lips searched for hers, and seconds turned to minutes. As they pulled apart Richard gently stroked her cheek. 'I'm very fond of you, Betty. I hope you feel the same about me. Perhaps once we are settled and working in Ramsgate, we can make plans? I would like you to meet my children and get to know them. What do you say?'

Betty's heart skipped a beat, but before she could reply she heard a polite cough and Hobby entered the room.

'Don't mind me,' she said as she went to the dining table and started to clear it. Betty hurried over to help her while Richard turned to the window, straightening his tie.

'It's just a scratch meal of cold meat and pickles, but there's plenty of it. Perhaps you'd help me bring in the plates, Betty? You can take a seat,' Hobby instructed as Richard went to help.

In the kitchen, she turned to Betty. 'You can tell me to mind my own business, but I'll say this just the once. Do not rush into anything just to spite Harold Sayers.'

'I don't know what you mean,' Betty spluttered.

'I think you do. I wasn't born yesterday, and although I may not have experienced a relationship with a man, I know when they are being led along. You may like Richard, but don't fool the man into thinking he has a future with you just because you are lonely and still grieving Charlie's death. He too is grieving for his wife, and the pair of you could be throwing yourselves at each other for the wrong reasons. Do you understand me?'

Betty bowed her head. 'I do like Richard, but I've only ever loved Charlie; or at least, I thought I did.'

'Then I suggest you are not so free with your kisses,' Hobby said. 'Think of the message you are sending him.'

'You are right, I wasn't thinking. It will not happen again.'

Hobby was thoughtful as the two of them carried the plates through to where Richard was sitting. 'Eat up, lad.

You must be tired after the day you've had. I know I for one am ready for my bed, and Betty looks half asleep on her feet.'

Betty realized Hobby was not giving Richard the opportunity to stay long. She stifled a yawn. 'I've had a lovely day but must admit I'm exhausted. Thank you for the delightful outing, Richard. It was very kind of you.'

'As it looks as though we won't see you again until we've moved to Ramsgate, I'll also wish you a pleasant Christmas with your family,' Hobby said before urging them to eat up.

They made small talk for the rest of the meal until Richard was ready to leave. Hobby sent Betty to collect Richard's overcoat and gloves, which meant the couple were not alone again as Hobby stayed with them while he made his goodbyes at the front door.

Betty wished she'd been alone with Richard one more time, just for a small kiss goodbye. She enjoyed his company very much, as well as the kisses. As she went upstairs to prepare for bed, her thoughts went to Charlie and what might have been. With the war over, he would have been home very soon, and they would have been closer to making their plans a reality. So much had changed since she'd said goodbye to him two years earlier.

She still wondered why there had been so little communication from him once he left to go to war. Perhaps, as his life had changed so much, he'd begun to reconsider marrying her . . . She felt so confused. Climbing into bed and closing her eyes, she found herself picturing Richard and Charlie standing side by side as if asking her to choose:

a man who would only ever be a memory, and might not have married her at all, or another who was offering her a ready-made family?

26

Summer 1919

'Miss Billington,' a young assistant gasped, hurrying up to Betty as she stood by a counter instructing new staff on the right way to display crockery on the polished wood counter.

'What is it, Daphne? Please remember not to run while you are on the shop floor,' Betty said, shaking her head. She knew that as soon as her back was turned, the young girl would forget her words.

'There's a woman who wants to speak to you most urgently. She said to tell you her name is Mrs Billington, just like yours.' The girl giggled, and the new staff members Betty was talking to joined in.

'Ladies, please. You must remember to behave like adults. Whatever will our customers think of a group of counter assistants acting in such a manner? Daphne, please show Mrs Billington upstairs to the office and give her a cup of tea. Tell her I will join her shortly,' Betty said, wondering what could have brought Kitty to Ramsgate. She had not mentioned a visit when they'd last corresponded.

'Yes, Miss Billington,' the girl said, hurrying away, the full skirt of her overall rustling as she did so.

Betty shook her head. She couldn't scold the girls too much, as they all worked hard and were keen to learn. That reminded her to have a chat with Richard about the gossip regarding the store being haunted. The stockroom lads had started to taunt the younger girls and frighten them with stories. Checking a list she held in her hands, she divided the six new staff members into three pairs and gave them their duties, telling them she would be back within the hour to see how they were doing.

With a certain trepidation, she hurried upstairs to see her cousin's wife. There had been no mention of Egbert or indeed the baby being with Kitty, which piqued her interest, although she hoped nothing was wrong back at Charlton.

'Betty, my dear, it is lovely to see you,' Kitty said, hurrying towards her and hugging her. 'How well you look. The sea air seems to be good for you.'

'Oh, it is. We simply adore living here. As you know from my letters, Hobby is involved in all kinds of committees and groups, and it feels as though we have lived here for years.'

'Yes, she was telling me when I was there earlier. I was relieved when she offered to care for Charlotte while I came to see you.'

Betty chuckled. She could not imagine Hobby caring for a young child alone, and imagined that their cook had already been summoned to take over. 'I would love to see her caring for Charlotte. I suppose the baby is too young to take much interest in talk of women's suffrage,' she chuckled.

'I'll bring her back when she is old enough to understand,' Kitty smiled.

'Why, Cousin Kitty, are you joining the movement? Whatever would Egbert say?'

'Egbert is intelligent enough to appreciate that I have my own views. He even agrees with some of them,' Kitty smiled. 'The war has changed many things, although I doubt he will ever approve of me having a career like you.'

'Then he is certainly a Billington,' Betty replied with a smile. She liked Egbert very much, but in some ways he reminded her of her late father. 'I will say that if I had such an adorable daughter, I would give my career up in an instant.'

'And if I didn't have a family I'd be working here with you,' Kitty chuckled. 'We are a fickle pair. I must say, this is a very smart office; everything seems to have a place,' she added, looking at the rows of shelves with their neatly labelled files and ledgers.

'One of the joys of working in a new building,' Betty replied, running her hand across the polished wooden desk. 'From what I saw of the offices in the Woolwich store, all branches are not the same.'

'I'm sure you have had a hand in making this office so tidy. I take it this is where Richard works?'

Betty felt herself start to blush and quickly changed the subject. 'Tell me, how is Egbert and why is he not with you?'

'He is a busy man, what with new staff to train at the office. There were such severe losses during the war, and then this Spanish influenza has taken so many people.'

Betty fell silent for a few seconds. 'I heard recently that

314

Vicky and her two babies succumbed to the influenza. I can't believe that she has gone. She was the closest thing I had to a true friend when I lived with my parents, even though she was our housemaid. This flu is relentless.'

'It certainly is, and I'm fearful of it coming into our home. I confess to having hired another maid in the house, just to clean. We are told that cleanliness is next to godliness, but now I feel it is more about staying alive.'

'You are right. We still have a counter just for cleaning products, although there does not seem to be the panic there was when I worked at the Woolwich store. Richard makes sure our stockroom still has plentiful supplies.'

'Where is Richard today?'

'He has taken the day off to be with his children, so I took the liberty of using the office to chat with you. I do work in here sometimes, as he is showing me more of the paperwork relating to the hiring of staff and their training. I'm finding it most interesting.'

'I can see you managing a Woolworths store yourself one day,' Kitty smiled.

'You sound just like Hobby. She never stops saying there should be more women in managerial positions in the Woolworths company. I dare not tell her when we have visits from head office, as she may well come and march up and down outside with one of her homemade placards calling for more rights for women workers. I would die of embarrassment. Ah, thank you, Daphne,' Betty added as the young sales assistant came in with fresh tea for Kitty and a cup for Betty.

The girl blushed and bobbed a curtsy as Kitty thanked her, before dashing out of the office.

They both chuckled. 'You are teaching your staff very well. I may just pinch Daphne and whisk her away to work for me.'

'You wouldn't dare!' Betty warned her good-naturedly. 'I doubt she would go for all the tea in China, as I hear she has set her cap at one of the lads in the stockroom.'

'Talking of setting one's cap, have you met Richard's children yet?'

Betty ignored Kitty's barbed comment, but answered her question. 'They've been to the store several times, and twice I've joined them for afternoon tea on my half day.' She didn't add that she had been to their home to celebrate the birthday of the eldest, or had helped the middle child with her reading.

Kitty nodded knowingly. 'It is rather cosy, Betty. Are you sure you are completely over your loss of Charlie? How do his sisters feel about you being so friendly with Richard?'

'I've not heard from Olive or Peggy since the day I dropped off their Christmas presents. I have written several times, and sent some colourful postcards of Ramsgate so that it's quite clear where I now live. I had hoped that now summer was here, they might come and visit me – my last letter to them included enough money for the train fare,' Betty said, looking sad. 'Whatever my circumstances in the future, I would like to remain friends with them. After all, they would have been my sisters-in-law if Charlie had survived and we'd been married.'

'Do you feel their father has a hand in their silence? From what you told me, he was rather aggressive with his words when he saw you with Richard?'

'Yes; it rather frightened me at the time.'

'It must have done,' Kitty agreed.

'Now, you know it is always a delight to see you, but I'm wondering why you sought me out at work rather than wait for me to return home this evening?'

'I wanted to have a word with you alone, and that would be almost impossible with Miss Hobson clucking around us.'

'She is a darling, but she can fuss,' Betty agreed. 'Pray tell me, what it is you came here for? I'm becoming rather alarmed.'

'There is no need. I have two pieces of news that we felt should be told face to face rather than by a letter.'

'Two?' Betty exclaimed, looking concerned.

'Do not fear. The first is purely a family matter: we are making plans to have the baby christened, and I wanted to check that you are still agreeable to being a godmother?'

'I'm honoured you have thought of me and would never change my mind. I will take my duties most seriously,' Betty said, reaching out to hug Kitty. 'You must give me the details so that I can book leave from work and decide on the perfect gift . . .'

'There is plenty of time, so fear not. Now for something that I hope won't alarm you too much. Egbert has been offered a promotion, and it means we shall be moving away from London. As we will be living in Edinburgh for the foreseeable future, he has decided to put the house on the market so that we can set up home in Scotland. I'm sorry, Betty; this means you will no longer be able to visit your childhood home.'

Betty raised her hand to stop Kitty's apologies. 'Please,

there's no need for you to apologize. The only thing I value about that house is your presence there. We may have discovered each other later in life than expected, but I will miss you. However, I have heard that Scotland is a lovely part of the world, and if I may, I will visit often.'

Kitty looked relieved. 'I insist you visit as much as you are able. In fact, if you ever have a fancy to move to another part of the world, there will always be a home for you with us.'

Betty felt tearful. She adored her cousin and would genuinely miss her. However, she would not miss the house in Charlton at all. 'You are so kind to me,' she stammered. 'If there is anything I can do to help with your move, please don't hesitate to ask.'

'There is something,' Kitty said, looking worried. 'I had wanted Egbert to mention this to you . . .'

'Goodness, whatever can it be?'

'The house is selling for a much higher price than we expected it would – it has astounded us both. We feel some of the money should come to you. Egbert is going to arrange to invest it for you, so that it's there when you wish to invest in your own property.'

'No, there is no need to do that,' Betty said, looking startled. 'Miss Hobson has made a very generous gesture to me in her will. I am well provided for. Please use your money for my godchild and any future children. Who knows what the future will bring?'

Kitty looked flummoxed. 'I don't know what to say.'

'Then say nothing.' Betty stood up with a smile. 'I must return to my work. Goodness knows how the new counter staff are coping.'

Kitty rose too, straightening her hat. 'I intend to have a leisurely walk around the harbour before returning to Miss Hobson's house to see if she has spoilt my child. I hope to see you before I catch the train home?'

'I will leave spot on half past five and run as fast as I possibly can,' Betty promised. 'This is just a thought, but why don't you stay overnight and catch a morning train home?'

'That is a good idea. May I use your telephone to contact Egbert at the office?'

'Of course you may,' Betty said, kissing her cheek and leaving her cousin to place her call through to London. Straightening her overall and pinning a smile to her face, she stepped through the door and returned to her work.

'I must say, this has been very nice,' Kitty said as she put down her knife and fork before dabbing at her lips with a napkin. 'I could easily abandon my husband and move to the seaside.'

'You are always welcome,' Hobby said as she rang a bell to summon their maid, who also served as cook and general help. 'Now we are settled, and Betty is enjoying her job, we are ready to entertain more. I may even advertise a room to rent to holidaymakers. I quite fancy being a seaside landlady.'

Betty hooted with laughter. 'I could just see you banging on a gong to summon people to dinner and checking your watch if they come home late.'

'I'm sure Hobby would be a very good landlady. If you do decide to rent a room or two, I can inform my husband's colleagues in London. A few days' holiday in Ramsgate would sound very attractive to many Londoners.'

'I'll keep you posted,' Hobby said with a glint in her eye.

'You had best make your plans quickly, before my cousin departs to Scotland,' Betty said, not for one moment thinking Hobby was serious about her plans.

'Please tell me more,' Hobby said, turning her attention to Kitty.

Betty listened as Kitty explained about her and Egbert's plans.

'You are selling the house? That is interesting; at the moment I am renting out my house next door to yours. May I ask if house prices are reasonable? I know mine is much smaller, but even so . . .'

'I don't mind you asking at all. Egbert was very surprised by what we have been offered. It seems we are far enough outside the city of London that people wish to move after putting up with the bombing in the capital.'

'We had our fair share,' Hobby said.

'Yes, but our road was mainly untouched. Buyers are attracted to the nearby parks and railway stations.'

'Who'd have thought it?' Hobby said, as the maid collected the plates.

Kitty waited for the maid to leave the room before she turned to Betty. 'I spoke to Egbert about you refusing our gift, and he is most insistent you accept. He told me to inform you he will not change his mind.'

'This sounds interesting,' Hobby said. 'Am I allowed to ask what it's all about?'

Betty sighed. 'Cousin Egbert wishes to settle some money on me once the house is sold. I told Kitty I would prefer it if they save the money for the future, for their children; however, it seems my dear cousins will not take no for an answer.'

'It is their money to do with as they wish,' Hobby told Betty. 'I know that you will be comfortably off from my will, but as I don't plan on going anywhere any day soon, to have a little money of your own courtesy of your cousins would be very handy. You never know when it might be needed.'

'Miss Hobson is right,' Kitty said, looking serious. 'Egbert and I would be much happier knowing you are taken care of; after all, the property was your parents'. Under different circumstances, everything would have gone to you.'

Betty was thoughtful. She knew that to have some money tucked away in a bank would be handy for a rainy day. Granted she lived with Hobby in a very nice house, and had her wages from Woolworths, but who was to say her circumstances wouldn't change? 'Very well, I will accept your generous offer,' she said. 'I don't feel I deserve it, but I don't want this to come between us.'

'Are we supposed to shake hands?' Kitty said with a grin.

'Why not celebrate with steamed pudding and custard?' Hobby suggested as the maid returned with a laden tray.

27

Christmas Eve 1919

'You look glum,' Richard said, as he met Betty in the staff room during her afternoon tea break. 'I'd have thought our first Christmas in Ramsgate and a new store would have put a smile on your face.'

'I'm sorry,' she replied as she indicated for him to take the empty seat opposite her. 'It's just that I'd hoped to hear from Olive and Peggy, and Hobby has just popped in to tell me there was nothing in the midday post. I know it has been almost a year since I last saw them, but as it is Christmas, I thought perhaps a postcard or a letter . . . just to let me know they are keeping well.'

Richard looked sympathetic. 'I don't know what to say. Do you think their father has poisoned their minds against you?'

'I truly hope not. Olive is old enough to know her own mind, and she does have my address. I've been diligent in writing to them and have sent small gifts on their birthdays. Last week I posted a box containing two new frocks and other items I thought they would like.'

'Perhaps you will hear from them after Christmas? They are bound to send a note to say thank you for your generosity.'

Betty considered his words. 'You may be right, and I should not burden you with my glum thoughts when you are so busy in the store.'

'Don't give it a second thought.'

'It isn't really that I want their thanks; I'd rather just know they are keeping well. Olive is fourteen now; surely she will be starting work soon, and I thought I might be able to advise her in her choice of occupation.'

Richard turned briefly to speak to a staff member, who wished him a happy Christmas, before returning to Betty's problem. 'You should have accepted your cousins' invitation to visit them in Edinburgh. The break would have done you good.'

'Oh, Richard, it is out of the question. How could I not be here on one of the busiest days of the year? I would have felt as though I'd abandoned you. Besides, Hobby has so much arranged for today and tomorrow that she needs my help. She is like a mother to me, and everyone should be with their mother at Christmas.'

Richard gave her a gentle smile. 'I like that you will not abandon me,' he said.

'Oh, for goodness' sake, you know what I mean. And don't look at me like that, as you will give the staff ideas about us,' she laughed. 'You know how the girls like to talk; we don't need to fuel the gossip.'

'Even though you wear Charlie's ring?'

'You know it isn't Charlie's ring, just a ruse to stop people asking me questions. I thought it would be a good idea,

323

but it doesn't seem to have worked. The younger members of staff see me as some tragic figure doomed to live a loveless life. I've had numerous suggestions to meet their brothers and uncles, and on one occasion a grandfather.' She laughed as she thought of their matchmaking. 'Bless them, they mean well.'

'So when they see me taking up your time, they put two and two together?'

'Exactly,' she chuckled. 'They only raise their eyebrows when I say we are just work colleagues and good friends.'

Richard raised his eyebrows, which made Betty laugh again. 'Please, don't you start. Be off with you, go back to your work.'

'Haven't you forgotten something?'

Betty gave him a puzzled look. 'Have I?'

'This evening. I have an invitation to Hobby's Christmas soirée, don't forget.'

'Are you sure you have time? I thought you would want to be with your children before they go to bed.'

'And I will; I plan to change in my office and arrive with the first guests. I will stay for one hour, then leave to be with the children.'

'We are honoured that you can fit us into your schedule,' Betty smiled. 'Hobby thinks so much of you and will be delighted you are able to attend. She's even had someone come in and move the furniture so that we can all dance; and there is to be a caterer.'

'Then I will claim my dance with you,' he said as he stood up. 'Now, I will get back to my work, otherwise I will still be here on Boxing Day.'

Betty watched him leave the staff room, stopping several

times to shake hands and wish the workers a merry Christmas. He was popular with the staff, taking an interest in their work and their home lives. The summer bank holiday had seen staff and their families enjoy a picnic on the beach, while only last week he'd handed out hampers to all employees and allowed the mothers a full hour off, with pay, to do their Christmas shopping. No wonder all the female staff adored him, and the male staff looked up to him too. She had to admit she had a soft spot for him herself.

Hobby had made a marvellous job of turning their house into somewhere fit to celebrate Christmas Eve. Betty had rushed home from work and quickly admired everything that had been done before hurrying to her bedroom to wash and put on her new dress. She brushed out her hair, which had been confined to a tight bun at the nape of her neck, and left it to fall into loose waves, only clipping back the sides to show more of her face. Her dress was something even her mother would have approved of, simple and elegant in a delicate shade of eau-de-nil. Dabbing a little perfume at her throat, she checked her appearance in the full-length mirror before hurrying downstairs to join Hobby as she greeted her first guests.

Betty's head was in a whirl as she was introduced to all the neighbours and people Hobby had befriended since they moved to Ramsgate. Hobby seems to have met more people than I have, she thought to herself, even though I work in such a busy store.

'You look beautiful,' Richard whispered over her shoulder, causing a shiver of excitement to run down her spine. She closed her eyes for a moment, enjoying the sensation, before turning to face him.

'And you, sir, look extremely handsome,' she smiled sweetly, admiring his evening attire.

Hobby hurried over to them. 'What a splendid couple you make. Won't you start the dancing for me?'

Richard held out his arm to Betty. 'Would you do me the pleasure?'

Betty smiled. 'I would love to,' she said as he led her to the room Hobby had cleared of furniture for her guests to dance. It was at the back of the house, opening out onto a small orangery and the garden. Candles were dotted amongst the shrubs, giving the scene a romantic air. A young man tasked with overseeing the gramophone noticed them enter the room and placed a recording of a waltz onto the turntable. Richard swept Betty into his arms and held her close as they waltzed round the room. 'Have I told you you are adorable, Betty Billington?'

'Once or twice,' Betty giggled. 'You are always generous with your compliments,' she added. He pulled her even closer, so that she could smell his cologne.

'I mean every word,' he whispered as his lips brushed her forehead.

Betty fell silent, enjoying the moment. Richard was a good dancer; she felt as though she was floating on air. A fleeting thought that she had never danced with Charlie was swept away as her thoughts were consumed by Richard. She was oblivious to the room filling with other couples until he paused for a moment.

'Shall we take a walk outside?' he said as he led her by the hand through the orangery to the garden.

Betty was speechless. It felt like such a magical evening. With the war behind them, there was a feeling of looking towards the future, and standing here with Richard still holding her hand, she wondered what it held for her.

Richard lifted her hand and gently kissed it. 'Betty, I feel as though the time is right for me to ask you a very important question.' He led her to a garden seat below an arbour, where she sat looking at him as he knelt before her. 'Elizabeth Billington, will you do me the honour of becoming my wife? We both know we have a closeness and friendship that for me has turned to love. I hope you feel the same?' he said as he held out a diamond ring.

Betty felt breathless. Of course she knew Richard was fond of her, and she enjoyed his company. Perhaps she had been wrong to imagine she would never love another man after losing Charlie. Recently, as she had revisited her memories of their time together, she had come to realize that he had never declared his love for her in any of his correspondence after their parting. In fact, she had received very few letters from him in the months before hearing of his death; to this day, she wondered whether he might have had second thoughts. Theirs had been a sweet romance with a promise of things to come, dreams for the future and snatched kisses behind her parents' back.

Charlie would have grown up a lot once he joined the army, she thought. He would have been influenced by his comrades and his new experiences abroad. He might even have thought more about her parents, and the class difference between their families, and come to realize that their marriage could never have worked – there was so much standing in the way of their happiness. Now that she was a little older and had had the luxury of some time to think about their relationship, she wondered whether if he hadn't died, he would have returned from the war and gently let her down. If only he had written to her to say he no longer wished to marry her.

'Betty? Do you accept my proposal of marriage?'

She patted the seat next to her and Richard joined her, still holding her hand, a pleading look in his eyes. 'Oh, Richard, I would so much like to accept your proposal, and I do feel we could have a happy future together . . .' She stopped speaking, her head still full of thoughts of the past.

'It's Charlie, isn't it? A man I never met is still coming between us,' he said sadly. 'I do understand how you feel, and in many ways I felt the same after Harriet passed away. The difference is that she and I had the chance to marry and have a family; I have my memories of that time to look back on. Until I met you, I wasn't thinking of marrying again. But as the years have passed, you have been on my mind so much; and despite Charlie, I think you've had similar feelings for me.'

'I can't lie; I have had romantic thoughts about you, dear Richard. It's only recently that I've begun to question whether my love for Charlie was real. As time passes, I wonder more and more whether it was perhaps a one-sided love, just a young girl's dream.'

Richard smiled. 'Then will you consider my proposal?'

'I'll do more than that,' she said, holding out her left hand. 'I accept your proposal of marriage. Although we do have one small problem to overcome.'

He was about to slip the ring onto her finger, but stopped and almost groaned. 'Don't tell me you love another?'

'Be serious, Richard. You have forgotten I am not yet twenty-one years of age.'

He frowned. 'I'm confused . . . if you are referring to my asking your father for your hand in marriage, I'm afraid that is impossible.'

Betty kept a straight face. 'Nevertheless, I feel you should do things properly and ask somebody for my hand.'

'I never gave it a thought. Perhaps I should take a trip to Scotland and speak to your cousin Egbert?'

'There is no need, as the person you need to ask lives closer to home.'

Richard looked perplexed. 'Please give me a clue, Betty.'

'I would like you to ask Hobby for my hand in marriage,' Betty told him with a smile. 'She is like a parent to me, and I value her thoughts on my future.'

Richard roared with laughter as Hobby ran from the orangery, where she had been standing behind a large plant. 'I give my approval,' she cried out, almost dancing around them as she kissed Betty and then Richard. 'I have felt for some time that the pair of you would make a happy marriage. I had my doubts when you first appeared, young man. But since we've all moved to Ramsgate and settled into a new life, I have waited patiently for this day. I truly feel like a mother handing her only child over to the man who will care for her for the rest of her life. This is the happiest I've ever been.'

Betty watched as guests started to flood from the house to offer their congratulations. 'I'm beginning to think this party is not to celebrate Christmas, but to celebrate our engagement,' she said. 'Hobby seems to have had an inkling of your intentions already. Have you been plotting with her?'

Richards raised his hands in surrender. 'I confess, she

has hinted a few times that you might be ready to accept my proposal if I were to offer it. However, if I had really had a hand in the planning, surely my own family would have been here to celebrate with us . . .' He turned towards the house as Hobby appeared again, this time with his family.

'Oh, Richard, you did know about it all along! What if I had said no?'

'I would have been a broken man. However, if that had happened my family were primed not to say a word about it, and to simply enjoy a Christmas party.'

Betty chuckled. 'I have been truly duped. Thank goodness I accepted your proposal,' she said, admiring the sparkling ring on her left hand. 'I do wish Egbert and Kitty could have been here. You haven't hidden them behind an aspidistra in the orangery, have you?' she asked, peering playfully over his shoulder.

'Sadly not, but I do have this,' he said, reaching into the inside pocket of his jacket and taking out an envelope. 'It arrived yesterday.'

Betty tore open the envelope, recognizing Kitty's handwriting. She quickly scanned the letter before holding it to her breast. 'Oh, Richard, they say they are thrilled to hear we are engaged and wish they could be here with us to celebrate. However, in her delicate condition they fear the journey would be too much.' She checked the page again. 'She thanks you for writing to her, and feels very much as though she is part of our party this evening . . .'

'Another baby?'

'Yes, their second; it is due in the spring, and she hopes to be well enough to join us for the wedding.' Delighted,

Betty held out the letter for him to read. 'I almost wonder if you've arranged the wedding as well,' she chuckled.

'I wouldn't dare do such a thing. That, my dear, is for you alone to organize.'

'And Hobby; we mustn't forget her,' Betty said as he wrapped his arms around her and gently kissed her.

'Come, we must go inside and join our guests. The children are eager to talk with you about the wedding and where we will all live once we are wed.'

'Goodness,' Betty said. 'However will I cope with work as well as a wedding to plan, and a home to find for our family . . .'

In the early hours of Christmas Day, after all their guests had left and Betty had said goodnight to Richard, she sat with Hobby in the kitchen drinking cocoa. This was a much grander kitchen than the one in Hobby's old home in Charlton, with a large cooking range, floor-to-ceiling cupboards and a walk-in pantry. The pair both enjoyed nothing more than drinking their cocoa there at the end of the day.

Hobby kicked off her dancing shoes and sighed with delight as she placed her stockinged feet on the tiled floor. 'I've been wanting to do that all evening,' she said. 'I should have listened to you when you said they would pinch my toes.'

'They do look pretty, though perhaps you should wear something more comfortable for my wedding,' Betty said as she stood up and padded to the pantry, bringing back a tray of petite sandwiches and pastries the caterers had left behind. 'Eat up, or we will be having these for our Christmas dinner and probably our Boxing Day meal as well.'

'I'm pleased with the caterers; perhaps we should use them for the wedding, too. What do you think?'

'Gosh, Hobby. Richard has only just put a ring on my finger. I want to enjoy the feeling for a while before I even think about setting a date. There's no rush.'

Hobby frowned. 'I was speaking to Richard's in-laws, and they told me they plan to travel next year. There was talk of the Grand Tour – not that it is possible to visit every country, as one used to be able to do.'

'Then who will care for the children?' Betty frowned. 'I suppose Richard could hire a governess . . .'

'There's nothing to stop you marrying before they set off on their travels,' Hobby suggested.

'But I will still have my job to go to. I have so much more responsibility now. How can I care for a young family?'

And do you want to? Hobby wondered, as she saw the confusion on Betty's face.

28

May 1920

'That is certainly different,' Hobby said as she watched Betty twist and turn in front of an ornate full-length mirror as the shop owner fussed around her. 'It was worth you waiting while you made up your mind about what to wear,' she added, while privately thinking that three weeks before the big day was cutting it rather fine.

The lace cloche hat with a veil flowing from the back, reaching down to the bottom of the calf-length satin dress, hung on Betty perfectly. 'I'm very pleased with it,' she murmured to the lady helping her. 'Please convey my thanks to the dressmaker.'

'I wasn't sure about the new short style, but it suits you,' Hobby said as she ran a hand over the heavy satin. 'It's not my cup of tea, but you young things do tend to buck tradition.'

Betty was as pale as the dress. The pressure of organizing a wedding had left her drained. 'I was unsure what to wear as I'll be escorted down the aisle by Richard's children, which is somewhat unusual.'

'Mademoiselle has chosen beautifully,' the shop owner said as she stood back to assess Betty while she walked up and down the length of the shop. 'The dress is so versatile, as it can be dyed and worn again some day. Perhaps to the christening of your first child?'

Hobby raised her eyebrows as Betty ignored the comment. 'I must change, as I'm due back at work soon,' she snapped. 'Please have it delivered.'

Outside, Hobby said, 'Do you have to hurry off, or can you spare me ten minutes to take tea?' She nodded to a nearby teashop that looked out over Ramsgate harbour.

'Of course, I have time,' Betty said. 'I'd just become tired of that woman fussing around me. Come on —' she tucked her arm through Hobby's — 'I'll treat you to a toasted teacake.'

Once they were seated at a table by the window with their order being prepared, Hobby removed her gloves and looked across the table at Betty. 'Isn't it time you told me what is wrong? For the past few weeks your mood has deteriorated to the point I feel as though I'm walking on eggshells around you.'

'I'm sorry; I have so much on my mind now. I feel as though I could simply run away and be free from it all,' Betty replied with an apologetic smile.

'Then let me help you. I'm supposed to be the mother of the bride, taking care of you. A blooming good mother I am, when I've let you get yourself into such a stew over planning the wedding. Or is it just the wedding? I overheard you arguing with Richard when he dropped you home the other night. I'm surprised the front door is still hanging on its hinges. Now, don't tell me you are sorry, as that solves nothing. Talk to me, Betty,' she said gently.

Betty was silent for a while as she looked out towards the sea. 'I've been offered a promotion at work.'

'Why, that's wonderful news. Tell me more.'

'You may recall we had a visit from head office. It was more to see how the store is coping under new management, and to show the area to members of the delegation who had not visited Thanet before. There is talk of more stores being built in this area of Kent.'

'That is good news, but I don't see why this is a problem?'

'I was called into the office for a chat about what it's like for young women moving away from home to work for Woolworths. They wanted to know about any difficulties I'd experienced, so that they could try to make things a little easier for others. My suggestion was that Woolworths could compile a list of suitable lodgings in each area, to help their staff settle in.'

'I like that idea. Why I never thought to offer rooms to your staff is beyond me. We should talk about this more.'

'Thank you, I did suggest you might be able to help. But then they asked me about my plans for working with Woolworths in the future.'

'Once you are married, do you mean?'

'No, it was more general. I said that I hoped to move into management one day, and until then I would like to learn as much as possible about the company and experience different departments.'

'That sounds sensible. You must have been excited to be able to put your case across?'

'I was . . . until an older member of the team pointed out that I was to be married to Richard shortly, and my experience would mean I would be ideally placed to support his career . . .'

'Oh dear! I do hope you held your temper?'

'You would have been proud of me,' Betty smiled. 'I did point out to the man that my imminent wedding has no bearing on my career with Woolworths. Thankfully he did not bring up having children, as I might have ended up mentioning Marie Stopes' advice on birth control and embarrassing everybody.'

Hobby burst out laughing. 'That's my girl.'

'There was one ray of sunshine, though. There was a woman in the delegation. She pulled me to one side after the meeting and asked if I would consider working in another store after my marriage. She told me she felt I would do better in a different location, not working in my husband's shadow after the wedding. I told her I was agreeable to that.'

'She makes a very good point. You are your own woman and should not be judged by your husband's career. I take it the loud words and the slamming of my front door came after you informed Richard of this?'

'What you heard was the culmination of an evening of talking about the future. Richard is away now for several days, and we have agreed to discuss it again once he returns. I've not given him an ultimatum, but I fear I may have to if he cannot see my point of view.'

Hobby patted her hand. 'You are both sensible people and I am sure you will find a way forward. Apart from that, are all your plans running smoothly?'

'Thank goodness they are, although . . .'

'You've still not heard from Olive and Peggy Sayers?' Hobby asked, knowing this was playing on Betty's mind.

'No; and I so wished they would be my bridesmaids. I just hope they are well.'

'We can only pray they are,' Hobby said, as an idea came to her.

Hortensia Hobson completed the tasks that had taken her back to Charlton and, after enjoying lunch with a friend, set off for Woolwich. She was a formidable woman at the best of times and was determined to get to the bottom of why the Sayers family were not replying to Betty's letters. She had not mentioned her quest to Betty, hoping that if she was successful she could return to Ramsgate bearing good news.

Never having visited this particular area of Woolwich, she hired a cab to take her to Railway Terrace and approached the first door she came to, not being sure of the address. It was opened by a young woman carrying a baby on her hip.

'My apologies,' Hobby said politely. 'I fear I have come to the wrong address. I was looking for the Sayers family, who have lived in Railway Terrace for some years. There is a Mr Harold Sayers and his two daughters, Olive and Peggy.'

The woman's forehead wrinkled in thought as she soothed the fractious child. 'We've only lived here a couple of months, but there's a Harold who drinks with my husband at the railway club. You could ask further down the terrace.'

Hobby tried one more house, and this time she was pointed to the Sayers home. She reached their gate at the same time a young girl crossed the road, heading for the same house. 'Can I help you?' she asked politely.

'Would you perhaps be Olive or Peggy Sayers?'

'Why do you wish to know?'

'I'm a friend of Betty Billington's.'

The girl looked worried. 'There's nothing wrong with Betty, is there? It's just that . . .'

Hobby smiled. 'I take it you are Peggy? Betty is well; she's been wondering why no one has replied to her correspondence, and as I was in the area I thought I'd call and see if you were all well.'

Just as Peggy began to reply, the door opened and a woman called to her to come in immediately. 'Sorry,' she said to Hobby, 'it's rather difficult,' before hurrying inside.

'Perhaps you could ask your sister to get in touch?' Hobby called out as the door closed. 'Oh, well; I tried,' she sighed, before heading off to find another cab to take her to the station. She wouldn't say anything to Betty, but she hoped that her few words with Peggy might at least prompt the girls to get in touch.

'Don't you wish to marry me?' Richard asked, searching Betty's face for a response. 'You've been like a stranger these past few weeks, and I can't understand why.'

Betty stared ahead, through the windscreen of his motor; the sunset over Ramsgate beach was beautiful. They'd been to have Sunday lunch with his children and listen to his in-laws' plan for their trip to Europe. Betty had been shown the children's rooms, along with closets full of clothes and lists that had been made about their food likes and dislikes, along with routines. Her head had been spinning, and the more she thought about running the household, the more she knew she was not capable. She knew for certain that there would be changes once she was living there.

'Richard, this is a big step for me, in fact, for any bride. However, I have additional worries, the first being about my ability to run the family home. I have decided we need more help, as I plan to carry on working.'

'I knew this would happen,' he sighed. 'You have no need to work. I know you have enjoyed your time with Woolworths, but most women leave work when they marry and have a family . . . We won't be short of money. I want you to enjoy getting to know the children and create a family home where you will be comfortable.'

'I understand that; but Richard, I love my job. I do not wish to give it up.'

'Perhaps a few hours a week would satisfy you?'

Betty gave an exasperated sigh. 'A few hours a week will not help me to further my career.'

'I knew it!' Richard exclaimed. 'Someone spoke to you when we had that visit from head office, didn't they? You've been in a dream world ever since then. I'll bet it was that Jean Blake; her head is full of ideas about creating more female managers,' he scoffed.

'Women are able to run stores just as well as men,' Betty said calmly. 'You've always agreed that they could, that is until I wanted to have a career with the company.'

'I should have known you'd have these ideas about careers and suffrage and the like, after living with Miss Hobson.' He emphasized the word Miss. 'It was perfectly sensible to consider having a career while you were single, but now you're going to have a husband and family.'

'Honestly, Richard, I thought better of you,' Betty hissed. 'Next you will be mentioning Charlie.'

'Let's face it,' he said, running a hand through his hair,

'the chap is never far from your thoughts, is he? Even four days before our wedding.'

Betty held back her tears at the mention of Charlie's name. 'That is an unfair comment. Charlie played a big part in my life. I would never have imagined I'd hear you speaking to me like this,' she said as she opened the door and stepped onto the pavement. 'I can walk home from here. No, please don't follow me. I'll see you at work tomorrow.' And she turned and walked away.

29

Betty's mind was in a whirl as she walked away from the seafront, through the town and towards the house she shared with Hobby. As she passed the Woolworths store, she stopped to look at one of the window displays and noticed that it had changed. Instead of the arrangement of pretty crockery that had been there when she'd left the store late on Saturday afternoon, there was a wedding scene. The staff had used items for sale in the store to construct a bride and groom leaving a church. For the first time in hours, she smiled; the bride had been made from a mop, and her white dress was a linen tablecloth. Hanging above the scene were the words 'Good luck for the future, Betty and Richard!'

'The future,' Betty said out loud to herself as she walked on. She knew then that her future was bleak. Although she was fond of Richard, she could not imagine living out her years in his home with his children – and possibly some of their own. 'What have you done, Betty Billington?' she asked herself, turning onto the road where she lived. 'What have you done?'

Letting herself into the house, she wondered if she could

creep upstairs to her room without Hobby knowing she was home. If she had an hour to rest on her bed, she would be refreshed and possibly have a plan. She hadn't climbed more than four steps when the door to the drawing room opened, and Hobby spoke.

'Good, you are home. You have visitors.'

Betty couldn't even pin a smile to her face and, ignoring Hobby, walked into the room.

'Betty, my love,' Kitty declared as she hurried over to hug her. 'We managed to leave a day early, so I'm at your disposal as cousin to the bride.' Behind her, Egbert smiled a greeting.

Betty felt as though she was engulfed with love and couldn't hold back her tears. 'I'm so pleased to see you both,' she said, when she could speak again.

'I'll take a walk and leave you ladies to chat amongst yourselves. You must have a lot to talk about,' Egbert said as he left the room, only stopping to pat Betty on the shoulder. 'It's good to see you,' he said, before hurrying out the door.

'Tears will always clear the house of men,' Hobby said as she passed a clean handkerchief to Betty and led her to a chair. 'Sit yourself down and tell us all about it.'

Betty told them about her conversation with Richard that afternoon, and how she'd walked away from him.

'I must admit, it is a big step to move into another woman's home. I felt the same when we moved to Charlton,' Kitty said. 'Would Richard consider a new home for the family rather like a fresh start?'

'His late wife never lived there. It's her parents who have been living in the house to care for the children.

They are nice people and have done a marvellous job, but now they are about to leave for Europe and won't be available.'

'It seems rather convenient to me,' Hobby muttered, and received a look from Kitty that could curdle milk.

'No doubt just a coincidence,' she said with a bright smile.

Betty blew her nose and looked at the two women. 'They have been planning this for a long time.'

Kitty and Hobby nodded their heads knowingly.

'Well, I'm sure you will do a wonderful job being the children's new mother. Think of it as having junior staff to train. You are wonderful with new staff, from what I've heard,' Kitty twittered on.

'Or organizing a committee,' Hobby added.

'I'm not sure I love Richard enough to marry him,' Betty blurted out, silencing the pair at once.

'Good grief, what a pickle,' Hobby declared.

'Are you sure it isn't just pre-wedding nerves?' Kitty asked.

'I don't know. I only know I'm not sure what to do – please help me.'

Hobby disappeared from the room and returned with three glasses and a decanter. 'We may as well have a sherry or two while we decide what we are going to do about Betty's dilemma.'

'You see, I'm not sure Charlie ever really loved me. If he had, surely he'd have written to me once he went away? He was always sending me little notes and pretty cards up until he left for the front. Even after we were notified of his death, I thought his letters would arrive, what with the war holding up the post. I can only think I was someone to dally with . . .'

'That is a possibility,' Kitty said, as she finished her third sherry. Hobby gave a slight snore, her head drooping onto the arm of the sofa where she sat. 'How would you have felt if Charlie had kept in touch right up until his death?'

'I would have known he truly loved me and that would have been enough to hold onto throughout the years ahead, until we met again.'

Kitty reached for the decanter and topped up their glasses. 'Are you telling me you would never have married? And that your memories of Charlie would have been enough to sustain you into your old age?'

'Hobby has never married, and she has been very happy.'

Kitty frowned. 'That is completely different, and you know it.'

'It is,' Hobby mumbled.

'Tell me why you decided to accept Richard's proposal of marriage? I want to support you, but we must think of him in all this.'

Betty bowed her head. 'I know; and I feel awful. Without a real reason, I feel I may just have to marry him and forget about my own dreams for the future. It's not as if it will be a hard life, and he does care for me. Many women have had much worse lives.'

'That's not a good reason to marry,' Egbert said as he came into the room. 'I'm sorry, I couldn't help but overhear some of your conversation.'

Betty was embarrassed. 'I apologize that you have heard about my dilemma, Egbert. What do you suggest?'

'I suggest we ring for the maid to serve a light supper. Then, dear cousin, you are to take yourself to your bedroom and try to sleep. Be assured, I am here to support you.'

'I feel quite tearful, but in a good way,' Betty said. 'Thank you, Egbert.'

'So do I,' Kitty said as she hugged her husband.

Hobby gave a loud snore.

Betty woke the next morning to the maid softly calling her name. 'Miss . . . there are people here to see you.'

'What time is it?'

'Almost midday, miss.'

'What? I should have been called for work this morning,' Betty said, trying to sit up. Her head started to spin, and she groaned.

'Mr Billington sent a note to your workplace to inform them that you are indisposed. Flowers have been delivered from Mr Richard. Would you like them here in your room, or should I leave them downstairs?'

Betty couldn't think straight. 'I need to dress and go down to see my visitors. Did you take their names?'

'They didn't say, miss. There is hot water for you to wash, and I've left a cup of tea here,' she said, pointing to the bedside table before she hurried away.

Betty sipped her tea and felt better almost at once. She quickly washed and dressed before hurrying downstairs. No doubt it was the caterers, or someone concerned with the wedding – the wedding, it was a day closer, and she was still unsure . . .

'In here,' Hobby called from the dining room. 'I have a surprise for you.'

As she entered the room, Betty was praying that it wouldn't be Richard. 'Oh, my goodness,' she exclaimed as Olive and Peggy ran to her.

'We came by train,' Peggy said excitedly.

Olive nodded her head. 'Miss Hobson has given us breakfast.'

Betty looked towards Hobby, who seemed a little pale after the excesses of sherry the evening before, but nonetheless was eating.

'You could have knocked me down with a feather when the pair of them arrived. They have some news.'

'News? Does your father know you are here?'

'He's dead,' Olive said. 'Two weeks ago. It was the Spanish flu.'

'I'm so sorry. You can stay here for as long as you wish.'

'I told them that,' Hobby said, 'but they said they've only come to see you, then they are going back.'

'Please explain,' Betty said, as she sat down opposite the girls. 'It's not that I'm not pleased to see you, but you seem to have come here for a reason.'

Olive put down her cup. 'The railway told us we had to move out of Railway Terrace, as it was only our home while Dad worked for the railway. Our mother's sister kept in touch, and she is coming to collect us. We are going to live in Somerset with her.'

'Thank you for coming to let me know,' Betty said. It was a relief to imagine the girls being cared for by someone from their mother's side of the family, unconnected to Harold. 'That was quite a journey; why didn't you write me a letter, instead of travelling all the way here?'

'I have something to explain to you,' Olive said, reaching for a box she'd put on the seat next to her.

'I recognize that,' Betty exclaimed. 'Wasn't that the box

your dad was going to give me the last time I visited Railway Terrace? I'd completely forgotten about it.'

'Yes, I came across it while I was tidying, and I made Dad promise I could give it to you. But after he saw you with your young man, he was very angry and told us he'd thrown it away.'

'I don't understand . . .'

'They are Charlie's things,' Peggy said.

'Oh my goodness,' Betty said faintly. 'Then . . . your father didn't throw them away?'

'No. I found a suitcase under his bed after he died, and inside it were all the letters Charlie had sent home to us that were meant for you.'

'You mean to say, Charlie was writing to me all the time he was away?' Betty asked.

'Some letters came after we heard he had died, but Dad never told us. We weren't allowed to open the post and had no idea until I came across them recently. Even then, he threatened to kick me out if I said anything to you. That's why I dared not write to you. Dad was always jealous of Charlie and wanted what he had. That included you.'

'He slapped Olive so hard when she asked about the letters that I thought he had killed her,' Peggy piped up. 'That's why I couldn't speak to you the day you knocked on our door. I was afraid he would hurt me too.'

'Well, I never,' Hobby said. 'I just wish I could have helped you.' She mouthed 'later' to a puzzled Betty before asking, 'Are you going to open the box?'

'Later,' Betty replied. She chatted with the girls about their aunt, hearing about how Olive would be returning to school for a little longer before deciding what she wanted to do for work. She was pleased when Olive asked about working for Woolworths. All the time she chatted about the girls' future, her eyes kept straying to the box containing Charlie's letters.

Hobby wanted to put the girls up for the night, but they refused.

'We have our return train tickets and must catch the late afternoon train back home. Our aunt will be expecting us. She's been wonderful since Dad took sick; she even moved in with us to help care for him.'

'She sounds like a good woman,' Hobby said, thinking that must have been the woman she spotted at their door. 'Promise me that if things don't work out in Somerset, you will come and stay with us?'

The girls agreed. After feeding them a substantial lunch, Hobby and Betty walked them back to the train station and waved them safely off.

Hobby turned to Betty. 'I suppose you will be busy for the rest of the day?'

'I will be. I want to read all of Charlie's correspondence, from the first letter to the last. I hope they will answer my questions.'

She sat up late into the night, sustained by the cocoa Hobby and Kitty brought in to her at regular intervals. Each envelope was laid out on her bed according to the postmark date, so that she could read them in order. She showed the others some of the pretty silk-embroidered cards he'd sent, although they didn't read his private words to her. Eventually Betty fell asleep fully clothed, surrounded by the love letters from her Charlie.

The next morning she was up bright and early, ready to

head to Woolworths. She refused breakfast, which worried Hobby.

'You need something in your stomach before a busy working day,' she insisted.

'I'm not expected at work. I have the day booked off for wedding preparations,' Betty replied.

'So you do plan to go ahead with this wedding?'

'I'll tell you when I return home,' she said, giving Hobby a big hug. 'Thank you for everything.'

'Don't talk like that; it sounds as though you're thinking of throwing yourself off the harbour wall.'

'I promise you, I won't do anything rash,' Betty assured her, giving her a kiss on the cheek before heading out into the early morning sunshine.

Ten minutes later she was outside the Woolworths store, tapping on the front door to get the attention of one of the cleaners. After being let in and chatting briefly with the women, she went upstairs to Richard's office to await his arrival. While she waited, she wrote three letters, putting all but one into her bag. Hearing movement in the staff canteen, she went down to collect a tea tray to take back to the office.

'I didn't expect to see you,' Richard said when he walked into his office soon afterwards. His face was pale, and he'd cut himself while shaving.

'I needed to talk to you,' she said, before explaining her feelings two days earlier, when they'd had words and she'd walked away from him. 'I've been so confused,' she said. 'Then, yesterday, I had two visitors; Charlie's sisters came to see me.'

'I'm pleased they contacted you. I know you were worried

about them,' he said, before listening while she told him what they'd had to say and what they'd brought with them.

'So, you see, it changes everything for me. Charlie did love me, and it wasn't as I thought, and he hadn't changed his mind. There was a letter that he probably wrote on the day he was killed. Even on that day, his thoughts were of me. He was a regular writer and there were just a few gaps where post could have gone astray, or perhaps he wasn't able to write. But whatever he wrote, his love for me shone through. I hope you understand what I'm trying to say.'

'You are saying you do not wish to marry me, and you are going to spend your days knowing that you were loved by a man who died for his country.'

'Yes, that is what I'm saying.'

Richard gave a harsh laugh. 'He was a lucky man to have your love, Betty. I can't compete with that and have no wish to. To think this would not have happened if Harold Sayers had not been such a jealous old man.'

'I pity him; grief and jealousy can do terrible things to people. May I ask, will you release me from our engagement?'

'I wouldn't dream of holding you captive when you wish to spread your wings and fly,' he said sadly. 'It will make things difficult here. Have you seen the window display?'

'I have; and that is why I'm leaving this store. Here's my notice,' she said, handing him the letter. 'I hope you will release me at once.'

'But Woolworths is your life. Please stay, I'm sure we can work something out,' he said, looking concerned.

'I have no wish to embarrass you, and you know how the staff will gossip. I have written to head office to request a position at another store; they've offered me a chance to move before, but I declined. Who knows, it could be a step up the ladder for me. But whatever happens, I know it will be for the best. Thank you for being so understanding, Richard,' she said, standing up and holding out her hand.

'I don't suppose there's a chance you will change your mind if I get down on my knees and beg . . . ?'

'Please, Richard; you know this is the right decision.'

He gave a wry smile. 'I do, but you can't blame me for asking.'

'Dear Richard. I will always have fond thoughts of you.'

He took her hand and raised it to his lips. 'Goodbye, Betty, and good luck in all that you do.'

Epilogue

December 1938

Betty looked at the application forms in front of her, putting a face to each of the names. Several she put to one side; they weren't suitable as counter staff, either through lacking experience or having failed the arithmetic test. On two of the forms, she added a positive tick in the right-hand corner; Sarah and Freda would be assets to Woolworths as counter assistants. She read again Maisie's answers to the arithmetic questions and thought about the woman; she was different from the others, but then, hadn't Betty too been different from her colleagues when she'd started work at the Woolwich store? Maisie was a possibility.

She smiled to herself as she thought of the younger women who seemed so in awe of her. Was it that long ago she'd been in their position? Counting on her fingers, she realized that indeed it had been more than twenty years since she'd applied for her first job at the Woolwich branch. She shuddered at the memory of those early morning starts, scrubbing floors. Thank goodness for Richard seeing her potential, offering her promotion and so much more.

Dear Richard. What would her working life have been like, if she hadn't met him? Indeed, she had been fortunate to have the support of so many people: Hobby most of all, for giving her a roof over her head and being like a second mother to her. Hobby had been gone for five years now and was very much missed; a day didn't pass without Betty thinking about her friend and how supportive she had been all her life. Nothing could have surprised her more than when, after she'd left the Ramsgate store, Hobby upped sticks and followed her, settling again in Charlton when Betty's next position turned out to be at one of Woolworths' London branches. She chuckled as she wondered if Hobby would have followed her to Erith, and the first position where she did not have to wear a uniform. Ramsgate was a lovely town, but once she left, she had never felt the urge to return to Thanet. That part of her life had become a blur, as had her memories of Richard. Their paths had never crossed again.

Looking up at the clock on the wall of her small office, she realized she would have to hurry with her decision; there were applicants waiting in the staff canteen and she had other work to attend to. Her new position did not allow much time for quiet contemplation. The job was all she'd ever dreamt about, but even so it had its challenging moments.

Quickly checking the rest of the applications, she sorted them into 'yes, no, or possible' piles. Some of these applicants had husbands and young families to get home to. Betty only had her own little house to return to each night, but it was her home, her sanctuary. Her hand went to the brooch she proudly wore on the lapel of her jacket. Under different circumstances she would have had her Charlie and their family to care for, but she wasn't bitter, wondering what life would have been like if her one true love had survived the Great War. Indeed, storm clouds were gathering once more over Europe and she would be here to support her staff, her Woolworths girls, as they too faced an uncertain future. Hadn't Charlie's last letters insisted she should promise to have a good life if they were never reunited, and to follow her dreams?

She smiled to herself. 'I've kept my promise, Charlie.'

Acknowledgements

I have so many people to thank for supporting 'Team Elaine' that I don't know where to start . . .

My agent, Caroline Sheldon, and her team at Caroline Sheldon Literary Agency Ltd, who take such good care of me and my writing career. I'm lucky to be cared for by such a knowledgeable lady who is dedicated to the publishing world.

My editor, the fabulous Wayne Brookes at Pan Macmillan, along with the wonderful assistants, cover designers, publicists, sales department, editing staff, and not forgetting Susan Opie, whose input at the structural stage of editing is second to none.

I love listening to audiobooks; they've been a godsend for me in the past year. A very big thank you to award-winning Annie Aldington, who has narrated all my books and brings my characters to life.

I mustn't forget to say thank you to the book buyers in supermarkets, major bookshops, independent bookshops, online sellers as well as book bloggers and reviewers who make sure everyone knows about my books.

Magazines are very important to an author, as we are invited to write short stories that reach out to readers, so thank you to *The People's Friend, My Weekly, Woman's Weekly* and *Your* magazine, just to name a few. In fact, before I was a novelist, these magazines hired me to write short stories and articles at the beginning of my writing career.

I'm lucky in that I get to chat on the radio about my books and everything 'writerly', as well as dogs and other subjects. Many thanks to Pat Marsh at BBC Radio Kent for my very first interview and following my writing career ever since I was their 'short story writer of the year' way back in 2003.

Before I forget, I do need to say a massive thanks to our libraries who stock my books and invite me to visit and chat. Floods, storms and hold-ups on motorways haven't stopped me from getting to meet readers. Please do support our libraries as much as you can before we lose them completely.

Thank you also to readers and followers on social media. Where would I be without you? So many have become good friends over the years, bringing joy to my life when you chat about my characters, seeming to know them better than I do at times.

Friends, family, as well my dear students, past and present, who put up with my constant talk about books and are ready to hit 'share' and 'RT' on social media.

Next my writing friends, especially the Strictly Saga Girls. We got each other through lockdown with our chats and support. It was a hard time for many authors and a shoulder to cry on is always welcome.

I'm sure I've forgotten someone – oh yes, the home team. Thank you to my husband, Michael. You put up with late dinners and a miserable woman at times, help brainstorm stories and point out when I have made a mistake – not that I agree with you. You keep the home ticking over while I sit in my office with Il Divo blaring away while I write. Perhaps I should thank Il Divo as well?

Henry the dog is the final part of the home team, and he is such good company, especially when he comes to visit me in my office and points to his biscuit tin for a treat. If only he could type, he wouldn't be such a freeloader!

I know I must have forgotten many people, and I do apologize.

You are all part of my book tribe, so don't let anyone tell you a writer's life is a solitary life.

Thank you!
Elaine xx

Keep in Touch

I love to hear from readers, and there are many ways you can not only follow me but contact me to chat, as well as enter competitions.

Twitter:
Find me as @ElaineEverest

Facebook author page:
Come and chat and hear my news on Facebook.
www.facebook.com/ElaineEverestAuthor

Instagram:
I have an account on Instagram, so why not find me and say hello?
www.instagram.com/elaine.everest/

Website:
This is where you can not only read about me and all my books, but also read my blog posts where I chat about my life and everything to do with my books.
Go to www.elaineeverest.com

My newsletter:
Sign up to receive a copy of my monthly newsletter, where I not only give you the latest news about my books but also run some fab competitions. In the past there have been competitions to win a sewing machine, leather handbag, hampers, jewellery and signed copies of my books. You will find the link to sign up on my website: www.elaineeverest.com